Madhouse Fog

Also by Sean Carswell

Train Wreck Girl
Barney's Crew
Glue and Ink Rebellion
Drinks for the Little Guy

Madhouse
Fog

Sean Carswell

Manic D Press
San Francisco

for
Wendy Bishop, Sheila Ortiz Taylor,
and
Jerome Stern

This is a work of fiction. All characters and locations appearing in this work are fictitious. Any resemblance to real persons, living or dead, and places is purely coincidental.

Cover photo by Nino Andonis

Madhouse Fog ©2013 by Sean Carswell. All rights reserved.
Published by Manic D Press. For information, contact Manic D Press,
PO Box 410804, San Francisco CA 94141   www.manicdpress.com
ISBN 978-1-933149-75-2   printed in the USA
Cataloging in Publication data is available from the Library of Congress

1

I'd been hearing a voice in my head lately. Not voices. One voice, and I didn't want to listen. It still somehow convinced me to take a job at the Oak View State Psychiatric Hospital.

The first thing I did on arrival at Oak View was to take a seat in the back row of a large lecture hall. All of the hospital administrators and a good chunk of staff were having the beginning-of-the-year meeting there. I sat between two empty chairs and scanned the hall for Dr. Bishop.

Despite what the voice in my head might tell you, I was not a patient at the hospital. I was a new employee. Dr. Bishop had hired me to write the grants needed to keep this facility humming.

All the other voices in my head—which were all mine; I usually refer to them as thoughts—had told me to stay in Fresno, to find a way to breathe life back into my suffocating marriage, to keep writing grants that would fund the community space I'd helped to create and dedicated fifteen years of my life to running. For some reason, I listened to Dr. Bishop's voice. I took this job at Oak View and joined the staff at the staff meeting.

An exceptionally short woman sat down next to me. She said, "You must be Mr. Brown."

She offered her tiny hand for me to shake. I shook it. It felt like a canary in my palm.

"I am. How'd you know?"

She swept her bangs sideways above her right eyebrow. "I know that everyone else in here is not Mr. Brown so I made an educated guess."

I nodded.

She said, "I'm Dr. Benengeli."

I didn't exactly follow. I thought she was giving me a first and last name but she didn't strike me as a Ben. I asked her to repeat her name. It didn't help. I asked, "Is your first name Ben or Benen?"

She said, "Mr. Brown, on hospital grounds, my first name is Doctor." I winced as if I'd been scolded.

She patted my forearm. "We don't use first names on hospital grounds. This way it's tougher for former patients to Google us and drop by our homes in the evening."

Before I could respond, her phone buzzed. She read the screen and started typing with her thumbs. I went back to scanning the lecture hall.

Dr. Bishop had emailed me and told me she'd be there. I knew a few things about her. I knew what she looked like from the first time we had met a decade and a half earlier. I knew what her voice sounded like over the telephone and what it sounded like in my head without the telephone's electrostatic buzz. I knew she used Verdana as her chosen email font and had email stationary with a George Burns quote that said, "The most important thing is sincerity. If you can fake that, you've got it made." None of these things helped me to pick her out among the nurses and medical doctors and psychiatrists and psychologists and administrative assistants populating this meeting. All I saw was a bunch of too-ordinary-looking employees: sweaters and slacks and big cups of coffee and worn down briefcases and hard shoes and falling socks.

In the room behind me, the chief of staff and a couple of IT guys worked furiously to get the computer and overhead projector to speak to each other. The screen at the front of the room flickered with their successes and failures. Most of the staff chatted with each other or talked on their phones or texted. At least three women knitted. Another woman read a paperback. She was brutal about it, folding it in half at the spine as if it were a magazine, really taxing the glue that bound the paper together.

Amidst this scene, The Professor appeared. Who could he be but a professor, with his bow tie, starched dress shirt, v-neck sweater vest that was maroon (of all colors), blue blazer, pleated tan slacks, argyle socks, and fuzzy bedroom slippers? He walked to the front of the lecture hall, stood in front of the podium, mimed the actions of opening a briefcase and placing his notes on the podium, and said, "Good morning, class."

The staff quieted down somewhat. A low murmur buzzed through the hall. Everyone looked at everyone else, perhaps waiting for someone to do something. Glances ricocheted off one another. No one took action.

The Professor spread his arms as if to hug the entire hall and boomed, "Can I get a huzzah?"

One of the knitters paused mid-stitch to shout back, "Huzzah!"

"All right!" The Professor stepped away from the podium. "One student is awake this morning. And it's okay if you're half-asleep because we're here to talk about that realm between sleeping and waking." He put his arms behind his back and paced in front of the screen. The light of the overhead projector flickered on. It broadcast an error message, then faded away. The Professor drifted into a lecture about Chuang-tzu and his famous butterfly dream. The story was familiar to me and far less interesting than The Professor's conviction. He seemed convinced that he was really in front of a classroom, really teaching a class at this moment.

I have to say I got a little excited. This was exactly the type of madness I was hoping to find with my new job at a psych hospital. Several of the staff were less amused. They pulled out cell phones and put their thumbs to work, either dialing or texting psych techs. Dr. Benengeli leaned over and whispered, "Well, this wasn't on the agenda."

"Should I go down and put a stop to this? Escort this guy somewhere?" I asked.

She shook her head and patted my knee. "Relax. Sometimes things don't go as planned."

I met her glance and smiled. How could I not? Look at those eyes. Such a deep, rich brown, like an old rosewood fretboard.

The Professor continued his lecture. He recited a Chuang-tzu poem:

> "The one who dreams of drinking wine,
> In the morning may be crying.
> The one who dreams of crying,
> In the morning may go hunting."

I actually recognized this poem. I'd majored in Religion, with a focus on Eastern Studies way back in the college days. The final lines of the poem rang in my head. I raised my hand. The Professor pointed at me. "Yes? You in the back row."

I recited the last two lines: "This kind of talk / Its name is 'bizarre.'"

Dr. Benengeli whispered in my ear, "You said it."

Several staff members shot me dirty looks.

The Professor smiled and said, "Someone did his homework."

Before he could say more, the screen behind him reflected the image of a PowerPoint display: a fake notebook page with a pencil in the corner and a computerized script reading *Happy New Year!*

Another man emerged from a doorway in the front of the lecture hall, just to the left of the screen. He wore the uniform—boots, blue slacks, work shirt, and polyester jacket—of a Roads and Grounds employee. He walked up to The Professor, touched him gently on the elbow, and muttered in his ear. The Professor nodded. "I apologize," he told us. "Today's class will be cancelled. Be sure to consult the syllabus for Thursday's reading."

The Professor and the Roads and Grounds guy headed for the exit. A psych tech in his scrubs waited there. The three walked into the crisp January day.

The meeting ended at 10:30, which gave me more than six hours to figure out what to do on my first day of work. The staff ambled out of the lecture hall. I sat there searching for a bright idea and waiting for Dr. Bishop. When neither emerged, I moseyed out of the hall, too.

I wasn't prepared for the winter day that greeted me outside. It was one of those coastal Southern California days that looks so beautiful when you see it through a window but when you step into it, it's wet and cold. The wind cut through my skin. I wasn't wearing the right clothes for this. Or more precisely, I did own the right clothes. I had jeans and hoodies and even a leather motorcycle jacket with a rusty X-Ray Spex pin on the lapel, but none of these were going to help on my first day of work in a professional setting. And though I'd been more or less a "professional" during my whole time working at the community space in Fresno, I was my own boss. I could dress however I wanted. This new job at an institution was different. I felt like I needed a uniform of sorts. So I dug out my tan Dickies slacks and a white dress shirt that someone had left at my house years ago. The shirt hung loose on me in that hand-me-down way. I probably didn't look very professional. I probably looked like my dad was a professional and I raided his closet, dressing up as him for Halloween. My brown loafers had dust in the seams.

Dr. Benengeli looked professional. She came up to me, warm and confident on this January day, wearing a stylish wool pea coat she'd probably picked up in the juniors' section of an upscale department store. She said to me, "You look lost."

"I am, a little," I said.

"A psych hospital is a bad place to look lost. Someone will find a room for you, sooner or later."

And don't you know that's exactly what I was thinking.

Dr. Benengeli nodded vaguely in the direction of some buildings to the east of the hospital. "Come on, I'll show you to your office."

"I'm waiting for Dr. Bishop," I said.

She nodded. "Dr. Bishop isn't here today. She asked me to show you around."

I paused a second to chew over this information. Dr. Benengeli started walking without me. I said, "Wait." She stopped walking and turned to face me. "If you're supposed to show me around, why'd you let me wander out here, lost?"

She smiled. "Just to mess with you," she said. Those beautiful eyes of hers made her smile all the more sinister.

We walked together across the hospital campus. The grounds were a bit of an anomaly with their red brick and white wood buildings, their ancient black oaks and white firs and ficus trees that cast enough shade to house a small village underneath. The whole place looked more like the campus of an Ivy League university than a Southern California psych hospital. I'm sure that if elms could've survived drinking only the fog of this dry, rocky valley surrounded by cacti-covered hills, someone would've planted them. I'd researched the facility before all my phone and email interviews just to get a sense of what I was getting into. Nothing told me about the history of this place. It was a new facility but the buildings and some of the trees looked more than a century old. I asked Dr. Benengeli about it.

She said, "This place used to be Winfield University."

"Really?" I had heard a little bit about Winfield U, but only a very little. RW Winfield was some kind of 19th century plutocrat. Made his money on railroads or oil or steel or something. Probably most of the money came from shady government deals and exploited workers. He had started this university at the end of his life. That was about all I knew. I said, "I thought Winfield University was still up and running. It closed down?"

"Of course," Dr. Benengeli said. "There was a big scandal and everything."

"Really?" I said again. I couldn't imagine something so scandalous that it would close a university, especially a fancy private one like Winfield.

"It actually had to do with old RW Winfield," Dr. Benengeli told me. "Apparently, some of the students claimed he was haunting the dorms. No one paid much attention. Students at old schools are always talking about ghosts. But then the stories became more and more commonplace. Old Man Winfield's ghost would pop up and shout at kids making out in the arboretum. He'd be seen wandering the halls late at night. He'd sneak into the girls' dorm and chase co-eds from room to room." She waved her hands vaguely in the direction of a cluster of buildings to the east. Perhaps these had been the girls' dorms. Perhaps she just spoke with her hands.

A cool wind sifted through my white dress shirt. I crossed my arms against the chill. "You're pulling my leg," I said.

Dr. Benengeli's eyes got big. She kept walking across the thick carpet of grass, talking. "That's what most people thought," she said. "A lot of locals would come by to see if they could catch a glimpse of the ghost. These four kids in particular showed up in their van, trying to hunt the ghost down. And for some reason, the ghost went right after them. Scared the hell out of their dog."

"Oh, yeah?" I said. The van and the dog were too much. I'd spent enough time as a little kid with a big bowl of cereal and Saturday cartoons to recognize the plot of a *Scooby Doo* episode when I heard it. I played along. "Only it turned out that the ghost wasn't a ghost at all, right? It was a local land developer who wanted to put up a strip mall where this university was."

"Exactly," she said. "And he would have gotten away with it, if not for those meddling kids."

I laughed. We wandered past a small concert shell with a stage just the right size for student productions. The concrete floor of the stage was worn smooth like the seat of an old rocking chair. "What really happened to close this place?" I asked.

Dr. Benengeli smiled again. "Oh, it's fucked up. It is a crazy story." Apparently such a wild story that Dr. Benengeli needed to add a third syllable to "crazy" when she said the word. She shook her head. "If you don't know about the scandal," she said, "I'm not going to be the one to tell you."

Fair enough. It would all come in time.

I gathered that Dr. Benengeli felt like blowing off work for most of the morning because she showed me every nook and cranny of the hospital grounds. She walked me through the therapy rooms, the doctors' offices, the medical hospital, the gym, the cafeteria, the Alzheimer's lab, the arboretum, the cottage once inhabited by the robber-baron himself RW Winfield, the psychiatric technician school, the post office, the library, the art gallery, the different dorms that housed patients according to their varying degrees of craziness, the chapels and synagogues and confessional booths, the archives, the canteen, the administration buildings, the Roads and Grounds office, the volleyball courts, the swimming pool, and the weight room. When it was all done, we headed in the direction of my office in the Williams Building.

"Your office," she told me, "is just behind the dual diagnosis dorm." She explained that "dual diagnosis" meant patients suffered from both addiction and mental illness. "It's not as bad as it sounds," she said. "We like to pathologize everything these days. We can always find a diagnosis for you if you need one."

"That's what the voices in my head keep telling me," I said.

"Right? Psychotic Disorder NOS." Dr. Benengeli opened the door to the dual diagnosis ward and led me through. We passed a therapy room with a group session in progress. I peeked inside. The patients looked like the type of crowd you'd find at the county fair: overweight men in overalls, middle-aged women with thick makeup and cheap hair dye, skinny young women with exposed midriffs, skinny young men with flat-brim hats and sunken eyes, old men with the chalky skin of day laborers. They slumped in plastic chairs and lit one cigarette off another and sucked on coffee in styrofoam cups. I paused a second too long because there, in the middle of this group, with her own sad eyes and styrofoam cup, was Lola Diaz: the second woman I ever loved.

Dr. Benengeli grabbed my elbow. "Quit gawking," she said. "It's time for us to get back to work."

2

On my first day off from the psych hospital, I bought work clothes. I was aware all the while of Thoreau's warning to beware of the enterprise that requires new clothes. I was also aware that Thoreau's mother baked him cookies while he was living out on Walden Pond. And Ralph Waldo Emerson—or Thoreau's aunt or mom, depending on where you get your story—paid Thoreau's taxes when he was in jail for not paying them. Since I had no one but myself to bake me cookies and pay my taxes, I couldn't be too wary of this enterprise. Since I didn't want to walk around for weeks smelling like a discount department store or from the body odor of days gone by, I gathered my new clothes and old clothes, and walked down to the laundromat.

This was a particularly tough day because it was the day my dog was going to die. My dog lived with my wife back in Fresno. I wanted to be there. For her. For him. I wanted to see him one last time and hold my wife when she cried but I couldn't find a bus or train or any other conveyance making its way from where I lived on the Southern California coast out to inland Fresno. So, on my dog's last day, I walked down the hill from my apartment to the nearest laundromat. I stacked my clothes on empty washers, slid dollars into a machine that gave me quarters, and slid those quarters into washers that filled with water. I filled them with detergent and clothes and the laundry bag that held the clothes. When the washers were loaded, I sat on a white plastic chair between the laundromat's front door and its side door. Santa Ana winds blew in one door and out the other. I leaned back, opened a book, stared at the words, and thought about my dog and my wife.

The dog's name was Nietzsche. He was so old that he dated back to

13

a time in our shared life when my wife and I were too young and stupid to realize how pretentious it was to name your dog after a philosopher, much less a German one with five consecutive consonants in his last name. That would put our adoption of Nietzsche at the summer between our freshman and sophomore years at Fresno State. If you count the years backwards from the time of this story to that particular shared summer, and then apply those years to Nietzsche's life, you'd realize that he was nearly eighteen years old. He had a permanent scab on his back just north of his tail. His hair matted up as it dried from his bath. He could not see. He could not hear. He was able to digest less than half the food he ate. The rest of the food came out as vomit or diarrhea. Since his hip was pretty much shot and he couldn't walk too well, he generally lay around within a few feet of this vomit or diarrhea. He smelled like death. It was time.

The only thing keeping the poor Nietzsche alive was my wife's love and her patience with the necessity of cleaning up his vomit and diarrhea daily. I had loved Nietzsche, too. I saw him as a portal into greater things in my life when we first adopted him. As his health deteriorated, Nietzsche came to be a reminder of my own mortality and the futility of life. He also came to represent all of my life's failures.

I sat in that laundromat and thought about Nietzsche and my failures until the washer cycled through and I transferred my clothes to the dryer. I returned to my white plastic chair between the Santa Anas and stared at the blurred ink on my paperback.

A young woman came into the laundromat at this point. Her hair had been dyed Jayne Mansfield platinum, her bangs cut high across her forehead. They were dyed black. She wore a little white dress tailored to look like something from a '40s stag magazine. Her high heels clumped across the laundromat linoleum. A barbed wire tattoo wrapped around her ankle. The Santa Ana winds blew through her sheer dress. Goosebumps formed on her pale legs. She plopped her clothes on the three washers closest to me. My glance drifted back to the blurred ink of the paperback. My mind returned to the chart of the typical American lifespan.

If you're tracking this with me, you'll see a couple in their mid-thirties. They have graduated from a state university. They're both gainfully employed. They have health insurance, vision benefits, and retirement plans. They've shared a dog for nearly eighteen years. This should be a time in their lives when they've proven that they can be nurturing, that they're responsible enough to have a life dependent upon them for food, shelter, etc. They've garnered stability. At this point, they should be focused on taking the next step: breeding. Instead, you see the couple living in two towns separated by hundreds of miles. One half of the couple takes the responsibility of killing the dog (humanely; it's the best thing for the dog after all). The other half sits in a laundromat washing the new clothes he needed for his first job in a mainstream, white-collar environment. Inspect this development chart more closely. You may realize that, by now, the couple should be four or five years beyond this point. There should be a child. Nietzsche's demise should coincide with the child's adventures in kindergarten. At the very least, there should be a washing machine and dryer at home and laundromats should be a romanticized memory of the lean, post-college days. You may look at me, the one in the laundromat with discount department store clothes, and cast the blame. This would not be the right time to defend myself. I would be too distracted.

I snapped out of the chart and my blame when I saw a vague white fluttering in the far right recesses of my peripheral vision. The Santa Anas played with the pin-up girl's white skirt. It floated up her pale, goose-bumped thighs. She set down her detergent and flattened her skirt. I glanced lower down her leg, watched that barbed wire tattoo twist around her ankle. That barbed wire allowed me to do more math. An unspoken fashion moratorium must have passed on the barbed wire band tattoo sometime around 1995…'96 at the latest. It reached the apex of its popularity, though, around '92. The recipient of a barbed wire band tattoo would likely be no younger than eighteen, no older than twenty-three. Looking at median numbers, factoring standard deviations, discarding data too wildly errant to be relevant, I decided that this woman would likely be around my age. Around my age and also at a laundromat, but wearing high heels and a sheer dress that was no match for the January California winds. Her development chart had to be lagging behind mine. I tried to take a little comfort in that and returned my gaze to the paperback.

It was no use trying to read. Nietzsche was surely dead at this point. My life compared to a pin-up laundromat girl meant little to me. I worried more about my life compared to what I wanted, what I dreamed, where I found meaning under this crushing wave of mortality. At what point would *I* be broken-hipped, blind, deaf, picking at perpetual scabs, and sleeping next to my own vomit? Will someone have the humanity to put me to sleep? Will I have the courage to accept an end to this life? Did Nietzsche know where he was going this morning? Did he shake and quiver in my wife's arms? Did she wrap him in a blanket and try to convince herself that Nietzsche was shaking because of the cold, not because of the great unknown he was facing? Did that white dress just flutter up higher?

I shot my glance over just in time to see the pin-up girl's hand smoothing her dress down. Surely, the corner of my eye didn't deceive me. Surely, the Santa Anas had swept that dress high enough for me to realize—despite my fractured consciousness—that the pin-up girl was not wearing underwear. Surely, it was better that I didn't see it. This woman deserved her privacy. She didn't need some sad psych hospital grant writer with a dead dog staring at her ass.

I kept my eyes glued to the paperback that my mind wouldn't let me read. I told myself that my eyes needed to stay there because this young woman deserved her privacy, that she should be afforded the opportunity to sort her laundry into three machines without my lecherous stares. To be more honest, though, I kept my stares off her because I was convinced that people could feel it when you stare at them. A breeze grazes their necks. Their scalps feel lighter. They know. They look around to see who's looking. I didn't want this to happen to her, either for her own comfort or because the wind still blew through the laundromat doors. Either one.

I set my paperback down on the white plastic table adjacent to me and my white plastic chair. I picked up the paperclip I'd been using as a bookmark. I used it to dig at the dead skin around my cuticles. I thought of Nietzsche. The breeze picked up. My glance shot over. All mysteries were solved. The pin-up girl was not wearing underwear. Her hands were occupied with the sorting of her laundry. She let the wind blow and her dress flutter. She effectively, maybe unconsciously, mooned me. I watched until I felt a bit embarrassed. My mind drifted. My eyes followed the waves of the dress as it floated like a white streamer trapped between the wind and a tree branch. I wanted to look away, but at the core I was still a heterosexual male of the species, prone to all of the instincts inherent to my role in the animal kingdom. The wind died down within a few seconds anyway.

My mind kept fluttering, wondering if it meant anything that the dog named after the man who declared God dead was now dead himself, wondering if any of this added up to anything. Wondering why I hadn't just rented a car and driven to Fresno. This last thought killed the breeze in my mind because it seemed every other time in my life, I would have acted that way. I could imagine no point in my life when I would not have accompanied my wife in the task of taking Nietzsche on his final journey to the vet. But this time, for some reason, it was like someone had gotten into my head and insisted I stay here. It was that voice—the one that sounded like Dr. Bishop's—motivating me to act against the way I typically acted. Thinking about this hurt. It sent my eyes back to the pages of the paperback. I still couldn't make out the letters.

Then the wind picked up. It inflated her dress to the point where I could see above her ass. I could see the dimples where her lower back tied into her pelvis. Again, the pin-up girl did nothing to smooth her skirt or fight the wind. She dropped a handful of quarters into her washer. She selected the proper water temperatures. I wondered if perhaps she could feel my glance, if she knew and she was letting it happen, if she wanted me to look. A wave of anxiety crashed on the shores of my stomach. I swam under it. After all, this wasn't a situation that required anything of me. I was married. I was happy enough about it. If I had been single, I would've felt the pressure to talk to this woman, to invite her to the coffee shop down the road, to buy her a pastry and listen to her life, to maybe get wrapped up in all the drama promised by someone who wore high heels to a laundromat and unabashedly advertised one of the most embarrassing tattoos from the early '90s. As things stood, I enjoyed a flash of divinity. My dryer buzzed. I pocketed my paperback and went to fold laundry.

Tall double-washers stood between me and the pin-up girl. She picked up her gossip magazine and pink laundry basket, and sat down in the white plastic chair I'd just vacated. She was no longer visible through the double washers. I folded my laundry. I dwelled again on the thoughts of my wife taking the responsibility that I dodged, on the distance between me and Fresno, on my uncharacteristic inability to be in Fresno at this crucial moment, on the fact that I'd spent a hundred dollars on three pairs of slacks, five button-up shirts, and a brown belt to match my dusty loafers. The next day would be Sunday. I'd go to the psych hospital to feel less lonely and use their computer to search out more funding possibilities, to find something to distract me from the death of Nietzsche.

3

The residents of the dual diagnosis dorm were on an afternoon smoke break when I arrived on hospital grounds. There was something lopsided about the whole group. They were like an oft-patched bicycle inner tube held together by bulky squares, stretched thin at the weak points, full of a wary optimism that this dried-out, cracked old rubber could hold it all together if it just had the right tire wrapped around it, if it were only asked to maintain the right amount of pressure and no careless or cruel bastard came along to over-inflate it. I had a smile and nod at the ready for the lot of them.

One young white guy in a FUBU sweatshirt held my glance so long that I felt like I had to say something. "Hi."

He replied, " 'Sup," and kept looking.

I took this as an invitation to cross the line past what was likely appropriate, considering my probationary status as an employee and my perhaps shaky status as a husband now that my wife was balking on making the few-hundred-mile move to Southern California. I said to him, "Lola's not taking her smoke break, huh?"

"Who?"

"Lola Diaz?"

"She a nurse or something?"

"A patient."

The dude shook his head. "Ain't no beaners in this dorm."

I winced, either at the word "beaner" or at the usually repressed notion that something about me in my white skin and discount department store clothes suggested that I was an okay guy to say "beaner" around. I thought about making a comment about his comment and taking this conversation to the next level. I stopped myself when I realized that this dude was a patient at a mental hospital. "A *patient*," I told myself. "In a *mental hospital*." Besides that, he was a white guy in a FUBU shirt. I let it all slide, cut through the dual diagnosis dorm, and headed for the Williams Building.

Originally, the Williams Building had been built on the bottom of a hill. Small white Doric columns framed the entranceway. The building stretched three stories above the classical entranceway, its ancient brick bleached by the California sun, reinforced by rusty sand filling in porous gaps, and worn smooth by Pacific winds. The original building carried an addition the way a horseshoe crab carries its young. The addition stretched halfway up the hill, supported by newer brick, flanked by newer windows, topped by a black shingle roof that was sloped slightly steeper than the original. Sunlight bounced off the ghost of a long-forgotten contractor who surely must have put an arm around a cost-conscious university president saying, "We can save you thousands of dollars this way and who's gonna know the difference? You and me. That's it." And perhaps a younger ghost of that older university president was looking at the finished addition, thinking, *No. Everyone will notice.* All in all, the building didn't look too bad. Another twenty years of sun and dirt and wind might even the score.

The toughest thing about the addition came from the building's inside layout. The Williams Building was four stories high but it had eight different levels. Nine, if you counted the basement. The first floor of the original building was roughly six feet lower than the first floor of the newer building. All of the ceilings were about twelve feet high. The hallways from the newer building didn't exactly match up with the older hallways. Shrinking faculty offices, wide open halls for lectures, subdivided rooms for graduate assistants, and reroutes through the old classrooms that had been cut into newer, smaller ones added to the overall maze of the guts of the Williams Building. Six-foot stairways would surprise me. Halls would lead to dark recesses yet to be remodeled for the building's new job in the psych hospital. Simple errands during my first week caused me to pause and reflect on who might own a complete blueprint of this building and whether he'd sell me that blueprint. At times, I dreamed of drawing the Williams Building treasure map and placing a giant red X on my office. I toyed with the idea of bringing string to work, letting it unravel from the front door to my office. Breadcrumbs seemed too unreliable. My office was on the third and a half floor.

I wound my way through the Williams labyrinth, counting my steps. Twelve paces to the right to reach the stairway, up four levels of stairs, then to the left. I fumed about that cracked inner tube of a kid calling the second girl I'd ever loved a "beaner." I cut through the interns' lounge and counted seven more steps to the left. I tried to remind myself that I have to give people more leeway in a psych hospital. That argument didn't work. I still fumed. I successfully reminded myself that those last seven steps to the left were always a mistake and turned around, repairing those seven mistaken steps and adding an additional thirteen to them before reaching another half-stairway that led me to the familiar right turn into what on Sundays was apparently a dark hallway. For whatever reason, this reminded me of Nietzsche again. The dog, not the philosopher. I closed my eyes and counted my last steps thinking about the now-departed pup. At the count of eight, I opened my eyes again, turned to the right, and opened my office door.

The Professor sat there. He faced my desk, back to the door. He did not turn to look at me as I entered the office. I walked around my desk, sat in my chair, and faced him. "Professor," I said, and smiled.

This is a problem of mine: I smile when I don't know which emotion to express. I've been doing it at least since I was a little kid. I distinctly remember smiling when my mother told me that my grandmother—her mother—had died. Not because I wasn't sad. I was very sad; I'd just lost my favorite grandparent. I was old enough at the time to know what death meant. I just wasn't old enough to know what to do with that sadness and my mom usually cheered up if I gave her a smile. So I gave her an absolutely inappropriate smile.

Thirty years of life hadn't taught me much about what to do with my sadness. The best I could come up with on this Sunday was a trip to a psych hospital and a smile for The Professor, who, to the best of my knowledge, was a patient with the potential to become dangerous.

The Professor stood and offered his hand. I stood and shook it. We both sat again. The Professor didn't say a word. He regarded me. I took in his bow tie, his blue blazer, his maroon sweater vest, his crisp white shirt. Crumbs clung to the fuzz of his sweater vest, gathered along the little crest formed by his stomach when he sat. My eyes lingered on the crumbs. Toast? A Reuben for lunch, perhaps?

Time passed. That stupid smile stayed glued to my face.

Finally, The Professor said, "You must be the new grant writer."

"I must be," I said.

"Your timing couldn't be better," he said.

I waited for him to go on, but he didn't. He seemed somehow smaller in that chair, facing my desk. In front of the lecture hall on that first day, The Professor had beamed with a well-honed stage presence. Or classroom presence. He'd had that style, that cool of a shy person in his element. Sitting in the chair across from me, he lost that style. His body language seemed to tell a familiar story about being on the wrong side of a desk in all the places we find ourselves in the smaller chair: when we're sent to the principal's office, when we buy insurance, when we file a report at the police station, when we petition a professor for a higher grade or a boss for a raise. A transference from all those small moments of supplication weighed down The Professor's shoulders.

I didn't like my position—that of a principal, an insurance salesman, a cop, an authority of any kind. I wanted to put him at ease but I didn't know how. I watched him and kept waiting. When the pause stretched into the recesses of uncomfortable, I said, "How can I help?"

The Professor stroked the edge of his bow tie. "I'm sure I don't need to tell you about the scandal."

I shrugged. I hoped it was a vague enough gesture to get the three-syllable-crazy story from him. Apparently, The Professor read my shrug differently.

"Needless to say, Winfield University has seen better days. What this university needs is something dazzling, an academic statement that will reestablish us among the elite private universities on the West Coast. I propose to make this statement."

I picked up a pencil from the cup on my desk. I rolled the pencil between the pads of my thumbs and forefingers on both hands. The

Professor watched the pencil's slow roll. His eyes met mine, looking for an answer. I said, "Please, go on?"

Perhaps it was a little cruel for me to humor The Professor in this way. Perhaps I should've led him back through the maze of the Williams building and into a psych tech's arms. I couldn't help myself. My life's problems had gotten to the point where denial wasn't working any more. I either needed to face them head on or find a distraction. The Professor seemed to be the perfect distraction.

"Now, I know you're familiar with the works of David Hume. I recognized this when you visited my Monday lecture a few weeks back. I'm sure you're aware of the fundamental ontological problems raised by Hume and other modern philosophers, going all the way back to Descartes."

I was not, in fact, familiar with any of that. I'd never heard of David Hume. I didn't know what the word "ontological" meant. I ran over the word in my mind, just to travel its ridges and humps. I said, "Sure. Sure. Go on." Was that dopey smile still on my face? I'm sure it was.

"Well, I propose to solve that problem." The Professor said this so definitively that, for a split second, I felt a little foolish for not coming up with this conclusion myself.

I responded the only way I could think to. "Great!"

The Professor stood and took two steps to my bookshelves. I'd taken my books with me when I moved down from Fresno. The shelves were full of a hodgepodge of books on Buddhism and Taoism, grant-writing manuals, political books that I'd likely never read, newer versions of mid-20th century crime paperbacks, contemporary Japanese fiction, a few classics whose spines knew no wear, one crazy novel about carpenters in Florida, and, let's face it, a lot of junk. The Professor took his time examining the spines. He pulled out Thomas Merton's translations of Chuang-tzu. "Have you heard the butterfly story?" he asked.

"Yep," I said. "The guy couldn't be sure if he was a man dreaming he was a butterfly or vice versa."

"The transformation of things," The Professor said. He clasped hands behind his back and started pacing. My office was only about ten feet wide. His paces were short. His classroom presence had returned.

His transformation was complete.

"In essence, this question is endless. It doesn't matter if it's Chuang-tzu wondering if he's butterfly or man, or if it's Descartes staring at his hands, wondering if they really are his hands. The result is the same. We learn that everything we believe to be real isn't necessarily real. We pause for a second and wonder: if the past is gone, if the future has not yet happened, how can we be sure that our entire existence isn't simply this moment right now? How do we know that we didn't make up our past to explain our present? How do we know the future will resemble anything of the past?"

The Professor paused to look for my reaction. Who knows what my external expression was or what he read on my face? Internally, I liked the argument. I liked the idea that the whole universe could be wrapped up in this moment and my past could be a fiction. If it were all fictitious, if there were no past or future, I'd be off the hook. I could let it all float away and just enjoy this one moment: my own private philosophy lecture.

The Professor carried on. "Take you, for instance. You sit at that desk. You imagine yourself to be a grant writer employed by a private university. You have a vague sense that you went to a university yourself. You imagine memories of that university experience. Perhaps you have an idea of classes you took. Perhaps, when you dig through the crevices of your mind, you can unearth little treasures of knowledge from those classes. Perhaps you don't even dig through these parts of your brain. Perhaps it's something else, something personal. Your mind lingers on some problems with your love life, or with a sick child, or with unresolved feelings about your parents. Who knows? Maybe your dog just died. Anyway, you know you have this feeling of loss or longing. It's vague. You don't really understand where it comes from, so you assign it to a lover or child or parent or pet. But are they real? Are they here? Can you show me this loved one? Can you be certain that it's not all a fiction you created in your mind? Maybe this isn't a university at all. Maybe it's a mental hospital. Maybe you're an inmate…"

"Patient," I said.

The Professor stopped pacing. "Excuse me?"

"Residents of psych hospitals are called 'patients,' not 'inmates.'"

The Professor nodded and resumed pacing. "If your dream calls them 'patients,' we can go with that. Nonetheless, by any objective criteria, you cannot prove to yourself or me right now that any of it exists. The whole universe may have been created for this split second. There may be no past and no future. This may be everything."

I nodded and smiled. If only that were the case.

"What's the smile about?" The Professor asked.

"That idea," I said, "of the past being an illusion and the future a false hope. It's funny."

"It's not funny," he said. "Not if you can't prove otherwise."

"It's okay," I said. "I trust that I witnessed my past, and the future will come along, more or less in the way I expect it to. Whether I want it to or not."

"And what's the basis for this trust?"

I shrugged. "I don't know."

"How do you know that this moment isn't everything?"

"I don't know." But I did take a second to think about it. Okay, I figured, maybe there would be a bit of a respite if this moment were everything. Maybe it would be nice to relegate my past to a fiction and not deal with it. But I'd want the future part. Sad and lonely as I was feeling at this moment, I still had hope that things would get better. So I answered The Professor honestly. "It would suck if this moment *were* everything."

"It would more than suck. It would drive you mad. It would be unbearable."

I actually saw where he was going with this. "It would be so bad," I said, "that I'd probably create a fictional past and a belief in the future, just to keep from going mad."

"And so there's no distinction." The Professor pointed a finger to the sky, I guess to illustrate his point. "You can never know if there is any reality to reality, or if it's all a fiction created to ward off madness."

I leaned back in my chair. My pencil commenced its rolling between the pads of my fingertips. "This is the problem that you seek to solve?"

"Exactly."

It was too much for me. Curiosity had completely taken over my better judgment. And besides, this discussion was proving to be exactly the distraction I was seeking. I asked, "How are you going to solve this problem?"

"A series of objective experiments to show that the world does not necessarily operate the way you imagine. Of course, I'd need funding. Which is where you come in. I have proposals, hypotheses, prospectuses, you name it. It's all outlined and available for your perusal." His pacing led him to the window behind me. He opened it. A gust of January filled the room. I spun my seat to watch him.

"I'd like to see it," I said. I wondered for a second if these documents really existed, or if they were the elaborate pantomimes carried over from the front of the lecture hall.

The Professor snapped his fingers. I watched. He climbed out the window and floated away.

An hour later, the bare wood above the point of my pencil had turned black from pencil lead and the oil of my fingers. I continued to roll it between the pads of my fingers. I still sat in my chair, gazing out the closed window behind my desk. Of course, The Professor hadn't really floated out of it. He couldn't have. It's not humanly possible. He walked out the front door of my office and counted his footsteps to the exit of the Williams Building. There was no other way to explain it.

Still, our conversation had my head reeling. How did I know anything? More particularly, The Professor seemed so genuine in his beliefs, so convinced these grounds were still part of a university and I was a university grant writer that I didn't know what to think. Which one of us was the crazy one? Could it be that I was the patient? That there was no wife in Fresno, no Lola Diaz, no dead Nietzsche? I thought about the woman in the laundromat. Surely that had to be part of my overactive imagination, no? Surely American women at the beginning of the 21st century are more careful about exposing their backsides. Or...

Hmmm. I set the pencil down and turned to my computer. After several minutes of searching through the tangled lines of the internet, I found a story about Descartes. The story had been written by a professor and posted on his university web page. According to this professor,

Descartes admitted that there were moments in his life when he spent so much time wrestling with these questions about existence and reality that he could actually make himself believe that his hands weren't really his own. According to this professor's web page, when Descartes had these crises of faith, he generally left his lonely office. Being around people seemed to hold these deeper questions at bay.

At this point in my day, I was leery of the stories professors tell and sick of these questions. I decided to find some people to be around. And preferably not psych patients. I stood and forced opened my window. It creaked. Dust and flecks of old paint fell.

Outside, a woman with gray hair and a dark business suit approached the Williams Building from the direction of the dual diagnosis dorm. I watched her approach. She waved to me. I waved back. She kept waving. I realized that she was signaling to me. I closed the window. It dropped smoothly. I counted my steps, winding my way down through the labyrinth.

The woman sat in a plush, dark leather chair in the front lobby of the building. "I've been meaning to meet you for a week," she said.

"Oh?"

"Yes, indeed," she said. "I'm Dr. Bishop."

I gave her a broad smile and offered my hand. "It's a pleasure."

She grasped my hand. Her fingers were slim and cool as fresh asparagus.

"Did it seem sincere?" I asked.

"What's that?"

My smile hadn't waned. "My greeting. Do I seem sincerely pleased to meet you?"

"I suppose."

"Good. I figure sincerity is everything. If I can fake that, I've got it made."

She gave me a flustered look as if to say, "You are the grant writer, right? Not a patient?" But, no, I realized. Dr. Bishop was a professional. A psychologist. All of her facial expressions must be carefully calculated.

I explained myself. "The signature on your email. It's that quote from George Burns. 'Sincerity is everything…'"

Dr. Bishop smiled again. "Oh! I get it. A joke. I'm sorry. My secretary—ex-secretary—put that on my email. It was funny to her. A geeky psychologist joke. I can't figure out how to get rid of it." She pointed out the two plush chairs with her cool, slim fingers. "Please have a seat."

I did. We discussed hospital business for the next half-hour: forms, departments, hierarchies, donors, social events that were encouraged, social events that could be ignored, insurance plans, retirement benefits, staff projects, research projects, administrators' jurisdictions, the secretaries who really ran the joint, the charge nurses whose good sides I'd do myself a favor to get on, places to get office supplies, where to pick up the paycheck that had been waiting for me in payroll for 48 hours, Hawaiian shirt Fridays (the first of each month), vacation days and the best time to take them, and everything else that Dr. Bishop could think about. At the end of it all, she said to me, "You know, I'm not an administrator. I just volunteered to lead the search committee for a grant writer."

I did know that and told her so.

She continued, "Which is one of the reasons I wanted to talk to you. I've been engaged in some recent fascinating research myself."

I wasn't sure I was ready to hear about it, what with my earlier encounter with The Professor and all. Besides that, I knew a bit about her and her research. I'd suspected as much when I was going through the hiring process, but now, sitting face-to-face with Dr. Bishop, I realized that I did know her. I'd experienced her research firsthand. It had been years ago but it wasn't an event I was likely to forget. If she remembered me, she didn't let on. Without dredging up the past, I prodded her into the present. "Oh, yeah?"

She paused. "Let's not get into that now." She patted my knee. "Do you like dogs?"

"Yes, I do."

"Would you like a puppy?"

I laughed, surprised. "As a matter of fact, I would."

Dr. Bishop clapped twice. Each clap was as sharp and definitive as a period at the end of a sentence. White space separated them. She said,

"You look like a dog lover. And we just admitted a patient. A suicide attempt. When the paramedics picked him up, they found the saddest little dog in his apartment. Just a puppy. And, well, long story short, the patient is no longer with us. No longer among the living. But the puppy is living with me. My cats do not like him. He needs a new home. You're the guy to give it to him." Dr. Bishop popped out of her seat. She said, "Follow me."

I had no idea what I was getting myself into.

4

The next day, I sat in my wooden office chair, gazing at the fog outside my office window. I had a three-ring binder on my lap. It was full of papers I had printed off the internet, punched three holes in, and stuck in the binder. I had ordered the pages logically, highlighted them appropriately, made notes in the margins. On the computer behind me, I had computer files that held the drafts of various proposals. The phone on my desk could show a list of my last ten outgoing calls; all to people whose names were in my three-ring binder. Surrounded thus by all the signifiers of the consummate professional, I watched a bluebird.

The bluebird perched on the high branch of a fir sapling on the hill across from me. The young branch sagged under the bluebird's weight, swaying in the gentle breeze. I wondered if bluebirds were indigenous to this part of California and if it was odd to see a bluebird in January. Or, perhaps, was this the south where the bluebirds flew in the winter? Are bluebirds migratory? If so, where was the rest of its flock?

Letting go even further, I indulged in more thoughts, wondering if a group of bluebirds was called a flock, or, perhaps like crows, a group of them could be called a murder. A murder of bluebirds? It didn't have the right ring to it. And while I was on the subject—or nowhere near it, if you don't follow my random loose associations—where were all the palm trees on the grounds of this Southern California psych hospital? Wasn't it state law that palm trees had to be visible in every glance here in Southern California?

Dr. Benengeli snapped me out of my ruminations. I heard her voice in the hallway outside my office. "Are you supposed to be here?" she asked.

A male voice responded. He did not answer her question. He just said her name in that warm and jovial way that sets off alarm bells. He said, "Dr. Benengeli."

"Walters," Dr. Benengeli said. She paused. I set my feet on the floor and perked up my ears. "Are you supposed to be here?"

"I just wanted to say hello."

"To whom? To me?"

"Well, who else?"

"You know where my office is. You know it's not in this building." Dr. Benengeli had a lilt to her voice that I'd never heard. I thought of her exceptionally short stature and the lack of psych techs in this building and of the castor oil coating the barbs of this strange man's voice. I rushed into the hallway. The fluorescent light above my office door flickered. Dr. Benengeli and the strange man both stopped talking and turned to face me.

"Do you need a hand, Doctor?" I asked.

Castor Oil Walters gave me a smile. "You must be the new grant writer," he said.

I looked to Dr. Benengeli. Her eyes were like polished stone. I couldn't read anything in them. She didn't wait for subtleties to play out. "Okay," she said. "I see how it is. Come on, Walters. It's easy to get lost in this building. Let me show you to your car."

Walters walked toward me. He wore smoky dark glasses, even in the dark hallway, and he waved a white cane in front of himself. The cane didn't touch anything. The tip just floated a few inches off the ground and away from the wall. Walters didn't exactly look in my direction. I gathered that sight wasn't the sense he was relying on, anyway. He pulled a silver case from the inside pocket of his blazer and opened it. I looked to see what the silver case held. Business cards. He slid a card out like it was the end of a magic trick. *Ta-da*. The card was in my hand before I could think to refuse it. Dr. Benengeli spun Walters and led him down the hallway away from me.

I read the card:

FRANK WALTERS
CONSUMER LIAISON
DICKINSON AND ASSOCIATES

The address was on Wilshire Boulevard in Los Angeles. He had an office phone number there and a cell number with a 212 area code. I thought, 212? Manhattan?

I looked back down the hall. Dr. Benengeli and Frank Walters were gone. I scratched my chin with the card. Something seemed off. I couldn't put my finger on it. I returned to my seat and faced the window. The bluebird still sat on a high branch of a fir sapling. The sun burned away at the gray of the morning. Mist from the Pacific that had settled on the rocky hills around me started to fall away like a silk slip falling off the back of a chair. I tried to make sense of things.

Could Walters be a patient? Patients weren't allowed into the Williams Building. That would explain Dr. Benengeli shooing him away. But what was she doing up here? How did she know there was an errant patient? And why would she go after him herself? Wrangling wandering patients was the jurisdiction of psych techs. And what about that business card? Why would a patient be carrying a business card? While I was no authority on clothes, I had spent some time in a discount department store lately. That jacket Frank Walters wore had not come off a bargain rack. There was money behind the purchase of a blazer like that. His sunglasses alone must have cost more than my whole wardrobe. And it's not that people who own these items don't show up in a psych hospital; it's just that they don't wear their big money clothes here. Most patients show up wearing the clothes they'd wear if they were changing the oil in their car. Also, Dr. Benengeli had offered to walk him to his car, not to his room. Which would make a certain amount of sense if she knew he didn't have a room in the hospital, but why would she assume that a blind man had a car? Something was fishy.

Before I could figure out what was going on, my phone rang. It was someone from the Beatty Foundation for Mental Health. A grant possibility. I got back to work.

Ten minutes later, my phone call was done and Dr. Benengeli poked her head into my office. She didn't offer a greeting or loiter with any small talk. She got right to the point. "I don't want to tell you how to do your job or where to look for funding," she said, "but be careful around that guy."

"What?" I closed my three-ring binder and leveled my eyes at hers. "Why?"

Dr. Benengeli looked at her watch. "Crap. I have a ten o'clock group. I've got to run. Just be careful." She vanished down the hallway.

My phone rang. The caller ID told me the call was coming from the 212 area code. I answered. "This is Frank Walters of Dickinson and Associates," he said. "I'd like to talk to you about donating money to your institution. Can I take you to lunch on Thursday, say, one o'clock?"

"Sure," I said. I opened my nearly empty appointment book. Under the page listed for Thursday and the time listed for 1:00 PM, I wrote: *Frank Walters. Lunch.* I also wrote the name of the restaurant where he wanted to meet. And then added *Be careful.*

5

Of course there was a catch. Dr. Bishop gave me the puppy, sure, but she asked for a favor in return. She promised it would be a small favor but now I had a Roads and Grounds guy hooking up a timer and a surveillance camera in the front entranceway of my apartment. I wasn't sure what to make of this either.

The Roads and Grounds guy's name was Eric. He was a white guy with one of those autobiographical faces: hard and rocky, full of crevices and ravines and the lingering effects of time. It was a face that told the story of a man who'd had his feather earring and his Trans Am with an eagle painted on the hood, who'd smoked his Camels and drank his CC and Ginger, who'd learned the after-hours secrets of women who spent their evenings in dive bars, who'd surfaced on the other side worn and scarred but without regret. Or at least without any regret he'd admit to. It was the kind of face that I would hire if I were hiring because you don't get a face like that if you don't find a way to show up for work every Monday morning after spending a Friday, Saturday, and Sunday blowing the lion's share of what you'd earned the previous week. Perhaps it was this face that led Dr. Bishop to trust Eric. Regardless, he looked very trustworthy as he capped wires and double-checked connections.

The surveillance camera fit in the drawer of the small side table positioned by the front door. Eric had brought the table with him. It was the kind of furniture purchased from a big box store; the kind you take home and assemble with a Phillips-head screwdriver and a hammer for the tiny nails. The newspaper rack/table actually matched the rest of the cheap furniture in my apartment perfectly. I wondered how Eric or Dr. Bishop had known this would be the case. Then I remembered that

I was a man in my mid-30s who lived in an apartment, wore discount department store clothes, and waited patiently for his wife to leave Fresno, though signs were pointing more and more to the notion that she was not going to leave. Of course I'd have assemble-it-yourself, pressed-wood furniture.

Eric took the knob off the drawer. He asked me to hold one edge of his tape measure flush against the drawer, where the knob had been. He pulled his end of the tape to the middle of the tile foyer adjacent to my front door. He sized up the angle of the tape. He told me I could let go. He then positioned a drill to enter the table at roughly the angle that the tape had shown him. He drilled a hole there. The lens of the camera fit in Eric's new hole. Using door shims, Eric supported the camera in the drawer. He filled the rest of the drawer with styrofoam peanuts. When all seemed sturdy, he shut the drawer, saying, "You won't even notice this."

"And the whole idea is to film my floor?" I asked.

"To film what happens on that floor in the fifteen minutes prior to you coming home."

"What do you think is gonna happen?"

"It's not what I think. It's what Dr. Bishop thinks that matters."

"And what does she think is gonna happen?"

"She thinks your pup here is gonna sit in that spot and stare at the door."

"That's it?"

"Maybe wag his tale."

"That'll be one exciting movie," I said.

Eric smiled. His teeth were shockingly white, the kind of bleached bones you can get from over-the-counter teeth whiteners. His eyes backed up the smile. "It actually could make for an interesting movie, if you give it enough time."

I raised an eyebrow. Clearly there was something more going on here that I didn't understand.

Eric kneeled in front of his toolbox. He carefully arranged his tools, in order. With a four-inch paintbrush, he swept the shavings that his drill had left on my foyer tile onto a sheet of paper. He folded the shavings into the paper, careful not to let any slip out. He stuffed the paper and paintbrush into his toolbox. He stood up. "That'll do 'er," he said.

My new pup came over at this point. Perhaps he sensed that Eric was about to leave and it was time to go for a walk. He trotted over with his little legs and big paws. In another year, he'd be a decent-sized dog. He'd grow to maybe forty or forty-five pounds. I'd have to get a place with a little yard so there'd be enough room for the two of us. For the time being, he was still small enough for me to scoop up and hold on my forearm, if I wanted to. I didn't at the moment. The pup nuzzled against my leg. Eric bent to pet him. He said to the dog, "You must be the little gift from Dr. Bishop."

I watched Eric rub his fingers through the pup's short fur. It was the same brownish gray of a koala or the hair on my head. This was one more thing I liked about the pup: when I found short gray hairs around the apartment, I could tell myself that they were the pup's and not mine. As long as I stayed away from mirrors, I could believe it. "The timing couldn't have been better with this guy," I told Eric. "We had to put Nietzsche to sleep the day before."

"Nietzsche?"

"That's what my wife and I named our last dog. Nietzsche."

Eric looked around my front room. A few scattered newspapers, a couch I'd picked up at a thrift store, a once-nice recliner with dark armrest stains from the oil of my hands, an assemble-it-yourself, pressed-wood coffee table, an ancient television with a rabbit-ears antenna and a dial instead of push-buttons sitting on a two-tiered rolling cart, a turntable underneath the TV, and a cardboard box full of old LPs. "You got a wife around here?"

"In Fresno. She should be moving down here any day now," I said. I don't know if either of us believed me.

Eric nodded politely. "That's a lot of weight to put on a little dog's shoulders, naming him Nietzsche."

"I learned my lesson." Though maybe I hadn't. I named the new pup Clint Dempsey, after the kid who scored the only goal for the US national team in the 2006 World Cup. Clint Dempsey. Maybe that name is a lot of responsibility to give a dog, too. But if you didn't see the US/Ghana game when Clint Dempsey scored, let me tell you, it was one hell of a goal. "Anyway," I said, "it was a lucky coincidence, Dr. Bishop coming along with this pup when she did."

Eric gave me half a smile, a little bit of bleached bones squeaking out. "Coincidence?"

I nodded. "Yeah. Coincidence."

"If you study metaphysics, there are no coincidences."

"I don't study metaphysics."

Twenty minutes later, Clint Dempsey and I walked through the park near my apartment. Eric's truck sat parked in front of my apartment building. I did not know why but I didn't give it much thought either. I threw an old tennis ball for Clint Dempsey. The tennis ball possessed him. Nothing would stand between him and that ball, once it started moving. He crashed through little stands of bushes, he danced over the century-old roots of a gnarled oak, he shaved the lint off the jeans of passing park goers. All in pursuit of that ball. He knew no obstacle. At one point, he even gathered such a head of steam going downhill that gravity thrust him into a somersault. He regained his feet and still scooped up the ball before it stopped rolling. Just like his namesake. Clint Dempsey would win the ball.

I sat at the top of the park's hill, throwing the ball anew every time Clint Dempsey returned. The park spread out in front of me, lush and green. A paramedic lay in the grass, napping while his partner wandered around, listening to headphones. A couple held hands and meandered downhill. Four young men—flannel-shirted, beanies pulled down over their ears, fingers black from a day's work on the row crops east and south of town—gathered around a park bench, a joint passing between them. Ancient flat gravestones caught the occasional flash of the waning sunlight. These gravestones had long been abandoned by loved ones, the graveyard too spooky to build on but too beautiful to leave alone. Hence, this park. On the horizon, the sun scraped the ridgeline of islands on the horizon, leaving the Pacific aglow in orange.

A beer would taste good right now. Clint Dempsey brought me the ball. I threw it. He darted off. A woman jogged by on the sidewalk below me. The #6 city bus shuddered to a stop in front of the park. The farm workers crushed their joint and hurried over, bus passes visible before the doors were open.

I heard footsteps behind me. I turned to look. Eric was back. He had a plastic bag from the nearby convenience store. "What's the law on drinking beer in this park?"

"I guess that depends on who's drinking it and how much they're drinking."

"You and me." Eric pulled a large bottle of brown ale out of his bag and handed it to me. He stripped the plastic bag off a second, identical bottle. "And one apiece."

I dug my key ring out of my pocket. I'd kept a bottle opener on the key ring from the days when drinking used to be a bit of a hobby. The bottle opener still came in handy occasionally. I opened my bottle and traded with Eric. He handed me the unopened bottle and I solved that problem. "I guess it's all right," I said.

Clint Dempsey came back and I threw the ball again.

"Tell me about metaphysics," I said.

"What do you want to know?"

"What's up with the camera you installed in my apartment?"

"Didn't Dr. Bishop tell you?"

"She gave me a form to sign. I didn't read it, though."

"But you signed it?"

"Yep," I said. "I didn't care what the form said. I just wanted the dog." Which was half the truth. I still wasn't fully ready to face the other half. Just as I hadn't been able to bring myself to drive to Fresno for Nietzsche's last day, I couldn't bring myself to read the form Dr. Bishop had given me. That little something in my psyche prevented it. For the third time, I acted counter to my typical self. The third presence of that little voice in my psyche left me a little worried.

"He's a good dog," Eric said.

I watched Clint Dempsey leap over the napping paramedic and snatch the ball on a short hop. "That he is."

Eric lifted his baseball cap, scratched his gray-blond hair, and replaced the cap. He sipped his brown ale. He dug his work boots into the park grass. He did not say anything more about the camera. Clint

Dempsey came back. I threw the ball again.

"Southpaw?" Eric asked.

"I don't know what kind of dog he is," I said. "Mostly mutt, I think, but it looks like you can see a bit of hound in his face. Those droopy eyes, you know."

"Not the dog. You." Eric mimed a throw with his left arm.

"Yep. I'm left-handed."

A moment of silence passed. In honor of what, I don't know. The earth kept spinning to fill the space between the sun and me. I asked Eric again, "What's up with the camera?"

"I'm not good at explaining it."

"Do your best. No judgment here."

Eric fiddled with the bill of his ball cap. "Dr. Bishop is doing an experiment about the way we talk to one another without talking. Non-verbal communication."

"Okay."

"Like, do we talk to our dogs?"

"We give them commands. I know that's verbal but I don't think they speak the language."

Eric smiled. "But beyond that?"

"I don't know," I said. "I'm sure our body language says a lot."

Eric shook his head. "Dr. Bishop is looking for something less direct. She's trying to figure out if we talk to them in another realm of communication. Like, do they know when we're coming home? Can they somehow sense this?"

"How could they?" I asked.

Eric paused and took a sip of beer. Clint Dempsey returned with the ball. I tossed it down the hill. He took off in hot pursuit.

I asked, "So what's this other realm of communication? Telepathy?"

Eric winced. "Not telepathy. Dr. Bishop hates that word."

I smiled. "Okay." A little, embarrassed laugh slipped out. "So she's not testing to see if we're all sending telepathic messages to animals like we're Aquaman. But she is seeing if there is some sort of non-verbal, non-physical communication that we have with our pets."

"Something like that."

It all seemed silly to me. I didn't want to say so to Eric. Something in Eric's wince signaled that he was somehow invested in this research. I backed off a little. "So you set up the camera to click on at a certain time, right before I'm supposed to come home, and film to see whether the dog reacts?"

"Exactly."

"But wouldn't there be obvious problems? Like, how do you know that the dog isn't reacting to the sound of the camera turning on?"

"That's what the packing foam is all about. To muffle the sound."

"Dogs hear pretty well."

"There is an element of classical conditioning," Eric said. "To get around that, Dr. Bishop has me set the time to click on a few hours before you typically get home. Mostly we want to see if the dogs react."

Clint Dempsey reacted. He dropped the tennis ball between Eric's legs. Eric tossed the ball downhill. Clint Dempsey pursued.

I took this little break to come to a quick conclusion. I analyzed the comfort with which he used the term "classical conditioning." I chewed on his use of the second person plural pronoun. *We*. As in "we want to see." Not that Dr. Bishop wanted to see. Eric wanted to see, too. He must've had some kind of stake in this research. So I tested him. "Does this have anything do with the collective unconscious?"

"Yep. That's exactly it," Eric said. The orange light of the sunset settled into the crevices on his face. He stared off toward the Pacific. He didn't say more. It seemed like he'd given me my first clue but I wasn't sure what to do with it.

6

On the Wednesday before my Thursday lunch with Frank "Castor Oil" Walters, I dined alone on a picnic bench on psych hospital grounds. A cool Pacific wind sifted through the thin fabric of my discount department store clothes, but the warm sun countered the wind. It created a nice balance. About twenty yards to my left, a group of patients engaged in a pseudo-game of croquet. Psych techs kept a close eye on the game. One doctor patiently explained the rules, showed the patients the proper way to swing the mallet, and showed them the non-threatening way to hold the mallet between their turns. The patients were not high functioning. They wandered away from the course. Psych techs wrangled them back.

To my right, squirrels darted in and about a knotty manzanita tree. They barked and ran. I ate my sandwich. Salami and provolone on rye bread. A little bit of mustard. One squirrel had an acorn in his mouth. He seemed to lead the pack. The other squirrels chased him. I wondered what was behind it all. What thoughts ran through the tiny brains of these squirrels? Did they want to steal the acorn from their neighbor? With so many oak trees on the premises, so many acorns on the ground and in the trees, why take the time to steal this one? Why not just go snag an easily accessible acorn? Or maybe this was a game, like rugby or something. Catch the Squirrel with the Acorn. Maybe they had elaborate rules for Catch the Squirrel with the Acorn. Maybe goals could be scored, winners declared. Maybe they had practices and tournaments, acorn-holding champions and retired acorn-holding stars who thought wistfully about the glory days of running with their acorns, never getting caught. And, if so, there must be defensive stars as well: burly squirrels who knew the proper angle of pursuit to capture that acorn with the least amount of effort, fearless squirrels willing to forgo their own safety to launch out of acorn-filled trees in pursuit of the acorn runner. Or perhaps this was no game at all, but an elaborate mating ritual. Perhaps, in the squirrel kingdom, the male squirrel demonstrates his value by carrying the acorn; the female shows her love in the pursuit. Perhaps this one squirrel winding around the knotty branches of the manzanita tree was actually a lucky dude. Two females in pursuit. He'd let one catch him.

No, I didn't want to think about that. Personifying squirrels as jocks was all easy enough. A harmless daydream. Personifying love in squirrels, though, brought me to that sensitive area of my mind that I was trying to dodge. In fact, the mental activities of my lunch all had to do with an elaborate game of repression and evasion. I didn't want to think about Dr. Bishop's camera in my foyer or the experiment behind it; I didn't want to think about my meeting with Frank "Castor Oil" Walters; I didn't want to think about The Professor or my existence or how much of it might be my imagination protecting me from madness. And I definitely didn't want to think about Lola Diaz, whom I hadn't seen since my first day at the psych hospital.

Lola had spent a good deal of time lately wandering through the alleys and passageways of my mind. Old memories were dragged to the surface of my consciousness. Lola unearthed thoughts and feelings long ago discarded. When this happened, I sought solace in The Professor's philosophy. I tried to convince myself that maybe it was all a fiction. Maybe there was no Lola Diaz. Maybe I'd just created all the thoughts and feelings and memories as a way to ward off the madness inherent in a fleeting, meaningless existence. Maybe...

"Is it really you?"

I'd been so lost in thought that I hadn't heard her walk up. It was almost as if she glided in on the wind of my thoughts. I turned to look, though I already knew.

I said, "Hey, Lola."

She sat next to me in a blur of past and present. She'd spent the last twenty years frozen in the amber of my memory, forever sixteen years old. Now I had to update her in my mind. Some things hadn't changed:

that cute little nose, her plump lips, her irises the soft brown of Sugar Babies. She still didn't wear make-up. In general, everything about her had gotten a little bit bigger. Her cheeks were a little rounder; her breasts took a wider curve. With her low-cut polyester shirt showing me so much of those particular curves—the olive skin going pale in the sunlight—I had to make sure that my line of vision shot up to less invasive regions. Her brown hair still hung ironed straight with that precise part right down the middle. At first, I thought she'd dyed highlighted streaks in it. Looking closer, though, there was no hair dye. Gray hairs had infiltrated in too great a number to pluck but not with enough force to take over. So this was Lola Diaz at thirty-seven. I had no idea she'd be so beautiful.

Lola smiled. "It is you," she said. "I thought I'd seen you around. What are you doing here?"

I held up the remaining half of my salami and provolone sandwich. "Just having lunch."

"I meant here." Lola pointed down at the table. "You know. *Here*."

"You mean in the psych hospital?"

"Exactly."

"I work here. I'm a grant writer."

"I see." Lola nodded. I wondered if that was a look of disappointment on her face. Was she let down by my employee status? Had she hoped for me to say, "I'm a patient," and share my tale of woe? She stared down at the table. I tried to figure out what she was looking at. Nothing lay in front of her but rough planks of wood and flaking paint. I thought to ask her what she was here for but I couldn't bring myself to. She deserved her privacy.

I started to lift my left hand to scratch my cheek. Halfway to my face, Lola reached out and grabbed the gold band on my left ring finger. She touched it with her thumb and middle finger in a way that kept her skin from touching my skin. Still, I felt like I could feel her skin so close to mine, like the static electricity of her fingers were making the small hairs on my hand rise. Lola let go of my wedding ring. She said, "Pack up your lunch. I want to show you something."

When I think of the stories that my mind has created to explain how

I got here, I remember things this way: Lola and I had gone to high school together. That was in Folsom. There wasn't much to Folsom when we lived there. Not much to make it different from any other farming town in that middle California agricultural belt. We had a prison that Johnny Cash made famous in a song. We had a lot of hills and rocky pastures that made for good dirt bike paths. That's about all I remember. And I don't even remember the prison so much as I know the Johnny Cash song. I've heard that Folsom became more suburban since absorbing the Sacramento overflow, nurturing outlet malls and chain restaurants and big box stores. I can't say for sure. My parents moved away from Folsom when I was in college. I haven't been back since.

Swimming in that shallow pool of Folsom memories is sixteen-year-old Lola Diaz, already looking like a woman even though I still look like a gangly, skinny boy who hasn't quite mastered the mechanics of a body fresh from a teenage growth spurt. The womanly Lola Diaz comes up to the kid version of me at my locker. I brush my long hair out of my eyes. In my sixteen-year-old mind, I look like a Ramone with my tight jeans and leather motorcycle jacket and shaggy hair.

With the perspective of the impossible number of years that had passed since then, I realized that I looked nothing like a Ramone and Lola didn't care about the Ramones, anyway.

In that pool of memory, she says to me, "I heard you were going to take me out to a diner for pie and ice cream after school." Her cracking voice undermines the confidence of her words.

I say, "You heard right," trying hard to sound cool and failing to an equal degree.

Out of that exchange, a first date was born. That first date doesn't really swim in my shallow pool of memories. I remember more an amalgam of dates and meetings and times at the diners and slices of pie and doing everything we could do before six o'clock but never going out on an evening date with Lola. Not even on weekends.

I remembered sixteen-year-old Lola asking me out as thirty-seven-year-old Lola led me across the psych hospital grounds toward the largely unused North Quad. Perhaps it had something to do with the way her hips swayed when she walked, so brazen and smooth that there had to be a Pandora's box of insecurities behind this practiced confidence. Or maybe not. Maybe she was just walking. "Are you taking me to the Alzheimer's lab?" I asked.

"I don't remember," she said.

She smiled to show me she was kidding. Crow's-feet crinkled around her eyes, so striking for a mind that had barely updated Lola to an adult. I got the joke.

Lola led me through a parking lot that held no cars. The pavement was worn down to that point where it couldn't be smooth again. Tiny pebbles jutted out of the eroded tar. Weeds grew through cracks.

Beyond the parking lot stood an ancient red brick dorm that hadn't been renovated with the rest of the hospital. This dorm was so forgotten that the administration hadn't mentioned it when they talked about finding funding for renovation of various hospital buildings. Lola stopped at the side entrance of the dorm. "I need you to open the door," she said.

I reached for the ring of keys on my belt. "I'm not sure if I can."

"It's not locked. It's just heavy." Lola showed me how to grab the handle and told me to lift up, then pull out. I tried it. The door groaned under its own weight. Dust and flakes of weather-stripping rubber fluttered onto my hand. I pushed in with my shoulder and yanked up. The door broke free of the spontaneous seal of paint where its edge rested against the doorframe. I tugged the door back to me. It obeyed.

Just as Lola said, the door was heavy. The main problem being a broken hinge on the top of the door. I gently let the door rest, its bottom edge on the concrete ramp leading to the entrance. The sun cut a broad swath of light down the otherwise dark hallway. Lola led the way inside.

"This building was the art dorm back in the Winfield University days. I used to live here."

"You went to Winfield?" I said. It wasn't a question so much as an inarticulate way of saying, "I didn't know you went to Winfield."

Lola didn't answer. She led me down the dark hallway. Both sides were flanked by barren rooms: closets without closet doors, linoleum floors stained where feet rested in front of long lost chairs and scuffed by the legs of desks and beds that had long been auctioned off. Only dust and spiders stayed in these rooms. Even the doors lacked doorknobs. We passed a former bathroom. A few bathroom stall walls still stood, but the sinks and toilets were gone, the plumbing capped off. The lobby adjacent to the stairway was equally naked. Not even the carpet remained. Just swirls of ancient glue stuck to the concrete floor.

Lola climbed the first flight of stairs. "My room was on the third floor," she said.

"Is that where you're taking me?"

"No," Lola said. "I don't live there anymore."

We headed down the second floor hallway, directly above where we'd just come from. Without the light from the side door, I couldn't see much. I asked myself the following two questions: is Lola a patient here? And, if so, is it advisable for me, an employee of the psychiatric institution, to walk down a dark, deserted hallway with a patient, particularly if said patient is the second woman I ever loved? I wrestled with the first question first.

I figured that Lola must either be a patient or an employee. I hadn't noticed her at the all-staff meeting on my first day, but it had been my first day and I had been nervous. Surely I hadn't looked at everyone in that large lecture hall. And all the staff hadn't been there anyway. I hadn't seen her at any other employee function or in any of the places where the employees typically congregated to avoid the patients. There was the key test, too. Dr. Benengeli had told me on the first day that, if in doubt whether someone was a patient or an employee, look for keys. All of us employees carried a huge ring of keys so that we could get into and out of the various administration buildings. A huge ring of keys usually signified an employee. We were forever locking and unlocking doors. Sometimes patients picked up on this and did what they could to assemble a ring of lost keys. So the test wasn't foolproof. Still, it worked well enough that the staff kicked up a fuss when the administration proposed replacing all the keys with a single key fob that could get you in and out of anywhere on site.

Lola carried no keys. I couldn't ignore this. Also, if I'm going to be honest here, I should admit that I'd searched the faculty directory for her name. Her name was not listed. Clearly the chances were less than fifty/ fifty that she was an employee.

I'd seen her in the group session in the dual diagnosis dorm on my first day. It was possible she was an intern sitting in on a group. If I really wanted to believe this, I guess I could make myself believe it. The evidence pointed otherwise so it seemed likely that Lola was a patient. Her presence in the dual diagnosis group session suggested that she was a high-functioning patient. That was a plus. Her presence there also suggested that she had some kind of chemical dependency as well as a mental illness. I added it up. Based on the information at my disposal, the answer to my two questions would have to be: yes and no. In that particular order.

I walked behind Lola in that dark hallway, watching the brazen sway of her hips, and wondered what chemical she was dependent on. She had too much flesh around her bones, she was too full-figured of a woman to be addicted to speed or crystal meth or crack. Which was good. I wanted to eliminate those possibilities as soon as possible. Heroin was another possibility, but surely that would've been painted on her face right from the beginning. I would've noticed the tracks on her bare arms when she touched my wedding ring. I would've seen the sunken eyes when I met her glance. So what then? Marijuana. Maybe. It seemed far-fetched to think someone would need rehab for weed, but it didn't even take a week at the psych hospital to learn that courts order rehab for potheads. And my last job in Fresno showed me that you don't have to be physically addicted to a substance for it to deteriorate your life. So maybe weed. Cocaine was a possibility. If she were in the early stages of addiction, she could still have both a problem and all those curves. And, of course, there was always alcohol: the Occam's Razor solution to this.

Lola reached the end of the hallway. A sheet of plywood leaned against the window there. Lola grabbed one side and said, "Give me a hand. We'll lean it up against the wall behind you."

"Got it," I said. I picked up the plywood and moved it away from the window. The new light brought to life a series of icons and comics and colors and logos.

"Now, I don't want you to judge me by this," Lola said. "I was in college. Fifteen years have passed. I'm much better now."

I nodded. "Did you do this?"

"Guilty."

"I wasn't expecting this at all."

"How very evasive of you to say."

"Give me a second," I said. "Let me drink it all in."

The window cast light on a series of portraits that stretched from floor to ceiling, door to door, on the west wall of the dorm. In one mural, Marilyn Monroe played strip poker with John F. Kennedy. Styrofoam fast food cartons and waxed paper cups with prominent logos littered the poker table. In another, Bill Gates emerged as an infant from a computer screen, his coiled umbilical cord leading to a keyboard. Another mural featured Jesus, the Buddha, Confucius, an eight-armed Shiva, a gray-haired and white-robed Western God, and various other deities waiting in line at the DMV. They held tickets in their hands that read, "Your number is…" All of their numbers were between 161 and 169. A sign behind the DMV counter read "NOW SERVING: 003." And so on. Clever, well-executed bits of obvious satire. Nothing for a fine art gallery, but perfect for a college student to paint in a college dorm.

"I'm impressed," I said.

Lola pointed at the open window. "I started at that end and finished over there by the stairs," she said. "The better paintings are down there."

True to Lola's word, I found the most striking mural nearest the stairs. It was a simple scene: two cartoon squirrels at a picnic table, eating sandwiches and watching a bunch of tiny humans build a city in a gnarled oak tree. The landscape around them mirrored the campus outside the dorm. The painting itself mirrored my thoughts at the exact moment when Lola approached me earlier. I remembered Eric's words: "If you study metaphysics, there are no coincidences." I thought, nope. It's too simple. If you believe in common human experience, that the campus occupied these grounds for more than a century and over the course of that time, surely hundreds of people sat at the picnic benches, eating sandwiches and watching squirrels. That's what the picnic benches were for: to eat at. Sandwiches have long been the most popular American lunch food. And surely the squirrels had been around for as long as the acorns had. Nothing metaphysical was going on here.

"How'd you get the school to let you paint on the dorm walls?"

"I told them it was a celebration of my cultural heritage."

"Are murals big in Puerto Rico?" I asked. Because I recalled this from my puddle of Folsom memories: that Lola was Puerto Rican.

Lola smiled, a sharp mouth on a round face. Trouble. "You think a bunch of white liberal arts professors know the difference between Mexican and PR?" Lola shook her head. "Hell, no."

"Well, well done," I said. "I'm impressed."

"I'm better now," Lola said. "I still paint. You should see my new stuff." She looked at her watch. "Oops. I better scoot. One o'clock group."

I followed Lola down the stairs to the first floor. She checked her watch again and looked up at me. "I'm really late," she said. She reached out for my left hand, touched my wedding ring again, shot me with a dose of static electricity, and trotted off.

I stood in the hallway and watched her go. She turned into a silhouette in the doorway and vanished in the California sun.

7

I spent the morning before my lunch with Frank Walters in my office, doing research on the computer. I looked up everything I could find on Dickinson and Associates. I checked their company website, read all the easily available information on them from a quick web search, then dug deeper, reading about them in articles written for business journals, checking reports for stockholders—though, of course, I wasn't a stockholder. I also did several searches for a Frank Walters, but the names were just too common and I couldn't find anything that matched who I thought this Frank Walters was. No luck with Francis Walters, either. I slipped and tried Frank "Castor Oil" Walters. I actually typed it into a search engine and clicked "search" before it occurred to me that the "Castor Oil" part of his name only existed in my mind. I searched and read steadily from seven o'clock that morning until ten thirty. This is the long story short of what I found:

J. Reginald Dickinson, an Australian who'd cut his teeth interning in the upper echelons of a mass media corporation there, founded the firm. After the internship, he moved into advertising. His first big break came in a United Fruit campaign for which he developed the slogan "Life Is Good When You Have a Big Banana." I found a series of ads featuring this cartoon monkey in some presumably Latin American jungle, happy as hell about the big banana in his hand. The ads were actually a bit more subtle than I expected, though they were not subtle. The United Fruit campaign catapulted Dickinson into the advertising big time. He moved his upstart company to New York City, actually landing an address on Madison Avenue (though apparently a bit south of the insiders' stretch of Madison Avenue). From this location, he developed other projects that have surely burrowed into your subconscious: The Cattle Ranchers of America's whole "You Can't Beat Our Meat" campaign; Big Sugar's "Even God Has a Sweet Tooth" push. His loosely veiled dick jokes and pseudo-religion moved the company up to a more fashionable address. From there, Dickinson created the two most controversial and short-lived Miller Beer campaigns: "Drink Her Pretty," which featured 30-second TV spots with geeky, frumped-out women gradually losing their disguises and transforming into strippers while fat men who were way out of the women's leagues got drunk, and "If Moms Made Miller, You'd Still Be Breastfeeding"—a series of billboards with sloppy, unshaven men in diapers tugging at giant apron strings, the apron barely covering a pair of dazzling legs in high heels. He was even the guy behind Taco Bell's "Heaven in a Taco" campaign, the one with the striking Chicana's face appearing in the lettuce of a fast food taco, apparently some reference to the Virgen de Guadalupe, only this lady says, "Eat me." And so on.

He expanded the company into public relations with his specialty being the shadow campaign, in which he'd create a manufactured buzz surrounding a product or an idea through non-traditional means. For example, in the '80s when a certain congressman from North Carolina was in hot water for some unethical practices with lobbyists and he was trailing dangerously behind in his re-election campaign, the congressman hired J. Reginald Dickinson to clear things up. Since even Dickinson couldn't spit shine this congressman's image, Dickinson attacked the congressman's opponent. The opponent, among other things, was campaigning to dedicate more money to AIDS research. Dickinson and Associates created a team of writers to produce opinion pieces that promulgated one simple catch phrase: "AIDS is God's Will." For the more radical publications, the writers would argue that AIDS attacked a demographic that needed to be attacked. In publications that welcomed unambiguous brutality, writers would make assertions like, "I'll worry about AIDS when it kills people I don't hate." Non-Dickinson writers started to pick up on the trend, attacking the new wave of writers and their hateful opinions. This created exactly the kind of buzz that the congressman needed to inspire his homophobic constituents to get to the voting booth that November. He won a narrow victory and was back to getting blowjobs from lobbyist-funded hookers in no time. As far as I can tell, none of those hookers had AIDS. There was no delicious irony here.

When word of the first Dickinson and Associates shadow campaign spread, the company really took off. They were able to employ radio and television personalities whose opinions were for hire. They worked on political campaigns large and small, from several different points on the political spectrum. They became masters of digging at the loose hangnail of America's id. They also became more subtle because I couldn't find much information on who they worked for or what they worked on. Dickinson and Associates clients clearly valued their privacy.

The last big campaign I could find that Dickinson and Associates had their fingers in was the re-imagining of School of the Americas. The School of the Americas was a facility on an army base in Georgia. Some of the alumni of this school included Chilean dictator General Augustus Pinochet and the men behind the brutal El Mozote Massacre in El Salvador. Congressional investigators had even unearthed SOA training manuals that taught the finer intricacies of torture. Every year, protestors gathered in huge numbers and rallied outside the gates of the SOA demanding its closure. After several years of protests, the US Army hired Dickinson and Associates to clear this mess up. Dickinson and Associates came up with a plan. They suggested that the army close the SOA, just as the protestors asked, but to start a new facility with the same teachers, classrooms, students, and curriculum. This new facility would be called the Western Hemisphere Institute for Security Cooperation. WHISC. This way, no one could complain about the SOA, no one could remember the name of the new facility, and if they tried to use the new acronym, it would sound pleasant. WHISC. Like a breath of fresh air.

The army changed the signs. This fractured all the sound bites around the protests. Everyone was happy. Well, except the protestors and the people who were tortured by WHISC alumni. But now they sounded like whiners because what more did they want? The SOA was closed. WHISC didn't have that horrible history. Et cetera.

At ten-thirty that morning, I'd had enough of my internet searches. I wasn't sure what to believe and I didn't really want to believe any of it.

I wanted to shrink the world back down to my little office in the maze of the Williams Building, to federal grants and psych hospital patients and January California breezes. I wanted to think about my shallow pool of Folsom memories, afternoons whiling away in the Diaz family's formal living room, sitting on an embroidered couch under wrought iron candleholders and a painting of San Juan city streets, watching Lola slide a Cure record into its sleeve, careful to touch only the edges of the record. Lola would spray all her records with rubbing alcohol and gently brush the grooves before putting them on the turntable. She would sit on the wooden living room floor, stare at the zigzag patterns of the area rug, and sing all the sad words of her favorite British pop stars. I had come to love music I would've otherwise hated, if only because each familiar wail made me feel like Lola was in the room.

Piggy-backed on that memory, of course, was the old living room grandfather clock striking five-thirty, the harried look of Lola saying, "My dad will be home soon," the rush of sweeping me out and clearing away any sign of my presence before her father's six o'clock return time.

I cracked open my office window to feel a little January breeze. A psych tech and The Professor strolled along the walkway that stretched between the Williams Building and the dual diagnosis dorm. I tried to imagine what The Professor might say about Dickinson and Associates. Would he tell me to question the sources, ask how reliable the websites of corporations, protestors, and business magazines really were? Would he take the larger road and ask me what it meant to develop a view of the world beyond my own, based upon the ephemeral words I read off a glowing screen? Would he chastise me for developing opinions about places I'd never go and people I'd never meet when all the while I couldn't prove to him that my hands were really mine or that I was more than just a butterfly dreaming I was a grant writer?

I needed to talk to people so I called an old bandmate of mine, a guy named Brandon Burch. Two things about Brandon Burch: 1. We'd been friends a long time ago, and as years stretched away from the original point of the friendship, I spent a lot of time questioning why we'd ever been friends; and 2. He worked down in Los Angeles on Wilshire Boulevard, where a bunch of advertising agencies are gathered. The area is known as the Miracle Mile, though there is no miracle about that stretch of Wilshire Boulevard, and it's not a mile long.

Brandon was in his office and picked up on the second ring. First things first, we dealt with small talk. "What's up with you?" Brandon asked. "Still trying to save the world?"

"Nope," I said. In a way, even answering the question was a confession that I had once been trying to save the world. I did not intend to make such a confession. I didn't believe it to be true. I never lived through a period so idealistic that I thought I—the wannabe Ramone from Folsom—could save the world.

"So you're not at the nonprofit anymore?"

"Nope."

"What was it again? A hippie commune?"

And, see, this was exactly why I wondered how I'd ever become friends with a guy like Brandon Burch. He knew that I'd worked at a community space, that there was nothing hippie about it, and that we weren't trying to save the world. We held free resume-writing workshops for blue-collar people, provided lunch for the homeless, hosted art exhibits and poetry readings for the Fresno State students. That kind of thing. I was the only employee of the space, and I only got a salary because I wrote the grant that gave me the salary. And, truth be told, I wrote all the grants that kept that place up and running. I knew that in the next minute, Brandon would make fun of my very modest salary. Which he did.

He said, "Still paying yourself Cup-O-Noodles wages?"

"Those days are over," I said. "I'm working as a grant writer at a psych hospital now. It's pays a good salary, benefits, you name it. I have a tie around my neck as we speak." Which was true. I had put on a tie that morning.

"I'll be damned." A few seconds of silence filled the line. An intentional pause. Brandon ended it with, "How's your wife? You still married?"

"Yep. She's doing good. We had to put Nietzsche down, though."

"I'm sorry to hear that." He paused again, for a shorter moment this time. "What does the afterlife hold for a dog that believes God is dead?"

"Do you think Nietzsche the dog believed that?" I asked.

Brandon said, "We better get to the point. You didn't call me to talk about dogs and philosophers. So what is this all about? Shoot."

"You know a guy named Frank Walters? Works for Dickinson and Associates?"

"Who's asking?"

"I'm asking."

"Why?"

"I'm supposed to have lunch with him today."

"Ouch," Brandon said. The pain was clearly non-physical. "Be careful."

"And why is that?"

"He's a dangerous dude."

"Dangerous how?"

"He's a guy who wants something so bad he can taste it, and he'll tear up anything between him and it."

"And what does he want so badly?"

"Oh, the same thing everyone wants: more money, more power. He works on the fifteenth floor and wants to work on the nineteenth. He lives in Agoura Hills and wants to live in Malibu. That kind of thing."

"Those floors and towns don't mean anything to me," I said. Of course, I gathered that the top brass worked on the nineteenth floor and people who wanted to be top brass were on the fifteenth. I knew what Malibu was. I'd have to look up Agoura Hills.

"Put it this way," Brandon said. "Walters just turned fifty. In advertising years, he's a hundred and sixty-seven. The guy's like Fu Manchu hatching fiendish plots to take over the company before his expiration date."

"What happens when you expire in advertising?"

"You spend the rest of your life as a mid-level executive in an office with a window overlooking a parking lot and a doorway with a view of smirking shits who get promoted over you because they know how to use urban slang to sell cleaning supplies."

"Are you telling me my paper towels aren't the shiznit?"

Brandon groaned. "What does Walters want with you anyway?"

"He says he wants to give money to the hospital."

"No one gives money for free. What's Walters trying to buy with his donation?"

"I don't know. Maybe he's just rich and generous."

"He's neither. The fucker tips fifteen percent and he isn't half as rich as he looks. He's got a lot of money; don't get me wrong. He probably made more this month than you would in a year at your stupid little hippie commune but he doesn't have big money to give you. Not run-a-hospital money. Though I guess he does have bribe-a-grant-writer money. And he definitely has put-a-grant-writer-in-the-hospital-if-he-doesn't-do-what-he's-told money."

"Thanks for the heads up." I took a second to process this last comment because in the world of my little desk in the maze of the Williams Building, with a window overlooking a dual diagnosis ward, advertisers who hired thugs didn't seem to fit. I asked, "Does a guy who works in advertising really have access to hired muscle?"

"Strange things happen north of the fourteenth floor. And a dude like Walters has no sense of humor. Oh, which reminds me." Brandon suddenly sounded animated. It was the first time in our conversation when his voice triggered those memories of our original friendship a decade and a half ago. "I have to tell you this. I was at an awards thing one time. An industry function, and I ended up standing next to Walters at the bar. I was all liquored up and knew I shouldn't do it, but in my booze-addled mind, I'm like, when am I gonna get this opportunity again? And I was curious. So I just asked Walters." Brandon paused.

I didn't want to bite, but I bit. "What did you ask him?"

" 'How do blind people know when they're done wiping their ass?' And you know what he said?"

I blurted, "When the toilet paper doesn't stink anymore?" I didn't want to say that. I didn't want to get sucked back into the early-20s Land of Dude that seemed to surround old friends like Brandon. I wanted to take higher ground. I just couldn't resist.

"Nah," Brandon said. "It's one of those jokes that's funnier without a punch line."

A short silence lingered between us. I didn't see any real need to rescue the conversation from the silence. I said, "Listen, I gotta go. I appreciate the info."

"No sweat," Brandon said. "And I know you're not asking for my advice but I'll give it anyway. Cancel your lunch with that fucking guy. No good can come from this."

"I may do that," I said, knowing I wouldn't cancel that lunch. Because here it was, a voice in my head for the fourth time. It insisted I act against my nature and my better judgment. The same thing that held me here instead of going to Fresno on Nietzsche's last day, the same thing that kept me from reading the release form I signed for Dr. Bishop. It was a little creepy how insistent it was, how strangely directed. Maybe something was slipping inside. I had to be aware of that possibility. It wasn't enough to keep me from lunch with Frank Walters, though.

Brandon said, "Keep in touch."

"You got it." I pulled my appointment book closer. I underlined the words *Be careful.*

8

Frank Walters had asked to meet at a chain restaurant, the kind of place you could find lingering on the edge of most American suburbs and dotting Southern California freeways every twenty miles. Our meeting was scheduled for one o'clock. This had put me in a bit of a pickle. Due to the bus schedule and time allotted for walking to the big box shopping center and across its vast parking lot, I had a choice of either arriving for our lunch meeting fifteen minutes early or fifteen minutes late. I erred on the early side.

A hostess sat me at a four-top round table. On the wall above me hung one toy tricycle too small for any rider with the exception of an organ grinder's monkey, one railroad crossing sign, one candy-striped clown horn, one autographed picture of Mets legend Ron Swoboda making a diving catch in the 1969 World Series, one stuffed owl, and six black-faced Russian nesting dolls on a tiny shelf. A toy airplane hung from a rafter above my head, supported by fishing line. An absconded carousel horse stood at the end of the hallway, its nose pointing to the bathrooms. I tried to think of a story that encompassed all of these items, or some sort of theme that could tie together clown horns and nesting dolls and railroad signs but came up with nothing.

In front of me lay my white, three-ring binder with all of my grant information. I couldn't concentrate on it or anything else in the clutter of surrounding kitsch. I closed my eyes and tried to think of something more peaceful: the cemetery park by my house, Clint Dempsey chasing a tennis ball, the soft flesh of my wife's earlobes, Lola's wall of college art. It calmed me long enough to open my eyes again. My gaze rested on a sign across the room from me. It showed a clip-art man from the

'40s. He had a huge head, a tiny body, and a cane that must've been for decoration judging from the way he held it. Below the clip-art man, the sign read *Hats Cleaned, 6¢*. Clearly, the interior designer of this restaurant was afflicted with that random madness brought on by a complete lack of imagination. I could make no other sense of it.

Luckily, the waitress snapped me out of it. She approached my table from behind me and said, "Hey, you. I'm glad you stopped by."

I looked up at her. Nothing about her eyes struck me as familiar. I wondered if she knew me from the psych hospital, or if the tone of her voice was affected, claiming to know me in an accepted insincerity, much in the way that this particular big box restaurant claimed to be "Your Neighborhood Restaurant" though it was in hundreds of locations throughout the US, none of which could accurately be called a "neighborhood." I gave the waitress my best noncommittal smile.

"What can I get you to drink?" she asked. She set a cardboard coaster that doubled as a beer advertisement on the table in front of me. Her fingernails were painted black.

"An iced tea, please."

"Mango or passion fruit?"

This question struck me as nonsensical as the decorations. It took me half a second to understand that mango and passion fruit were my choices of iced tea. I didn't know how to choose one. I said, "Whichever one you recommend."

The waitress smiled. "Passion fruit." She winked and walked away. I watched her pale legs swish as she left, her saddle shoes and frilly white socks a blur on the dark, matted carpet.

I'd brought my three-ring binder with me to the restaurant for two reasons: it gave me something to read on the bus and it served as a reminder that the funding for the hospital was going well. I was negotiating with both a pharmaceutical company and our research scientists about a large endowment to drive their Alzheimer's research. A psychologist turned legislator had set aside a good deal of money from last year's state budget to cover hospitals like ours, and early conversations with various members of the Department of Mental Health led me to believe that a lot of that money would be heading our way. I had irons in several promising fires.

The indicators I could read all pointed to the notion that I was doing a good job so far and that the hospital didn't necessarily need money from Frank Walters of Dickinson and Associates.

I flipped the pages, re-read my own notes, kept my eyes down. A blur crept into my peripheral vision, white trails from a waving cane. I looked up to see Frank Walters. He paused at my table, pulled out a seat, folded his overcoat the long way and the short way and hung it over the back of the seat next to him, unbuttoned his jacket, and sat down without a word. He retracted the length of his cane into its handle.

I said, "Mr. Walters."

He offered his right hand. I shook it. I wondered how he knew how to find my table, how he'd gotten to the restaurant, all of those things. He moved with such ease and confidence that, for one shameful second, I wondered if he truly was blind. What a perfect coup for someone in his business: to soften the barbs associated with being an advertising guy by faking blindness. A nice dose of pity to dilute the contempt. If it was his personal campaign to advertise himself, it would be an effective one. I'd buy it. As soon as I finished wondering this about Walters, I felt like a jerk for even thinking it.

Walters adjusted his tie. Everything about him was immaculate: pressed silk shirt, matching handkerchief in his front pocket, suit jacket tailored to fit, manicured fingernails, hair so sculpted by product that a Santa Ana wind couldn't muss it. His sharpness was intimidating. I'd even dressed up a little for this lunch. I wore my best dress shirt, tie, and slacks. It was the outfit I wore for job interviews, the suit my mother had bought so that I wouldn't embarrass her at formal family functions. Only minus the jacket. I'd left that at home. Of course I recognized the irony of getting dressed up to meet a blind man.

Walters said, "I'm sure you're wondering why I invited you to lunch."

"I am."

"My firm is willing to make quite a generous donation to your mental hospital."

"I appreciate that."

"We understand that some of your scientists are engaged in very compelling research. We are willing to completely fund one of these scientists."

I tried to see the angle in this. The first research scientists I thought of at the facility were the Alzheimer's biologists. Why would an advertising firm be interested in Alzheimer's research?

I said, "That's very generous of you."

"And would you like to know why we are willing to make such a generous donation?"

The waitress returned with my iced tea. She leaned over the table to set it down, her left shoulder close to my nose. I caught a whiff of some kind of laboratory chocolate body wash. It sparked something deep in my unconscious. A rush of excitement. Expectation. I took another deep breath, barely looking at the waitress. She took Walters' drink order and vanished again.

I gathered my wits. "It's not my place to ask," I said. "By its very nature, a donation has no strings attached to it. It's a gift with no implied return. That's what 'donation' means. Donations with implied returns are called 'payments.' If you want to pay the hospital for something, you took the wrong guy out to lunch."

Walters laughed out twin guffaws. His voice was deep. His smile seemed sincere. His eyes, hidden behind the smoky dark glasses, gave no hints. He wagged his finger in my general direction, though the actual point of his finger was directed over my left shoulder. "You're not new at this game. I appreciate that."

Perhaps this was meant as a compliment, but it struck me as condescending. I shrugged it off.

"How did you come to work at the mental hospital?" he asked.

I decided it was best not to tell Walters anything that wasn't readily obvious. I left out all the bits about my wife finding work down here, pressuring me to leave Fresno and find a better-paying job, my job search which landed me at the psych hospital, my wife balking about the move, Nietzsche's health being at the point where we were afraid to move him, my wife's job falling through, and so on. The whole tangled mess was none of his business. As my personal drama continued to unfold in my mind, it seemed unreal. I avoided talking and even thinking about it as much as I could. I said to Walters, "Psych hospitals like this one are becoming a thing of the past. I'd like to help turn that trend around."

"Tell me about it. A place like yours saved my mother's life."

"Really?"

"It's true. I know electroshock therapy gets a bad rap, especially around people who don't know anything about it. But when I was a child, my mother was haunted. I don't know what it was, but I know she wasn't able to let it go. Something had a hold on her and made her life miserable. She went away to a facility for several months. She underwent a series of electroshock treatments, and when she came back home, whatever had haunted her was gone. Or at least held at bay. Either way, her transformation was amazing. I owe a great deal to these hospitals."

"When was this?"

"A long time ago. I was just a kid."

"So when are we talking about? Late '60s? Early '70s?"

"Try early '60s." Walters reached out to the table in front of him. He grabbed his silverware and unwrapped it from its paper napkin cocoon. He set the fork and spoon to the left of where his plate would sit, and his knife to the right. He set the napkin on his lap. "It's still in use, though. Electroshock therapy."

"Oh, I know," I said, though I wasn't at all certain he was telling the truth.

"And a damn good thing it is. You can't let public opinion drive your science."

"That's true." Apparently, I was agreeing with anything this guy said.

The waitress returned in her subtle cloud of laboratory chocolate. The unconscious jolt hit me again. Walters said to her, "Can you tell me what the woman at the table behind me is having? It smells wonderful."

The waitress glanced over at the table to her right. I took a good look at her face, the Jayne Mansfield white hair, the black bangs, her thin, pale neck stretching from the collar of her uniform shirt. Conscious memory overtook my déjà vu. I knew who this woman was. I'd seen her white skirt flutter in the Santa Ana winds that blew through the laundromat. No wonder these jolts shot through my brain. She said to Walters, "The jambalaya?"

"The Me Oh My-a Jumbo-laya?" Walters said. "I'd like that."

I wondered for a second how Walters knew the actual name that the menu gave for that dish. The menus were not in Braille. The woman behind us had ordered before Walters arrived.

The waitress turned to me. "And what can I get for you?"

"A burger and any side that's not fried and doesn't have mayonnaise on it."

"Fruit cup?"

"That's okay with me," I said.

"You don't want the Cheese Please Burger?" Walters said, seemingly trying to up-sell me, though it was understood that he'd be paying the bill.

"Cheese and a hamburger is an unholy union," I said, although I'm not Jewish and don't have dietary restrictions designating the separation of dairy from meat. I just don't like cheeseburgers.

The waitress smiled and fluttered off, her barbed wire tattoo buried under a frilly white sock.

I said to Walters, "I imagine you must know a lot about psychology, what with the business you're in."

Walters shook his head. "Not much," he said. "I know about operant conditioning. It's one of the basic principles of advertising. I know quite a bit about behavioral psychology. Ever since John Watson defected to Madison Avenue in the '20s, behavioralists have overrun the industry. I know that there's something psychological about restaurants like this applying musical names to their food that makes it sound better than it will likely taste. But that's not much psychology."

"Still, you're interested?"

"More on a personal level than a professional one. Advertising today isn't quite as psychological. It has more to do with demographics. Watch this." The waitress clomped by in her saddle shoes. Perhaps hearing the clomps, he waved her over. She paused at our table. He said, "Excuse me, Miss. Would you mind telling me your zip code?"

The waitress glanced around the nearby tables. Everything seemed in order. She didn't seem to be in a particular hurry. She said, "93003."

"Midtown?" he said.

She nodded.

He likely didn't need affirmation and couldn't see the nod, regardless. He said, "Tell me how many of these things are correct. You like cashmere sweaters, but only purchase them when they're on sale. You're registered at Sephora and when they send you a birthday coupon, you redeem it and buy expensive bottles of shampoo and body wash. You're not interested in tires and tend to buy whatever is on sale at the local Firestone. You don't eat much fast food but you can't resist the occasional Crispy Chicken Caesar Wrap at Wendy's. You dye your hair and occasionally like to mix in fun colors. You really like the looks of those new Mini Coopers and you're considering purchasing one. You own two pairs of Uggs. Both are factory seconds purchased at an outlet. You rarely purchase books. You only purchase music online, and you do that one song at a time. You have never voted in a special election. You don't use public transportation. You have a bicycle, but the tires are flat and you don't have a bike pump. You own the complete box set of *Sex & the City* and think the main character made a huge mistake when she broke up with the furniture maker. Am I close?"

"Wow," the waitress said. "That's pretty good." She looked at me and raised her eyebrows, then went back to work.

"Demographics, not psychology," Walters said.

Bizarre was more like it. Everything he said was a spot-on description of my wife, with the exception of the Wendy's wrap. My wife never ate at Wendy's though she did work at their corporate offices in Fresno. I wondered what was behind this little parlor trick he'd pulled, and how much of his description of my wife's purchasing habits was a coincidence. If I were to believe in metaphysics, or at least in Eric from Roads and Grounds, there are no coincidences.

Perhaps not coincidentally, at this exact moment the servers started clapping and singing a birthday song that was not "Happy Birthday" and therefore did not owe royalties to the artist who wrote "Happy Birthday." One of them carried a mound of chocolate and cream and high fructose corn syrup with a candle on top. They gathered around a corner booth near the window with the neon Blue Moon sign. An overweight woman in a flowered polyester blouse yelped and gushed, "I can't believe you guys."

Her friends—all similarly large women with similar polyester blouses—laughed and goaded the birthday girl. The servers continued to sing with bright smiles stuck on their faces. Suddenly, the madness of this big box restaurant made a little more sense. It was all a blend of performance and willful ignorance: the birthday girl acting like she was genuinely surprised when she likely came to this restaurant specifically for this song and dessert, her friends acting as if this were all spontaneous and not a repeat of previous birthday episodes, the servers trying to mask their humiliation with big smiles and an off-key song. Even the beer sign, Blue Moon, advertised one of those beers sold as a microbrew despite the fact it was made by a huge multinational corporation that owned half of Colorado.

The biggest performance, though, was enacted by me in my silly shirt and tie and slacks, acting as if I were anything but an aging punk rocker trying to find a way to keep his soul intact while making a living, as if I wasn't a failure of a husband who gave up my second greatest passion to save my marriage. I wondered how much of this Walters could see, blind or not.

The servers finished their song. The birthday girl blew out her candle. About half of the diners in the half-full restaurant applauded. Walters applauded. I did, too.

I didn't say anything about my little epiphany. I kept it to myself and let Walters talk and eat. I assumed that his more or less idle chatter was better than me giving away anything I didn't want to give away. After Walters had polished off his Me Oh My-a Jumbo-laya and I finished my No Cheese Please Burger and fruit cup (without a cute name), Walters selected among the three credit cards in his wallet and handed one to the waitress. He then got back to the point.

"I know that you're not a man for subtleties, so I'll just say it. I'm personally interested in the research that Dr. Bishop is doing. Extremely interested. I'm in control of some discretionary funds at Dickinson and Associates, and I'm willing to use those funds to cover the complete expenditures of her experiments and make sure she has the necessary means to continue her work."

This seemed the most random thing he'd said. I couldn't imagine why a man like Walters would want to fund a batty old doctor investigating telepathy in dogs. I didn't ask him why he was interested. I just said, "That's very generous of you."

"In exchange, I'd need access to any and all paperwork accompanying these experiments. And this is important: only I get access to her information." He pointed at his chest with his thumb to emphasize the "I." "No one else in my organization does."

"I'll pass your offer on to Dr. Bishop."

Walters reached across the table and grabbed my hand. The arm of his tailored suit rested less than a quarter-inch from a clump of rice and tomato sauce that had fallen off his bowl of Me Oh My-a Jumbo-laya. "Make no mistake. Though we both represent larger agencies, this offer is between you and me. Exclusively between you and me."

I gently slid my hand from underneath his. "I'll think about it," I said.

The waitress came back with the credit card slip and a pen for Walters. He asked her what the total had been. She read the number off the credit card slip. He said, "Can you put your finger by the lines where I add the tip and total?"

She did.

He set his finger on top of hers, softly enough for her to slide her hand out from underneath. He then added the fifteen-percent tip and total. As I watched him do this, the waitress handed me a slip of white, glossy cash-register paper. I unfolded it. Inside, in bubbly handwriting, were her phone number and her name. I smiled a false and inappropriate smile. I raised my left hand up to my chin and tickled my wedding ring with my left thumb, hoping she would get the hint. She just smiled and fluttered away.

I looked back to Walters. He pulled a thick, booklet-sized yellow envelope out of his pocket. The envelope was sealed. It had no names or markings of any kind. The paper was thick enough to prevent postal carriers or nosy roommates from peeking inside. He set it on the table in front of himself. He drummed his manicured fingers on it. "Look, I understand the situation from your perspective. You're an idealist. You spent your twenties trying to save the world. You spent even longer than that, right? You worked for that nonprofit well into your thirties. A guy with your particular skill set, you could've made a lot of money during that time. You wouldn't have to live in an apartment and ride the bus around town. You could own a home by now, your own car. And, I don't mean to presume, but maybe that extra bit of money you could've been making would make things smoother between you and your wife."

I stared at Walters, happy at this moment that he couldn't see the surprise on my face. So he knew everything. Just like me, he'd done his research prior to this meeting. I said nothing. A few seconds ticked off the clock. Walters let the empty time pass. He drummed the envelope in front of him. "I hope I don't offend you," he finally said. "I don't mean to bring your wife into this."

Though, of course he did mean to do just that. He wanted me to know how much he knew about me. He wanted me to use my imagination to fill in the blanks left by his little hints. I waited for him to make his point.

"Like I said, I understand somewhat where you're coming from. You're reaching that point in your life when you realize that the world can't be saved. You know now that idealism has its place, but a time comes when realism takes over. It becomes time to move on. It becomes time to start making the world better for yourself and for your wife. Maybe it's time to settle into a comfortable life and have kids. Again, I don't want to presume. I'm just letting you know that, if you work with me on this, you will reap financial rewards." His manicured fingernails slid the envelope across the table. I did not pick it up.

"Of course, you'll keep thinking about this," Walters said. "You'll wonder what I might want with Dr. Bishop's research. Perhaps you'll make some presumptions of your own. You'll imagine sinister intentions. Understand that there's nothing sinister here. I'm just a guy trying to get a jump on a discovery that I think I can make a buck on. You're in a position to profit off it, too. That's it."

I said nothing in response. I didn't take my eyes off his smoky dark glasses. I couldn't let all the effluvia of this big box restaurant distract me. I couldn't watch that waitress's pale legs flutter by another time. I was too busy wondering whether or not I was being careful. And what the hell could this have to do with dogs knowing when their masters came home?

Walters didn't wait for a response from me. He said, "There's one more thing I want you to keep in mind. It is this: I am a very powerful man."

I took a second to wonder how powerful. If he were genuinely big time, he wouldn't be in this big box restaurant eating with me. Someone with real wealth would've sent a car to pick me up and would've taken me to a much nicer restaurant. He would have dazzled me with his wealth. He wouldn't have had to tell me he was a very powerful man. He would have showed me. Or he would've sent a henchman to meet with me. So, at best, Walters was the henchman to a powerful man. Brandon had said Walters was only rich enough to bribe me or pay someone to put me in a hospital. And, well, there was a power in that I couldn't ignore. I didn't know who to believe or how to figure out what to believe. I asked Walters, "What does that mean?"

"It means, if you say no to me, you're saying no to an extremely powerful man."

"Okay," I said. Or maybe it was, "Okay?"

Walters stood. He buttoned his jacket, transferred his folded overcoat from the back of the chair to the crook of his arm, and extended his cane. "I'll keep in touch," he said. He followed the white sway of his cane out the door.

In the midst of this big box restaurant, Walters looked as if he were exiting stage left. I took a second to think about this: about his spotless clothes and his awkward way of talking with all those crazy transition words—*of course, perhaps, like I said, again, understand.* No one talks like that. No one dresses like that. Walters came at me as if he were trying play the role of the bad guy in a movie. He acted as if he were on stage, his costume selected for him, his dialog written by some hack. It raised all kinds of questions in my mind, like, if he's the actor, who's the director? Who's in charge of this performance? Or was this his own vehicle, the play he was writing, directing, and producing himself to catapult himself to the nineteenth floor? And, of course, since I was in a place that blended willful ignorance with performance, I could imagine that I was just being overly suspicious, paranoid.

I opened the flap of the envelope and peeked inside. A stack of one hundred dollar bills. Enough of them to solve a number of my problems. I didn't count them. I closed the envelope and stuck it in the front pocket of my pants. I stuffed the waitress's number next to it. I knew I wasn't going to call her. I guess I just didn't want to hurt her feelings by leaving the number there for the bus boy to stack on top of all the other trash.

I walked out of the big box restaurant, my pockets weighed down by things I didn't want and didn't feel right throwing away.

9

A week and a day later, my wife appeared.

I returned from work on Friday night, unlocked the door, and dropped my keys on the newspaper rack/table. Clint Dempsey greeted me. I squatted in the foyer, in front of the surveillance camera, and tried to pet him. Clint Dempsey jumped up and down, twisting, wagging his tail, trying to lick my face but missing, looking for affection but unable to settle himself long enough for me to give it to him. I did my best. I said, "Wanna go for a walk?"

"Sure."

I knew that voice. It wasn't Clint Dempsey's. It was my wife's. I looked up and there she was. She sat on the thrift store couch, legs crossed. She wore black tights, a plaid skirt, and her white cashmere sweater. I knew the sweater well. She'd found a cashmere sweater very similar to this one in a thrift store several years ago and purchased it for three dollars. She made a big deal about it when she got home, about what a great find it had been and a bargain and all, and that, new, the sweater would cost three hundred *dollars*, not three hundred *cents*. That particular thrift store cashmere sweater was already wearing through. If she wore a dark bra, shadows would drift through more threadbare parts of the sweater. So she replaced the thrift store bargain sweater with a nearly identical new one. She didn't tell me about her new purchase. I wasn't sure why not. I wouldn't have been angry. She wanted to keep it a secret, though, so I respected that. She pretended that she'd bought her $300 sweater for three hundred cents and I pretended I didn't know the difference. Anyway, it looked good on her. Stunning, really.

"You look nice," I said. "A little dressed up for a long drive."

"I came straight from work."

"Hungry?"

"Yeah."

Clint Dempsey jumped up against my leg. The surveillance camera caught it all. I said, "Come on. We'll take a walk, get this guy some exercise, pick up some food. The works."

My wife stood, smoothed her skirt, and walked toward me. We briefly hugged and exchanged a kiss in the foyer. The camera picked up the shot of her stockinged legs and my slacks and fake suede loafers. She knelt to put on her shoes, clunky leather oxfords with flames sewn on to the toes. I leashed Clint Dempsey. We headed out the door.

We strolled downhill toward the little independent grocery store. My wife filled me in on what our friends were up to in Fresno, who was leaving town, who was having kids, who went back to graduate school, who got fired, who was being an asshole at work, that kind of thing. I knew most of it. She'd told me most of this stuff the last few times we'd talked on the telephone. And, like most of our telephone calls, she avoided discussing anything deeper in our lives. She stayed on the surface.

About halfway down the hill, Clint Dempsey had to poop. We stopped at a tree in front of a lawyer's office. All of the lights were on inside. Next to the heavy wooden door at the front of the adobe-style office was a sign that read "Notary Public." My wife and I looked at each other to avoid looking at Clint Dempsey. I noticed for the first time that she'd lost a little bit of weight in the month or so since I'd seen her. Even her face looked thinner, skin wrapped tightly around the line of her jaw. I tested the waters below the surface a little. I said, "How are things at the community space?"

"They're closing up this month."

I winced. I had a feeling the center would close after I stopped writing the grants to fund it. I just didn't think it would happen this quickly. "That stinks."

"Yeah, well…" My wife turned her gaze away. She focused on something vaguely in the direction of the law offices behind me. "If you had cared about making it work, you would've stayed in Fresno."

I tried to meet her gaze because the tone of her voice wasn't much of a clue. I couldn't tell if she was talking about the community space or implying something bigger. I said, "Oh?"

She pointed at Clint Dempsey. He'd done his business in the little square of sand surrounding the tree. "Are you gonna scoop that up?"

I reached into my pocket. In the rush of leaving the apartment, I'd forgotten to grab a plastic poop bag. "I don't have anything to scoop it up with," I said. "We'll get it on the way home."

"Don't forget," she said.

We walked the rest of the way down the hill trying to avoid sensitive topics of conversation, though they did creep up. I talked about the town, how pretty it was, how close the ocean was, the nice weather, the beautiful sunsets, Southern California, etc. I bragged about how central everything was, how I could walk everywhere except work, but a bus ran up to the psych hospital. I even pointed out the bike paths that lined the streets. "You're going to love it here," I said.

She gave me back a noncommittal shrug. I would say it was a taste of my own medicine but I'd picked up that gesture from her. When we got to the store, she stayed outside with Clint Dempsey. One of us had to. Since I knew where everything was inside the store, and since I knew what I'd be cooking that night, I did the shopping. True to my word, I asked the cashier for an extra plastic bag. I scooped up Clint Dempsey's poop on the way back.

If I had known that my wife would be coming, I would've prepared more. Not that the place was dirty or that we hadn't lived together for the better part of fifteen years. Not that she didn't know me and how I lived. I just wanted to do something special. So I'd picked up a few extra items at the grocery store, and I got to work in the kitchen.

First, I made a syrup by boiling water, adding sugar, honey, a bit of lemon peel and a stick of cinnamon. While the syrup boiled, I chopped about a pound of walnuts and almonds into tiny chunks. I mixed the chopped nuts with more sugar and cinnamon. I turned off the flame under the syrup and left it to cool. I melted a stick of butter. One at a time, I laid sheets of phyllo in a shallow baking dish and brushed melted butter on them. All the while, my wife sat at the kitchen table, rolling a ball for Clint Dempsey, waiting for Clint Dempsey to fetch and return, rolling the ball again.

I layered the phyllo and the mixed nuts, sugar, and cinnamon. The ceremony of it was somewhat comforting: the slow, methodical act of building one of my favorite things. I had to admit there was an aspect of showing off here, too. For a long time, I didn't have money to make this kind of treat. Bags of walnuts and almonds cost too much for my humble budget. A twenty-dollar dessert was too decadent.

My wife looked at me for the first time since returning from the store just as I layered the last sheets of phyllo. She said, "Lucky me. I get baklava tonight."

Once the baklava was in the oven, I cleaned the kitchen and started dinner—another ritual of boiling water, peeling shrimp, chopping garlic, dicing tomatoes, cooking angel hair pasta, sautéing and mixing it all together. All the while, my wife rolled the ball into the living room. Clint Dempsey retrieved it.

I drained the pasta and mixed it together with the olive oil, garlic, tomatoes, and shrimp. My wife and I ate at the table. She fed Clint Dempsey shrimp from her plate. She said, "I love this dog."

"I'm glad," I said. There had been a few uncomfortable phone calls right after she'd put Nietzsche down, right after Dr. Bishop had given me Clint Dempsey. First, my wife expressed her anger about me not being there on Nietzsche's last day. I accidentally fueled the fire of her anger by telling her about the laundromat girl. I guess there were more than a few uncomfortable phone calls. Once the Nietzsche argument died down, my wife expressed her fear about my quick transfer of emotions. One dog down, a new dog in his place. I tried to explain that my love for Nietzsche and my love for Clint Dempsey were two different kinds of love. All she would say is, "I hope you wouldn't replace me so quickly."

What I didn't say and she didn't acknowledge, was that she had replaced me so quickly. At least that's what one particular friend in Fresno kept telling me. I chose to ignore the rumors.

After dinner, I pulled the baklava out of the oven and dripped the syrup onto it. My wife pulled my new bicycle off its hooks it and set it on the carpet. She said, "When did you get this thing?"

"Yesterday."

She rolled it around the carpet, leaving little tire tracks, little traces of dirt. "It's nice. Top of the line, huh?"

"Not exactly."

"But it's a hell of a bike." She examined it more closely, mentioned the brand name, the model. "I remember looking at these at the Bike Doctor. This was what you called your dream bike, right? It's what you said you'd buy if you suddenly came into a lot of money." She had a good memory for all those things we said we'd buy if we had the money. She held the bike at arm's length and marveled. "Did you suddenly come into a lot of money?"

I didn't mention the envelope from Frank Walters. I still wasn't sure what I was going to do about that, but I wanted to keep it to myself until I figured it out. I said, "The hospital pays me three times what the community space did. You know that."

"Still." My wife whistled. "This is nice. It must have set you back six hundred dollars."

"It was on sale."

"So what, then? Five-fifty?"

"Something like that," I said. To the woman wearing the $300 cashmere sweater.

"Plus tax?"

"Yeah."

"Which does bring it up to right around six hundred, right?"

I shrugged. Never marry an accountant. I said, "Baklava's ready."

She said, "I brought the divorce papers. You know that, don't you?"

Of course I knew that. I'd known it for months. I had hoped that maybe we could work things out when she got that job down here. We could move to a new place, start fresh, all that business. After I had gotten hired at the psych hospital and her job fell through the cracks, I knew. And even though I knew, even though we'd had all the roundabout conversations and fights and resolutions that it couldn't be resolved, even though I'd noticed that she didn't have enough love left to even hate me over any of this, when she told me she'd brought the divorce papers, I said, "What? Because I bought the bike?"

"Don't be an asshole," she said.

She leaned my bicycle against the two-tiered cart that held my television and record player and returned to the kitchen table. She opened her purse. I sat at the table across from her. She pulled out an envelope and handed it to me. I opened the envelope. "This is it, huh?"

"There's nothing to split up," she said. "No need to bring lawyers into this."

I nodded.

"You've already moved out."

"It's not like that. You wanted to move down here. I was just doing what you wanted."

"We've been through this a million times." She handed me the pen. "Just sign the papers."

I looked through them. Everything came at me in a blur of legal jargon. I took several deep breaths. I focused on the dark ink, the swirls on the paper. I cleared my mind enough to read. Everything seemed fair. Nothing looked underhanded. I thought about what I'd left in Fresno, and it was a lot, of course, but I narrowed my thoughts down to what material possessions I had left there. The only thing I still cared about was my record collection. I asked my wife to box it up and mail it to me.

"I can't," she said. "I sold it on eBay. You had some valuable stuff there."

"Christ, I know that."

She tucked her hair behind her ear. I watched the flow of the hair all the way down to her white, cashmere sweater. "Well, anyway," she said, "the money's already spent. No use crying over it."

I held her glance for a minute, looking not so much at her eyes as at the thick eyeliner painted above her lashes. Images of album covers flickered in my mind, fighting images of Fresno and fifteen years of marriage. They whipped up a tornado and spun through the alleys of my brain. I signed the papers. I said, "There's a notary back by where Clint Dempsey pooped. I'll get this taken care of right now. Have some baklava."

She nodded.

I rolled my new bike out the front door and raced down the hill. Wet ocean air cut through my long-sleeved t-shirt. Red lights of passing cars mingled with the white lines of the bike path. The bike shifted effortlessly into the highest gear. I reached the notary just as he was closing up for the night. For one green picture of Alexander Hamilton printed on US mint paper, he ended my part in the marriage.

I raced the bike back up the hill to my apartment. When I got there, the apartment was empty. The only traces of her were the dirty dishes in the sink and the stamped envelope for the clerk of courts back in Fresno. She took the baklava with her.

She took my dog, too.

10

I wanted to get in touch with Eric from Roads and Grounds, but I didn't know how. He had no direct extension. I could only contact him through Roads and Grounds, and what I wanted to talk to him about had nothing to do with Roads and Grounds. Hunting him down on the roads and grounds of the psych hospital was a futile pursuit. Eric was a veteran from the Winfield University days. He knew every hiding space on the hundred-acre campus. If you wanted to talk to Eric, you had to wait until he wanted to talk to you.

I spent a week figuring that out. One week of keeping my head down, writing grants, making follow-up calls, preparing budgets, meeting with administrators, dotting i's, crossing t's, dodging the dual diagnosis dorm, not calling the waitress and in fact putting her phone number through the paper shredder because I knew enough to know that the last thing I needed wrapped above the heels of a divorce was a barbed wire tattoo. One week not catching the bus to Fresno to make things work, to get back my wife or my dog, to give up the pursuit of reclaiming my middle class status and return to the halcyon days of trying to save a small part of the world that didn't want to be saved, at least not in the way I wanted to save it. One week of looking at an envelope full of hundred dollar bills—a hundred of them—and drumming my fingers.

I wanted to talk to Eric because the next step was figuring out what Dr. Bishop was up to and whether or not I wanted to go against all better instincts and sell that information. Since I seemed to have no other recourse, I squeezed my eyes tight and thought as hard as I could. I envisioned a corkboard floating in the ether above the psych hospital covered with flyers and notes and notices advertising the futile endeavors and unanswered claims of the patients and staff. I pinned my own note on that corkboard. It read, "Eric, contact me." Within an hour of pinning that unconscious note, there was a knock on my office door. Eric poked his head in the doorway. "Routine smoke alarm check," he said.

I waved him in.

Eric opened the metal door, strolled across the concrete, though carpeted, floor of my office, and went over to the smoke alarm that was bolted to one of the four concrete walls in my office. Concrete walls that supported the concrete floor above me. I drummed my fingers on my metal office desk and added up all the flammable things in front of me: one stack of grant paperwork, files of other working grants in a metal file cabinet, three pieces of crumpled paper in the metal trash basket, the wooden office chair I sat on, and perhaps the acoustic ceiling tile. I even doubted that you could draw a flame out of the flat, synthetic fiber carpet glued to the floor. It would probably just melt.

Eric said, "Cover your ears." I did. He pushed the test button on the smoke alarm. A loud, shrill, continuous beep bounced off the four concrete walls. I hadn't hung up so much as a picture in my office so there was nothing to absorb the alarm sound except the books on my bookshelf, which, on second thought, could've been used for a little fire. An auto-de-fé all their own. The alarm vibrated throughout the room for a few seconds until Eric took his finger off the button. "Everything looks good here," he said.

"Safety first."

Eric shook his finger. "Safety never takes a back seat."

I smiled.

Eric took a seat in the chair in front of my desk. He crossed his legs. His fingers stroked the heel of his brown work boots. "Sorry to hear about your dog," he said.

"How did you know?"

"The surveillance camera. I saw him walk out your front door with a pair of stockinged legs and clunky shoes."

"That he did."

"Too bad. Good dog. He'd wag his tail like a motherfucker when he knew you were coming home."

"The camera showed you all of that?"

"That's what it's for."

"And what does it show you now?"

"Nothing. An empty floor. Your legs walking in the door. You don't even go outside like you used to."

"I don't have a dog to walk anymore."

"You still have an outside to go to." Eric had a week's worth of stubble on his cheeks sticking out like sagebrush on a hard-packed desert floor. He scratched his new beard. His fingers grazed the barbs of hair. "I stopped watching. You're so depressed, you're depressing me."

I nodded. "You can come back to get your camera anytime you want."

"Nah." Eric shook his head. "Hang on to it. Maybe you'll get your dog back."

I picked up my stack of papers, tapped them against the desk even though they were already in order and formed a perfectly rectangular pile, and set them back down. I picked up a spare pencil and dropped it into the pencil cup. With nothing else left to straighten up on my desk, I grabbed a toy. It was a tiny plastic wind-up bird. When its spring was wound, the bird slowly dipped his beak down to the desk, came within a breath of actually touching the desk, and did a back flip. My wife had bought it for me at some long forgotten toy store. She'd said, "It was so cute, I just had to have it." But she gave it to me instead even though I didn't have to have it. Now the bird was a nervous habit of mine. I wound it up. I let it forever peck at a non-existent worm. I condemned it to the Sisyphean task of doing a back flip at the exact moment when it came closest to reaching that phantom worm.

I wound the toy and let it flip. I said, "Can I see that surveillance tape?"

Eric stood. "I don't see why not." He headed out the door. I followed. The wind-up bird performed back flips without an audience.

Dr. Bishop had set up an office for Eric in an abandoned storage room in a forgotten building on the north end of the North Quad. The room shared the same design scheme as my office: barren, off-white walls, one smoke alarm (presumably tested and in working order), and metal furniture. Pure utility. On the single metal desk sat a computer. Eric sat in front of that computer. He invited me to pull an office chair up next to him. I did. He focused his gaze on the computer screen, flicked his mouse thither and yon, and brought up a series of jerky video images of foyers. Nothing moved in any of them. Eric said, "These are some of the homes that we're monitoring. Obviously, I don't need to watch right now. And, obviously, this isn't all of them. Dr. Bishop has 47 volunteers in this experiment. Forty-eight, including you and your dog, if he comes home. I scan through them and look for action. It's pretty boring, so I listen to music. You want some music?"

I shrugged. I assumed a blue-collar guy like Eric would blast classic rock or pop country. I didn't particularly care to hear either. But, after all, this was his office.

Eric pushed the "play" button on the CD player next to him. First, an accordion blasted out of the speakers, then drums, then rhythm guitars. The music was norteño all the way. I looked closer at Eric. He still had all the northern European features I'd noticed in him initially. His hair still mixed that dirty blond and gray. I'd even learned his last name when he typed it into his computer to log in. Jurgenson. Eric Jurgenson. You didn't get much whiter than that.

Eric raised his voice so I could hear him over the norteño. "I edit everything out but the action. I store the little videos in files for Dr. Bishop."

"Do you have the one of my dog leaving?"

Eric flicked the mouse and opened a file named after me. "It's right here."

"How big is it?" I asked. "Can you email it to me?"

"No, but I can burn it onto a CD." Eric pulled the plastic cover off a stack of CD-Rs and grabbed a blank. "It'll only take a second."

I watched Eric slide the mouse around and work the CD burner on his computer. As I did this, a voice that sounded suspiciously like Dr. Bishop's said, "You should volunteer to work with Eric and Dr. Bishop on this." Was Dr. Bishop in the room? Was she speaking of herself in the third person? I looked around the barren little office. Dr. Bishop was not there.

I asked Eric, "Did you hear something?"

"It's this computer," he said. "It gets hot in here, so I installed a couple of extra fans inside to keep the hard drive cool."

It wasn't the fans I was hearing. It wasn't the norteño. It was that same voice once again saying, "You should volunteer to work with Eric and Dr. Bishop on this." I couldn't imagine why I should. I hardly felt like leaving home at all these days. I hardly felt like doing anything.

The voice said, "You could ride your bike up to the hospital. It'd give you a chance to ride your bike more." Which was a good point. I loved that bike, and I was hardly riding it. I figured I should listen to this creepy little voice. I asked Eric if he and Dr. Bishop could use any help.

"Sure, man," he said. "I'll talk to Doc about it and get back with you."

I spent the next day in front of the computer in my office. I watched a pair of stockinged legs and clunky shoes walk in the front door of my apartment; slender fingers slide the clunky shoes off the stockinged feet; a rough-edited chop; four minutes of Clint Dempsey sitting in the foyer, wagging his tail; my cheap brown loafers stepping into the foyer; Clint Dempsey twisting and jumping and licking; my slacks and jacket as I squat into the frame to pet Clint Dempsey; my slacks as I stand; the stockinged feet sliding back into leather oxfords with flames sewn into the toes; my hand attaching the leash to Clint Dempsey's collar; all three of us leaving; a rough-edit chop; all three return; another rough chop; my bike tires rolling out the door with my shoes and slacks alongside; a final rough-edit chop; stockinged legs and oxfords walking out the front door; and my lonely brown loafers walking in the door and stopping there.

I went further than that, even. I duplicated the five-minute file so that it would repeat perpetually for the length of a seventy-minute CD. I watched that CD four consecutive times.

When I was done, I addressed a postcard to both my wife and Clint Dempsey. To the left of the address, I wrote, "I love you. Please come home."

Neither dog nor wife answered.

11

I sat in my wooden office chair, feet propped on the window ledge, staring blankly in the direction of the sunny March day outside. A slight breeze blew through my slacks, tickling the hairs on my legs. The first fragrances of spring floated around: an impending evening rain mixed with hints of flowering shrubs. I wondered how much a Greyhound ticket to Fresno would cost and if I would make my situation better or worse by showing up in Fresno on a Greyhound. I even thought about renting a car despite the fact that I hadn't driven a car in years. I still knew how to drive, more or less.

A pebble pinged the upper pane of my window. It snapped me out of my thoughts, but I didn't move. Another pebble missed the upper pane, flew in through the open lower half of the window, and skittered across my desk. I stood and looked outside. Dr. Benengeli stood on the walkway, three and a half stories below me. She waved for me to come down and meet her.

I locked the office door behind me, turned left and counted eight steps, reached the half-stairway and walked down, strolled thirteen more paces, took a right through the interns' lounge, took another right to the stairs, trotted down four levels, and counted twelve paces out the door. Of course, I didn't need to count my steps anymore. I knew my way through the maze of the Williams Building. I knew it so well that I could've drawn that treasure map that I coveted when I first started at the hospital. But such is the nature of maps: by the time you can draw them, you don't need them anymore.

I met Dr. Benengeli under the Doric columns at the entranceway to the Williams Building. She smiled and said, "You need a break."

"I do," I said. "How did you know?"

"It's beautiful out. Spring is in the air. Everyone needs a break."

She strolled down the pathway and into the dual diagnosis dorm. I followed. I didn't ask her where she was taking me. She answered just as if I'd asked. "I'm doing an arts and crafts group this afternoon. Finger-painting. I thought you might want to join in."

"You thought I might want to finger-paint?"

"Yes."

I scratched my head. "Is there something about me that indicates that I want to return to kindergarten?"

Dr. Benengeli stopped abruptly in the lobby of the dual diagnosis dorm. I stopped, too. I looked over her head at a water cooler. The hairs on the back of my neck felt light. I glanced down. Dr. Benengeli held my glance. She said, "Everyone wants to go back to kindergarten."

I waited for her to elaborate. She started walking again. Little kindergarten memories flashed through my mind: climbing monkey bars, rolling wooden trucks around the classroom linoleum, walking the balance beam and getting a candy bar because I didn't fall, the PE teacher leading us all in a round of jumping jacks, a woman playing an acoustic guitar and everyone singing along with no notion or care about being off-key. Coloring. Fair enough. That was exactly the kind of day I'd like to have again. I followed Dr. Benengeli through the double glass front doors.

As we cut across the springtime hospital grounds, I thought about Dr. Benengeli throwing pebbles against my window just when I needed to get out of my office, as well as the videotape and Frank Walters and Dr. Bishop. I said, "What are your thoughts on Dr. Bishop's research? You know, with the dogs and all."

"Why? Is she trying to get you to fund it?"

"She hasn't said anything about that. I did participate in the study for a while."

"Oh, that's right. I heard about that. And your wife stole your dog." Dr. Benengeli tried to cast a sympathetic glance in my direction, but the suppressed smile betrayed her.

"You guys gossip way too much."

Dr. Benengeli touched my forearm with the palm of her hand. She grazed it so gently that I barely felt her touch. I slowed down. She said, "Are you taking care of yourself?"

"I'm fine," I said. "I'm just curious about Dr. Bishop's research."

"You know, you can talk to me about the divorce if you want. Not in a formal capacity, of course, but just as friends."

"Thanks." I did appreciate Dr. Benengeli's offer to take a busman's holiday with me, I just didn't feel like doing it at that moment. "But why would I want to talk divorce when I could talk about telepathic dogs?"

"You mean Dr. Bishop's research, of course. You know it's not really telepathy. She calls it the collective unconscious."

"You don't call it that?"

"Well, what she calls the collective unconscious and what Jung used those words to describe are two different things."

"I don't understand."

"You don't need to. Between you and me, it's all a crock. I mean, even if she's right, it's all a crock. The last thing we need to be investigating is a new form of communication." She swept her hand in front of her. Two other doctors cut across the narrow street between red brick buildings. Both doctors spoke on cellular phones, presumably not to one another. "Look at how much we talk, talk, talk these days. Emailing and texting and cell phones and landlines and blogs and on and on and on. And nothing gets said. We aren't exchanging anything deep or meaningful. We aren't even communicating in the genuine sense of the word. We're just chatting. Or maybe chattering. I don't know. I just think if you really want to help people communicate, you find a way to sit them down together, face-to-face. That's what I think we need."

"Hmmm," I said, because I wasn't sure how else to react. On the one hand, I agreed that we'd all be better off with more face-to-face communication. On the other hand, Dr. Benengeli was losing me. I didn't understand what Dr. Bishop meant by the collective unconscious; I didn't understand what it had to do with dogs or Eric's version of metaphysics. I still needed to understand what Walters wanted with it all. But Dr. Benengeli's mind was clearly drifting in other directions on this sunny afternoon, so I let the subject drop. Dr. Benengeli led me to the south quad.

Eight fiberglass and aluminum picnic tables had been grouped together in the yard in front of the dual diagnosis dorm. Two or three patients sat at each one. Assorted jars of finger paint were arranged in the middle of each picnic table. Psych techs distributed white sheets of 11" x 17" paper, one sheet per patient. I scanned the picnic tables for a place to sit. At the table nearest me sat The Professor and Lola Diaz. I tried to think of a smooth way to sit at any table except that one. Dr. Benengeli touched my elbow and said, "You can sit right here." She directed me to the seat next to The Professor. That settled that.

I took a seat. The Professor nodded. "You picked the right class to sit in on," he said. "Dr. Benengeli has the reputation of being the top Art professor here at Winfield."

Lola shot me a conspiratorial smile. I returned the sentiment. The Professor said, "Have you two met?" He motioned a hand toward Lola. "She's one of our shining stars in the Art Department. She recently finished a mural over in McCabe Hall. I would suggest that you stop by and view the painting. However, as you know, McCabe is not a co-ed dorm."

"It is now, Professor," Lola said.

He rubbed the edge of his bow tie. He straightened his vest. "It is?" he said. "When did they change that?"

"Last year," Lola said, without missing a beat. "Only girls are living there now, but boys are allowed in during visiting hours." Lola turned to address me. "You could stop by between three and four this afternoon and take a look."

I wasn't sure if this was a real invitation and I wanted no part of a subterfuge. I played their game. I said, "I have class at three today. Maybe sometime next week."

The conspiratorial grin spread across Lola's face.

Dr. Benengeli started the session. She said, "Today, we're working on sharing. Not only are we sharing our paints, we're sharing our thoughts, our feelings, and our artwork. I'm going to be coming around and joining each of your tables. I'm looking forward to hearing what you have to say and seeing what you produce. Are there any questions?" Dr. Benengeli glanced around the group. No one said anything. She clapped her hands once. "Great. Let's get started."

The Professor reached first for the jar of red paint in front of him. I waited for Lola to choose her color. Eric swept in next to Lola. He swung his brown work boots over the faded turquoise fiberglass seat of the picnic table, sat down, unzipped his blue Dickies jacket, took it off, folded it, and set it on the bench seat between him and Lola. He said, "Finger-painting. All right! You guys mind if I join you?"

"Not at all, Eric," The Professor said.

I looked at The Professor's eyes and tried to follow the line of their stare. Had The Professor read Eric's name off the embroidered nametag sewn into his Roads and Grounds shirt? Did The Professor remember Eric from the Winfield University days, or did they know each other from wandering around hospital grounds? Did all three of my tablemates have a history that stretched back to the Winfield era? Was everyone else in on it? In on what?

Lola took the jar of black paint. Eric raised his hand. A psych tech came by and handed Eric a sheet of white paper. He said, "Don't you ever work, Jurgenson?"

Eric grabbed the jar of yellow paint. "I'm working right now," he said. "I'm working on my finger-painting."

The psych tech raised an eyebrow, shook his head, wandered off. Eric smeared yellow paint haphazardly across his white paper. I took the jar of green paint. I was never much of an artist and didn't really have any vision for this day's finger-painting. Since I had green, I painted some grass. Or, to be more specific, I painted the bottom third of my paper green and imagined it to represent grass.

Eric said, "So, Professor, how are classes going this semester?"

"Wonderfully."

"Good group of kids?"

"There's always a good group of kids. But, yes, this year we have some exceptional students. In fact, you're sitting next to one of them."

Eric looked at Lola. Lola had dipped her clean fingers into both The Professor's red paint and Eric's yellow paint. She mixed the two together to create orange. She spread the orange paint into little circles that would surely add up to something soon. Eric said, "I don't think we've met. I'm Eric."

She barely looked up. She said, "Lola."

The Professor said, "Lola is the student who painted the mural in McCabe Hall."

"Really?" Eric said.

"Really," I said.

Eric looked me in the eyes. He said, "Really?" again, but with more conviction this time.

"Really," Lola said, without looking up.

"It is hard to believe," The Professor said.

I tried Lola's trick of blending paint. I dipped my fingers into the yellow and black paints and mixed them together to make a tree trunk. Or, to be more specific, I made a brownish vertical line that stretched up from the green bottom third of my sheet.

Eric crinkled his brow. Long eyebrow hairs jutted up in the sunlight. He said to Lola, "Were you at Winfield in the early '90s?"

Lola nodded.

The Professor said, "The early '90s? What year do you think this is, Eric?"

"Touché," Eric said.

I went back to painting. In my mind, all four of us at the table returned to kindergarten. I imagined us all as kids, but in that restricted imagination way. It was like when someone whom I've only known as an adult tells me a story about himself as a kid, and I think of the kid in the story but he's mostly just the shrunken down version of the adult in front of me. Eric returned to a time before the sun and smokes had cured and wrinkled his skin. His face became flush with baby fat. His hair was trapped in a gray-blond bowl cut that hung down to his shoulders. He sat with one leg underneath his butt, little kid work boot pressing up against little kid blue Dickies slacks. His shiny teeth bit his bottom lip and something about the way he smeared the paint around gave me the sense that recess was just around the corner. Good times ahead. The Professor regressed to kindergarten size in my mind's eye, too. He kept his bow tie and sweater vest and blazer, but they became new. Glistening polyester from the kid's department. His hair had been slicked back, except for the one strand that dangled over his forehead no matter how many times his mom licked her palm and pressed that wayward strand against his scalp. The kindergarten version of The Professor became so fragile in my mind, like a kid with brittle bone disease or hemophilia; the little boy who I want to invite into the game of tag the rest of us are playing, but I know that if he falls or gets cut, it's curtains. So we paint and he stares so intently, so seriously at his paper and the colors he can't seem to blend into anything that makes sense to the rest of us. Lola was the easiest to imagine back in kindergarten, because I'd known her then. We'd run in different circles thirty-plus years ago, but the image of her flashed from some long-ignored neurons. Her chocolate brown bangs. The rest of her curly hair pinned back with butterfly barrettes. The dimples on her round cheeks. The sundress with the white lace collar that her mom sewed for her. Those tiny, delicate brown fingers that I just wanted to wrap up in my hands…

I couldn't call up the kindergarten version of myself. The harder I tried, the more I stayed a mid-30s grant writer. A guy whose wife just left him. And took the dog. Someone with nothing to go home to except the dust of nameless tenants trapped in the paint and carpet fibers of a generic Southern California box apartment.

I left my imaginary kindergarten class and focused on my painting.

Dr. Benengeli visited our table last. By this time, The Professor had elaborated on his classes this semester. He'd given us the lowdown on Leibniz and his notion of the best of all possible worlds. Eric and I nodded along. Lola kept painting. She created a beautiful, round-faced, brown-skinned woman with huge brown eyes handing a bouquet of sunflowers to a tiny, yapping dog. Because she used her fingers carefully and even used her fingernails to create fine lines, it was hard to believe that her painting had been done without the aid of a brush. It was stunning. She had gotten much better since the days of the McCabe mural. Eric painted a big yellow dump truck. The Professor painted a bunch of smears that I couldn't assemble into anything unless Dr. Rorschach asked me to and then scored me based on my responses. Dr. Benengeli inspected each painting in order. She responded with appropriate "ooohs" and "aaahhs" and pointed questions and concerned listening and unconditional positive regard. She appropriately downplayed the superiority of Lola's painting, even though we could all see it.

She inspected my painting last. On top of the grass, next to the tree, I'd painted a stick figure with yellow skin. She wore a black skirt and black shoes. Since I couldn't paint a white sweater on white paper, I painted the background all blue and left the paper white where the sweater would be.

Dr. Benengeli lifted my left hand and inspected it. A smattering of paint covered my fingernails and burrowed into the cracks and wrinkles of my skin. The ring on my left ring finger suddenly felt like it weighed a hundred pounds. It looked huge to me, like a glowing paean to my failure and denial. Everyone at the hospital knew about my divorce by now. Gossip traveled faster than I'd ever thought it would among a bunch of people who barely knew me, among a bunch of people who took confidentiality oaths and dealt daily with pedestrian issues like the divorces and deaths of expendable lives like mine. I felt like everyone at the picnic table was looking at my ring, though I knew it was ridiculous, though I knew no one really pays that much attention to what's going on inside anyone else's head. Dr. Benengeli set my hand back down. She said, "You look like you need a hug?"

"Isn't that inappropriate? For a doctor to hug her patients?"

"I'm not your doctor," she said.

I nodded. She was right. And, sure. Yeah. Definitely. I could use one.

12

A long, black BMW pulled in behind me as soon as I hit the bike lane in front of my apartment, and by pulled in behind me, I mean my bike was in the bike lane and he drove at the same speed with two tires in the bike lane and two tires in the road proper. This suggested either the driver of the car was a very bad driver or that he was following me. I picked up my pace. He did, too, but no faster than I did.

Every Saturday and Sunday morning since I'd gotten the bike, I took long rides. I often daydreamed about how far I could take this bicycle, about making it all the way to Fresno. I did the math, figured out how many miles I would have to ride each day, how many days it would take me. I figured that I'd need to get into good enough shape to ride fifty miles a day. So far, I was up to twenty. Not a bad ride. Not good enough to make Fresno, but good enough to get out of my apartment and clear my head on weekend mornings. Only it was tough to clear my head when there was a long black car with two tires in the bike lane behind me.

I blew through the first stop sign I came across and took a sharp left. So sharp that my left pedal scraped the pavement. I pedaled quickly down that hill. The black car followed. I took a sharp right, crossed the four-lane road, left onto a side street, over the railroad tracks, and onto a pedestrian bridge that stretched over the freeway. The black car was only able to follow as far as the parking lot in front of the pedestrian bridge. From there, he'd have to make a U-turn, head back to the four-lane road, and circle around. By the time he got over the freeway and to the other side of the pedestrian bridge, I'd be long gone. He wouldn't be able to find me again unless he knew where I was going. I figured he didn't know where I was going. If he did, why would he be following me, right?

The pedestrian bridge emptied out at the town's pier. A promenade stretched along the ocean below the pier. I rode my bike down to the promenade. A light onshore breeze threw a glancing blow across my face. The ocean's surface had the slightest texture, like a cotton t-shirt straight from the dryer. Surfers, mostly black in their full wetsuits, gathered like squadrons of seals around the two point breaks, one on the south end of the promenade and the other beyond the northern tip. I rode slowly down the promenade. A young woman in a gray, high school soccer t-shirt jogged toward me. I drifted close to the wall above the ocean and let her pass. A man in a black hoodie and his probable wife in a pink hoodie walked in front of me. He pushed a sleeping baby in a stroller. She talked on her cell phone, loud enough for me to hear her tips on how to get a baby's vomit out of a white carpet. I wondered for a second why anyone would want both a baby and a white carpet at the same time, why people would be concerned with such things before seven o'clock in the morning, why I paid any attention to this at all, but I quickly shook off those thoughts and rode past. The promenade opened up for me in streaks of early dawn: palm trees; white sand to the left; green grass to the right; surfers waxing their boards in the parking lot; old men in shirtsleeves sitting on wooden benches, thumbing through paperback spy novels and casting glances over their left shoulders at the sunrise over the Santa Susana Mountains in the east; women on the menopausal edge of middle age, power-walking in yellow sweat suits, tiny dumbbells swinging in each hand, chatting away; dogs at the end of extendable/retractable leashes sniffing at the trunks of skinny white oaks in planters along the walkway; a homeless guy casting off the odor of a campfire, pushing his shopping cart overflowing with plastic bags full of aluminum cans; serious bicyclists in loud colorful spandex suits full of advertisements that the cyclists paid to wear, riding bikes that cost thousands of dollars and would do a lot in the way of getting me to Fresno, but it wasn't my kind of riding. In a way, it was all typical Southern California. A little too early, too cold, too far north of LA to be full of the stereotypes, but sand and waves and pier and promenade nonetheless.

I kept riding past the promenade, around the northern point, down the riverbank trickling snow runoff from the Santa Ynez Mountains, across a bridge, past an RV campground, through a state park, along a bike path that ran halfway up a hill and looked down at the ocean, at the waves crashing on the rocks. The first Amtrak of the day rumbled by on the train tracks that ran parallel to the bike path. A morning fog settled on the ocean, making it seem like the world ended two miles to the west. It was all so beautiful that I forgot about the long black BMW until the bike path ended and I pedaled onto the Pacific Coast Highway and crossed a bridge over the railroad tracks and found, once again, a car behind me with two tires in the bike lane and two tires in the road proper. This meant that he did know where I was going.

So why follow at all? I decided I didn't care. I pedaled along, letting myself get lost in thought, letting the car putter along behind me, letting the string of traffic gather behind him and the other drivers get impatient and whip past at the first opportunity. This scene repeated itself two or three times. I thought to flee, but there was nowhere to go. A steep incline leading to the railroad tracks flanked me to the right; the Pacific Coast Highway, the beach, and the ocean flanked me to the left. There were no side streets, no trails, no ditches, nothing... just a long, straight ribbon of road for the next several miles. I pedaled along, trying to ignore the car, but really, how could I ignore it? It was scraping my mind's back tire.

About halfway between the state park where the bike path emptied out onto the PCH to the south and the multimillion-dollar houses that teetered over the ocean to the north, traffic emptied out. The long black BMW left the bike lane behind me, whipping around my bicycle and skidding to a stop in the bike path in front of me. His front bumper kissed the short, steep incline to my right. The rest of his car blocked any escape route to the left. I skidded to my own stop.

I couldn't see inside the tinted windows. The car itself was pristine, washed and waxed to such a fine sheen it mirrored my reflection. The driver jumped out, a real ape of a man with arms the girth of an adolescent girl's waist and chest like a beer keg. He had no hair on top of his head and a thick beard that obscured the tribal tattoo on the left side of his face. His beard hair was red. His fists were clenched. He stomped his way around the car. I got off my bike and leaned it against the incline to my right. I clenched my fists, too.

The Ape Man said, "Get in the car."

I didn't say anything. I raised my fists and stood on the balls of my feet. If there was going to be a showdown, I figured the sooner, the better. I'd fight and probably lose, but I wouldn't drag this out.

The Ape Man kept stomping in my direction. "What the fuck is this?" he said. "Get in the fucking car."

Blood raced through my muscles. I felt loose, ready. The bike ride had probably helped out. I harbored no real delusions about being able to take this guy. But maybe. Maybe no one ever stood up to him. Maybe, when you looked like him, so big and threatening, you never had to fight. Maybe I could get in a cheap shot or two and buy enough time to skedaddle. I watched his legs. I reckoned my best bet was to try to kick him in the side of his knee. He didn't get close enough, though. He stopped about a yard in front of me. I kept my fists up.

"Look at you, tough guy. What? You gonna hit me with your purse?"

I didn't move. We'd fight or he'd back down, but I had nothing to say. He balked. I stepped forward, drew back my right arm, and started a punch. He backed off.

"All right, then, tough guy." Ape Man unzipped his bomber jacket. He wore a white t-shirt and red suspenders underneath. Just past the red suspenders, he had a gun in a holster. A pistol. I had no idea what kind of pistol it was, other than it was the kind that could shoot bullets.

I started to think quickly and clearly. Okay, this guy has to be with Frank Walters. It's the only possibility. Who else but a blind man would give this guy a job? So he's a thug for an ad man. It didn't add up to likely gunshots. No way. Like everything in advertising, Ape Man was a façade, more image than substance. I held my ground, arms still bowed, legs still balanced on the balls of my feet. Still with nothing to say.

A few tense seconds passed. A growing rumble emerged from the direction of the multimillion-dollar beachfront homes to the north, the unmistakable sound of an approaching eighteen-wheeler. Ape Man glanced in that direction. He zipped his jacket back up and tapped the trunk of the BMW with his two left knuckles. The tinted window closest to me rolled down. Frank Walters' castor oil voice drifted out. "Park the car across the street," he said. "We'll all be gentlemen and have a civilized chat there."

The Ape Man left me standing with my dukes up. He got back into the driver's seat and swung the car into a wide U-turn, parking it across the street. I entertained the notion of making a run for it, but the nearest side street was a mile away. My bicycle was fast, but not fast enough to outrun a car in a mile-long drag race. Fleeing would just postpone the inevitable conversation with Frank Walters. And, let's face it, if I'd known it was Frank Walters in the car, I would've just pulled over and talked to him. All these theatrics were completely unnecessary.

I walked my bicycle across the street and locked it to a sign that read NO PARKING 10 PM TO 6 AM." The Ape Man opened the door for Walters. He climbed out of the back seat. He was immaculately dressed: crisp gray business suit, all natural fibers, pressed, tailored to fit; silk tie and matching silk handkerchief in the pocket; black leather loafers polished until they sparkled like a crystal ball. To be dressed like this on a Saturday morning took some effort. When I factored in that it was seven o'clock on that Saturday morning, that Walters had to ride a half-hour north of Agoura Hills to get outside my apartment at 6:30 so that he could follow me, and that he was blind to boot, I was nothing short of impressed. Which I guess was the whole point of the suit. The whole point of following me, even.

The Ape Man carried a black and silver beach towel, with an Oakland Raiders logo barely visible as the towel hung over his forearm. He took brief, cautious steps alongside Walters. Walters strolled over to the boulders that separated the PCH from the beach below. His cane floated just above the gravel, touching nothing until he reached the boulders and the plastic cane tapped once against the nearest one. Click. At this point, the Ape Man helped out. He stood on a wide, flat boulder, touched Walters' left elbow, and gently guided Walters onto the boulder. Ape Man arranged the Raiders beach towel on the edge of the flat boulder. Walters collapsed his cane and sat on the towel. His shiny loafers dangled off the edge. Ape Man waved me over. I sat on a boulder next to Walters. Ape Man cleared out.

Walters said, "Beautiful morning, isn't it?"

"Yes, it is."

"I love the waves here."

I looked out at the ocean. Waves rolled in slowly across the light wrinkles of the Pacific. As they approached the shoreline, the waves stood and, in a moment of violence, collapsed into whitewater. They broke almost simultaneously along the beachfront. Because of this, they were all but useless to surfers. I took a second to experience the waves from Walters' perspective. I closed my eyes, listened to the sudden crash of a wave, followed by a fading grumble as the whitewater scraped the shoreline.

"So, you're having a little ethical crisis? You're wondering if you can be bought. You're seeing me as The Man, maybe, and you somehow equate selling me information with selling out. Is that it?"

I shrugged, even though I knew he couldn't see it. His zipcode parlor tricks weren't working with me. I'm not a demographic. I'm an individual. And my hesitancy wasn't an ethical crisis. I knew my ethics. It was a crisis of bad information. I didn't know what Dr. Bishop was really studying or how it could be used. I didn't know what Walters was up to. I only knew that I was trying to be careful, and I was unsure how to do that.

Ape Man opened the driver's side door of the long, black BMW.

Walters called out to him, "Remember to crack a window."

"Got it, Boss."

Ape Man climbed into the driver's seat. All four windows of the car opened, leaving about an inch between the top of their smoky glass and the doorframe. Music drifted out of those cracks: loud, aggressive, exactly the type of stuff I listened to in my early twenties, though I couldn't place the song or band and it was mostly drowned out in the wind, the rumble of passing traffic, the crashing of waves.

Walters said, "What do you think of my muscle?"

"The Ape Man in the car?" I jerked my thumb in that direction. Again, Walters couldn't see it. "He's all right," I said, "if looks, charm, and personality don't count for anything."

Walters smiled. "Are you talking about his face tattoo? I've heard about that. Of course, I can't see it, but in my mind's eye, it's hilarious. A Maori tattoo on a suburban white kid from Irvine. And you hear his music, right? All of that British working-class noise. Sometimes I let him listen to it when we drive. The way he sings along… I can just hear it. He believes every word. He thinks he lives it. His dad is a lawyer. His mom's a mortgage broker. He grew up in a two-story house at the end of a cul-de-sac. Not exactly what I have in mind when thinking about the proletariat." Walters raised his palms and shrugged. "What are you going to do, right? He's my sister's youngest. She didn't know what to do with him, so I took him in."

"Very big of you."

"Yeah, well, one thing you'll learn about skinheads: they're loyal as can be. That kid would take a bullet for me. Not that anyone is shooting, but still. It's nice to know he'd do it. And he can rupture your kidney with one punch. He's good at making people bleed internally."

I tried to ignore the last thing Walters said. I said, "Plus, he's your target audience, isn't he? Isn't all of advertising about molding the anger of the enfranchised? Taking the middle class suburbs and selling them on any dream that'll rescue them from the cul-de-sac? Finding some kind of lifestyle they can associate themselves with—SUVs or cheap beer or thirty-dollar t-shirts—so that they don't have to associate their lives with the banality of dead end streets?"

"You sound like you've thought about this. You *are* having an ethical crisis." Walters ran his right index finger along the crease between his collar and his tie. He pinched the knot of his tie between his index finger and thumb. Satisfied that everything was in order, he let his hand rest on his thigh. "I know we've talked about him before, but let me tell you a bit more about John Watson," he said. "Watson was a prominent psychologist back in the first half of the 20th century, a behaviorist. His whole idea was that human actions are essentially programmed the same way as other animals' actions. If we could study human responses the way we study animal responses, we could predict and control human behavior. So Watson took the baton from researchers like Pavlov and Skinner and really ran with it. You know all about Pavlov and Skinner right? Classical conditioning? Operant conditioning?"

"I do. Yes."

"Good. Good for you. You're an intelligent man." Walters reached across and patted my knee. His own bit of operant conditioning. He went on. "Watson was Chair of the Psychology Department at Johns Hopkins. He was the editor of the premier psychology journal of his day. He was a very impressive, though, at times, judging from our current perspective, controversial researcher. A hell of a guy, really. An important historical figure. Left to his own devices, he would've been a top-flight academic. But you know how vicious academics can be. They build little castles around their ideas and defend them with all the dogma of a medieval knight. This kind of thing makes it tough when you're tearing down castle walls the way John Watson did. So, when Watson had an affair with one of his students—a grad student, mind you; whom he later married—well, shit hit the fan, so to speak. Watson's wife published Watson's love letters to the grad student in the local newspaper. Johns Hopkins fired him. The psychology community turned their back on him. What could Watson do? What do you do with that particular skill set if you're blacklisted from the psychology community?"

"You go into advertising?" I remembered this much about Dr. Watson from my first conversation with Walters.

"Exactly. That's exactly what he did. He revolutionized advertising. At first, when he was a researcher and academic, he'd been focusing on controlling human behavior for therapeutic reasons: finding ways to quell the anger, the frustration, the meanness, the petty jealousies, and backbiting. When he got into advertising, he shifted gears. He realized that he could use this meanness, these petty jealousies to sell products. He set up advertising in essentially two stages: first, you make the consumer feel as if what he has isn't good enough, make him suddenly worry about things that otherwise wouldn't matter at all in life: dandruff and ring around the collar and what your car says about who you are. Second, you offer a simple solution. Make the consumer feel as if he's forever one purchase away from happiness."

I thought of my wind-up bird, always a breath away from his imaginary worm, perpetually doomed to back flip. I translated this into terms Walters would recognize. "Like a donkey going after a carrot on a stick."

"Exactly. It's so simple, now. We all know it. But fifty, sixty years ago, it was revolutionary. And that leads us to the problem of today: we all know it. Advertising has become an accepted lie. No one believes it any more. The only way advertising agencies can get through to people is with a constant barrage of ads."

"Throw so much shit against the wall that some of it has to stick."

"If you want to be vulgar about it, yes. That's exactly it. But that leaves advertising professionals like me in a bind. It's too inexact. People start to know better than to feel a specific shame, that their clothes are too cheap, for instance, or that their teeth are too yellow. Instead, we all start to feel a more general form of inadequacy. We feel vaguely like losers, but we can't place why. This general feeling does leave the typical consumer more vulnerable to advertising, but not necessarily vulnerable to what we're trying to sell. This is the problem. Advertising needs a new paradigm."

"And so you're looking to me?"

"Sure. Why not? You. Dr. Bishop. Maybe you're on to something."

"You know she's trying to talk telepathically with animals?" I said. Of course, Dr. Benengeli and Eric had both corrected me about this, told me that it wasn't telepathy, exactly. I couldn't follow what it was supposed to be instead. I figured using the word "telepathy" would make Walters see the foolishness of what he was up to. I added, "You know that, don't you?"

"Come on," Walters said. "You're not stupid."

"I just don't understand. I don't know what you're after."

"I'm after Dr. Bishop's research."

"But why?"

Walters wagged a finger in my general direction. "It's probably nothing. Think of it this way: the money I'm giving you amounts to about the salary of an entry-level researcher. If what you give me doesn't pan out, no big deal. I'm just asking you to give the research to me."

"Then why all the theatrics? The muscle man, stalking my bike ride, snooping around my personal life. Is this how you treat your entry-level researchers?"

"Come on," Walters said again. "You're not stupid."

But I did feel a little stupid. Or at least like I needed more information. Walters raised his smoky sunglasses and rubbed the bridge of his nose. He kept his eyes closed as he did this. He lowered the glasses again. Silence washed over us.

The morning's first surfer walked along the beach below us. The soft-top board he carried and his choice to surf these waves that closed out so quickly indicated to me that he was a beginner. He wore the logo of his wetsuit manufacturer on his chest, carried the logo of his surfboard maker on the top of his board. I looked around, at my shoes and the logos there, at the long, black car and the BMW logos stuck to the hood and trunk, at the portajohn alongside the PCH and the logo and phone number of the portajohn company that supplied it. Even my bicycle was plastered with logos. I'd stuck bumper stickers of bands I liked over the brand name of the bike, but really, I'd just substituted one advertisement for another. So even here, a mile in any direction away from anything but the road and the beach and the boulders and the train tracks, advertisements papered the landscape in any direction I chose to look. A cool ocean breeze swept across my bare calves. I shivered.

Walters made a whistle out of his thumb and index finger, and he whistled. Ape Man climbed out of the driver's seat. I remembered Walters' words: *he's good at making people bleed internally.* Ape Man said, "Yes, Boss."

Walters said, "Let the dog use the bathroom before we go."

"Yes, Boss."

Ape Man's ass hung out of the open doorway of the car as he grabbed something. He clumped over to us, the soles of his Doc Martens scraping the gravel, the bottoms of his jeans rolled up. In his right hand, he lugged a dog carrier.

"Take the dog down to the beach," Walters said.

Ape Man climbed down the boulders, quick and graceful despite how steep the boulder wall was and how off-balance the dog carrier made him.

Walters reached into the inside pocket of his jacket. He pulled from it an envelope, opened the envelope, and handed me the white sliver of paper from inside. It was the receipt I'd sent him for his donation to the hospital.

Walters said, "Of course, you recognize this."

"You should keep it," I said. "For tax purposes."

Walters' hands rested on his lap. He did not reach for the receipt. He said, "That ten thousand dollars was not a donation. You knew that. If you want to give it away, that's your prerogative. I can find other ways to motivate you." He pointed at the beach in front of him. A wave stood up and crashed. The whitewater tumbled over the beginner surfer and his soft-top board. He rolled over and lost grip of his board. It bounced in the water.

Surely, this wasn't the scene Walters intended to show me. I scanned the shoreline. Off to my right, Ape Man tossed a tennis ball in a short arc and caught it again. The dog carrier sat at his feet. Paw prints led away from the carrier, over to the boulder wall. The dog stood there, one leg propped up, a stream of urine bouncing off the rocks. He was unmistakable. Clint Dempsey.

My left arm ached for a phantom ball to throw to him. I asked the obvious question. The one I knew the answer to:

"You stole my dog?"

"Of course not. I bought him."

"How?"

Walters pointed at the ocean in front of him, ostensibly meant to indicate Ape Man below us and to the right. Ape Man walked away from the carrier. Clint Dempsey finished his business and ran to Ape Man's feet. Ape Man rolled the ball into the carrier. Clint Dempsey chased it down, going all the way inside the carrier to get the ball. Ape Man raced behind Clint Dempsey and locked the dog into the carrier. Ape Man made his way back toward us.

"I sent my nephew up to Fresno. He met your wife. He said she was quite a beauty, by the way. His exact words, I believe, were 'She was one fine piece of ass.' But there's no need to get vulgar. Regardless, a few hundred dollars was all it took to separate her from your dog."

Just to torture myself, I asked, "How many hundred?" I guess I had to know how much Clint Dempsey was worth to her: the price of a new cashmere sweater or a new bicycle or a round-trip, first-class plane ticket to Hawaii.

Walters winced. I caught him off guard and he seemed to be thinking through his response. "Well," he said softly, as if he pitied me. "Actually, only one hundred."

Damn it. She sold Clint Dempsey for the price of her monthly cell phone bill. I would've doubled that. I would've tripled it. Hell, I would've given her Walters' whole envelope full of Franklins to have my dog back.

Ape Man's boots clunked off the boulders as he climbed up again. Walters stood and folded the towel.

"The deal is simple. We'll have lunch in two weeks. It's on me, once again. If you give me information on Dr. Bishop's research, I'll give you back your dog. If you don't give me the information, my nephew will kill him." Walters extended his white plastic cane with a quick flick of the wrist. He stepped off his flat boulder with confidence and walked over to the long black car, his white cane fluttering inches above the ground. Ape Man and Clint Dempsey met him there.

I wondered for a second whether or not I could jump Ape Man and get my dog. I took another second trying to come up with a plan. In the third second, the doors of the long black BMW were closed and the engine started.

They drove south down the ribbon of road, vanishing into a wall of fog enveloping the railroad bridge. I unlocked my bike and picked up my ride from where I'd left off.

13

"Charles!"

My name bounced off the concrete walls, echoing down the hallway of the Williams Building's third-and-a-half floor. At first, I was sure I'd imagined it. No one uses my first name on hospital grounds. Then I heard it a second time: "Charles!" Some things can be striking in their reality. There was something in the tone of that voice calling out my name. A ring of fear or panic. Wind striking a vocal chord to sound a slight alarm. I paused outside the interns' lounge and looked to my right. No natural light hit the hallway at this point in the building, only the shroud of yellow fluorescents that flickered the same, day or night. The person connected to that voice was Lola Diaz.

I turned to face her.

"Oh my god. Get me out of this building." She rushed toward me, her wooden sandals clomping on the concrete floor, the plastic sunflowers on the sandal straps in a race for daylight.

I put out my hand, gently, carefully, always a little skittish about touching a patient at all, even if the touch is only on the shoulder, even if said patient is the second woman I ever loved. My fingers rested on Lola's slick, shiny blouse.

Lola took two deep breaths, her eyes closing, mascara tearfully sliding into the grooves of nascent crow's-feet, her chest rising and falling with the bellows of her lungs. She said, "I thought I'd never find my way out of here. I've been wandering around these halls for an hour, going up and down stairways and getting in and out of elevators. I'm so lost. What's half a floor? How does a building have four and a half floors?"

The Williams Building actually had nine floors, counting the basement. I didn't tell Lola this. She was confused enough as it was.

"Please tell me you know the way out of here."

"I know the way out of here," I said.

Lola opened her eyes and smiled, the corners of her mouth twitching, unsure whether or not this smile was a little premature. I turned and walked her through the interns' lounge and to the staircase that led to the exit. Lola set one sunflower-sandaled foot on the first step down. "Are you sure you know where you're going?"

I nodded and pointed at the yellow flickering hallway behind me. "My office is on the third and a half floor. I know this building pretty well."

"Third and a half floor? How?"

"It's a strange building," I said. "But you already know that."

"I wasn't here looking for you," she said, her words falling flat from her mouth.

I took her denial the way we all take denials offered in response to unasked questions. I said, "Okay."

We stood in the dead air of the older half of the Williams Building. A few seconds passed. Half a minute. She set her other sunflower-sandaled foot to moving. We climbed down the stairs, across the lobby, and out through the entranceway.

As soon as the sunlight hit Lola, she was a new person. Her tension evaporated. Her hunched shoulders and lowered glance bloomed open. A smile grew on her face. Even her sunflower sandals seemed to perk up. "I'm so glad I'm out of that building," she sighed. "You don't know."

She kept walking. I paused. My lunch hour was over and it was time to get back to work. Not that the afternoon promised much. I had to check my email, though likely there was nothing pressing. I had to… Well, I didn't really have to do anything. I'd planned on shutting my office door, leaning back in my wooden chair, propping my feet on the windowsill, and whiling away the afternoon with a paperback. Still, I half-turned and said, "I, uh…"

"Are you busy? Do you have a little time to take a walk with me?"

I thought to lie, but really, the afternoon promised me nothing more than time and I would've felt sinister lying to a patient of the psych hospital. "I have time," I said.

Lola reached out for the pinky of my right hand. She tugged me along just enough to get me going, then let go. We took the long way around the dual diagnosis dorm and made our way to the campus proper. March was halfway between coming in like a lion and going out like a lamb. In fact, we were right in the middle of the month, March 15th, the ides of March. Why was the word "ides" plural when it only referred to one day? Why wasn't it the *ide* of March? Why couldn't you have just one ide? I let it go. Lola and I strolled across the grass carpeting the south quad, among the knotty oak trees and the old brick buildings and the squat shrubs and the cracked sidewalks that represented the legacy of RW Winfield.

"This takes me back," Lola said.

At first, I thought she meant that walking in the afternoon took her back to the days of our high school sweetheartship when we squeezed in as much life as was possible between the end of school and the return of her father in the evening. Walking with Lola, feeling her tug on my pinkie, had given me a jolt of that feeling.

Lola rode the current of a different memory. She pointed to the basketball courts on the south end of the south quad. "I played on a co-ed basketball team. An intramural league, you know? It was me and a bunch of dorks from Art School. We lost every game we played. It wasn't totally our fault because those outdoor courts over there were the only place you could practice. And there were always guys playing, all the time. Come out at midnight, two in the morning, guys would be playing basketball. And the way they played, you called out if you wanted to play in the next game. The winner got to stay on the court. So we'd all come out here, ready to practice, then we'd get in a game, play for, like, five minutes, lose to the team that beat everybody, and have to wait an hour for a new game to open up. It wasn't fair."

"Doesn't sound like it."

"And to make matters worse, this one guy on our team, a painter who wasn't nearly as good as he thought he was—at anything: painting, basketball, anything—broke the index finger on his painting hand. After that, we were all too scared that we'd hurt our hands. Our awful team got worse." She shook her head, glanced up at me. Her ironed caramel hair swooped over her left eye. "It was fun, though. College was fun." The toe of Lola's wooden sandal clicked on a rock in the grass. She knelt down and picked it up. She rolled the rock between her fingers, getting the feel of the ridges, then threw it in the direction of the basketball court. The rock flew for about twenty feet and fell into the grass. "Who would've known then?"

"Known what?"

"All of it. That Winfield would close down. That the state would turn this campus into a mental hospital. That I'd be a patient here." She hung her head. I watched her feet as she walked, one foot in front of the other, sandals and toes getting lost in the tall grass, the sunflowers resting for a second, then rising to plant themselves again in front of her. With her head still hung, Lola said softly, "How could I tell little eighteen-year-old Lola that we'd be back here in another eighteen years? It would break both our hearts."

I didn't know how to answer. I wanted to ask why she was at the hospital, what had happened. I knew better than that. Back when I still ran the community space in Fresno, we'd get a fair number of ex-cons coming in to learn how to make a resumé and how to interview for a job and get the job despite their background. At first, I'd ask the ex-cons what their crimes had been. I quickly learned not to, not because the ex-cons wouldn't tell me. Ex-cons are usually quick to tell their side of the story. I learned not to ask them because it was nosy. They'd already served their time. They'd done whatever they'd done and accepted their punishment and did what we, as a society, asked them to do. That was enough, so I learned to leave that question unasked and do what I could to help them take the next step. Lola wasn't an ex-con and of course there was a world of difference between a prison and a psych hospital. The core principle still applied, though: she was trying to right whatever went wrong and that was all I needed to know.

The unasked question hung like a cloud. Silence rained down. My body felt heavy, as if I'd gone swimming in jeans and now had to walk around in wet clothes weighing me down. I didn't know what to do. Lola stopped walking. She turned to face me, but stared at our feet below us. I hugged her. She kept her arms by her side for a second, her face pressed against my chest, her breaths warming the fabric of my jacket and shirt, right down to the skin. That second passed. I loosened my hug, ready to let go. Lola wrapped her arms around me and squeezed. Time stuttered. Lola let go.

"Let's go to the north quad," she said. "Dr. Benengeli is having rehearsal." Lola started walking. I followed.

"What's she rehearsing?"

"She puts on plays as a form of therapy. I guess it's the same principle as Paxil, you know? You get people out of their heads and thoughts for a while, and when they come back from either the drug or the play, they have a little perspective. I did some little one-act stuff with her, but I didn't want to do a whole play. Hopefully, I'll be out of here before opening day."

Lola led me across the south quad, past the gymnasium and the lecture hall where I'd gone to that first all-staff meeting, across the street, around the main hospital building, and through the courtyard where a small owl sat perched on the red roof tile, shaded by an overhang and watching squirrels dart carelessly around the white fir tree. I used one of my many keys to open the door of the psych tech school. We cut through the lobby. I waved to the secretary there. She smiled and waved back. We exited through the back yard and into the overgrown north quad, past most of the main action of the hospital. Up ahead, about twenty yards away, Dr. Benengeli and a group of patients stood in front of a bandshell on the open-air stage. Lola pointed to a bench nearby, in the shade of a gray pine. The ground around the bench was matted with pine needles. We took a seat.

"If we sit here, we can chat and not bother the actors," she said.

"Good thinking."

Lola smoothed her skirt so that it covered her knees. I took my jacket off.

"Are you warm enough?" I asked. "Do you want the jacket?"

"I'm comfortable," she said.

In the distance, the actors took their places. A woman stood in the middle of the stage, speaking to a man. They talked for a few seconds, then stopped suddenly. The man rushed to the back of the stage and stood against the backdrop, stone stiff as if he were hiding behind an imaginary tree. A second man walked onto the stage. He argued with the woman. Voices raised. Two more women stood in the wings, chatting through the rehearsal. The woman screamed. The first man echoed the scream. The second man, the one who argued with the woman, pulled the foam sword from his belt and stabbed the hiding man. It all looked familiar, but was not instantly recognizable.

I watched as Dr. Benengeli rearranged the actors. She moved the hiding man more toward center stage. She had the woman start from farther downstage. The two women on the wings stopped chatting during Dr. Benengeli's direction. Dr. Benengeli had them stand so that they actually intruded into the scene. The actors ran through it again. More arguing, the hiding man getting stabbed again. I recognized the scene. My wife had played Gertrude in a small production when we were still early enough in the relationship that I faithfully attended every performance.

I turned to Lola. "Is she doing *Hamlet*?"

"Something like that."

"What's something like *Hamlet*? *Strange Brew*?"

Lola didn't get the joke. She said, "No. It's a weird play. It all takes place backstage during *Hamlet*, but not really backstage. It's like, the whole play is what happens to the characters in *Hamlet* when the play isn't really happening, and they're all confused because no one wrote their lives. If that makes any sense."

"Of course," I said. "*Rosencrantz and Guildenstern Are Dead*. That explains the two women on the side who keep talking through all the action. Dr. Benengeli must've cast women in the roles of Rosencrantz and Guildenstern. Interesting choice."

"Not really. Not many men sign up for these plays. She has to cast who she gets."

"Still," I said, and left it at that.

Lola ran her fingers through her hair. "How do you know this play? Did you read it?"

I shook my head. "Saw the movie."

"Any good?"

"I liked it."

"As good as a bunch of crazy people playing crazy people in a play?"

I smiled, declining to answer any more than that.

"You know, it's crazy here," Lola said. "You know that, don't you?"

"I'm in administration. I don't see much of the crazy."

"Oh, I see all of it," Lola said. "I had to leave my room earlier today because my roommate had a psychotic break. Her husband was coming in for couples' counseling at noon, and at about 11:30, she started going ape-shit. Yelling, screaming, breaking stuff. Breaking *my* stuff. The psych techs had to come in to restrain her. She's yelling, 'Fuck you. You can't touch me. You're all a bunch of cocksuckers.' Everything. The psych techs were black so she started calling them the n-word. It was horrible. She even bit one of the psych techs. Right on his forearm. Nasty girl." Lola shook her head and stopped talking.

I wanted to hear the end of it but I wasn't sure if she wanted to keep talking. I gave her a prod. I said, "She sounds nasty."

"Oh my god." Lola paused. "And you want to know what the worst of it was?"

I nodded.

"Okay, so she's going nuts. The psych techs come in. She bites one. They get serious. There were three or four of them. Plus a nurse and a doctor. Because my roommate was not a small woman. She was very large. And she was just wearing a hospital gown, you know, the kind with the open backs? So they flip her over to keep her from biting anyone and her gown opens up and she's not wearing any underwear and her big white ass is just glaring like a crystal ball. No, like two crystal balls. Like two crystal bowling balls with a hairy crack in between. And the psych techs are all trying to look away, but how can you look away? How can you look away from that big, nasty white ass?"

"How can you?"

"But wait, I'm just getting to the worst of it. They finally calm her down and the nurse gives her a shot of the booty juice…"

"The booty juice?"

"Yeah. The sedative they inject in patients' asses. They give her a shot in her big white ass and put her in the timeout room. Then, the nurse on duty meets with the husband. She tells the husband that he can either take his wife AMA or his wife is going into lockdown for the next week. You should've heard the intern. She was good. Because AMA means 'Against Medical Advice,' but to hear the intern, she was all but telling the husband to take that crazy bitch home. At least that's what one of the charge nurses told me later. She's Puerto Rican, too. She tells me everything. Anyway, so the husband signs all the paperwork and my roommate finishes her time in the timeout room and she comes back to our room and she's all acting like she'd planned it all along, like she went crazy just so she could get out of here. She's the worst."

"Sounds nuts," I said.

Lola groaned like there was a grapefruit of anxiety inside her and she was trying to choke it down. "That's why I went looking for you," she said. "I needed to talk to someone who wasn't crazy."

"Okay."

"So talk. Tell me about your life. What's life like on the outside?"

"I don't know if I'm the right one to talk to. My life's not exactly the screenplay for escapism."

"Why not?"

"Well, for starters, my dog died, then I got a new dog and I started feeling better until my wife decided to leave me and she stole my new dog."

"So you lost your wife and your dog?"

"Two dogs."

"Hmm."

"I know. I'm just as crazy as everyone else."

"You're not crazy. You're just a country song right now." Lola smiled to show she was kidding. I wondered if she really was. She should've known it was a touchy subject to tell anyone from Folsom that his life was turning into a country song.

I didn't bring that up. I didn't say anything.

Lola said, "I heard about all that, anyway."

"You heard about my dog?"

"No. About your wife."

"Who told you?"

"Eric. We're old friends."

So it was true. They did all have a history. Eric and Lola and probably even The Professor. I looked up to the stage. The two women who had been on the sidelines when Hamlet stabbed Polonius through the curtains now held center stage. They were talking to one another. I couldn't hear what they were saying. I knew the play well enough to know that it could've been one of any number of scenes. One of the women pantomimed flipping a quarter and catching it. I realized that Dr. Benengeli was rehearsing out of sequence. I remembered that scene from the play, when Guildenstern keeps flipping the coin and it keeps turning up heads, and he and Rosencrantz come to realize that no matter how many times in a row the coin lands on heads the chances of it landing on heads again are still 50-50.

This made me think of The Professor and all of his talk about the past being gone and the future being uncertain, about the possibility that the whole world was just this moment: me and Lola on a wooden bench under a pine tree, watching a play in the distance. Everything else could've been a fiction. Maybe I wasn't a grant writer and Lola wasn't a patient and that wasn't *Rosencrantz and Guildenstern Are Dead* up in the distance and it wasn't crazy people playing crazy people and nothing was as it seemed. Maybe I'd made all of this up just so it would make sense and, if that was the case, why would I make up such a world? Why would I create a fiction in which the beautiful woman next to me was unwell and all the people surrounding me were in pain and my wife was gone and my dog was gone and perhaps the craziest of them all—the blind man with the skinhead muscle—was threatening to kill my new dog and make me bleed internally? Why would I do that to myself?

"Are you okay?" Lola asked. "You didn't see a ghost or anything, did you?"

"I'm okay. Just thinking about the play."

"The Professor is going to love this play. L-O-V-E, love it."

I looked over at Lola, her tongue gliding across her lips, brown eyes searching the sky for something. "Do you know The Professor from the Winfield days, too?"

"I do. Me and The Professor. The two returning veterans of Winfield."

"Did he actually teach a class here?"

"Oh, yeah. He was great. He was like high priest of this joint. The Big Kahuna. A few hundred professors on campus, but everyone called him The Professor." Lola kept gazing off, as if the past lingered somewhere in that springtime sky. "I took his Metaphysics and the Mind course. It was trippy." Her cheeks tensed into pre-smile balls. Her eyes stayed glued to the sky. "I learned a lot, though. He wrote a book, too."

"Really?"

"Yeah. I'm sure it's still in the archives, if you want to check it out."

"Hmm." I rubbed my face. I'd shaved that morning, but already stubble poked through the skin. "Maybe I will." And, out of the blue, a thought flashed through my mind and words fell from my mouth before I could stop. "So you probably know all about the scandal here, don't you?"

"I can't believe you said that to me." Lola stood straight up. "We were having such a nice afternoon. Why'd you have to say that?"

My jaw dropped. No more thoughts rushed through my brain and out of my mouth. I honestly had no idea why I'd asked that. I didn't even care, really. I had very little interest in the scandal at Winfield. I hadn't looked into it. I hadn't whiled away hours researching it despite the fact that I whiled away hours nearly every day researching one thing or another. It didn't matter. Yet I blurted out that question and obviously touched a sore spot. Stupid.

Lola brushed the pine needles off her butt and straightened her skirt. She shot me with a dose of electricity from her chestnut eyes. She said, "Rude!" and she stormed off.

14

With ten days to go before I either spilled the beans on Dr. Bishop's research or the skinhead killed my dog, I took my first steps in the direction of resolving the situation. I went to a downtown pub, got a table on the patio, ordered a beer, and waited. Thanks to the newly appointed Daylight Savings Time, a six o'clock sun still hung in the sky. Warm rays blanketed my legs and feet while my top half remained in the shade of the patio. My own personal yin and yang.

As usual, I arrived early for our meeting. I'd brought a paperback of '50s poetry, *Gasoline* by Gregory Corso, to be exact. I'd read it a thousand times but still carried it in my back pocket occasionally to keep me company. People-watching was good enough on this Thursday evening to keep the book in the pocket. I watched a little drama across the street. Three gutterpunk kids dressed all in black, leather, studs, each wearing a t-shirt of a different British early punk band—the Vibrators, the Subhumans, and Crass—sat in the doorway of an abandoned storefront. They had a dog with them, a shaggy mutt with a bit of German Shepherd in its face and a black bandana around its neck. Two middle-aged women stopped to talk to the kids. The women wore clothes and jewelry from the local boutiques. One woman's outfit alone likely cost more than the sum total of what these crusty kids had made panhandling since the last time they ran away from home. The women stopped to pet the dog. One woman knelt and opened a styrofoam takeout container. She placed the container in front of the dog. The dog buried his nose in it. The three kids stared at the dog's snout, a choir of sad, hungry faces. The women patted the dog and made their way into the next boutique. The three kids had a quick, animated argument with a lot of pointing at the container and a lot of rubbing of their stomachs. The dog pushed the styrofoam container around with his nose, licking the final drops. That seemed to settle things. The kids sat back down in the doorway, dejected, ratty engineer boots splayed in front of them.

The rest of downtown played out like a parade: hot rods rumbling down Main Street followed by dentists on Harleys, big trucks driven by suburban white kids thumping the bass of urban hip hop, SUVs holding up traffic while they waited for parking spots to empty out, and angry men in sports cars honking their horns in a vain attempt to get the traffic moving again. There was even one young man in a red Mustang convertible, blasting Michael Jackson for all to hear. It didn't affect me because the song "Baby, Baby" had been lodged in my head since first seeing that Vibrators t-shirt on the gutterpunk kid.

More shoppers, homeless drifters, exercising locals, parents with baby carriages, cruising high school kids, and haggard dayshift employees walked past. I drank my beer. It was thick and malty and very strong, brewed at this particular pub in the vats behind me. Middle age and nearly a decade of clean living had killed my alcohol tolerance so I tried to pace myself. I sipped.

Out of the passing crowd emerged a woman wearing trouser jeans, a baby blue t-shirt with a picture of a big-eyed doll on it, and a navy corduroy coat. I would not have recognized her if not for her exceptionally short stature. I waved. She entered the little restaurant patio and pulled up a chair.

She said, "What's up, Chuck?"

"I almost didn't recognize you in your street clothes," I said.

"That's part of the point," Dr. Benengeli said. "I try to look like a doctor at the hospital and not like a doctor when I'm away from it. Life's easier when you're not recognized quite so often."

"Makes sense," I said, though it didn't, really. She was a pretty recognizable figure. "I like your shoes. My wife used to wear oxfords like that."

"With stars on the toes?" Dr. Benengeli's oxfords had stars on the toes.

"No. She had flames on her toes. But a similar style." I paused, looking at her shoes, which reached the ground only because Dr. Benengeli sat so far forward in her chair. "I think I like the stars better."

"I have another pair with kittens at the toes. But I have to be careful." She pointed at the picture of the big-eyed doll on her t-shirt. "Don't want to be too precious."

"I understand."

The waitress visited our table. Dr. Benengeli ordered a glass of wine. I ordered three grilled vegetable sandwiches and french fries to go. The waitress nodded and headed for the computer to type in our orders. Dr. Benengeli said, "Were you going to eat dinner here?"

"I hadn't planned to."

Dr. Benengeli's glance volleyed between the waitress and me as if she were watching a quick tennis game. The waitress served, I returned, she nailed a baseline volley and I apparently missed. Fifteen-love. Dr. Benengeli said, "Okay." She set her purse on the table. It had been woven out of seatbelt straps. Jet black. "I notice that you said 'my wife' when referring to your ex-wife's shoes. I thought the divorce was final."

"It's final."

"Still, you say 'wife' instead of 'ex-wife.'"

"Old habits are hard to break."

"Are you taking care of yourself?"

I shrugged. I didn't want this to become a therapy session. That's not why I'd invited Dr. Benengeli out for a drink. "It was a long time coming," I said. "Kinda like watching a loved one die of cancer. You know, the disease gradually eats them away and everyone does everything they can, but you can't beat the cancer. The end almost comes as a relief. Does that make sense?"

"It does."

I thought that would end the conversation. That's why I'd responded with the whole cancer analogy: because I wanted to end the conversation about my marriage. It didn't quite work.

"I notice that you still wear your wedding ring, too."

I reached down and spun the ring on my finger. "I'll take it off when I'm ready to start dating again."

"Half the nurses and secretaries at the hospital are waiting for that day. Did you know that?"

I dodged the question. "We don't have secretaries at the hospital. We have 'administrative assistants.'"

"See, now that pisses me off," Dr. Benengeli said. I knew it did. That's why I'd brought it up. I'd heard stories about Dr. Benengeli leading the push at the hospital to call the patients "patients." Apparently, there'd been a big debate as to what to refer to them as: patients or clients or residents. One group even wanted to call them "consumers." Dr. Benengeli made the strongest argument, though, and patients remained patients. Knowing that, I was able to end this therapy session. Dr. Benengeli said, "Why can't secretaries be secretaries? What's wrong with a secretary? Everyone knows that secretaries run most companies anyway. It's a respectable job. There's honor in it. There should be prestige in it. But lately, we've become condescending to all of these respectable blue-collar jobs. Garbage men become 'sanitation engineers.' Janitors are 'custodial engineers.' Secretaries are 'administrative assistants.' Handymen are 'maintenance facilitators.' It's bullshit. It's a way of attacking people's socioeconomic status. It's saying that blue-collar is not good enough, and we still want you to do blue-collar jobs, but we'll give you white-collar names so we can pretend we're not looking down on you. It gives me a headache."

"I understand," I said.

Another unpleasant situation narrowly averted. The waitress brought Dr. Benengeli the glass of wine. She took a sip. I leaned back in my chair. The procession of shoppers and cruisers in front of me started to thin. Most of the downtown shops closed around seven o'clock, and most of the shoppers cleared out about half an hour before that. I turned my glance to Dr. Benengeli, now sitting back in her chair, her starry oxfords swinging a couple of inches above the ground. Outside her work clothes, she looked several years younger. She looked, in fact, right around my age. Realizing this made a lot of the pieces of the Dr. Benengeli puzzle fit together more. Her references to Duran Duran cassette tapes and bikes with banana seats and top-loader VCRs and her brother's parachute pants and playing Coleco Electronic Quarterback in the backseat of her parents' Ford Galaxie while they waited in line to get gas at Tenneco all

115

matched up nicely with the group memories of my generation. I suddenly saw Dr. Benengeli as a more complete person.

She said, "Now, I know you didn't invite me here to talk about what we should call secretaries. So let's get down to the point."

"Okay." I nodded, more to something in my mind than to something outside of it. "I'm curious about Dr. Bishop's research. Can you give me the straight dope?"

Dr. Benengeli raised her wine glass and pointed at me with her pinkie. "I'll tell you this: it's a good thing she's already in a psych institution."

"Why's that?"

" 'Cause what she's doing is a little crazy."

"Okay?"

Dr. Benengeli took a sip. "Do you know what it's about?"

"Pets and pet owners, right?"

"Yeah. But there's more to it. See, Francine…"

"Who?"

"Dr. Bishop. Francine Bishop. She believes something different about the collective unconscious. When Jung discussed the collective unconscious, he wrote about it as if it were inherent in all of us when we're born. Think of it like a genetic trait, like eye color or male pattern baldness. One of your genetic traits is your personality. It holds your instincts, your deepest beliefs, your spirituality, your cultural heritage, everything. It's the core of who you are, but it's buried. Jung believed that the key to psychoanalysis should be to get the patient in touch with this core. The collective unconscious."

"Okay."

"That does sound right, doesn't it? I haven't studied Jung in fifteen years. I'm not a Jungian therapist. It's mostly Cognitive Behavioral for me."

"I see."

"So that's what the collective unconscious is, in a very brief, laymen's way. Okay? But Francine has a different idea. She asks the question: what if the collective unconscious isn't within us all? What if it's not at the core of our minds, but instead it's something outside of our minds? What if these ideas float around us in the ether, and we get our cultural messages, our beliefs, our spirituality from this floating ether?"

The waitress stepped into this pause. She handed me the three grilled vegetable sandwiches. They were each in their own styrofoam container. The containers were in a white plastic bag. I ordered another beer. Dr. Benengeli ordered another wine. I tied a knot out of the handles of the plastic bag and tucked it under my seat.

Dr. Benengeli picked up her lecture. "So that's the first distinction, right? For Francine, our shared unconscious is external, floating around us like radio waves or cell phone reception. All we have to do is dial it in."

"Okay," I said. Though I wasn't sure whether it was okay or not.

Dr. Benengeli asked, "Have you heard of the hundredth monkey effect?"

"I think so." A book with that title kept popping up at the community space in Fresno. "Is that the one with the monkeys on two islands and it had something to do with peace?"

"You got it. Researchers would show the monkeys on one island how to open clams with a rock, or something like that, and usually right around the time the hundredth monkey on that island learned how to open the clam, the first monkey on the other island would figure it out without the help of researchers. So they hypothesized that certain learned behaviors within one society can somehow be spread to other societies through some unspoken communication."

"Okay. That sounds familiar."

"So Francine is working off this premise: that you can somehow place notions into the collective unconscious and other people can learn from them. She's starting with animals, seeing if we send unconscious messages to them and they receive them. That's what the monitoring of pets is all about. She thinks that we send a message to our pets that we're heading home, the pets receive that message, and they wait for us at our front doors. And if she can prove that this phenomena does occur, then she can move forward and see how we place those messages, how we receive them, and how we can control them."

"And you think it's all a crock?"

Dr. Benengeli nodded. "It's like the telegram."

"What?"

"Like the telegram. Maybe telegrams do still exist. Maybe we can still send them. But who cares? Why the hell would you want to send a telegram?"

"Okay." We'd already had this discussion. More people need to communicate face-to-face.

"Francine is trying to get you to fund this madness, isn't she?"

"Not at all."

"Does this have anything to do with Frank Walters?"

"Who?"

"The blind guy I caught in the Williams Building. He gave you his card."

"I thought he was a patient. Is he a researcher, too?"

Dr. Benengeli shook her head. "Hardly. Why are you curious about all of this?"

"She was filming my foyer for a while to see if my dog reacted to me coming home."

Dr. Benengeli tilted her wine glass, pointing the rim at me. "Ah. The stolen dog." She emptied the last of her wine.

"Poor little guy," I said, my guard slipping down. "Breaks my heart."

She raised her eyebrows. "You miss him, huh?"

I saw what was going on here. I was not about to get trapped into any Rogerian reflective listening. I just smiled and shook my head.

The waitress came back with the second round and cleared away our empties. I sipped my beer. It seemed to go straight to my head. It also reminded me of the food I'd ordered. I turned to the table next to me. Sitting alone was a kid who looked about 13 years old. His mother had gone to the bathroom and his father was at the bar, talking to a friend. The kid played a handheld video game. I reached over and tapped him on the shoulder. He paused his game and glanced up.

I grabbed the takeout bag from under my chair and set it on the table. "You see those three kids in that storefront doorway across the street?" I asked the kid at the next table.

"Yeah," he said. His thumbs hovered over the controls of his game.

"I'll give you five bucks if you bring this food over to them."

The kid looked at the bag, looked at his game, looked around inside the restaurant. "That's all that's in the bag? Just food?"

I untied the knot and opened the bag. He reached inside, took out a styrofoam container, opened it, picked out a fry, ate it, and closed the container. "Five bucks?"

"Payable when you get back."

The kid stuffed his videogame in his pocket. "Deal." He swept up the food and set to jaywalking.

"How generous of you," Dr. Benengeli said.

I plucked a picture of Lincoln on US mint paper from my wallet and set it on the table. "I suddenly have more money than I've ever earned in my life and no wife to spend it all."

Dr. Benengeli swung her chair around. She leaned forward in her seat, arms crossed, elbows on the glass of the table. The big-eyed doll on her t-shirt stared at me. Through the glass and metal mesh of the tabletop, I could see Dr. Benengeli's oxfords flat on the ground. Her dark eyes locked on mine. "Are you sure you don't want to talk about the divorce?"

I groaned.

15

A week later, I sat alone in Eric's office in a more or less abandoned building in the more or less abandoned north quad. I'd spent almost all of my non-work hours since meeting with Dr. Benengeli volunteering for Dr. Bishop's study. I'd worked on it enough to gain Eric and Dr. Bishop's trust. I'd worked enough to get my own keys to this barren little office. Now it was time for me to do what I had to do for Clint Dempsey.

I'd purchased a small memory stick. Eric's computer transferred the bulk of the data from Dr. Bishop's experiments onto the memory stick. I also had photocopies of Eric's notes spread out in front of me. Eric had used a simple system of symbols to indicate different actions: an asterisk for the days when the pets reacted more than ten minutes prior to their master's return, a yen symbol for when the pets reacted less than three minutes prior to their master's return (because, ostensibly this would suggest that the pet might not be responding to unconscious messages but rather to something physical, like the sound of the master's car approaching), a cent symbol for when the pets reacted between three and ten minutes prior to their master's return, and an infinity symbol when the pet didn't react at all. The symbols didn't seem to have any inherent meaning. As far as I could tell, Eric had chosen these particular symbols because his handwriting was sloppy and each of these symbols was easy to distinguish. In the corner of the first page, I drew this legend:

∞ — pet reacts more than ten minutes prior to return
¥ — pet reacts between three and ten minutes prior to return
* — pet reacts less than three minutes prior to return
¢ — pet does not react

After drawing the legend, I went to work with white correction fluid, blocking out symbols randomly. I used the correction fluid sparingly, changing no more than seven symbols per page. When I got through all forty-eight pages, I drew stars over each blotted out symbol. The star was the only symbol I could convincingly write in Eric's handwriting.

Dr. Bishop knocked on the door while I was drawing seven stars on my 31st sheet of photocopied notes. I stacked my photocopies and slid them into my briefcase. The entire contents of my briefcase now added up to: forty-eight sheets of photocopied and falsified notes. I set my briefcase at my feet. "Come on in."

Dr. Bishop poked her head in the door. "Working on a Sunday?"

"I don't want to volunteer for you on the hospital's dime," I said.

"See, I could tell you were an honest man," Dr. Bishop said. "I could hear it in your voice when you interviewed for this job. That's why I hired you."

I smiled. I wondered if that smile seemed sincere. Could I fake sincerity with a psychologist, a researcher, someone so in tune with human behavior? I also wondered, not for the first time, if Dr. Bishop remembered me from our first encounter way back when, long before these psych hospital days. A printout of data sat on Eric's metal desk. I picked up the printout. Out of the corner of my eye, I noticed the little light at the end of my memory stick, glowing like a beacon to my honest man's theft of Dr. Bishop's information. If I accidentally tapped the mouse or any key on the computer, the screen saver would go away and Dr. Bishop would be able to see the dialogue box that tracked the progress of the file transfer from Eric's computer to my memory stick. I handed the printout to Dr. Bishop. She sat in the other office chair and slid on her reading glasses.

"Numbers look pretty good," I said.

Dr. Bishop's eyes darted back and forth as she skimmed the page. She nodded but didn't smile. "What's the bottom line?"

I didn't need to look at the sheet. The final numbers stuck in my head. I said, "The pets almost always reacted. I don't remember the exact percentage, but it was less than two percent of the time that the pets didn't react at all. About nine percent of the time, the pets reacted to their master's return within three minutes of the return…"

"Together, that's almost ten percent of the time." Dr. Bishop shook her head.

"A little over ten percent. Yeah. On the other hand, about seventy percent of the time… A little less than seventy percent. Sixty-eight point something percent of the time, the pets reacted more than ten minutes prior to the master's return. That's a pretty high return rate."

"It's pretty high. True. But is it a phenomenon?"

I shrugged. "Who can say? There are so many variables. Maybe the pets reacted because their masters came home at the same time every day, give or take ten minutes. Maybe they reacted because they heard the car rumbling down the street, and it took the masters five or ten minutes to park, put the club on the steering wheel, lock the doors, get out of the car, balance the groceries, get to the front door, fiddle with the keys, and so on. Maybe pets didn't react on certain days because they were mad at their masters. Who knows? It's so hard to isolate anything in this experiment."

Dr. Bishop took off her reading glasses. She opened her glasses case and took a swatch of silk cloth from it. Her fingers—long, thin, cracked and spotted with age but manicured to suggest an earlier, more fashionable time—rubbed the silk swatch against the lenses of her reading glasses. "It won't stand up to peer review, that's for sure."

I felt suddenly bad about being the one to point this out to her. I looked down at the floor, by the tower of the computer. My memory stick stuck out, the light a beaming tattletale. I pushed the power button on the computer's monitor. The monitor shut down, but not the computer. "Still," I said. "Seventy percent is pretty compelling. Almost ninety percent, really, if you count everything beyond three minutes. That's something."

Dr. Bishop wrapped her reading glasses in the swatch of silk and replaced them in their case. She handed back the sheet of data. "Did you run the numbers or did Eric?"

"I did."

"Off Eric's notes?"

I nodded.

"Not easy to read his handwriting, is it?"

"Not at all."

Dr. Bishop stood from the office chair. She brushed her cotton slacks and adjusted her coat. She placed her thin fingers on my shoulder. "Come get a cup of coffee," she said. "I need to talk this out."

I rolled the numbers of the combination lock on my briefcase and set it in front of the memory stick. If Eric came to the office while I was gone, he'd know that I was saving my own personal backup of this information. It would not be a good scene. I couldn't think of an excuse to get me out of coffee with Dr. Bishop. I've never been too good of a liar. Lying to a shrink seemed even tougher. I figured it was best to try to forget about the memory stick and take my chances with coffee.

Dr. Bishop and I left the more or less abandoned building and headed toward the campus lot where she parked her car. Between the two, we passed a little café on the edge of campus. The café accepted both money and vouchers earned by the long-term patients for doing chores around the living units. In a way, it was a little oasis of equality, where no one made the distinction between staff and patient, the keyholders and the keyless. We would all duck in for a quick rubbery hamburger with fries that contained more oil than potato. A lot of the staff, particularly the janitorial staff and the interns, kept cheap, beat-up bicycles on campus so they could go quickly from their offices to the places where they needed to work. No one locked the bikes and, for most of the staff, the origin of the bikes was a bit of a mystery. Eric had explained that several of the bikes had been abandoned during the mass exodus from Winfield University. Others had been donated by a psych tech who salvaged junk parts and reassembled them into working bikes as a hobby. Since no one technically owned the bikes, no one locked them or worried too much about theft. The only difficulties came when workers rode bikes across campus, did their work, and came back to find the bikes gone. It would be a drag, but nothing that couldn't be solved by a long walk. The bikes, it seemed, never left campus.

As Dr. Bishop and I passed the café, a middle-aged man with long flowing bangs that, with more care, could be used to craft a comb-over rode one of the bikes in big, slow loops. He had a round head and a grin like a jack-o-lantern. His loops were occasionally punctuated with a "Woo-hooo!" The man wore pajama bottoms, a stretched out V-neck t-shirt, and flip-flops. He was clearly among the keyless.

Another young man jogged behind the slow loops. He wore a blue button-up shirt tucked into khaki pants. His loafers flapped on the pavement. His keys jingled. Almost to the rhythm, almost as if it were a song, the young man said, "Come on, Danny. Give me my bike, Danny." Over and over.

Danny kept up his slow loops, bangs fluttering in the wind, up to and probably long after the time Dr. Bishop and I had gotten into her car and exited the campus.

To her credit, Dr. Bishop did not take us to Starbucks. She drove into the foothills north of the psych hospital and stopped at a coffee shop in the downtown area of the little artists' community there. The coffee shop made a big deal out of using beans grown in Hawaii and having fair trade everything. Even the girl behind the counter, with her white-girl dreadlocks and her sleeve tattoos and her pierced eyebrow and nose and lip wore a shirt with the words "fair trade" stretched across her breast. I lingered a second on all the possibilities and contexts available for interpreting the words "fair trade" stretched across a young woman's breast. Luckily, my glance had drifted up to the menu above the counter while I spaced out, only my mind's eye ogled the "fair trade" boobs. The young woman asked for our order. I got an iced tea. Dr. Bishop ordered a coffee, paid for both, and even tipped generously. We took a table on the patio.

The patio of the coffee shop was enclosed. A short metal fence almost completely swallowed by shrubs surrounded the patio. This ensured that the only people-watching would be done with people inside the patio. As for this Sunday afternoon, the patrons included Dr. Bishop, me, and one homeless woman counting her change on a wooden picnic table. Dr. Bishop said, "So this experiment proves nothing."

"No?"

She shook her head.

"Nearly ninety-percent of pets can predict their master's return and that doesn't suggest anything to you?" I asked.

"Oh, it definitely *suggests* something. It suggests that pets and their owners are communicating on some unspoken level. It even makes a compelling suggestion for one of the uses of the collective unconscious. But there's a big difference between suggesting something and proving it."

I dumped a packet of sugar into my iced tea and stirred. "So, what's the next experiment?"

"I'm not sure."

Part of me hoped that this was the end of it. That way, I could give my falsified data to Caster Oil Walters and get my dog back and life would go on. But I knew that wasn't the way science worked. I knew that if the phenomenon still suggested something to Dr. Bishop, then more research would follow. So I tested her unconscious a little. I said, "That must've been one expensive experiment, with all the surveillance cameras and everything."

"Oh, no. Eric rescued those cameras from the old Winfield scandal."

"From the scandal?"

Dr. Bishop blew on her coffee. "Let's stay focused here."

Which I wanted to do. The Winfield scandal seemed like gossip and what I really wanted was my dog back. And I wanted him back without having to do anything that would lead me to hate myself. So I said, "Do you need funding for this research? I'm sure I could get this funded."

Dr. Bishop shook her head. "Absolutely not."

"Why not?"

"Think of what would happen if this research fell into the wrong hands."

I'd thought about that. Believe me, I'd thought about it. But I was curious as to what Dr. Bishop thought. I said, "What would happen?"

"Well, if you haven't thought of a way to use this knowledge as a weapon, you're a good man."

And that was all she said on the subject.

A boy, maybe ten or eleven years old, took a seat at the patio, away from both the homeless woman and Dr. Bishop and me. He set a leather day-planner and a cellular phone on the table. He held on to his frozen coffee, which looked more like a milkshake with all the whipped cream, slivers of ice, and streaks of chocolate. His cellular phone rang. He answered and gave street directions to someone he referred to as "Mr. Steve."

The homeless woman, in the meantime, counted her change for the eighth or ninth time.

Dr. Bishop listened to the kid's phone conversation, then turned back to me. "Maybe I'm just hanging on to those core beliefs from the '60s. I don't know."

I wasn't sure if she was talking about the kid with the huge caffeine slurpee and cell phone or if she was talking about something to do with her research. I prodded her in the latter direction. "If you're worried about your findings falling into the wrong hands, why do it?"

"You have to think of the positives, too."

"I'm not sure what they are."

"A deeper level of communication, a way of tapping into the unconscious that allows us to both better understand ourselves as individuals and as social creatures. Think about how much better it would be to be able to delineate your personal beliefs that you've formed based on your own experience instead of the core beliefs that you've plucked out of a collective unconscious or group think. Do you see what I'm saying?"

I didn't, really. She was a lot further along in her thinking about all of this. I was still at the stage where I just saw dogs and a batty doctor, where I spent a lot of time questioning my own intelligence. I had thought I was a reasonably bright guy, but my time spent with Walters and the psych hospital crew was leading to a lot of self-doubt. "Most of this is over my head."

Dr. Bishop reached out with her bony fingers and tapped my hand. "You're a good soul," she said.

I smiled and looked down at the table.

Did I feel like a hypocrite, drinking tea purchased by Dr. Bishop and accepting her compliments while, fifteen miles away, my memory stick stole her research? Did I feel dirty knowing that I had a lunch meeting set up with Frank Walters exactly one week away? Did I feel whorish because I knew every man had a price and my price was apparently one dog? Yes.

Dr. Bishop lifted her coffee cup to drink, but set it down before it made the full trip to her lips. "This research is risky," she said. "That's why I'm only working with you and Eric. That's why I'm keeping everything hush-hush."

I swirled the tea in my clear plastic cup, watching the murky brown liquid create a whirlpool. "So what are you going to do next?"

"I have another experiment in mind. Will you help me?"

I nodded. I stood to do the only thing I could think of to assuage the tell-tale heart threatening to rip out of my chest: I bought a muffin and a cup of coffee for the homeless woman who clearly didn't have enough change, no matter how many times she counted it.

16

Eric led me through the rocky foothills east of psych hospital grounds. We hiked and climbed and stumbled through the bends of an all but forgotten trail, surrounded by manzanita, chaparral, sagebrush, and various other trees and shrubs and plants of Southern California that seem destined less for the landscape of this growing freeway culture and more for a future as the namesake of suburban streets ending in a cul-de-sac. Eric had assembled his arsenal. It contained:

- one five-gallon plastic bucket
- one fishing net with a six-foot pole
- one plastic dog carrier with a screen fastened to the door
- three bottles of water
- one plastic bowl
- four hollow metal poles, each about a foot and a half long

I carried the fishing net in one hand, using the pole of the net as a walking stick. In the other hand, I lugged the water, the bowl, and the four poles in the five-gallon bucket. It wasn't heavy, but the hike had been long enough for me to trade the load between hands a few times. Eric lugged the pet carrier. It was made of lightweight plastic, but the bulkiness made it cumbersome. Eric rotated the carrier from shoulder to shoulder and hip to hip. I tried to imagine how he'd tote that thing home once we filled it. If we filled it.

And who else was with Eric and me? My good little dog, Clint Dempsey. He darted in and around the shrubs. He sniffed trails. He raced away on unexplained missions, then raced back when he had strayed too far from us.

Eric had explained his plan before we set off on our hike. There was a lone oak in a clearing at the end of this trail. We'd rush the clearing, raise a racket, and scare all nearby squirrels into the lone tree. Eric would use the fishing net to scoop the brave or panicked squirrels trying to flee the tree. We'd escort the captives home in the pet carrier. "I'm not at all sure this will work," Eric said. He assured me of his lack of assurance several times.

I'd made my peace with that. I was up for the wild squirrel chase nonetheless. For me, it was more of a hike with a theme than an actual hunt. It was an excuse to get Clint Dempsey out into the woods, an excuse to have a little bit of fun with my newly returned dog. And there was another element to my decision to go on this little adventure. The voice had come back—that little nagging voice that kept popping up in the back of my brain, issuing instructions, making me question just how well I knew myself. I thought about skipping this venture just to shut up that little voice. Maybe if I stopped obeying it, it would go away. That's what I thought anyway. Maybe I was going a little nuts. I had to acknowledge that possibility.

We crested the final hill. The clearing opened up below us. Eric set the pet carrier on the ground, just off the hiking trail, and sat on it. I found a nearby log and took a seat. The five-gallon bucket sat between us, blocking the trail, but no hikers were in these hills, anyway. I grabbed the water bottles, handed one to Eric and kept two for myself. The springtime air in the foothills lay still. The day had begun with its obligatory fog, the sun steaming up the cold Pacific waters and swallowing the coastline in its cloud. As morning wore on, drier, warmer inland regions inhaled what cloud it could suck up, dreaming in vain for more water. This led to powerful midday breezes. And now, Eric and I sat in the late afternoon balance, when the ocean was warm enough and the land was cool enough, the coastline calm and the desert sated, everything at peace and ready for the setting sun. Just about squirrel-hunting time.

I took the little plastic bowl out of the bucket and filled it with water. Clint Dempsey raced over and started lapping it up. This reminded me of how thirsty I was, so I drank from my own bottle. Eric did the same.

Eric wiped his mouth with the short sleeve of his blue work shirt. The embroidered patch with his name on it caught the brunt of the late afternoon sun. "You want to go through the plan again?"

"Nah," I said. It didn't matter how many times I heard the plan. It wouldn't get any better.

Eric took a handkerchief from his back pocket and wiped away the sweat from his forehead. I looked at the rigid lines of his face, well worn as the rocks around us, casting shadows in the late afternoon sun. Clint Dempsey stopped lapping up water and walked over to Eric. Eric scratched Clint Dempsey behind the ears. "This little guy ought to help a bit, huh?"

"Probably." I wanted to say more. I recognized that Eric was stalling while he caught his breath. I looked for more to chat with him about, but I just didn't know the guy that well. Ideas for conversations kept coming up empty.

We sat there for maybe five minutes, not really talking, not really drinking much water. Just giving our bodies a few minutes to prepare for the madness. I gazed into the clearing. The oak stood among the high grass. Behind it lay the rotting trunk of the oak's brother, long since fallen. Nothing stirred. No breeze blew, no blade of grass flickered. The amber rays of the late afternoon sun trapped the scene. It could've been a painting. The world around us could've been oils on canvas.

Eric leaned over and tied the loose shoestring on one of his work boots. I leaned down to check the laces of my own shoes. Tight. I grabbed the four metal poles and passed two of them to Eric. He took one quick sip of water and stuffed the bottle back into the bucket. He said, "Let's hunt some squirrels."

If the clearing had been a clock and noon was in the north, I walked to the three. Clint Dempsey followed me. Eric waited for us at the nine. Hills framed the clearing. The growth around it was neither high nor dense. Just more chaparral, more cacti, more rocks. I climbed up the hill about ten feet. It was about as steep as the roof of a house. Eric did the same on his side. He smiled, his glowing white teeth shining in the late afternoon sun. I nodded. Game on.

Eric took off running through the hills, banging his metal poles together. He ran clockwise toward me. I ran clockwise away, banging my sticks. Clint Dempsey followed the arc between Eric and me, barking away. I watched my feet on the uneven terrain, skidding on rocks, hurtling over chaparral, scraping past cacti, up and down the hill, metal clanging, the shins of my jeans taking on a new skin of briars, tan dirt nestling into my jogging shoes. A murder of crows rustled from a sycamore in the distance. Rodents and reptiles fled into the tall grass of the clearing. I swung past six o'clock about the time Eric hit noon. The clearing came alive in fluffy tails. The vibrations of the metal echoed in the hills and rung in the palm of my hands. I made it to eight o'clock and saw, not four feet away, a rattlesnake coiled and poised to strike. This left me three choices: fight, flee, or freeze. I froze. Both metal poles in my hands, inches away from one another, halfway to contact, feet planted in the grooves of dirt I caused by skidding. The rattlesnake sounded his castanets. His black eyes met mine. We regarded each other. Clint Dempsey barked and darted among squirrels in the clearing. In my peripheral vision, I could see Eric nearing three o'clock. His ruckus rattled the clearing. I stayed stock-still. Ten seconds passed. Fifteen. The snake and I stared each other down. He moved first. He crept backwards, back down to his belly, uncoiled himself, and slid inches past my foot. I let him pass. As he climbed the hill above me, I slammed the sticks together again and took off into the tall grass of the clearing.

Eric and I swung large circles through the high grass, cutting off any exits into the hills. Clint Dempsey covered the ground we couldn't cover. Squirrels upon squirrels sought shelter in the canopy of the live oak. We spiraled toward it, our very own whirlpool of noise and madness. Eric reached the trunk first. I swung in behind him. Over the din of metal on metal, Eric yelled, "You stay here. I'm gonna get the net."

I nodded. Eric ran off, no longer banging his sticks. I settled into a rhythm at the trunk of the tree. In my mind, I knocked together the beat of the Clash song, "White Man in Hammersmith Palais." I sang along. *Midnight, to six, man. For the first time from Jamaica...* Squirrels darted through the branches, too many to count but seemingly hundreds. No squirrels chanced the seven- or eight-foot drop from the lower branches, especially with the barking Clint Dempsey right below them. A few skirted down the trunk, then turned tail and made for the branches. I kept banging out the tune and singing along. *They got Burton suits, ha, they think it's funny, turning rebellion into money.*

Eric returned with his fishing net and his pet carrier. He set the pet carrier down. He shouted, "Stop banging the sticks and step back. Let a few squirrels loose."

I took seven or eight steps backward, beyond the canopy of the live oak. Loose leaves fluttered down and settled on my shoulders. I stopped my tune. I scooped Clint Dempsey up in my arms. He stopped barking and licked my face. Almost immediately, the first few squirrels darted down the trunk and made for the hills. Eric took off in pursuit. He swiped his net through the high grass, racing thither and yon, sliding in his work boots, slipping down onto one knee and popping back up. Continuing the chase. He swatted the net three or four times and ran nearly out of the clearing before he yelled, "Got one!"

I set Clint Dempsey down and started banging the sticks together again. The second wave of squirrels raced back up the trunk, not ready yet to take their chances in the high grass with what could only appear to be a volatile Roads and Grounds employee in a moment of madness.

Eric dumped his one squirrel in the carrier and shut the gate. He made his way back to the tree trunk, his chest rising and falling in tune to deep breaths. He used the pole of the net as a walking stick. When he reached me, he stopped and leaned even more weight on the pole. The thin aluminum curved, but didn't give out underneath him. Between heavy breaths, he said, "Your turn."

We traded sticks for net. Eric banged out the tune. I picked a spot outside the canopy, held the net like a lacrosse goalie would, and said, "Let's do it!"

Eric stopped banging the sticks. He knelt and held Clint Dempsey. A new wave of squirrels raced down the tree. They beat a path for the hills, running everywhere except for where I was. I chased. I focused on one bushy tail popping above the high grass. He ran much faster than I could, but I had a bigger stride and I knew where he was going. I cut down the angle and made a diving swipe for him. He darted outside the shadow of the net just in time. I hit the ground, rolled, and popped up onto my feet again, searching for more squirrels. Eric banged the sticks again, holding any of the more timid squirrels in the tree for that much longer. Clint Dempsey stayed under the tree, barking. I locked into the next bushy tail and chased after it, both of us zigging and zagging through the clearing until I got him turned around. He raced for the tree, hit the shadow, got skittish, turned tail, and unwittingly ran right into my net.

His struggle to escape the net only got more tangled. His little teeth tried to chew an escape hole. I rushed him over to the pet carrier, flipped the fishing net, held the net high, and let the squirrel drop in on his colleague. I closed the gate and huffed and puffed my way back to Eric. His rhythm had slowed down. "I thought I was in decent shape," I said, "but this is hard work."

"No kidding."

Bang bang.

"How many of these squirrels does Dr. Bishop need?"

"A dozen or so."

Bang bang.

"I don't think we can chase down ten more of these."

"Nope."

Bang bang.

"You got a new plan?"

"Yep," Eric said. "Take the sticks."

We traded. I started back on the "White Man in Hammersmith Palais." Eric told me to keep banging. He stalked around the canopy of the tree, searching for low running squirrels, shaking the branches to knock them out of the tree, tracing the falling leaves and branches and rodents, and scooping up the dazed squirrels when they hit the ground. He managed to get three in the net before dumping them all in the carrier. I kept banging the sticks, but I changed my tune. I stuck with the Clash's first album, skipping ahead to "Janie Jones." *He's in love with a rock and roll girl.* Eric swept under the tree a few more times, whacking at the branches, knocking loose the leaves, scooping up the squirrels. I banged Clash songs and sang to myself and watched Eric and Clint Dempsey.

By the time I banged my way through "Bored in the USA," the pet carrier held thirteen squirrels. Eric hoisted the carrier onto his shoulder and hollered, "That's enough." He took to the trail.

I stopped banging the sticks. The rest of the oak, so alive with squirrels, cleared out of rodents. They raced to the hills. Clint Dempsey nipped at the heels of a few, but he didn't catch any. I picked up the net, returned my metal poles to the five-gallon bucket, and fell into line behind Eric. We followed the trail back to the psych hospital.

17

Several days later, I unlocked my apartment's front door, stepped inside, and dropped my keys on the newspaper rack/table. I'd returned the surveillance camera to Eric, but he and Dr. Bishop both encouraged me to keep the table. They contended that pressed-wood furniture with a big hole for a surveillance camera in the middle of the drawer was essentially worthless to them. It had worth to me, though. It held my keys.

Clint Dempsey was going nuts in my foyer. I knelt down to pet him. He twisted and squirmed, jumped and licked at my face, too excited to really get a dose of the affection I administered. It was good to have my dog back. Moments like this, I didn't even feel guilty. So what if I'd traded false information to a bully to save my dog? There were no innocent victims in that scenario.

I made quick mental plans: get the tennis ball, head to the cemetery park, give Clint Dempsey ample opportunity to chase, capture, and return the ball. Watch the sun hang low over the blue Pacific, trace shadows cast upon the islands on the horizon. Maybe drink a beer to celebrate another day. Relax.

"That dog has been sitting right there, waiting for you for fifteen minutes."

Ape Man stood on the middle of my brown rental carpet, posed like a soldier at ease: feet shoulder width apart, hands clasped behind his back, apparently flexing his chest. He was clean-shaven. This made the Maori tattoo on the left half of his face all the more prominent. Despite that, he looked somehow softer without the beard. He had a weak chin. Pasty white skin and freckles filled in the parts of his face that were unmolested by the blue tattoo ink. The top of his bald head was level with the top of the doorway behind him.

Frank Walters sat on my couch, a few feet to Ape Man's left. Once again, he was dressed immaculately: light tan suit, silk shirt such a deep brown that it looked black at first glance, a tie like a shadow on his shirt, a matching silk handkerchief emerging from the front jacket pocket. Not a hair out of place, not a scuff on his shoes. The photocopied notes I'd given him sat on his lap.

I scooped up Clint Dempsey. He squirmed in my arms. I said, "Come on in, guys. Make yourselves at home."

Walters thumbed the notes on his lap. "According to this information you sold us," he said, "Dr. Bishop's pets only responded to their owners within three minutes of their owners coming home. That was the case almost ninety percent of the time. Is that right?"

I stroked Clint Dempsey's head. "Sounds about right."

Walters handed the pages to the Ape Man. He softened his Army pose and rifled through the notes. When he found what he was looking for, he arranged that page on the top of the pile. Walters said, "So let's review. Connor is holding the page that charts this dog's reaction to your return. It must be your chart because the starting date is later than all the others and the ending date coincides with the day you signed your divorce papers. And based on this chart, that dog right there never, not once, waited for you by your front door for longer than three minutes. Not once. Is that right, Connor?"

Ape Man held up the paper. "That's what the sheet says." He looked at me for a reaction.

I said, "Your name is Connor?" This realization filled me with confidence. I felt like I could take him. How tough could he really be with a name like Connor? I pictured a chubby, twelve-year-old version of the Ape Man lumbering off a suburban soccer field, none of the kids talking to him because his slow, fat ass just cost them the game. Only his mother will go near him. She embraces him and says, "It's okay, Connor. Let's get a hot fudge sundae at McDonald's and forget all about it." That's what the name Connor made me think of.

Ape Man said, "Careful, tough guy."

"Staying focused here," Walters said. "We learn that our empirical observations of your dog blatantly contradicts the information you sold to us. What are we going to do now?"

I stood in my foyer, holding my dog, wondering the same thing, wondering what my next move would be. Hang on to the dog. Do that first.

Walters extended his white cane. He stood from my couch and held out his hand. Ape Man placed the notes in Walters' hand. Clint Dempsey squirmed. I hung on and wondered how I would fight and hold onto my dog at the same time. Ape Man took a tennis ball out of his pocket and rolled it into the bedroom behind him. Clint Dempsey launched out of my arms, darted between Ape Man's legs, and vanished into the bedroom. Ape Man followed. I ran across the floor. Walters stuck his cane out and tripped me. By the time I got back up, my bedroom door was shut and locked. That didn't stop me. I kicked the door, just to the left of the knob. The cheap cardboard door gave way, splintering, creaking, swinging open. Ape Man held Clint Dempsey in his arms. Clint Dempsey had the ball in his mouth. Ape Man stuck a hypodermic needle into Clint Dempsey's rump.

I paused just long enough to watch Ape Man gently place Clint Dempsey on the bed. The pup limped around in one big, slow circle, and then lay down, as if to sleep. Lights out for Clint Dempsey.

I stared for a second and snapped out of it in the next second. I rushed Ape Man. He pulled a gun out of his bomber jacket. The same pistol he'd threatened me with before, that Sunday on the Pacific Coast Highway. I tackled him anyway and slammed my fists into his head four or five times before he was able to gather up the gun and whack me in the jaw with the butt of it. The whole world—my bedroom, my dog, the Ape Man, his sweaty armpits and his discount department store cologne, Frank Walters, the flash of his white cane, the rumble of the dying American car on the street outside my apartment, the groan erupting from inside me—narrowed down to a flicker of light in a field of black. Then the flicker snuffed out.

I woke up about twenty minutes later. Bits of dust danced in the slices of sunlight that cut through my window blinds. I lay on the floor and watched them dance for a minute or two. A few brutal facts crossed my mind. First, Clint Dempsey was gone. I lifted my sore head high enough to see that not even the pup's corpse remained on my bed. As far as I could tell, the scoreboard now read:

Death   2
My dogs 0

Second, I got knocked out by a guy named Connor. The getting knocked out, I could deal with. My assailant was much bigger than me and he was armed. Fair enough. But the fact that his name represented all the weenie kids I'd spent my life trying to help out, befriending just because no one else would… It was too much. Couple that with the fact that the ape who'd grown out the skin of the weenie kid named Connor had killed my dog, and I couldn't stand it. Either Karma was dead or she just wasn't paying attention. Third, Frank Walters wasn't easily fooled.

I pried myself off the tan rental carpet of my floor. The apartment bore no signs of my visitors, no trace of Clint Dempsey. Nothing but cheap furniture, junk paperbacks, off-white walls, and the detritus of a lonely man's life. If not for the knot on my jaw and the splintered bedroom door, I could've made myself believe that it had all been a dream. That there never had been an Ape Man or a Frank Walters or a Clint Dempsey. That Dr. Bishop wasn't doing any research. That I was the butterfly dreaming I was a grant writer. Or so I thought at first.

The knot in my jaw convinced me that the pain, at least, was real and that solid food was out of the question for the night. I walked into the kitchen, took a can of tomato soup out of the cupboard, opened it, dumped the contents into a pot, added water and some spices, and put it on to heat up.

I spent an eternity watching the pot, waiting for the thick red broth to bubble. I tried to add up what I knew and see where that took me. I knew that Dr. Bishop was doing some kind of experiments, first with pets in their foyers, now with squirrels. I knew that her findings could be exploited in some way and that Walters wanted to exploit them. I couldn't connect, though, how talking telepathically to dogs—and maybe squirrels, too?—added up to money in advertising. And there was Dr. Benengeli's explanation, that it was more than telepathy. That it was some kind of fractured collective unconscious that was different from Jung's, which I didn't understand well enough to understand the differences. This had led to Dr. Bishop's optimism, her dream that her experiments could all lead to a higher form of communication. But, again, a higher communication with animals? I didn't see how that led to Walters. Pile on top of that a weird voice emerging in my head, a blow to my jaw that knocked me unconscious, and a dead dog…

Which brought me into a new train of thought all about that hypodermic needle in Clint Dempsey's rump. It didn't have to be fatal, did it? The Ape Man surely put my pup to sleep, but he could have put him literally—not euphemistically—to sleep. He could've knocked my dog out like he knocked me out. He did, after all, put Clint Dempsey down on the bed very gently. There'd be no reason to do that with a dead dog. And if they were trying to be intimidating, it would make more sense to leave the corpse as a reminder. But there wasn't a trace of the pup left behind. Thinking of this brought back the image of Clint Dempsey's sad, slow circle. No, the poor little guy is probably dead.

When the soup was finally hot, I poured it into a bowl and carried everything over to the kitchen table. I sat down to eat and saw the pictures for the first time.

There were three of them. The first showed my wife locking the front door of the apartment that we'd once shared and she still lived in. She wore a navy blue business suit and high heels. Her hairstyle had changed since the last time I'd seen her. The second photo showed Lola Diaz seated on a wooden stool in front of a canvas on an easel. The bricks of the dual diagnosis dorm rose behind her. Because of the angle of the photograph, I couldn't see what was on the canvas. Her tongue stuck out slightly as she dabbed the paintbrush. The third photograph showed Dr. Benengeli and me seated in front of the downtown brewpub. We both gazed off to the street scene. Dr. Benengeli wore her blue t-shirt with the big-eyed doll on front and the oxfords with stars on the toes.

I ate soup and stared at the photos. Frank Walters meant business.

18

The telephone rang through from another world and wrested me from my nap. I was in the middle of a dream in which I was a zombie and all of the living alive, I guess you'd call them, were out to kill me and the other zombies. I'd sought shelter in a college dorm. A girls' dorm. Another zombie hid with me. He was this kid I'd worked with at the community space in Fresno. A sad, quiet, punk rock boy who'd often complain about not being able to meet any girls, even though I'd introduced him to dozens of girls. In the dream, he complained about being a zombie and that everyone was out to kill him. I empathized. A goth girl came out of her dorm room. Young and beautiful in her dyed black hair and pale skin and eyeliner mask. She went right up to the other zombie, the boy from the community space, and invited him back to her room to listen to Siouxsie and the Banshees records. The saddest smile crept across his face. It was the kind of smile only a zombie in love could make. In the dream, I was thinking I sure hope this works out and he doesn't eat her brains. At that exact moment, the phone rang. There was no phone in the dream dorm, so I had to undergo the transformation of things. I went from being a grant writer dreaming I was a zombie to a zombie dreaming I was a grant writer. I answered the phone.

"What are you doing?"

"Napping," I said, not quite able to place the woman's voice on the other end of the line.

"Napping?! Come on. It's a beautiful day. Don't waste it inside."

"Where are you?" I asked, because her last dozen words were enough to recognize that it was Lola's voice on the other end of the line. I thought it strange that she might be calling from the psych hospital.

"I'm at home. Can I come over?"

"Yeah. Sure. Of course."

"Cool. I'll be there in a minute." Lola hung up, leaving me with a world of questions about where she was calling from and how she got my phone number and how she knew where I lived and everything else I wondered about this grown-up version of the second woman I ever loved.

I had no idea how long it would take her to get over to my place, but I wanted to get a shower in first. I tacked a note on my front door: *Lola, come in.* I gathered clean clothes so that I could dress in the bathroom, just in case Lola was close and got to my pad before I got out of the shower. I didn't want an awkward situation of walking out of the bathroom and giving her the full frontal shot.

I washed quickly, dressed, and by the time I got out of the bathroom, Lola sat in the new armchair I'd picked up a few weeks earlier. She wore a white long-sleeve t-shirt from one of the local surf shops and black warm-up pants, loose at the ankles and with white stripes running down the side of each leg. Everything about her seemed out of context. When I'd seen her at the psych hospital, she always dressed like a woman going to work. I guess, because, in a sense, she was. The updated, 37-year-old Lola, in my mind, was supposed to wear business casual and walk around psych hospitals. Genuine casual and sitting in my new armchair threw me for a quick loop. Her legs were crossed. She wore black and gray striped socks. A bit of an illustration peeked out from the bottom of her pant leg. I said, "What does your sock say?"

She lifted her pant leg and showed me the illustration: a heart with a dagger through it, wrapped around by a banner. The words in the banner read, "Hardcore Love." Bright red blood dripped from the dagger.

"Very cool," I said.

Lola smiled.

I addressed the elephant in the room. "So, you're out of Oak View?"

Lola stood. She spread her arms and did a little half-curtsy. "I'm cured."

"Congratulations," I said. "So what now?"

"Now, we go for a walk."

"Give me just a second," I said. I slid on non-striped, non-illustrated socks and running shoes. My wallet sat on the table by the door. I paused and stared at it for a second. It was a black leather wallet with a wallet chain. My wedding ring was hooked on the clip at the end of the wallet chain. More than sadness or denial, I kept wearing my wedding ring out of habit. Because the ring and the wallet were connected whenever I was inside my apartment, and because I put them on simultaneously when I left, the two objects were linked together in my mind. If I left the house without my wedding ring, I'd have a nagging feeling that I'd forgotten my wallet. So I kept wearing the ring and hooking it to the wallet chain when I got home and took both wallet and ring off. But here was Lola in front of me, a paean to broken habits and improved learned behaviors. In honor of her, I dropped the wedding ring onto the table by the front door. I stuffed my wallet in the back pocket of my jeans, hooked the wallet chain on my belt loop, and scooped up my keys. Lola and I went out into the light.

"Where do you want to go?" I asked.

"On an adventure."

"What kind of adventure?"

"Who cares? Do you have anything else to do today?"

The truth was, I didn't. I'd been napping when Lola called because I had nothing left to do. I'd taken a long bike ride that morning. I'd cooked a big breakfast and cleaned my apartment and washed my dishes. I'd gone to the beach and read a paperback for a while. I'd ironed my work clothes and listened to records and read a magazine and had my lunch and, by one o'clock, I was nearly out of options. Before napping, I'd even contemplated taking the bus to the psych hospital on my day off and checking in on Dr. Bishop and her squirrels. That's how little I had to do that day. "Let's go."

Lola slid on a pair of sunglasses with big, round, white frames.

"You look like a movie star with those glasses. Like you're hiding out from the paparazzi."

Lola snorted. "God forbid. Could you imagine a little Puerto Rican girl like me an actress? It'd be a lifetime of playing maids."

"You could've been Rosencrantz or Guildenstern. Hell, you could've been Ophelia." The second I said that last part, I regretted it. I'd only meant to say that she could play a classic role. I didn't realize that it was probably a bad idea to tell someone fresh out of a psych institution that she could play Ophelia.

Lola slid her glasses down her nose, looked up at me, raised an eyebrow, and pushed her glasses back in place. We kept walking. A slight ocean breeze crept up the hill in my neighborhood. The sun hung high, close enough to be warm but too far away to be hot. Wisps of clouds floated in the blue sky above. Every panorama was filled with rolling hills and palm trees and mission houses. We passed a schoolyard where three adolescents, two boys and a girl, rode their skateboards down a short walkway and tried to ollie down the stairs. They took turns. None of them could stick the landing, but still they raced up toward the edge of the stairs, launched into the air, kept the board stuck to their feet, and had faith that their visions and skills could defy gravity.

Lola watched the skateboarders, too. After we passed the schoolyard, she said, "Did you go see *Rosencrantz and Guildenstern Are Dead*?"

"I did," I said. "I thought they did a good job."

"Dr. Benengeli is an excellent director."

"I guess so."

"You *guess* so? She gets a bunch of mental patients to put on a three-hour play that questions our very existence, and the performance is *brilliant*, and you guess so?"

"It was impressive." So impressive, in fact, that I'd figured out how to send a telegram and sent one to Dr. Benengeli congratulating her. I guess my tone of voice didn't betray any of this, though.

Lola mocked me. " 'It was impressive.' Listen to you." She smiled and shook her head. "Don't let on any more than you have to."

I took her advice and dodged that last statement. Since there had actually been a famous actress in Dr. Benengeli's production, I said, "Did you notice who played The Player?"

"Oh, of course. I sat in a few group sessions with her. I'm not supposed to say anything, but, wow, I could tell some stories."

"It's amazing how many famous people pass through Oak View."

"Oh, I know," Lola said. "When I first got there, I thought maybe I was crazier than I let myself believe. I kept walking around the grounds and seeing actors and actresses and rock stars and thinking, 'Good lord, I'm hallucinating. Somebody stop this.' But then, you know, you think about it for a couple of seconds and realize that of course a rehab facility this close to LA is going to be filled with celebrities."

"It's like they say: if you want to see the stars in LA, go to an Alcoholics Anonymous meeting."

"No kidding."

"It must be tough keeping all those stories to yourself," I said.

"Oh, you know it. I got the dirt on a few of them." The side of Lola's mouth crept up into a little half-smile. She kept walking and the conversation faded. I didn't press for details because, to be honest, I didn't care about the dirt. Most of the time, I only knew that a celebrity was at the psych hospital because one of the Roads and Grounds guys would excitedly tell me that a famous person was there and then explain who the celebrity was and then get frustrated with me because I usually hadn't seen the celebrity's TV show or movie or heard the hit song. The only time I got excited to meet a patient was when an aging Orange County punk rocker was admitted. No one else seemed to know who he was, so suddenly I could feel superior, like, "You never heard this song!" and, "You don't have this album!" But that only served as a reminder that I no longer had that song or that album because my wife had sold them on eBay in the days leading up to our divorce.

I thought about that patient. I rubbed the bare ring finger on my left hand. Lola and I strolled down Main Street, half a mile east of downtown and cruising further east at three mph.

Mid-afternoon on a Saturday, outside the basic shopping and dining district of town, there wasn't a ton of action surrounding us. Cars whizzed by on the street beside us. A few motorcycles rumbled past, mostly the big money models with riders dressed in hundreds of dollars' worth of leather that looked new and crisp and ready for one of their thrice-annual rides. An occasional bicyclist would pedal along, sometimes atop feather-light road bikes and decked out in the full complement of spandex and logos, sometimes atop dented mountain bikes and decked out in baggy shorts and t-shirts. One girl rode by on a pink beach cruiser. The bike had a white wicker basket with plastic flowers. Lola pointed to it and said,

"That's what I need."

We ambled along past thrift stores and a guitar shop and a tattoo parlor and a barbecue joint and a locksmith and several empty shops. Main Street ahead promised a coffee shop and a Little League field. Lola said, "I have a plan."

She led me into the coffee shop and said, "What's your favorite fruit?"

"I don't know. Oranges."

"Oranges? That's no fun. How about mangos?"

"Sure. I love mangos."

"Perfect." Lola walked up to the counter. A shaggy, tattooed kid leaned against a cooler, flipping through a free weekly newspaper. He saw Lola, slowly set down the weekly, and acknowledged her with the slightest head nod. Lola kept on her big, round, white sunglasses. She really did look like a movie star. I daydreamed about her being a movie star. Or not so much her being a movie star but what it would feel like if she were and she'd escaped the limelight for a day and had her driver take her up to this quiet little beach community and gave him the afternoon off so that she could stroll down Main Street with me and buy a smoothie and talk about how nice it was to get away from the rat race for a day. And, for some reason, that daydream felt no better than knowing that she'd just gotten out of a psych hospital and sought me out and strolled down Main Street and bought me a smoothie. The tattooed kid blended fruit, juice, and ice together. Lola rested, hands on knees, checking out the pastries behind the glass. Movie star or mental patient, it was all the same. I sidled up next to her.

"You want a muffin?" she asked.

"Nah. I had lunch already."

"Brownie? Lemon square?" She pointed at the goods behind the glass. "Pumpkin crunch? Macaroon? It's on me."

"I'm fine," I said. "Really."

"Scone? Come on. Have a scone."

I realized what Lola was up to. Fifteen years with my wife had taught me how to recognize when a woman is feeding me just so she can feel okay about eating. And, come on, what kind of spoilsport is going to say no to dessert on a day like this? I said, "All right. Sure. I'll split a muffin with you."

Lola ordered a blueberry muffin from the tattooed kid. She insisted on paying for everything. When the kid rang up the two smoothies and the muffin, the total came to $8.05. Lola gave the kid nine dollars. She leaned over the counter and peeked into the register. "Can I get my change in nickels?"

The kid looked at Lola like she'd just gotten out of a mental institution. Somewhere in his brain was a manila folder labeled *Nutty Customers*. He filed this moment into that folder. Later, he'd tell his friends, "Seriously, dude. Nineteen nickels. What kinda crap? What can you even buy with a nickel?"

He counted the nickels out into her hand. She tipped him a dollar bill and poured the nineteen nickels into her pink and black checkered coin purse. Even with those big, round, white sunglasses, I could see her beaming like a kid on the first day of summer vacation. Here she was with a smoothie and a muffin and a purse full of change, strolling out into the fresh, crisp Southern California springtime. Seeing her with this smile not just on her face but in her shoulders and in her hips and in the balls of her feet, I flashed back to the Folsom High School afternoons when Lola and I would hang out, and this one day in particular when I took her out for ice cream. She'd ordered a triple scoop cone: strawberry, vanilla, and rocky road on the top. The ice cream towered over the tiny cone in her little hand. She glowed in the prospect of this absurd amount of ice cream and the guy who was cool with feeding it to her. She actually skipped once as we left the store. The three scoops shook but didn't fall. We sat on a bench in front of the shop. The sidewalk below was stained with drippings from cones of days gone by. Cars circled the vast parking lot in front of us. Lola attacked the triple scoop. So serious and determined about the ice cream that I actually started to worry that she'd lick too hard and the whole tower would topple. I imagined the scenario: the three scoops plopping on the stained sidewalk, the suddenly downtrodden Lola, my offers to buy her a new cone even though we both knew that a replacement cone loses all the magic. But the scoops didn't drop. She managed that little bit of joy in her hand, despite how fragile and fleeting it was. She took it all in.

Lola led me across Main Street to the Little League field. Nine players dressed in blue jerseys and white pants covered the field. Judging from their height and from the slow, loping pitch that floated across the plate and the late swing of the batter, I gathered that the ballplayers couldn't be more than ten or eleven years old. The batter stepped out of the batter's box. He took two practice swings. He chewed his gum and blew a bubble. He took one more practice swing and stepped back into the box, wearing the one red jersey in the field of blue. Lola led me to the top of the aluminum bleachers on the visitor's side. Most of the parents sat in the other set of bleachers. One father paced behind the home plate fence. His loafers kicked up dust, but he was otherwise clean and pressed. When the pitcher started his wind-up, the father lined himself up, outside the field of play but directly behind the umpire, in perfect position to view that second called strike. He pumped his fist.

Lola opened her change purse and dumped the nickels onto the aluminum bench between us. The coins pinged on the bleachers. Lola separated the nickels into two piles, one of nine nickels, the other of ten. She pushed the ten nickels in my direction. She pointed to the scoreboard in right field. The count on the batter was two balls, two strikes. Lola held up a coin. "A nickel says this kid strikes out."

I picked up two coins from my pile. "Ten cents says that he not only walks, but that intense dad behind home plate yells at the pitcher."

"No," Lola said. "We're only betting nickels."

I put a nickel down into neutral territory. She set her coin next to mine. The next three pitches brought a ball, a foul down the first base line, and another ball. The kid walked. The intense father kicked the home plate fence and shouted something about the umpire's shrinking strike zone. I picked up the two nickels.

Lola set another nickel down. "Double play. This kid's gonna get the blue team out of the inning."

I set my nickel next to hers. The next red batter dropped a bunt on the first pitch. The ball waddled down the third base line. The catcher leapt from his crouch, scooped up the ball, and winged it to second base. The ball flew about four feet over the second baseman's head. The center fielder had been watching traffic and didn't realize that the ball was coming to him until it rolled past. He chased it back to the center field wall. The first runner scored and the bunter jogged safely to second base. The intense dad laced his fingers into the chain link fence and shook it, screaming, "Come on! Defense! Come on!" I picked up two more nickels.

With every batter, Lola placed another nickel down and called another bet. I kept winning. I realized that I was going to win all of her nickels if I didn't call out the bets, so I called out a few. My bets were a little more risky. A nickel that Angry Dad offers his glasses to the ump. A nickel that the kid in right field scratches his balls before another pitch is thrown. That kind of thing. I even won most of those bets. Lola seemed to absorb any losses. When she won, though, she didn't get excited at all. She just plopped a new nickel down and made an even more outrageous bet.

After two innings, the smoothies had melted down to watery juice and I had all nineteen nickels in my pile. I tried to split them up again, but Lola said, "No. Gambling's only fun if you really win or lose the money."

So there I was, with a pocketful of nickels and a nagging suspicion that I was maybe enabling a gambling addict fresh out of the psych hospital. That second thought must have floated above my head in a cartoon bubble because Lola said, "If you want to ask me why I was in the hospital, you can."

"That's okay," I said. "I can respect your privacy."

"Aren't you curious?"

"Sure, I'm curious, but it's none of my business."

"If I showed up at your house with a cast on my leg, would you ask me what happened?"

"Yeah. I guess."

"So when I show up at your apartment straight from the psych hospital, why don't you ask me what happened?"

"I don't know," I said. I did know that, clearly, she wanted to talk about it. So I said, "What happened?"

"I'm an alcoholic. I've been clean for six months now. I moved away from my bad influences. I'm doing okay."

"That's great," I said. "Congratulations."

"It's not great. I'm an alcoholic. That sucks." Lola stretched out the plastic wrap that her muffin had come in. Tiny crumbs clung to it. She twisted the clear plastic and wrung it into a long, thin roll. She tied a knot in the center of the roll, pulled it tight, and tied another one. "I totally bottomed out about six months ago."

"I meant it's great that you're sober."

"I hope so."

I reached over and patted her knee. It was intended to be a friendly gesture. A bit of reassurance. But as soon as my fingers tapped those cotton and polyester warm-up pants, I felt a jolt and realized that it was the first time I'd actually touched a woman in weeks.

Lola took off her sunglasses. She pinched the bridge of her nose, one finger on the inside cusp of each eye. She slipped the glasses back on. "And I was sexually abused by my father. Repeatedly. When I was too young to do anything about it."

"I'm sorry to hear that. I'm sorry that it happened."

Lola nodded. The Little League game below us reflected in the lenses of her glasses. "I can talk about it now. There's no shame. It's not my fault, right?"

"It's absolutely not your fault."

"But for years, I carried it around with me. All that guilt and blame. And, you know, being as Catholic as I was, it really rattled me. And then he died. To be honest, I wasn't sad at all. I actually felt a little happy. Relieved, you know?"

"That's understandable."

"Not really. I didn't understand it. I felt so shitty, like everything was my fault. It was haunting. I honestly believed that Jesus died on a cross to forgive me for allowing my father to molest me. It was crazy. And so I drank and drank and drank. But it didn't help."

Lola leaned forward and rolled up her warm-up pants. Her striped socks had fallen down to her ankles. She pulled the socks back up. The black and gray stripes circled her calves. The red heart burned in the sun. I read the words on the banner again. Lola readjusted her pant legs.

"You know, you read Bukowski or you watch movies about alcoholics and it seems so beautifully tragic: this lost soul burying his problems in a bottle. But when you live it, it's not a beautiful tragedy. It's a slow, lazy death. Mostly, you're just watching basic cable."

I laughed a little at this line. Then I said, "Sorry."

Lola smiled. "I'm serious. We all have this image in our head of a troubled soul in his beautiful suicide, but the truth of the matter is, you just spend your days drinking and watching crappy reruns. I found myself crying during a sad episode of *King of Queens* and I said, 'That's it. I need help.'"

"Really?"

"Not quite. I'm kidding. Sort of. I never cried during a sitcom. But you get the point, anyway."

I guess I did. More or less.

"So now it's all like those nickels in your pocket. Sure, I lost something but it's gone now. I can make my peace with that." Lola sucked up the last watery remnants of her smoothie. Scattered drops rattled with the air in her straw. "And so, that's done. Let's go look for new adventures."

Lola stood, brushed the muffin crumbs off her black warm-up pants, and started down the bleachers. I followed, nineteen nickels jingling in my jeans.

19

Dr. Bishop sat on a small metal stool facing a squirrel in a cage. The squirrel skittered around half mad, knowing what was coming. I sat behind and to the right of Dr. Bishop, clipboard on my lap, pen in hand. She held a small gadget in her hand: a three-inch metal tube with a button on top and a wire running from the bottom. It was like the buzzers that game show contestants use when they have an answer. When Dr. Bishop pushed the button, an electric current flooded the squirrel's cage. The squirrel leapt. The leap didn't help him much. The current ran through him. His short hairs stood briefly on end.

Prior to putting the squirrel in the cage, I had tested the shock. I tested it first with a voltmeter. It barely registered. I tested it second by putting my hand on the wired bottom of the cage and pushing the button. The shock felt like static electricity. It wasn't pleasant but it was far from painful. I realized, of course, that my threshold for pain was much higher than the squirrel's. Still, there wasn't enough juice in that cage to do real harm to anything.

I had also fashioned a wooden platform in one corner of the cage. The platform was exactly big enough for the squirrel to stand on, but no bigger. Because the platform was wooden, it was impervious to the electric shocks. A wise squirrel would seek solace there.

After the squirrel leapt, I made a note in Dr. Bishop's notepad. We were investigating whether or not the squirrel would figure out when the jolt was coming and react prior to the jolt. It was an alternate take on Pavlov's classical conditioning experiment. Instead of setting off a buzzer to warn the animal that a shock was coming, Dr. Bishop sent a mental warning. She thought to herself and hopefully to the squirrel, 'Okay, little fellow, I'm going to shock you in three… two… one… Jump!' Then she pushed the button. My job entailed watching the squirrel to see if he jumped onto the platform before the shock hit him. Dr. Bishop went through the ritual of thought, countdown, shock twenty-five times. The squirrel never made it onto the platform at the right time.

Dr. Bishop stood from her stool and set the buzzer down. The squirrel darted around in his little 2' x 3' cage. He clearly had no idea where the shocks were coming from. Dr. Bishop reached for my clipboard. I handed it over. She examined the notations.

The sheet on the clipboard contained a simple chart. On the top was written the date, the number Dr. Bishop had assigned for the squirrel, the time, and various codes about where and how this experiment fit into Dr. Bishop's larger research project. The body of the page had fifty rows and three columns. The first column was labeled 'shock.' Each row in that column contained a number, starting at one and ending at fifty. The second column was labeled 'anticipation.' All of the rows were empty. The third column was labeled 'no anticipation.' The first twenty-five rows had checks in them.

Dr. Bishop's gaze drifted up and down the rows and columns. She tugged her earring. It was a dangling gold dreamcatcher. "I have another idea," she said. She went to the storage closet behind me. I swung in my chair to watch her. She pulled out a full-face motorcycle helmet. The face shield had been spray-painted black.

"What are you going to do with that?"

Dr. Bishop returned to her stool. "The problem is, we're dealing with Mindland, not telepathy. I'm trying to reach this squirrel on a deeper level. I worry that my conscious mind may interfere too much with my unconscious mind. So I got this helmet. When I put it on, I can hardly see or hear anything. Maybe the sensory deprivation will help me to reach Mindland and warn this little squirrel."

Mindland was the word Dr. Bishop had been using lately for the collective unconscious, though she only used it around Eric and me. I liked it. The word made me feel as if there were a land outside our bodies where our thoughts could vacation. The way Dr. Bishop said it was a bit curious, too. She didn't pronounce the two words separately, like a land of the mind. She blended them, said them with the familiarity of a native of Mindland, so that the word rhymed with island or Vineland. When she said it, I would sometimes get lost in daydreams about a little kid born in Mindland, growing up with no body to return to, learning to live through a series of mischievous misadventures that planted ridiculous thoughts and cheesy songs into the heads of all who so carelessly let our unconscious thoughts rest in his home land.

Dr. Bishop sat back down on her stool and set the buzzer on her lap. She removed her dreamcatcher earrings and tucked them away in her lab coat. She pulled the helmet over her short, curly gray hair. She even fastened the chinstrap. I don't know why. She picked up the buzzer.

I grabbed my clipboard and watched the squirrel's panic ensue. He ran two strides to one end of the cage, whipped around, raced to the other end, tried to climb out, stood on his haunches, gnawed at the metal bars, gnawed at the wooden platform, jumped when he got shocked, and spun around in three full circles. He did not, however, heed the warning that Dr. Bishop traveled into Mindland to pass on.

I gazed around the lab. A certain kind of loneliness descended upon it as soon as Dr. Bishop put on her sensory deprivation helmet. Thirteen squirrels, all in individual cages, surrounded us. They had hamster wheels that they could run on. A few squirrels ran on the wheels. The rest nibbled on hamster pellets or drank water from their tubes or napped or watched their comrade get shocked. I wondered—not for the first time—why Eric and I had gone on a wild squirrel chase instead of just buying normal rodents at a pet store. Mice, hamsters, and gerbils were all cheap. Surely, you could get a dozen rodents for thirty or forty bucks. And rodents were rodents. The only difference I could see between a squirrel and a hamster was the bushy tail. So why didn't she just buy them? Especially for a scientist who was concerned about her work standing up to peer review.

I watched Dr. Bishop push her buzzer. She sat upright on her stool. Her white lab coat flowed down. She wore beige slacks and dark brown penny loafers. Everything about her demeanor advertised her professionalism as a researcher except for the black motorcycle helmet and black face shield. And, of course, the thirteen caged squirrels flanking us. I made notes on the clipboard. I thought—not for the first time—that this whole enterprise was insane. For the past four weeks, I'd been passing the information off to Frank Walters without argument. I'd been taking his envelopes of cash and donating the money to various charities because I couldn't see the harm in it. He was paying to chart the progress of a woman who was trying to speak telepathically to squirrels. I felt certain that it wasn't going to lead to anything and that Walters wouldn't be able to tap into any collective unconscious and wouldn't be able to exploit it for advertising purposes. It was silly. It was absurd. It broke my heart that Clint Dempsey had been an innocent victim of this information war. Not that it would've been okay for him to be kidnapped and/or killed for a legitimate experiment. It just seemed, I don't know, even more heartbreaking that he was taken and possibly died because he somehow got caught up in the madness of a kooky old doctor and a power-hungry ad exec.

Dr. Bishop stayed the course. Lost in her black helmet, she sent out her warnings, gave the squirrel time to jump on the platform, and pushed the buzzer. The squirrel darted and gnawed and spun, but he didn't ever find refuge in time. I counted the shocks. Dr. Bishop had sent twenty-five shocks prior to donning the helmet, plus nineteen post-helmet shocks. Six more and my volunteer time on this experiment was over for the day. On the twentieth post-helmet shock, the squirrel leapt onto the platform. His timing was perfect. He didn't get shocked at all. I made my first mark in the "anticipation" column.

On the twenty-first shock, he timed it perfectly again and leapt to the platform. He did it again on the twenty-second. Three times in a row. Maybe there was a pattern here. Between each shock, he left the platform and wandered the cage, only to return exactly when the shock came. He avoided the twenty-third jolt. The twenty-fourth. The twenty-fifth.

Dr. Bishop paused before taking off her helmet. The squirrel squatted on his haunches and waited. I looked at the six marks in the anticipation column. Hmm.

I missed the last bus home. This happened fairly often when I volunteered for Dr. Bishop. Dr. Benengeli usually gave me a lift on evenings like this. I'd called her from the lab and she told me to head on over, she was just finishing up with her progress notes. I cut across the south quad. The last of the afternoon sunlight filtered through the ancient laurel oaks that outlined the quad. A group of patients gathered in a circle on the middle of the lawn. One of the psych interns led them in group therapy. Two psych techs walked another group of patients to the cafeteria. One patient walked across the quad alone. He was a big guy, easily six and a half feet tall. He wore brand new basketball sneakers, the kind that cost a couple hundred dollars. He wore basketball shorts, a Clippers jersey with a gray undershirt underneath, and a helmet. He was not the first patient I'd seen wearing a helmet. More than once, it occurred to a patient that he could rid his head of the demons if he simply beat them out. Most of the walls around the institution were concrete block. When head met wall, wall typically won. This led to the purchase of state-issued helmets that were designed for skateboarders. This patient had wires hanging from his ears, too. At first, I thought the wires had something to do with the helmet. As I got closer, I saw that the wires were attached to earphones and a portable mp3 player.

The patient steered a path straight for me. I could think of no reason to avoid him, so I kept on my way. I thought about that squirrel. Six times he avoided the shock. All six times he found the platform. As if he'd finally gotten the message. And he seemed so relaxed at the end. I wondered whether squirrels relax. Can they? I thought about those six leaps of his and I wanted to write them off as a coincidence. It was tough. Usually, when something happens six times in a row, it's a pattern, not a coincidence. I couldn't bring myself to believe that Dr. Bishop had somehow posted notes in the collective unconscious and a squirrel had read those notes and reacted. It was too much.

The patient approached me. I remained lost in thought. He smiled and nodded. I returned both smile and nod. He stepped closer. I thought about squirrels. He reached out and grabbed my scrotum.

For a second, I couldn't believe it. I looked down. His hand was buried in my discount department store slacks. He squeezed. Pain seared through me. I screamed.

The patient didn't let go. An image flashed in my mind. I remembered a police officer who had come to the community space in Fresno to discuss rape prevention. He'd said that an effective way to fight off a rapist who overpowers you is to grab his ear and yank. "You can pull someone's ear off without too much effort," he'd told us. It was such a gruesome image that it remained with me. Now, with 61/2' tall, helmeted patient clamping onto my scrotum, I took the policeman at his word. I dug my fingers past the strap of his helmet and grabbed the patient's ear. His earbud fell onto my palm. The tinny sound of a hip-hop bass filtered out. I yanked. The ear started to give. The patient's skin tore open. His blood trickled down my fingers. The pain must've seared through him because he clamped down even harder on my scrotum. I couldn't take it. I let go of his ear. He did not return the favor vis-à-vis my scrotum.

I kept screaming. Waves of nausea flowed through me. I almost passed out and actually wished I could. I tried to pull his hand off my scrotum, but he kept a firm grip. The harder I pulled his arm away, the more painful it was for me. I felt like the skin around my scrotum would tear away from my groin. I stopped pulling and dug my thumb into the soft spot in the middle of his wrist. His veins and tendons wiggled around underneath my thumb. He still didn't let go. I punched him in the nose so hard that my hand would have hurt if my scrotum didn't hurt worse. Blood flowed through his nostrils and from the back of one of his ears. Tears poured from his eyes. He screamed. Bubbles of spit escaped his gaping yaw and covered my face. He did not let go.

I had no idea how to react. I punched him in the nose again and again. His nose was long-since broken. Tears flowed from his eyes. He kept squeezing and screaming. An impossible amount of time passed. Hours. Days. Months. Or more likely, only thirty or forty-five seconds. But forty-five seconds of someone clamping onto your scrotum can be days and weeks and months.

Two psych techs and a nurse rushed toward us. One psych tech wrapped his arms around the patient. The other tech restrained the patient's legs. The nurse yanked down the patient's basketball shorts and jabbed a needle in his rear. I tried to stop punching the patient in the nose, but I couldn't. Three punches later, he passed out in the psych tech's arms.

I dropped to the grass and lay there. Done. One of the psych techs stated the obvious. "Steer clear of this guy."

An hour later, I sat atop a towel on my new armchair. On the way home from the psych hospital, Dr. Benengeli had purchased two bags of frozen peas from a market. She told me to keep one bag in the freezer and one bag in my lap. When the bag on my lap thawed, make the switch. She had dropped me off at my apartment with those bags of peas and that advice. I did what she said. Beyond that, I tried to not move.

My scrotum had swelled to the size of two tangerines. The medical doctor at the psych hospital had examined the injury. He said I would be okay in another day or two. The only challenge was to make it through that day or two. He had given me codeine to help with the pain.

I sat on my new armchair in my empty little apartment, staring at the off-white walls and the renter's brown carpet and the rabbit ears atop my television and my bare feet on the ottoman. I was in too much pain to read or watch TV or even listen to music. The codeine I had taken didn't exactly ease the pain. It made me care a little less about the pain, though. I guess that was something.

I picked up the book Dr. Benengeli had given me, *An Enquiry Concerning the Understanding of Knowledge and Existence*. I read the title several times. I wondered what the difference was between an "enquiry" and an "inquiry." If the dictionary had been closer, I would've looked it up. I wasn't about to move. I looked at the author's name. It meant nothing to me. The cover had no painting or illustration or image to give away the contents. It was simply a design of circles and lines painted in 1970s-style earth colors. I rested my head back and took a nap.

When I awoke, my peas had thawed. I hobbled into the kitchen, put the thawed bag of peas in the freezer, and took out the frozen bag. Every step I took back to my armchair hurt. I took one more codeine, sat, and picked up the book again. There was a photograph of the author on the back. He was a fairly young man, probably mid-40s. He had a goatee, the academic variety that was neatly trimmed and sculpted into sharp angles. The beard narrowed to a point. His hair had been slicked back. He wore a corduroy blazer, a sweater vest, and a bow tie. Even with the thirty years that had passed since this picture was taken and even considering the unfamiliar goatee and slicked back hair, the author was unmistakable. He was The Professor. This was his book.

In a day populated by telepathic squirrels and full-frontal scrotal attacks, this book would prove to be the strangest thing I encountered.

20

Lola took over my kitchen. Sausages crackled in a frying pan. Gravy bubbled in a small pot. The mixer whirred through milk and butter and boiled potatoes quickly on their way to being mashed. The off-white walls and renter's brown carpet of my apartment gradually ceded to Lola's vision. My anonymous box of an apartment was getting a life of its own, suddenly full of the aroma of bangers and mash.

I never would've expected it, but Lola was the queen of British cuisine. I learned this on the day that the mental patient attacked my scrotum. Lola had stopped by to find me codeined and sad on my armchair with a bag of frozen peas on my lap. I told her my story. She decided to nurse me back to health. Over the course of the next five days, she employed her own version of holistic healing. She started by taking the rabbit ears off my old television set, arguing that, if I couldn't get any television stations over the air anyway, I may as well abandon the antenna. She bought a cheap DVD player and brought some movies for us to watch. She hung a few of her own paintings on the walls. They were street scenes of some far-off city, full of short, chubby girls and vibrant colors and a million little details that I could get lost in while she watched her movies on the television. She brought over her suitcase record player. It was pink and plastic and had a faded cartoon of Strawberry Shortcake on the lid. I actually remembered the record player from the old Folsom days. She set it up on a short end table next to my armchair. This way, I could play records for us without jostling my tender scrotum. And, more than anything, she cooked a feast.

By the time the bangers and mash crackled, bubbled, and whirred in the kitchen, my refrigerator was full. Lola had put me on a diet of beans and toast and eggs for breakfast; shepherd's pies or pork pies or cottage pies for lunch; pot noodles or curry for dinner; spotted dick or bread pudding when I wanted something sweet. She punctuated her cooking and eating with stories of her time as an artist-in-residence at a gallery that was really more of a squat in an industrial district of London's East End. I listened to the stories. They seemed somewhat incongruous. I'm not sure why. I don't know if I was hung up on the idea of a Puerto Rican girl finding her artistic soul in the heart of the British Empire. I don't know if I was having trouble with the notion of a small town Central Valley girl finding her place in gritty, urban London. Or it may have seemed incongruous solely because I couldn't reconcile my image of sad, lost, sixteen-year-old Lola with this complete woman in front of me.

I had no trouble with the smell of bangers and mash, though. I liked that I was once again living in a place where personality hung on the walls, where meals were cooked for more than one, where sausages and gravy blotted out the residual smell of generations of nameless previous tenants. I leaned back in the armchair and took it in.

At this point, feeling totally relaxed with the way my life was repairing itself and the way my scrotum was mending, I tried to make use of The Professor's book. To be honest, most of it went over my head. I don't think it was the painkillers that kept me from understanding. I just didn't have the background knowledge. I hadn't read that much Western philosophy. Starting with The Professor's book was like starting to learn Spanish by reading *One Hundred Years of Solitude*. It would be better to take Spanish 101 first. Or, in the case of the *Enquiry Concerning the Understanding of Knowledge and Existence*, it would have been helpful to have an Intro to Philosophy somewhere in my brain. Which I did not have.

Not that The Professor didn't help out a little. He gave a primer on modern philosophy. He talked about how little we can actually know for certain. He talked about Plato, of course, and Descartes again. He doubted that we could ever find Truth with the capital T. He talked about the possibility of the world being wrapped up in this second, with the past and future just a story we tell ourselves to keep us from going insane. I nodded off a lot. At times while I was reading his book, my mind hurt worse than my scrotum.

But there was one thing I liked, one thing that I really hung on to. The Professor talked a lot about *how* we know things, and how much about these things we really know. This was something I hadn't really thought much about. I mean, when I hung out with the administrative assistants and they gossiped, I often wondered where they got their information. There's a difference between wondering where information comes from, and wondering how we construct our view of the world. The Professor, in his book, suggested that we practice understanding how we come to recreate the world inside our minds, and how much of it is a story we tell ourselves. So I decided to sit there in my armchair, surrounded by my suddenly homey apartment, and think about how I knew things and how much I knew.

I started by closing my eyes and listening to the sounds outside. I heard children playing in the schoolyard. Or, to be more precise, I heard sounds that I identified as human voices making words that I identified as the American dialect of the English language, and those voices carried a certain high-pitched tone that I associated with children. I stood and walked over to my apartment window and looked outside. Sure enough, three kids played on the swings in the schoolyard. I assumed they were somewhere around nine or ten years old because they were of a certain size and stature I associate with that age. In the field behind the kids, a teenage girl sat on a hill. Her friends sat around her. They chatted, plucked strands of high grass and rolled them in their fingers, and smoked cigarettes. One teenage girl kept an eye on the kids on the swing.

I decided that the girl was the caretaker of the ten-year-olds, probably either big sister or babysitter. Most likely big sister. A babysitter would normally take her job more seriously and sit closer to the kids on the swings. A big sister might resent that she can't just hang out with her friends, so she'd sit farther away and create a physical and emotional distance from her role as caretaker. Of course, I didn't know any of this. All I knew was that six humans were in the schoolyard across the street from me. Three of them swung on swings and three smoked something. Everything else: their ages and relationships, even what they smoked, was an assumption, a story I told myself.

I turned back into my apartment and kept playing The Professor's game. I walked over to a wall where I found one of Lola's paintings. I tried to look at it more deeply than I ever had. I focused on the young woman standing on the street. Her head was a little big, slightly out of proportion for a human, giving her a cartoon feel. She had dark brown eyes, eyes the color of an old leather flight jacket, one that has been worn, cleaned, well oiled, closeted, loved. The eyes shared that softness, that sense of comfort. In each eye was a fleck of ivory paint positioned just so to catch the glow of the moon above the street. These eyes are Lola's eyes. Of course, they weren't Lola's eyes. Lola's eyes were still in her head in the kitchen. These eyes in front of me weren't eyes at all. They were dried bits of paint on a canvas. But such is the power of art that I could stare into these dried bits of paint, and they became eyes and stared back at me. I could imagine those eyes wanted to say something, or maybe I wanted to say something to them. I could project a world onto those eyes. It's the world I see as Lola's. I could smell her bangers and mash and imagine her in London. These eyes in London.

But I had to ask myself what I imagined when I imagined London. I'd never been there. The only sense I had of it was an amalgamation of scenes I remembered from movies like *Rude Boy* and *Riff-Raff*, or pictures I created in my head when I read *Great Expectations* in high school, or photographs that I'd long since forgotten, or maybe even a bit of the gray and brick from this painting in front of me. And so London to me is almost entirely a fiction.

And what about Lola in London? Which Lola did I imagine? Was it the sixteen-year-old Lola I dated in high school or the thirty-seven-year-old Lola stirring brown gravy in my kitchen? Or had I somehow blended the two together in my mind to create a mid-20s London version of her? What did this London Lola wear? Was her hairstyle different? What song played in her head as she walked the *Rude Boy* streets? What did she fear? What did her daydreams hold? What place in her core identity did her father occupy: the monster of her adolescence or the meek man dying of cancer several thousand miles away? And when I thought of Lola's core identity, what was she made of? Was it only these paintings, these stories that she told me, my incomplete understanding of them, my faulty memory of what she said, my randomly projected images of scenes?

Of course, I didn't have to answer any of these questions. I was just playing The Professor's game. And I was stumbling upon the answer that he likely was guiding me toward: that, despite any feelings I might have for Lola, I had very little knowledge of her.

I stepped away from the painting and sat back down in my armchair. I glanced at the back cover of The Professor's book. I opened it and looked at the inside dust jacket flap. The Professor's biography stated that his story began in Cincinnati, Ohio. So I thought of Cincinnati, of what that term meant to me.

Unlike London, I'd been to Cincinnati. It was fifteen years earlier, but the town still had some meaning. I'd been touring with my band, Pop Culture and the References. This was in the early '90s. Our guitarist, whom everyone called Fester because he looked like a young Uncle Fester from *The Addams Family*, had started a feud with the bass player, who called himself Pop because he'd come up with the band name. Both Pop and Fester sang the songs. I played drums and stayed out of the feud. It was difficult to do this because the band was only the three of us. And the feud kept growing. Cincinnati was a long way from the Fresno we'd all eventually return to. I'd been on the road for thirty days, played twenty-eight shows in twenty-six cities, slept most nights on apartment floors belonging to people who I couldn't call friends because I didn't know them that well, but who I'd likely be friends with if time and geography and feuding bandmates hadn't prevented it. The road home would take us north through the states that bordered Canada. We still had shows to play in Chicago, Madison, Minneapolis, Fargo, Bozeman, Boise, Seattle, and, really, the whole West Coast. Pop and Fester were not going to make life easy.

First thing in Cincinnati, I left the van to Pop and Fester and moved off on my own, walking dirty streets, passing stares from crank dealers wondering if I was buying, lingering in the windows of tattoo parlors where college girls picked hearts and cartoons off the walls, and down to a record shop. The girl behind the counter had shockingly red hair. Not the natural, genetic, orange-red, but the bright, plastic red of brake lights. Perhaps it was too many days on the road and too many fast-food meals, but the red in her hair made me hungry. She was a little short and a little chubby, just like every girl I've instantly fallen in love with over the course of my life. I tried to focus on the records and remember the girlfriend in Fresno who, though I didn't know it at the time, would go on to become both my wife and my ex-wife. I could feel the girl's eyes on me as I browsed the records.

I picked out a copy of the Stiff Little Fingers album *Go For It* and brought it up to the counter. The record store girl wrote the title on a notepad. She said, "I love this record. 'Silver Lining' is a great song."

I smiled and glanced down at the silicone flaking at the edge of the metal frame and glass of the counter.

She rang up the record and charged me half price. When I pointed out that she'd charged me too little, she said, "Employee discount." She also handed me a flyer for my show that night. "Check it out. Should be a good time."

She reappeared in the front row that night. The venue was almost completely empty of audience members who hadn't been in the bands that shared the bill. It was almost completely empty of anything else, for that matter: just an old warehouse space with the concrete floor painted black, a three-foot-high stage for bands, vacant space where the PA was once rumored to have stood, some blankets hanging on the block walls to keep the echo from overcoming the music, a keg floating in a tub of melted ice in the back of the room, an empty trash can and a carpet of empty plastic beer cups, two geeky punk rock boys dancing in the middle of the floor, Pop abusing his bass, Fester battering his guitar strings, the two of them alternating their screaming vocals, me pounding the drums a little too fast. The extra speed seemed to match Pop and Fester's feuding anger perfectly. The record store girl danced, it seemed, just for me. In my mind's ear, music never sounded so good.

And so fifteen years later, that moment is forever frozen in amber and labeled as Cincinnati. When I analyze my concept of the world and think of the present day Cincinnati, it is forever this moment, though Pop died in the late '90s in a jet-ski accident and Fester's name reverted back to Brandon and he got a job in the advertising industry. The warehouse stopped doing shows in '93. The record store girl's story is forever lost.

The neighborhoods I walked through have likely either deteriorated completely or been gentrified. And so on.

But I remembered this long-ago night and thought of Lola's painting across the room and I projected these notions of London and Cincinnati onto the world. I coupled them with the nebulous understanding I have of everyone I know and the nebulous understanding I even have of myself. I started to understand how I came to know the world around me. My ideas of cities were based on movies and descriptions in books and paintings and neighborhoods I once visited and people who have long since moved on. My concepts of people were based on assumptions and stories and projections. It all seemed so fragmented and incomplete.

I'd thought that I was okay with how little of the world I knew. I'd read enough of the *Tao Te Ching* and Chuang-Tzu, enough Buddhism and Confucianism to confront that I knew nothing. But there was always this nagging part of me that said, "No, you know a little something." Reading The Professor's book gave me a perspective on how little that little something I knew was.

I stared at Lola's painting for a couple of minutes, letting it all sink in. I wasn't sure what to make of The Professor's book or the exercise I'd just gone through. It occurred to me that there could be a unifying force to our understanding. If Dr. Bishop was right, if there was a Mindland that tied us all together, then our understanding of the world didn't have to be as fragmented as The Professor made it sound. We could share ideas, thoughts, core beliefs. Mindland, as Dr. Bishop conceived it, would allow us to have an understanding of, say, Cincinnati that wasn't frozen in amber. It would allow us to tap into Londoners' perception of London, at least to some extent. It would bind us not only with our bodies but also with the minds of others. My understanding of Lola could have a stronger connection than just a grouping of fragmented stories. The core of my world could be floating in the ether all around me. Understanding it more deeply was simply a matter of tapping into it.

Lola snapped me out of all these thoughts, saying, "What are you doing? Dinner's ready."

I joined her at the kitchen table. She'd already plated the food. I didn't have to do anything but sit down and eat. I looked into the soft brown eyes across the table. The world of The Professor and Dr. Bishop faded away. I was back to me and Lola and all the things I chose to believe in.

21

The #6 city bus dropped me off at the stop in front of the cemetery park. The springtime sun hung high in the sky. A steady wind blew in from the west. Kite-surfers dotted the horizon, the vibrant colors of their mini-parachutes cutting a sharp contrast against the gunmetal gray and white-capping Pacific Ocean. After days of walking around with The Professor's enquiry steering my thoughts, I was gradually becoming okay with my fragmented ability to view the world around me. What difference did it make? My life was straightening up. Every day put more distance between me and my divorce and the loss of my dogs. My job was going well. Lola's leftovers filled my fridge. Lola herself helped ward off the loneliness that had lurked in the dark shadows and chronically knifed me since I'd moved here from Fresno. Even my scrotum had fully healed a week earlier. So what else was there? Life was good again.

I crossed Main Street and headed down a side street to my apartment. A long, black BMW idled at the curb in front of me. Ape Man exited the driver's side door, walked around the trunk of the car, and stood by the rear passenger door. He folded his arms across his chest. His sleeve tattoos bulged and distorted, as if they'd been drawn on a balloon inflated to the point of popping. He blocked my passage on the sidewalk like a cosmic reminder that my life wasn't necessarily good again, that I still had to contend with a mad scientist and her squirrel experiments. I still had to contend with Castor Oil Walters groping blindly for the fruits of the mad scientist's labor.

I ignored the Maori tattoo and freckles on the Ape Man's face and stared right into his eyes this time. The whites of his eyes had yellowed and were flecked with red from burst capillaries, but the irises were clear,

clear blue. We stood for a second on that side street sidewalk, eyes locked, his arms crossed, my fists clenched. I stood slightly uphill. This made me almost as tall as him. I waited for him to make the first move. He stood there like a statue dedicated to the foibles of a wasted youth and the dangers of not thinking critically. One second passed. Two. Three. Four. Then, bam! Someone was suddenly on my back, wrenching my arms and neck into the full nelson, sweeping my legs out from underneath me, pushing and dragging me to the rear passenger seat of the BMW. Ape Man opened the door. Whoever had jumped me shoved me inside. I stumbled onto the back seat. My assailant slammed the door behind me. I got my feet out of the way just in time. Through the tinted window, I could only see his stomach, his white t-shirt, and his red suspenders. Walters had a regular skinhead army.

Frank Walters sat against the door on the other side of the backseat. He turned his head to face me. My image was reflected in his dark glasses. I thought about taking a shot at him, sending my fist into his scrotum or my elbow into his nose or maybe trying to break a rib. Strike back in some way. But, of course, I couldn't do it. I couldn't attack a blind man. Not like that, anyway.

So I just tried to sound tough. I said, "What the fuck do you want?" The words fell flat from my mouth. I simply don't talk like that. I couldn't fake the sincerity.

Walters, on the other hand, could talk like that. He could sound tough. He said to me, "Squirrels? Motorcycle helmets? Do you really expect me to buy this?"

I answered with a nonchalant, noncommittal shrug. The gesture was wasted on Walters. I let the silence hang in the air. He could do with it what he wanted.

"I know Dr. Bishop's research. She didn't just stumble into this field. She built a career based on verifiable, highly reputable research. She is not senile. She is not crazy. She is not about to perform her greatest experiments with wild squirrels."

Frank Walters slid off his smoky glasses. He pulled the silk handkerchief from his suit pocket and cleaned the lenses of his glasses. The act led me to ask myself again if he were really blind, because, again, he was dressed immaculately: a forest green, tailored suit; tie knotted so perfectly that I almost wanted him to show me how he'd done it; a crisp shirt with just a hint of green to match the varying shades of his tie and jacket. The handkerchief not only matched his tie, but it seemed to be cut of the same cloth. And, of course, I didn't immediately understand why he would clean his lenses if he couldn't see out of them. I glanced into his eyes. The irises were a murky black, clouded over, out of alignment. I wanted to look away, but I couldn't.

Okay, so he was blind, but I had to know how he dressed like this. I wondered if he had a personal shopper or maybe an account with a tailor. Maybe he'd worked out some kind of advertising campaign with a fashion designer down in Los Angeles and traded ad copy for clothes. It had to be something. The clothes looked expensive and fit in a way that off-the-rack clothes don't fit. I wondered how much money he had. What could a mid-level advertising executive, a guy who worked on the fifteenth floor and plotted a path to the nineteenth floor, make in a year? My best guess was enough money to buy a house in Agoura Hills and to pay Ape Man a modest salary. Enough to dry-clean these suits, but not buy them. Enough to bribe me with the first ten grand, but not with the subsequent thousands. Enough to buy this BMW, but he probably leased it. And, of course, he could have money coming in from another source. There could be an insurance settlement from the blindness. There could be a trust fund or inheritance. There could be side scams Walters was running. I had no way of knowing. I knew that I had to stop wondering about these things and focus on the moment and not Walters' eyes or suits or money.

He replaced his smoky glasses. He set the handkerchief on his lap, folded it in threes, and replaced it in his pocket. Again, immaculate. And this, I gathered, was why he cleaned his lenses: to keep up appearances that even he couldn't see.

"Where would one even get research squirrels?" he asked me. "Connor called or visited twenty-four different pet stores in the greater Los Angeles area. Not one of them sold squirrels. Nor did they offer Connor suggestions as to where he could purchase squirrels. One enterprising pet store clerk offered Connor suggestions regarding how he could capture his own squirrels. He drew a rough diagram of a trap for Connor. The trap could be made from a box, a stick, a string, and a piece of food. I'm sure you can imagine how this trap would work. The pet store clerk also offered a warning. He told Connor to avoid the squirrels in Griffith Park. As you may or may not know, these squirrels are rumored to carry the plague.

"Regardless, I wonder. Am I expected to believe that a researcher of Dr. Bishop's caliber sat in the woods surrounding the mental hospital, waiting for a squirrel to take the bait, pulling the string, trapping the squirrel?"

I pictured the trap in my mind. It certainly would've been an easier way for Eric and me to catch Dr. Bishop's squirrels. We wouldn't have needed to hold the string. We could've just rigged the bait the way you rig a mousetrap and let the box fall on the squirrel when he grabbed the cheese or nuts or what have you. Come to think of it, baited, wooden lobster traps would have worked very well, too. Though, of course, neither of these ways would've been nearly as fun.

Even so, I couldn't tell any of this to Frank Walters. I didn't want to tell him anything, anyway. I spread my left arm across the top of the back seat and stretched my feet in front of me. Again, it was a gesture wasted on Walters. Giving the appearance of feeling relaxed still helped to relax me. I said, "Honestly, I don't care what you believe."

"Surely, this is no way to handle a business relationship. Things work much better between us when we keep them on a friendly level. When you remain honest."

"Is killing my dog a way of keeping things on a friendly level?" I figured there was no harm in adding, "Did you kill my dog, or just kidnap him?"

Walters offered me a tiny, half-smile. "I heard you met my friend The Claw."

"Who?"

"The Claw. He's a mental patient with whom we've had some dealings. The poor man has a tendency to clasp onto the private region of an unsuspecting passerby. This can be problematic when he's out on the streets. Luckily, he's contained within the confines of a mental hospital. He rarely attacks people now. However, if you give him gifts, say, basketball shoes, or an mp3 player, he'll clasp onto the private parts of certain specified individuals."

As Walters said this, I felt a bit relieved that all my non-verbal communication was wasted on him. He couldn't see the surprise and anger that took over my face. I'd suspected that the patient who attacked me was another of Walters' goons. I just didn't want to let myself believe it was true. I wanted to think I was being paranoid. I wanted to believe that the attack had been a simple, random consequence of working in a psych hospital, not more of Walters' madness. Forget it. Try to play it cool. I said, "And this guy. What did you call him? The Bear Claw?"

"Just The Claw."

"Is he supposed to be at Oak View? Should I avoid him?"

"Are you being coy with me, Brown?"

"Are you going to get to the point?" I sat back up in the limo and grazed the door handle with the pads of my right forefinger and middle finger.

Walters brushed imaginary dust off his lap. "I'll keep this as simple as possible: you're going to give me real information, or I am going to make your life miserable."

Walters paused. I knew he wanted to allow a second for his words to sink in. I barged into his pause. "I'm going to keep this as simple as possible for you. You can't really threaten me. I don't have anything left to lose. I have a job that I'm ambivalent about. My wife has already left me. You took my dog. Even if he's alive, you're clearly not giving him back. I don't have any possessions I particularly care about. Your money means nothing to me. I have a feeling it's running out, anyway. The only thing you have to lord over me are these little attacks by weak little men. You're not as powerful as you think you are. You don't have any power over me. So find another way into Oak View."

I tried to give my own dramatic pause, but Walters was right there with me. He said, "Everyone has one thing they can't afford to lose."

Before Walters' word balloon had popped, I was out the door of the limousine. Neither the Ape Man nor his skinhead colleague followed me. I stormed down the sidewalk, heading for home. The record needle of my thoughts got stuck. It skipped on one thought, repeating the words again and again. I'm going to get that guy. *I'm going to get that guy.*

22

The Professor wandered into the middle of Highway 33, clearly not seeing the traffic lights or cars or town around him. Perhaps he even interpreted the concrete under his feet as something other than a highway. It seemed like a situation that demanded some kind of action. Since I was in a position to do so, I acted.

I dinged the bell to alert the bus driver that I wanted off. He faced the windshield and spoke to the passengers behind him. "No one's going anywhere until this old timer gets out of the road."

"I know that old timer." I walked down the aisle to the front of the bus. "I'll get him home."

The bus driver didn't look at me or say anything. The only indication he gave that I was there at all came in the form of the opening of bus doors. I stepped out and into the highway in front of the bus.

The Professor steered his course directly down the right lane of the highway. Cars whipped by to his left. The bus lingered behind him, left blinker on. The bus driver stared in his rearview mirror, hoping to find an opening into which he could escape this situation. I jogged up to The Professor and touched him gently on the elbow. He looked up, surprised, confused, clearly not recognizing me.

"Can I help you, sir?" he asked.

I did a quick assessment of the situation. Clearly, The Professor was having some kind of episode. Alzheimer's? More general dementia? Senility? I couldn't say for certain what. I felt that it was best to play along. I said, "Professor, I hate to catch you on your way home, but I was hoping to talk to you about your book."

"*An Enquiry Concerning the Understanding of Knowledge and*

Existence? How do you know about that? It's not scheduled for publication until the fall."

This threw me for a loop. For one, I could gather that his mind was viewing the world from more than thirty years earlier. For another, I didn't know how I, an ostensible student, would know about a professor's unpublished book. Unless… "I overheard you discussing it with one of your colleagues."

"Hmmm." The Professor lifted his hand to his chin and rubbed. The bus driver found his opening. He whipped past. The guy in the car behind him saw The Professor and me standing in the middle of the slow lane, making things even slower.

He honked his horn and yelled, "Get the fuck out of the road!"

The Professor didn't respond. I held up a hand in a not-so-universal symbol of *hold on a second*.

"Would it be possible to head back to your office for a few minutes? I want to discuss your…" I looked up into my brain and tried to think of the terms he used in the book, something specific, something he'd want to talk about. More horns honked. More drivers yelled. I grabbed a floater of a thought, "Your ideas of matter and memory."

"Certainly." The Professor nodded to himself. "Certainly." He started walking again, following the same path down the slow lane. I tapped him on the elbow again.

"Uh, sir. Your office is this way."

The Professor gave me that same look of surprise and confusion. "Yes. Of course," he said.

I steered him back toward the sidewalk. Our heels had barely touched the highway's white line before cars started whipping by, horns still honking, middle fingers saluting a situation they perhaps didn't think about enough to understand or perhaps thought about exactly enough to trigger their own fears of Alzheimer's and dementia.

The Professor was in no position to notice any of this. These horns hadn't honked in the '70s. None of these cars and some of these people hadn't even been made yet. And, though the rest of us seemed to be several years into the 21st century, The Professor refused to be trapped in the tyranny of our time. His concern was on his new book and its inquiry into knowledge and existence.

"The thing about matter and memory," he began as we followed the sidewalk uphill toward Oak View State Psychiatric Hospital, "is our inability to reconcile the two. By the time a memory is constructed well enough to be triggered by some type of physical object, that physical object—that matter—has been altered by the changes that we refer to as time. The matter no longer belongs to the memory. And so when we think of the matter that it takes to corroborate a memory, we realize that that object is no closer to the time of the memory than we are. This validation of memory with matter is a strictly artificial construct. Do you follow me?"

I nodded. Did I follow him? That wasn't the point. The point was to lead him up the hill to safer ground. Which I did do. It took us about twenty minutes, but The Professor, quite fit for his age, expounded on his theory the whole way. Everything he said was remarkably close to what I'd read in his book. Amazingly close. Nearly word for word, as far as I could tell.

I thanked The Professor for his time and left him in the care of a psych tech who kept calling him "chief." As in, "All right, chief. Let's get you to the cafeteria. Come on, chief." The term seemed entirely too cruel for a man of The Professor's caliber, particularly when I considered The Professor's mental state, which had him floating through the early '70s as a highly respected scholar. He acquiesced, though. I let him make his mental adjustments to arrive at whatever time period his matter and memory let him occupy.

If I hurried, I could have caught the next bus back down the hill. But I didn't hurry. I lingered. I thought of The Professor's delusions. They were the madness I expected when I signed up for this job. It was diagnosable. Whether Alzheimer's or some other type of dementia, I didn't know. Either way, the choice was binary. One or the other. Easy enough. It was a madness that withered away loved ones and that researchers searched to cure. It had a name. It made a certain amount of sense. Still, I was shaken.

A cool fog drifted uphill from the Pacific. The last vestiges of sunset shone through. And it was moments like this: standing alone on psych hospital grounds with a head full of thugs who may or may not have my dog and thugs who could be hired to wound my scrotum; of scientists who meddle in the unconscious of squirrels and maybe humans; of a vicious ad man; of an absent wife; of the return of the second woman I ever loved; and now of a delusional old professor who seemed equally convinced about his world as I was of mine, so much so that the only thing that remained to validate me and designate madness to him was that people around us seemed to corroborate my story…

I thought about Don Quixote and acknowledged—not for the first time—that the only thing that turned Don Quixote's giants into windmills was Sancho Panza's perspective. If Sancho had seen giants, too, who would we be to deny them? And so, it was a moment like this, with the fog seeping into my brain, when working in a psych hospital seemed to be driving me crazy.

That's why I couldn't hurry to the bus and spend the evening home alone with my thoughts. I knew that Dr. Benengeli's patients would be performing their own one-act plays this evening. I started walking toward the stage on the north quad.

On my way there, I saw the silhouettes of an exceptionally short woman and another woman in a lab coat walking alongside her. I hurried to catch them, knowing that they'd be heading in the same direction as me—to the one-acts—and that Dr. Benengeli could be my own Sancho, verifying for me that the windmills were windmills and that I wasn't the Quixote here. They strolled north slowly. I overtook them in a couple of minutes. Dr. Benengeli saw me before I could say anything. She said, "Hey. What are you doing here so late?"

"The Professor wandered down into town, so I walked him back up the hill," I said.

"What was he doing in town?"

"Heading home, he thought. He thought he was in the '70s."

"He is in his 70s," Dr. Benengeli said.

I was almost shaken enough to miss this semantic slip, but not quite. I said, "No. He thought he was in the 1970s. He thought he was a young professor with a new book coming out in the fall."

Dr. Benengeli smiled softly. "Oh," she said. "Poor thing."

Which I took as a validation that The Professor was indeed the delusional one. Relieved, I turned my glance from Dr. Benengeli to her companion. Her face threw me back into my fog. I'd never seen her before, but her face was unmistakable. It had surfaced among the research I'd been doing lately. Her name was Dr. Toru. It had to be.

I'd been looking a little bit into Dr. Bishop and her days at Stanford, and I found pictures of her and her research assistant, Dr. Toru. Dr. Toru had a tea-colored birthmark on the side of her face. It still looked like the handprint of a very small child. The woman with Dr. Benengeli had the exact same birthmark. And, sure enough, Dr. Benengeli introduced this woman as Dr. Toru.

"Nice to meet you," I said. I reached out and shook her hand. I almost asked her, "What brings you here?" but my months at the psych hospital had taught me a bit more discretion. That is, I knew to look for keys or a visitor's badge before asking a question like that. Instead, I said, "Are you looking forward to the one-acts?"

Dr. Toru exchanged a glance with Dr. Benengeli and smiled. "Yes, I am."

"You're in for a treat," I said. I looked down at Dr. Toru's hip. No keys. Her lab coat was open in the front. Neither her blouse nor her coat wore a visitor's badge. The coat was clean but threadbare, like a lab coat that could've been purchased during the same year when The Professor's book was published. Keys would have been visible on the hip or in the lab coat pocket or in the pockets of her tight slacks. Keys would have been visible somewhere. Clearly, she had none. No badge, no keys.

Dr. Benengeli pointed at me and told Dr. Toru, "He's a big supporter of the one-acts. He even got an arts grant for my plays."

"Impressive," Dr. Toru said.

"Thanks," I said.

Dr. Toru shifted her weight from one foot to another. She seemed agitated or nervous. I gave her a second once-over, but it wasn't necessary. She had no keys. It was possible that she'd simply left her visitor's badge behind—possible, but doubtful. I could be reasonably sure that Dr. Toru was, in all probability, a patient.

I wondered if her madness dated back to her time working with Dr. Bishop. Perhaps she heard a voice in her head, too. Perhaps it was the same one I'd been hearing. Perhaps she attributed the voice to Dr. Bishop finding a way to post thoughts in our brains. Perhaps she struggled between self-diagnoses of schizophrenia and paranoia. Of course, I couldn't bring any of this up. Instead, I said, "Really, Dr. Benengeli made it easy for me. You should've seen her production of *Rosencrantz and Guildenstern Are Dead.*"

"Oh, I did," Dr. Toru said. "I was here for that."

Okay, then. She's either a chronic patient or a frequent visitor. Or, maybe, like so many psych patients, she just comes in for periodic checkups. In all probability, Dr. Bishop's former research assistant was a patient at a psych hospital. I thought about that and coupled it with the fact that Eric, Dr. Bishop's current primary research assistant, took me on a wild squirrel chase, and I, the ancillary research assistant, was hearing a voice in my head and perhaps suffering from delusions.

Maybe it was best to keep these realizations to myself. I wrestled with the small talk. Drs. Toru and Benengeli kept the conversation flowing. It was all pleasant enough in the springtime sunset. Still, between The Professor's delusions and Dr. Toru's presence, my imagination was up and running.

Matters were made worse when, later, Dr. Toru performed her own one-act. Typically, only patients wrote and performed the one-acts. Because they were part of Dr. Benengeli's theater-therapy program, the patients usually reenacted some drama that they were trying to release from their minds. The plays could be intensely personal. Sometimes uncomfortably so. Once I got over the intimacy, I tended to enjoy them. I didn't watch every week or even most weeks, but I'd seen a few productions. I felt like I knew what to expect. When Dr. Toru erupted into her silent interpretive dance that included, but was not limited to, her flopping on the stage with her legs immobile and her arms held fast to her side, creating a fearful mimicry of an elephant seal, she took my breath away. This act: its name was bizarre.

For the next week or so, I seemed to see Dr. Toru everywhere I went on psych hospital grounds. Her hip remained free of keys. She showed no sign of a visitor's badge. A week later, she was gone.

23

Lola knelt in front of the dollar bin, flipping through LPs. The baby blue and pink diamonds of her argyle knee socks peeked out from between the cuffs of her jeans and her baby blue low-top Chuck Taylors. Her straight cinnamon brown hair hung in front of her face. I didn't need to see through the hair to know that she was smiling. She'd had a grin glowing since she walked into the record shop, saw the pink plastic LP suitcase, claimed it as her own, and vowed to walk out of the store with her new record case full. Lola stopped at a record. She said to me, "Psychedelic Furs!"

I raised my eyebrows and smiled. It wasn't exactly a noncommittal expression on my part. All I meant to say with it was, "I'm glad you're glad."

Lola turned back to the dollar bin and commenced riffling. The afternoon settled into a pattern. She would call out the names of '80s bands, pluck the records out of the bin, and slide them into her pink case. I would raise my eyebrows and smile.

The record store clerk sat perched on a metal stool, watching Lola. Surely, he'd seen scenes like this unravel in front of him periodically: someone of our generation wanders into a record shop and realizes that she can purchase all of her favorite songs from when she was an adolescent, on vinyl just like she'd had them originally, before she became convinced that cassettes were the way to go and got rid of all her vinyl, before the cassettes warped or melted or were eaten by her car stereo and the albums were lost, before CDs came along and took over, only to be migrating to a trash bin now that mp3s are around. Here, like the dusted-off ruins of some ancient temple, sat the relics of a lost and beautiful time.

In all my years of record shopping, I'd seen shoppers reacting like Lola was now, as if she'd found a pathway into her past here at the end of the Main Street corridor. Usually, they picked up albums I'd hate to have to listen to again, or they'd purchase songs that had been in heavy rotation on radio stations for the last two or three decades. It wasn't the stuff that impressed seasoned collectors like the record store clerk or me. I enjoyed the scene, though. The clerk probably did, too. These moments kept the ancient temple of the record store alive and kicking.

In the end, Lola bought sixteen records, a couple of record brushes, cleaning spray, and the pink, 13" square and 4" deep LP suitcase. I bought two LPs and three seven-inch records.

We caught the bus home. For most of the bus ride, Lola showed me her records: The Cure, The Smiths, The Vapors, Psychedelic Furs, Elvis Costello, 10,000 Maniacs, The Pixies, Big Country, Adam Ant, Love & Rockets, Siouxsie and the Banshees, The Go-Go's, a Jane Wiedlin solo record, New Order, Joy Division, and Devo. It was her own personal tribute to New Wave, the New Romantics, and '80s college pop, all wrapped up in her pink plastic record case.

"I can't wait to get home and listen to all this!" she said.

I felt like I could wait. I hadn't heard any of those songs in several years. Some of them I did still love, or at least I thought I would still love when I listened to them again. Most of them, I could do without. Still, I caught a little bit of Lola's enthusiasm. "We'll have a dance party for two," I told her.

The #6 city bus stopped in front of the cemetery park. Lola and I disembarked, crossed Main Street, and took the side street to my apartment. I unconsciously checked the street for Frank Walters' long, black BMW or skinheads in the bushes before we headed down the road. The guy was starting to haunt me more and more as I felt closer to Lola. I kept remembering the point he made to win our argument: everyone has one thing they can't afford to lose.

I thought to tell the story of Walters and Dr. Bishop's research to Lola as we headed downhill to my place. I didn't, though. I felt like I couldn't warn her, or that warnings would do no good. I didn't know when Walters would strike next. I knew that, every time he had come after me, he'd taken a different tack and hit me in a different place and a different way. He had a good understanding of my patterns of behavior. He knew how to get into my apartment. He knew about Lola. He knew that he could jump out at me any time he wanted. How could I tell all this to Lola? What could she do?

Lola rescued me from my anxiety. She said, "I didn't even see what you bought."

I pulled my record store booty from the bag and showed her.

"I've never heard of these bands."

"They're new," I said.

"New? These are new records?"

I nodded.

"Who makes new records in the 21st century?"

"The bands I listen to."

"Strange," Lola said. We crossed the street to my apartment.

As I unlocked the door, she took my bag and looked at the records. "I thought the people at the psych hospital were weird," she said. "But they don't hold a candle to you and your odd little world."

"Thanks."

I opened the door to my odd little world.

Lola spent an hour playing disc jockey on her Strawberry Shortcake record player. She sprayed and brushed the dust off her records before playing them, gently laid them on the turntable, and picked out one or two songs. We would actually get up and dance to a few of the more upbeat songs. Mostly, we sat on the floor and tapped our toes. She saved Elvis Costello for last. She plopped it onto the turntable and said, "I think we'll listen to this whole album."

I picked up the record sleeve. A young, shorthaired Elvis Costello posed like a New Wave Buddy Holly. "I used to have this record," I said.

"What happened to it?"

I shrugged.

Lola looked at my small box of records. She said, "For a collector, you sure don't have a lot of records."

"No. I don't."

"Why is that?"

I shrugged again. Lola crawled over to where I sat on the floor. She folded her legs underneath her and stared into my eyes as if there were a diorama hidden in the irises. "You're hiding something," she said, "because records are a hard thing to lose. CDs, cassettes, sure. You leave them in your car, they get melted, stepped on, scratched, snapped in half, whatever. But you keep records at home, on a shelf. They only move from the shelf to the record player and back. How do you lose them?"

She had me there. I could see that I couldn't avoid it any longer. I said, "I lost them in the divorce."

"How did that happen? I thought you said you just signed papers, and it was over with."

"Before we signed the papers, she sold all my records."

"What? How many?"

"All of them. I don't how many. Fifteen hundred? Two thousand?"

Lola stood up at this. She put her hands on her hips and stared down at me. "Two thousand records! How much did she get for them?"

"I have no idea. It depends on how she sold them, if she knew what each one was worth, all that stuff. If she sold them to a record store or a collector, she probably only got a grand or so. If she sold them individually on eBay or something, she could've gotten a lot. Over twenty grand, if she were smart about it." I scooted back about two feet and leaned against the front of the couch. I stretched my arms across the couch cushions, as if I were totally relaxed. The move seemed affected, even to me. "I don't know how smart about it she was."

Though I knew my wife. I knew she was smart. She probably made more than twenty grand on the whole lot.

"Twenty thousand dollars! And you didn't get any of it?"

I shook my head.

"Not a dime?"

"Not a penny."

"I'd be furious." Lola stomped her foot. The Elvis Costello record skipped. "I am furious. Where is this woman? I need to have a talk with her."

I hooked my finger into the belt loop of Lola's jeans and gave her a little tug. "Sit down," I said. "It's okay."

"It's not okay," Lola said. But she sat down.

I put my arm around her shoulder and squeezed. Lola leaned into me. I thought about what she said. I'd thought about that record collection a fair amount, about where the records had landed and the malice behind the move. The only two malicious things that my ex-wife had done in all the years of our marriage and in the months of our divorce were selling my record collection and kidnapping Clint Dempsey. The moves seemed calculated on her part, as if to say, "I'm going to do these two awful things to you as a way of making sure that the divorce sticks, and we both get on with our lives." Or maybe she didn't articulate it that way. That was the effect, anyhow. When she told me about selling the record collection, I stopped arguing and signed the paperwork. When she kidnapped Clint Dempsey, I was done with her. The divorce stuck.

It was natural, too, for Lola to be bothered by the money. I wasn't. I'd made that much off Frank Walters and donated it all to charity. I made more money working at the psych hospital than I spent, anyway. And it's not that twenty thousand dollars isn't a lot of money. It is. It's just that I'm well aware that twenty thousand dollars wouldn't make my life significantly better or worse. I didn't need it. I wasn't particularly anxious to buy what it would pay for. I did miss the records, though. If I'd known that my ex-wife was selling them, I would've paid her asking price. But they had to be my records. Not just another copy of the same album. I would've only paid for the exact same records. I tried to explain this to Lola.

"It's like this," I told her. "We can get all this stuff as an mp3 now. The only real value in the record anymore is the artifact. The way it ties you to the past. Like, if the record has a familiar pop or crack on a favorite song. Or the artwork triggers memories, you know. Just looking at the checkerboards on that Elvis Costello record made me suddenly get a feeling like Folsom again. Or even, I bought this Stiff Little Fingers record in Cincinnati one time and the girl behind the counter charged me half-price for no reason at all…"

Lola pinched the tender area just below my bicep. "I know why she charged you half price."

I made a little show of ignoring her and kept going. "Sometimes when I would play that record—years later—I'd see the little green sticker with the price on it and feel like I was back on tour with my old band. That's what I miss about all those records. The memories they brought back. That's why it broke my heart when she sold them all."

Lola slid her hand under my t-shirt. She dragged her fingernails back and forth across my chest. Even in the warm springtime afternoon, goosebumps formed in the wake of her fingernails. "What a jerk," she said. "Let's go kick her ass."

I tucked a few locks of Lola's hair behind her left ear. "No need," I said. "We're here now. We'll make new memories."

Lola bit her bottom lip. She climbed over my outstretched legs and straddled me. We started kissing. I don't think my cheesy line led to this. It had just gotten to be that time of the afternoon: the time when we generally drifted into having sex.

We kissed for the rest of the Elvis Costello side, then Lola unfastened my belt and pulled my plaid shorts down past my ankles. She slid my shorts off my right leg and left them hooked on my left ankle. Her fingers undid her own belt. She pulled off her jeans and her argyle socks.

I lifted my t-shirt. By the time I had it over my head, Lola had straddled me again. She slid down and my heart raced with the initial rush of being inside her, that warm and wet feeling. And with it came a little apprehension. I was still a little pensive because Lola had been way too rough the first few times we had sex. She'd left several bruises from her bites. She'd grabbed hold of the long hairs on top of my head and pulled so hard it made my roots sore. And not just sore while we were doing it. Sore for a couple of days afterward. She also clawed me with her fingernails, leaving track marks up and down my back, drawing blood in places. Once, when she was riding me, she reached around and punched me in the scrotum. And this was after the Claw incident. So there was a bit of apprehension.

But then, maybe the fourth or fifth time we had sex, she just stopped doing any of those things. We hadn't talked it over. I'd planned to ask her to stop, but I hadn't asked yet. She just stopped. I was glad she had. I also kept in mind the old adage that things that go away for no reason come back the same way.

Lola nibbled my neck, traced the line of my spine with the pads of her fingers. I snapped back into the moment, letting all apprehensions drift away. I caught my breath and relaxed and followed Lola's flow.

She rode me on the floor until the rug started to burn her knees. We took it into the bedroom from there, Lola leading me with the sway of her hips. We climbed onto the bed, where we sweated and moaned and rocked back and forth. We'd been having enough sex at this point for me to know some of Lola's little hints: how she arched her back when she wanted me to cup both of her breasts in my hands, how she pinned and squeezed my shoulders when she wanted me to keep doing exactly what I was doing, how she got that sexy insincere look when she was faking it and how she didn't care at all how she looked when she really was in the throes of something good. When she got tired, when she'd had her fun, when she was ready, we rolled over so that I was on top. Lola locked onto my eyes and squeezed my ass and pulled me close. And when it felt like time to come, I let go of everything else in the world.

After a quick nap and leftovers for dinner, after playing my new records on Lola's Strawberry Shortcake record player, after our encore in the bedroom and going to sleep in earnest, I awoke. It was just before three o'clock in the morning. I went into the kitchen and poured myself a glass of water. Naked, with all the lights off, I drank the water. I noticed that one of the blinds in the front window was off kilter. I walked over to the window to adjust it. Because my apartment was darker than the street outside, I could see out the window. A large man sat on the schoolhouse lawn, across the street from me. He smoked a cigarette. The tip glowed orange, then seemed to vanish as he pulled it away from his lips. The man wore a white t-shirt, a bomber jacket, and tight jeans with the cuffs rolled up. His head had been shaven completely bald. He stared directly at my window. I stared back. I wasn't sure if he could see me, or if he wanted to see me. I felt vaguely like I was dreaming, but this was no dream.

Sitting next to the guy was a little dog. I looked closer and wondered if my mind and the moonlight were playing tricks on me or not, because that pup looked just like my old buddy Clint Dempsey. I looked more closely at the man's face. Of course, one side of it was obscured with a tribal tattoo. I flicked the blind back. A fire burned in my brain. I ran into my bedroom, hopped into a pair of jeans, pulled on a hoodie, and raced out my front door.

Both man and dog had vanished.

24

On the farthest reaches of the psych hospital grounds stands an abandoned arboretum. Dr. Benengeli had told me about it on my first day at Oak View, a mischievous smile painted on her face. She'd said that when RW Winfield, industrialist and primary patron of Winfield University, was still alive, he had a little cottage on the northeastern edge of campus. Of course, he'd had his home where he lived with his wife and entertained guests and all, but he also had this little cottage where he spent his time alone. Apparently, he'd spent so much time there that, when he died, his wife had placed his ashes in the cottage. Out of respect for the dead, or perhaps fear of the dead, very few people went near the cottage. Painters and handymen kept the place standing, but that was it. University administrators left the cottage and the grounds around it more or less untouched for a couple of generations. In the '60s, a botany professor decided to turn that untouched ground into an arboretum. He wrote a small grant, bought a few local trees, and planted them. As time went on and funding grew, the botany professor expanded his collection of indigenous trees. Graduate students joined the project, trees were catalogued, placards were engraved and installed, and a walking path was paved between the trees and shrubs. Eventually, park benches dotted the walking path. It became a popular spot for students on first and second dates to show off a small chunk of the knowledge they were paying over thirty thousand dollars a year for. More importantly, it became a popular make-out spot. By the time scandal struck Winfield, the botany professor had long since retired and moved to Florida. No one took on the voluntary upkeep of the arboretum.

Dr. Benengeli had reveled in the story when she'd told it to me.

She loved the idea that RW Winfield, the man who'd hated everything Southern Californian so much that he'd banned palm trees from campus in the university's charter, should spend his eternal rest surrounded by all the indigenous trees of the state he hated. Well, all except the palm tree, which was still conspicuously absent when Dr. Benengeli told me the story.

Now, several months after Dr. Benengeli had told me the story, after I'd become fully enmeshed in the madness surrounding my new life as psych hospital grant writer, a baby palm tree stood at the edge of the cottage. The presence of the palm tree combined with the tree's exceptionally small stature convinced me that Dr. Benengeli had planted it. I sat on a bench in front of the cottage, watching that exceptionally small palm tree wave in the light morning breezes and letting my mind drift. I wondered about Dr. Benengeli and what play she'd direct next. I wondered about the history of the arboretum. Had an eighteen-year-old Lola walked these paths with an upperclassman Lothario? Had she succumbed to his charms? Had she been a seductress here? Had she returned to walk this path during her stay as a patient at Oak View? Would she like to come here with me now, find a private spot among the shadows, make love among the fuzzy blooms of the black elder, atop a bed of needles scattered from a Monterey pine?

I let my mind drift into daydreams. I did not wonder about Dr. Bishop and her squirrel experiments. Dr. Bishop was on her way to this bench in front of this cottage. It certainly was a mysterious place to meet. Still, I figured that she would offer answers when she got here.

I strolled around the arboretum. Weathered placards helped identify the blue, bottlebrush flowers of lupine (*lupinus*), the vibrant yellow flowers of the flannelbush (*fremontodendron*), and the cottony, soft blue flowers of the deer brush (*ceanothus*). I checked the leaves to distinguish the difference between a California black oak (*quercus kelloggii*) and a coast live oak (*quercus agrifolia*). I kicked acorns against the door of the cottage. And, when I finally sat back down and started daydreaming again about a stroll through the shadows with Lola, Dr. Bishop hustled down the path. She looked winded, like this walk had taken everything out of her. A thought flicked in my head: why didn't she ask me to meet her somewhere more convenient? I let that thought pass and reminded myself that surely, she'd brought me here to answer some questions.

I stood to meet her. She stretched out her hand. I took it. Her fingers felt like a bag of ballpoint pens in my palm. She gripped tightly and used my hand for leverage in sitting down. She took several deep breaths. Tiny beads of sweat formed on the borderlands where her short, curly, gray hair met her forehead. I sat next to her. I retrieved a bottle of water from my backpack and offered it to her.

"It's not real bottled water," I said. "I filled it from the water fountain in the Williams Building."

Dr. Bishop took the bottle in one hand and patted my thigh with the other hand. "Thank you, hon," she said.

I watched Dr. Bishop drink the water. Her fingernails were manicured as always, but her fingers looked bonier than ever before. In fact, Dr. Bishop had been getting gradually thinner as this experiment went on. I'd noticed but hadn't paid attention. I watched the skin under her chin go up and down with each gulp. The stress of her crazed experiments must have been getting to her.

Dr. Bishop finished half the bottle of water. She tried to hand it back to me. I told her to keep it. She thanked me and took a few more deep breaths. "I'm sorry," she said. "Give me a few seconds to recover."

She took a handkerchief from her purse and dabbed the sweat along her forehead. Small blotches of foundation dotted the white handkerchief. She folded it and returned it to her purse. She took one last deep breath, filling her lungs completely, swelling her chest, then letting it all out in a long, fluid exhale.

"I heard you read The Professor's book," she said.

"I did," I said, wondering how she'd heard that. The only person I'd talked to about that book was The Professor and that was in the middle of his episode. Surely, he didn't remember and tell Dr. Bishop.

"Interesting, huh? All about how we come to believe things, about how many possible ways there are to view the world. All that jazz."

"You didn't know The Professor when he was faculty here at Winfield, did you?"

"Heavens, no," Dr. Bishop said. "I spent most of my career at Stanford.

I came here only when the hospital opened. This is my retirement job." She winked at me, though I wasn't sure why. Still, the wink unleashed a rush of paranoia inside me. "But back to The Professor's book. Here's my question: when you read it, did it open you up somewhat to new possibilities? Did it make you think there might be whole worlds around us that we know nothing about?"

"Somewhat." I shrugged. "I think I felt that way even before reading the book."

"Good. Good. That's why I made sure to hire you down here. I could sense that curiosity in you. You're open to new ideas. You're more intelligent than you let on. You're a very special person."

I smiled. "Flattery will get you everywhere."

"I don't mean to flatter you," Dr. Bishop said. "I'm just about to tell you something very odd. I want you to be prepared to take in what I'm about to tell you."

I stared down at my feet. An acorn sat between my sneakers. I stepped on it with my right foot and dragged the acorn in a circle underneath the ball of my foot. Pangs of guilt stabbed me. I knew Dr. Bishop was about to give me very sensitive information about her experiment, and I didn't want that information. I said, "Listen, before you start, I have to tell you something." I took my own deep breath.

Dr. Bishop cut in. "You've been selling information to Frank Walters. I know. I'm sorry about that."

"No. I'm sorry about that." I paused and let her statement sink in. "I don't know what you would be sorry about."

"I convinced you to do that. I know you didn't want to. I know you fought against him and forged the information and he even stole your little dog over it. I'm sorry. I didn't want any of it. But, please understand, I needed you to sell the information—the real information—from these experiments to Walters. I needed to throw him off the trail."

I kept staring at my feet, grinding the acorn under my shoe. "Wait. Hold on a minute. This doesn't make sense. How did you know about Clint Dempsey? What do you mean *you* convinced *me*?"

Dr. Bishop patted my knee, gently poking the skin with her bony fingers. "I need you to relax and listen for a while. Imagine you're listening to my story just like you read The Professor's book: you're passive, just taking in information and digesting it before you decide whether or not to believe it. Can you do that?"

"I guess."

She lifted her hand from my knee, took another sip of water, screwed the top back on, and took one more deep breath. "Okay," she said. "Here's the story. About twenty-five years ago, I became a full professor at Stanford. My teaching load became nearly nonexistent and I was able to spend my time largely doing research. Since I'd been a Jungian scholar, I narrowed my research interests down to the collective unconscious. I conducted several experiments with the collective unconscious, I published articles, I wrote books on it, all that jazz. I was an authority on it. I *am* an authority on it. I know it sounds pompous to say that, but there it is. So, I came to feel like I knew the collective unconscious well. I started to ask further questions. For instance, if we really do receive cultural messages from beyond our conscious mind—which we really do; I have a body of scholarship to prove it—then who puts those cultural messages up there for us? Can we post our own messages? Can we consciously enter the realm of the collective unconscious? Or, more specifically, can we visit the place I call Mindland?

"Now, as you know, once a scientist starts asking questions like this, she has to search for answers. That's what being a researcher is all about. So I started searching. With the help of a junior colleague, I spent six years exploring ways to enter Mindland. I couldn't find that way. But I was getting closer. I started to believe that it could be done, that I could find my way there. It was exactly at this time, nearly six years ago, when Frank Walters came into my life. I noticed that, as the experiments went on, my junior colleague suddenly had money that she was spending on luxuries. They weren't extravagant, per se. She wasn't coming to the lab in jewelry and designer lab coats, but she was buying art, new furniture, a koi pond in the back yard... these types of things. Purchases atypical for a research professor. I also noticed that she was having regular lunches with a blind man who stood out not so much because he was blind but because he was always impeccably dressed. Have you noticed that about him?"

"Oh, of course. You could feed a starving nation with the money he spends on clothes."

"See, you think about these things. That's why I brought you here. But we'll get to that. Back to Frank Walters and my junior colleague. I noticed her lunches with him and I looked into who he was. When I saw he worked in advertising, my blinders fell off my face and I saw the dangers of my research. Namely, if I could visit Mindland and post messages that others would receive unconsciously, then so could other people. Anywhere people can post messages, advertisers creep in. But here's the danger. I want you to listen closely. This is the scariest thing about the world you're about to enter: when we receive a message from Mindland, we don't recognize it as a message. We recognize it as our own thought. Do you see the danger there?"

It took me a second to digest all this. A pine needle fluttered down and landed on the bench between Dr. Bishop and me. I picked the needle up and rolled it between the pads of my fingertips and thumbs, releasing a subtle pine scent. "Basically, then, what you're saying is that if there were commercials in Mindland, they wouldn't be like commercials now. It wouldn't be like someone saying to us, I don't know, 'Buy a car,' for example. It would be someone making us think 'I need to buy a car,' for no reason whether we wanted one or not. Like a voice inside our heads, not outside."

"Exactly," Dr. Bishop said. "So, for the first time, I saw the tremendous danger of consciously entering Mindland: you could give people thoughts, and the people would think that the thoughts were their own. I don't know that this is an ability people should have."

"So did you abandon the research?"

"I gave all appearances of that, yes. I broke from the junior colleague. I retired from Stanford. I took all of my personal research with me and moved down here. This was shortly after Winfield University had closed. The State took over the campus as part of the bankruptcy settlement. My son was employed here again as the head of Roads and Grounds…"

"Wait a second. Your son? Eric?"

"Yes. Eric is my son."

"But his last name is Jurgenson. How can that be?"

193

"His father's last name was Jurgenson. Technically, my last name is, too, but I use my maiden name in professional settings. After all, I'm the one who earned the doctorate, right?"

"Yes, ma'am."

Dr. Bishop gave me a little smile. "Moving on…

"Eric was employed down here and essentially had the facilities of an abandoned university at his disposal. Well, I guess he didn't 'essentially' have the facilities at his disposal. He literally had them. Think of it: a whole university open to no one but me. So I came down here and worked with Eric. I championed the cause of making this a long-term psychiatric hospital. I brought in doctors who had no interest in my research, found funding, and kept the place alive so that I could tinker with my own little projects completely under the radar. And, guess what? Walters came back.

"He started sniffing around. He tried to get Dr. Benengeli to inform on me. Luckily she thinks I'm crazy. Thankfully. She's also honest enough to tell me everything. About Walters. About me being crazy.

"Walters pursued Eric, too, until Walters' nephew got a little too rough with Eric, and Eric stabbed him."

"What?" I asked. I was surprised. Not that Eric would stab a guy. That didn't surprise me at all. I was surprised to think Walters would back off that easily. "All I have to do is stab Connor and Walters will leave me alone?"

Dr. Bishop shook her head. "Eric also shot at Walters. He blew out four of Walters' car windows. Walters and his nephew were in the car at the time. We're all lucky Eric didn't hit one of them."

"You said it," I said. Hope deflated inside me. Maybe I could bring myself to stab Ape Man, but gunplay was beyond me.

"I was so close to Mindland, though. I felt like I was within a year of finding a way in, but that also meant that, one way or another, Walters would be a year away from finding a way in. I needed someone to throw him off my trail. That's why I sat on the hiring boards of this hospital. This way, I could interview employees and get a real sense of who he or she was and what they wanted in life. And when I interviewed you, I thought, here's my guy. Here's the guy who's going to shake Frank

Walters for me. And that's why I brought you in."

Dr. Bishop paused again. She'd worked up a sweat with all this talking. She took her foundation-dotted handkerchief out of her purse and patted her whole face dry.

I thought about what she'd been telling me. "So, wait," I said. "When you first started talking, you said that you'd convinced me to sell information to Frank Walters. But if you and I have never had a conversation about all of this before, and I've never heard you mention Walters' name until just now, then... Wait." I chewed on it all for a few seconds. "That means you found a way in, didn't you?"

Dr. Bishop nodded. "That's why we're here today," she said. "To show you the way into Mindland."

I nodded along, but I wasn't sure what to believe. Most of me still resided in Dr. Benengeli's camp. I thought Dr. Bishop was crazy. At least, I wanted to think Dr. Bishop was crazy. It was too creepy to think about her slinking into my unconscious and convincing me to do things that were more or less against my nature. But then again, I couldn't be sure. So much of the world flutters along without my comprehension of it. Why not this point, also? It did seem at least somewhat possible. It would explain why I broke completely from who I was and sold information to Walters. It would explain the voice in my head that had been guiding some of my actions since it convinced me to stay down here on Nietzsche's last day. But it also raised questions. The first of which I asked Dr. Bishop. "But if you can enter into the collective unconscious and convince me to do things, why not just do the same to Walters? Why don't you just go make him think that you're crazy, that none of this could happen?"

"It's not that simple. The thoughts I plant are clumsy. You noticed when I did it. You blamed yourself and wondered if it were some sort of thought disorder, but you were in a special situation. For one, you work in a psych hospital, which makes you and everyone else who works in a psych hospital just a little bit paranoid that you may have one of these mental illnesses. For another thing, you didn't know what kind of research I was doing, so it didn't occur to you that I could really be the voice in your head. Even though the voice sounded just like me, you attributed it to your imagination or something deeper. Walters wouldn't be so flexible.

He'd never blame himself. He'd know it was me." Dr. Bishop smoothed a wrinkle on her slacks, then looked up at me. She added, "Also, you can only plant thoughts that people are capable of having. You can only make people believe what they're willing to believe. Frank Walters isn't willing to believe that my research is all a hoax."

"So that's why you got the squirrels? That's why you painted the shield on the motorcycle helmet?"

"Exactly. That's why all of this happened. Talking to pets? Come on. I'm a researcher. I'm a scientist. I'm a professor emeritus at Stanford University. I'm not going to genuinely waste my time with such things."

"Only problem is, when I sold all this to Walters, he didn't think you were crazy. He thought I was lying."

"Yes. That is our problem."

"And the solution?"

"I don't know." Dr. Bishop lowered her head, staring down at the needle-strewn path at her feet, at the way her slacks hung from her bony knees. "I think that's a problem you're going to inherit."

"So then you don't have answers for me?"

"No more than I've already given you."

"Then why are we here?"

"So I can burden you with my load," she said. She pulled an ancient key out of her purse. It looked like a miniature version of the keys to cities that mayors give out to dignitaries, with two prongs jutting down one end and a heart-shaped loop for a handle. The key was made of brass, but the brass had turned mostly green over the decades. Dr. Bishop stood and took three steps toward the cottage. She smiled. "Come on," she said.

Not much light shone inside the cottage. It had been built prior to the days when houses were wired for electricity, so the only light we had was the little pinpoint shining from the end of Dr. Bishop's penlight. Based on what I could see from that light, the cottage was pretty sparse. White sheets hung over a few pieces of furniture. A dark wood, roll-top desk sat in the corner beside a window. Wainscoting surrounded the four walls, giving way only for the doors and a small fireplace wrapped by a large, ornate mantle. The hardwood floors looked worn more than battered, like the seat of a favorite old rocking chair. In the back of the room was another door. Dr. Bishop opened it and led me inside. She said, "Watch your step."

I followed her down a steep and narrow staircase. Her penlight did little to illuminate the room at the bottom of the stairs. When we got there, she shone the light around a room I absolutely did not expect.

"What is this place?"

Dr. Bishop traced a long, hardwood path a little more than three feet wide, flanked by rounded gutters about twelve inches in diameter. At the end of the path, ten small circles formed a triangle. "What does it look like?" Dr. Bishop asked.

"A one-lane bowling alley."

"And therein lies RW Winfield's long-hidden secret: the guy was an avid bowler."

"And his bowling alley is the gateway to Mindland?"

"Something like that."

Dr. Bishop sat in the chair at the little scoring table. I sat on a footlocker that was almost six feet long. Dr. Bishop explained to me that there were nineteen steps one took to enter Mindland. She offered to guide me through. I think she would have insisted if I refused, but I wasn't about to refuse. I didn't need a voice in my head to make me want to go along with this.

The first seventeen steps were bizarre, to say the least. She had me touch my toes ten times, perform eight jumping jacks, kneel down to untie and tie the laces on my shoes, hum "Ode to Joy" while picturing a loved one from my past, walk down the bowling lane and touch the circle first for the seven pin and second for the ten pin, sit on the triangle and imagine a ball rolling my way, imagine the ball rolling through me as if I were not made of matter, return up the alley through the right gutter, turn and bow to the lane, take five deep breaths, open the footlocker I was sitting on, climb in, lace my fingers with the right forefinger on top, switch hands so that the left finger was on top, close the lid of the locker, and prepare to travel. The last two steps were very similar to practicing meditation. I repeated a mantra in my head until my conscious thoughts were held at bay. From there, I unconsciously found an external current for my conscious thoughts to ride out of my brain, and I let my thoughts ride along that current.

25

At first, you don't know if you've arrived or not. It's like when you enter into total darkness and you can't quite tell if your eyes are open or closed. You reach up with a finger, gently touch the eyeball or eyelid, and realize that in darkness like this, it's a moot point. What matters is only what the other four senses can tell you. Likewise, when you follow Dr. Bishop's directions and enter into Mindland, it looks just like your conscious mind. You see exactly what your mind saw the moment before entering. What matters is where you can go from there.

So I arrived into the bowling alley, still in the footlocker I'd laid down in, still in complete darkness, my mind still reeling with Dr. Bishop's anxieties about the discovery of this place and the threat of Walters forever looming. I stood up and realized that, if I could stand, then I had to be somewhere beyond the footlocker I'd laid down in just a few minutes earlier. I looked around the faint light of the alley. Something else was in there with me. It panted. Its nails scraped against the hardwood floor. I thought of a tennis ball and a tennis ball was in my hand. I dropped the ball onto the floor. It ricocheted and landed back in my palm. The creature yapped. I knew that yap. Hello, Clint Dempsey.

I remembered Dr. Bishop's first instruction: look for a door. Of course, I knew where the cottage door had been, but I didn't head up the stairs to it. Dr. Bishop had told me that wasn't the door I was looking for. I tossed the tennis ball towards the back of the alley and listened. It floated for a few seconds, landed, bounced once, twice, and then hit something that sounded wooden and hollow. I followed that sound. Clint Dempsey padded down the hallway in front of me, retrieved the ball, and returned it. I threw it again. I followed the sound. Everything remained dark. I measured the distance between the door and me by how far I could throw the ball. Pretty soon, the ball was ricocheting off the door, and shooting back at me. Clint Dempsey would have to actually run behind me to get it. And, then, I was at the door.

I knelt down to pet Clint Dempsey. "You stay here, boy," I said. "I need to go through this door alone."

Clint Dempsey yapped again. I tossed the ball back down the alley I'd just crossed. Clint Dempsey shot off after the ball. I opened the door in front of me.

Daylight blinded me for a second. I stepped out into it. Dust from the gravel street rose with every step. A meadow opened up in front of me, dotted with squat, knotty trees similar to the California landscape but somehow shorter, drier, more jagged. A hill rose directly in front of me. Something resembling the Parthenon, or at least a replica not in ruins, stood atop the hill. I wandered toward it and found a group of bearded white men wearing white tunics, chatting and laughing.

One of the robed men sat afar from the rest. His back rested against the trunk of an olive tree. He used a flat rock for a desk and wrote on a small papyrus scroll. I could see his thoughts appearing like a hologram in front of him. He was constructing a chariot with a white horse and a black horse that seemed at odds with one another. I reckoned I could see his thoughts because they were already well known to me. I also figured he was the guy to help me make the most of Mindland. I interrupted his train of thought to say, "I hate to interrupt, but…"

The hologram of the chariot dissipated. He didn't seem bothered. He said, "That's the beauty of writing. It exists without time. Once the words are written, you can always go back to them, build on them, revise them, expand them."

"That's true, I guess."

The man stood. "Well, then," he said. "Maybe we should ride that chariot." He whistled and, from some place I couldn't see, the white horse and black horse emerged. He stepped up and took the reins. "Ride with me," he said.

I stepped onto the chariot and grabbed hold of the handrail. The man cracked the reins. The horses started running. He had one rein attached to each horse. I could see he had to give them different cues to make them act together. Regardless, they ran side by side, nearly in step. We raced across the dusty ground for maybe fifty yards before the ground started to give way below us and we ascended into the sky.

"Holy shit," I said.

The man looked at my white knuckles clutching the handrail. "You don't have to grip so hard," he said. "You're metaphysical now. The physical laws don't apply. There's no falling off this chariot."

I believed him enough to loosen my grip, but not enough to let go. The ground grew smaller below us. We left the land that could've been Oak View or Athens or any Mediterranean-type environment: rolling hills of mostly brown and defiant shades of green; tough, tenacious trees that hardened their trunks to weather droughts; dry washes and thin rivers racing to empty all their water into the sea; the sea and the islands on the horizon. We continued our ascent out of the atmosphere and toward the sun, leaving the reflective glow of the earth and moving into the darkness that led to the sun. The wind raced through me, not the way winters in wet climates seem to creep into your bones, but more the way you can feel cold water slink down your esophagus on a hot day. I was neither particularly hot nor cold. I had no trouble breathing even though technically I seemed to have left the atmosphere as well as all the oxygen that implies. I began to see what he meant by metaphysical.

The man spoke about the soul and its descent to the earth and our search for Truth and Wisdom. At first, I said, "Part of what you're talking about is writing, isn't it?"

The man nodded. "Our search for perfection is marred by imperfect forms. Through language. Through writing. Words are imprecise tools to shape the true meaning of things. It is only as we ascend to heaven that we can find Truth and Wisdom."

I nodded and spoke thoughts as quickly as they came to my mind. "So we're ascending to heaven now?"

"In that general direction."

"Well, I appreciate the opportunity to see perfect forms and all," I said. "But metaphysically riding a chariot to heaven while my body is lying in a footlocker the size of a coffin creeps me out. I'd like to go back down."

The man shrugged his shoulders. "Suit yourself," he said. "Take the black horse."

I looked at the empty space around us, the stars, and the shrinking globe. "You mean just climb out there onto its back and ride it home?"

The man nodded. That's exactly what he meant.

"I've never even ridden a horse," I said weakly.

"You're an American living in the 21st century. You've been riding metaphysical horses your whole life. This should be a piece of cake for you."

So I trusted him. I climbed along the leather strap and onto the horse's back. She was connected to the chariot by straps and buckles that were all easy enough to maneuver. I unbuckled everything buckled and untied everything tied until it was just me, bareback on this horse, hanging onto the coarse hair of her mane because I'd accidentally untied her rein. As soon as she felt herself free, she turned and raced back toward earth. I held on.

The horse brought me somewhere far away from Oak View. It was a dense, old growth forest. The ground was carpeted with fallen leaves. My horse slowed to a stop and looked to her left. An anthropomorphic coyote stumbled on two legs. He was covered in feces, blinded by it. He held a small box in one paw. With each tree he approached, he asked, "Please, tree, tell me which way to the water." The trees guided him from oaks to willows to the stream. Coyote stumbled like the last patron let out of a bar that over-serves. The horse and I followed. Coyote jumped into the water and scrubbed at his fur with a porous rock, cleaning off all the feces. My horse headed for the stream, too. I stopped her and climbed off. She went upstream for a drink. I stood on the shores, watching Coyote clean himself and clean the box and clean the penis inside the box and reattach his penis. An elderly, dark-skinned woman came up behind me. She wore a dress with a broad sash around her waist and necklaces that hung nearly to the sash. Long ribbons and decorative patterns adorned the dress. "So, you've met the Trickster," she said.

I nodded. "He's in a bad way."

"For now," she said. She smiled as she watched him shake the water out of his fur and walk out of the stream on the opposite bank. "He'll forget this soon enough and get wrapped up in further madness."

Which is what I knew to be true about Tricksters. I asked her, "Can you guide me around here? Help me understand this place?"

She shook her head. "I only tell a specific type of story. It's rooted to the land. It teaches you to live a way of life you don't live anymore." She waved her hand to point out the space left by the now-vanished Coyote. "That's all I can do."

I climbed atop my horse, waved to the woman, and headed west, hoping that metaphysical space didn't take as long to traverse as physical space. We passed through high plains and mountains and desert. The air was full of songs in 3/4 time. The ghosts of slaughtered Native Americans and cowboys and coal miners floated around. I tried to comprehend it all, but my horse ran too fast and everything was too fleeting.

Finally, I made it back to the meadow near the cottage. I saw the bearded men in the distance, and all around the meadow, little groups of mostly children gathered around teachers. I dismounted. The horse headed back to where she'd come from. I wandered from group to group, catching bits and pieces of lectures. An Elizabethan man waxed poetic about love and treachery with a candle in one hand and the hilt of his sword in the other. A 17th century aristocrat discussed gravity, etching a diagram in the ground in which the dot falling on the stick figure's head extends to the core of the Earth and the moon above. A Renaissance man explained the mathematical calculations showing that the sun was the center of the solar system while in front of him models of six planets spun in a heliocentric system around the model of the sun. An unkempt German physicist discussed time and space; the children seemed to understand time's relativity only by recognizing how slowly it passed when he spoke. An African woman sang songs of pain and redemption. Some clapped along. Some danced. Some stared at their feet and shook their heads. The circus of the mind continued farther up the hill, where the teachers seemed more ancient, more Roman, then more Greek. I followed them up to the crest and looked down on the other side. Most of the teachers down there were women in clothes I couldn't recognize, outlining the rituals and festivals that ran through all the world's religions, hanging bells on trees, dancing around maypoles.

Somewhere among all of this had to be Dr. Bishop. Wouldn't she have come in here with me? Surely she didn't send me in here to fly around on horses and watch a coyote take a bath. And these teachers all around me were certainly brilliant, but I'd heard it all before. It all seemed a bit obvious.

In a way, that made sense. If this really were the land of our shared thoughts, then I would've been through all of this before. This would be the core of what our culture is. Of course I'd recognize it. I would've been one of the children gathered at the feet of the teachers. The child in me probably still attended these lectures on some level. The child in all of us probably does.

I strolled down the hill, back to the door I entered from. I thought to just head back, to tell Dr. Bishop, "Okay, I've seen it. It does exist. Now creep back into my mind and convince me that I dreamed all of this." I even spoke aloud into the meadow. I said, "I don't want to be here."

My words echoed throughout the meadow. The teachers behind me stopped their lectures and all looked at me. They nodded. I think they knew I was lying, that I couldn't wait to come here again with no one waiting outside the door, no one to judge me if I lingered among it all for hours and days and weeks.

I went back in the door from which I'd come. The hallway was dark. Clint Dempsey panted at my feet. I called out, "Dr. Bishop?"

I was answered by a light. A dull yellow bulb over a door, about fifteen feet down the room and to my left. I walked toward the light. Clint Dempsey walked by my side. When he got to the door, he scratched on it. "Why not?" I said. We walked in.

The door opened into the Williams Building. I followed the hallway away from my office and toward the basement. I'd never been down to the basement of the Williams Building. For some reason, it struck me as off limits. I didn't hesitate this time. I headed straight for the staircase and descended.

Dr. Bishop was down there. She sat atop a bed in an examination room. The room looked like one in any American medical doctor's office.

She wore a white hospital gown open in the back. I stepped up behind her and tied the strings of the gown in shoelace-type knots. She looked over her shoulder and smiled. I took a seat in the generic plastic examination room chair. A doctor walked in. He flipped through the chart and looked everywhere but at me or Dr. Bishop. He said, "This is never easy."

Without having to listen to what he said, I knew. He was there to tell her that the cancer had spread into her bloodstream. It was time for her to get her affairs in order and make peace with whatever God or loved one could help her into the next world. This stunned me. It was all too clear. I even said aloud, "Cancer? This can't be!"

The words echoed in the examination room. They banged on the door. They shook the world around me. The banging got so loud that it yanked me out of this room and this world and landed me back into the footlocker. Total darkness once again.

I tried to stand and bumped my head against the top of the locker. That was all I needed to know. I was back.

I opened the top and climbed out. Dr. Bishop stood above me, shining her penlight in my face. She was sweating, exhausted. She said, "Stay out of my mind."

I hugged her. My fingers rested in the spaces between her ribs, just shy of where the rib cage tied into her spine. Dr. Bishop hugged back. So that was it. Cancer was in her bloodstream. Now it was up to Eric and me to bury her life's work and throw Walters off the trail. Dr. Bishop released me and said, "Let's go."

She led me back up the stairs and through the cottage and outside again. I waited in the arboretum while she locked the cottage door with her ancient key. She put the key into her pocket.

I walked down the needle-strewn path with Dr. Bishop. We took slow, careful steps. At times, she hung onto my bicep for balance. We didn't talk. Late springtime breezes fluttered through the oaks. I wrestled with a thousand thoughts. What I'd been told. What I'd seen. What lay before me. I tried to make sense of it all. The answers were far from forthcoming. Dr. Bishop slipped once. I was too lost in thoughts to see her slip, but I felt it. She caught herself by grabbing onto the pocket of my slacks and held on for a second. I reached out to help her keep her balance. She took two deep breaths. Her hand was still halfway in my pocket. I waited. She recovered. We walked on.

We met Eric at the end of the trail. He nodded to me. I nodded back. Dr. Bishop and Eric walked in one direction. I walked in the other.

When I got to my bicycle, I reached into the pocket of my slacks for the key to unlock it. I felt the cool brass of the long, slender cottage key. Dr. Bishop must have faked her stumble on the pathway and slid the key in. It was a smart move on her part. I never would've taken the key if she'd simply tried to give it to me. Now I had it, though, and I had a sense of what I had to do.

26

Perhaps it's time to explain how I knew Dr. Bishop way back when. I'll rewind back to the summer of 1991. I had just finished my junior year at Fresno State. Nietzsche was a pup. The woman who became my ex-wife was my girlfriend, and we had a future instead of a past. I also played drums in the band Pop Culture and the References. We had big plans for the summer. We would record five songs, release a seven-inch record, and tour the West Coast. The cost of recording was covered. Our guitarist Brandon—also known as Fester back in those days—worked at a little studio in Fresno. As long as we recorded between the hours of 2 and 6 AM and paid for our own tape (which Fester had filched, anyway), the studio was ours. We also figured that we'd be able to pay for the tour with the cover charges at shows and record sales. What we really needed, though, was six hundred bucks to press the records. Two hundred each. These were the days when two hundred bucks was a very difficult sum for me or Pop to raise, particularly when it came on top of things like food and rent. Fester had his share covered.

Pop and I had another plan, though. Pop had come across an ad in the back of the student newspaper soliciting human research subjects. He called the number. A one-week gig. We could take the week off from our regular campus jobs and do the study. If everything worked out, we'd have enough for the seven-inch and the tour. The three of us—Pop, Fester, and I—piled into the band van and headed to Stanford for the week.

We arrived at the testing facility at the prescribed time. A research assistant interviewed us. She told us that she couldn't use any of us in the study. They needed anorexics. Clearly, we didn't qualify. "But," she said, "we also need more proctors: people to oversee the study, keep it running smoothly. The pay is the same. It's one week of work. If you're interested, you're hired."

The three of us nodded along. We produced pens and scribbled signatures on respective contracts. The research assistant led us to our rooms in the testing facility. We took a side entrance that led us up a flight of concrete stairs and into the blank hallway of a dormitory, low rent by Stanford's standards, swank compared to what we were used to. We passed the doorway to a communal bathroom, followed by rows of doors that led into box rooms, each with little more than bunk beds, a pair of metal dressers, and a pair of desks. There was a common room at the end of the hall, with couches darkened by the oils and dirt of a generation of students, but still in one piece, stuffing still stuffed and springs yet to have sprung. We sat on the couches and the research assistant explained our jobs.

The study explored a new approach to treating anorexia. The goal was to change the patients' relationship with food, to make food desirable again. In order to do that, the patients, or, in this case, research subjects, were housed in the dining room at the end of the hall. The research assistant pointed at the hallway that we hadn't walked down. The research subjects camped in the dining room, lived among the kitchen smells, and watched as proctors like Pop, Fester, and I ate elaborate meals. All the while, the subjects were not allowed to eat. The hypothesis, the research assistant told us, is that anorexia is a control issue. Anorexics stop eating because eating is one area in their life that they can have complete control over. If that control is wrested from them, they'll look for autonomy in a different arena and begin eating again.

Fester was the first to reframe this. He said, "So, basically, our job is to pig out in front of a bunch of starving people."

"Yes," the research assistant said. "That, and make sure the starving people don't eat."

I was a little stunned, not at all sure that I could be a part of this study. Fester, on the other hand, said, "How's the grub?"

The research assistant smiled and stood to leave. "Delicious. We hired the sous chef from Antonio's downtown." She winked at Fester. "Don't be shy. Ask for seconds."

She disappeared down the hall from which she came. Pop, Fester, and I headed to the dining room for a bite.

The study was already in progress. A group of proctors sat at a large table, serving themselves from communal trays of shrimp fra diavolo, eggplant parmesan, chicken cacciatore, sausage and peppers, shrimp and scallop scampi, puttanesca, various pastas in marinara or alfredo or olive oil and garlic sauce, rolls, loaves of bread, and a spinach salad. The proctors piled their plates high. The sous chef kept working in the open-air kitchen adjacent to the dining room. More food was on its way. Between the smells and the sight of those mountains of food, I wanted to eat like I'd never eaten before. I wanted to make a Thanksgiving feast feel like a light lunch compared to what I was going to do to those trays of food.

Then I saw the research subjects, gathered on their cots, staring at us with those hungry eyes. They were so skinny. Starving, really. Literally. One young woman among them called out, "Come on. You can't toss me a roll? One goddamn roll?"

One of the proctors looked me in the eye, shook his head, and said, "Fucking guinea pigs." He reached over to a tray I hadn't noticed yet and scooped up a lobster tail dripping with garlic-butter sauce.

I spent the rest of that night and all of the next day reading everything I could about anorexia, treatments, and this study. By dinnertime, sitting down to my fourth feast that would put the digs at Versailles to shame, barely able to touch any food, gazing into constellations of starving eyes, I decided to sabotage the experiment.

I borrowed the band's van that night, drove to a local bagel shop, ordered a sandwich, and chatted with the lone girl working. I told her about the experiment. She looked at me like she was unsure of what to believe. I asked her when she would dump the day-old bagels. She said, "When you're ready to leave, I'll give you a bag."

She gave me a few tubs of cream cheese to go with them, warning me to make sure I ate the cream cheese in the next week or so. I got the sense that she didn't believe me about the experiment, that she thought I was just hungry and had made up a clever story for free bagels.

At eleven o'clock that night, after the proctors were done with their gelatos and cheesecakes, I snuck into the dining room with my bag full of bagels and cream cheese. I crept into the middle of their circle of cots and knelt among them. "Okay, guys," I said, even though most of them were girls. "I know it's not as good as the food they're feeding us, but it's what I can bring you."

The research subjects looked at each other. For the first time, none of their hungry eyes would meet mine. Finally, the one who had called out for the roll the day before said, "Dude, you're crossing a line."

I stood. "It's okay by me," I said. I left the bagels and cream cheese on a little table among the cots. I crept back out of the room.

I couldn't sleep that night. I just kept thinking about the research subjects—the guinea pigs, as the proctors called them. I knew enough about anorexics to know they wouldn't tear into the food like a pack of wild animals. I didn't expect them to be ravenous. I did expect starving people to react more favorably to food, though. At least one of them should've reached out for a bagel. And that's when it occurred to me that the guinea pigs weren't that skinny. They were skinny, sure, but not anorexic skinny. There was something fishy going on. I thought about the proctors, too, because all of us seemed to have been hired on the spot, when we were signing up to be research subjects. I spent a lot of time that night lying on my dorm bed, staring at the underside of Pop's bed, wondering who the real guinea pigs were.

At about four in the morning, Pop got up to use the communal restroom. When he came back, I said, "Pop, does something seem fishy here?"

"Yeah," Pop said. "It seems fishy that it's four in the morning and you're trying to talk to me."

I didn't shy away, though. I said, "You remember freshman comp, when we read that essay about Stanley Milgram?"

"I didn't read anything for freshman comp."

"Well, we were assigned to read it. It was all about this experiment a guy did to gauge how far people would go in following orders. He

210

hired people to administer dosages of electricity to other people, like shock treatments, to see how much electricity someone would pump into another human being just because they were hired to do so."

"Okay, right. I remember talking about that shit in class. The teacher said that we all would've been Nazis if we'd been in Germany in the late '30s."

"Right, well, I think we're in the middle of an experiment just like that. I think the guinea pigs are actors, and we're really the guinea pigs. I think they're testing to see how much we'll eat in the face of starvation, how long it'll take us to start feeding the actors."

Pop climbed back into the top bunk. "I think you're being paranoid," he said. "And I'm going back to sleep."

Before breakfast that morning, I insisted on seeing the director of the study. It was Dr. Bishop. I told her what I thought of the study, told her that I thought it was unethical and I wanted out. Dr. Bishop was a bit different then. She was bigger and younger. She didn't have that grandmotherly quality. She projected a lot of authority, especially sitting in her black leather chair behind an oak desk in a huge faculty office at Stanford. She treated me as if I were being paranoid. She scolded me. She harangued me. She waved the contract I'd signed and threatened to sue. She placated me. She took every action she could to bully me, and when I didn't back down, she admitted that I was right. The study really was about complicity. That's why they knew about the bagels I'd brought in the night before, and about me explaining it all to Pop.

She told me, "We've been doing this study for six months. We've had over three hundred proctors. You're the only one who fed the actors."

Dr. Bishop's assistant pulled Pop out of the study. She paid the two of us for the week and sent us on our way.

Pop and I came back six days later to pick up Fester. His face was rounder and a genuine gut formed above his belt. He'd gained an easy fifteen pounds.

On the drive home, I explained to him about the experiment. He said, "Hell, I figured that out on the first day, but I wasn't about to give up a week of feasts by complaining about it."

I thought about the experiment again after my first night in the bowling alley footlocker. I rode my bike home from the psych hospital and wondered about paranoia and schizophrenia. It's hard to know what to do with paranoia when you realize that you really are enmeshed in a conspiracy; it's hard to know what to do with schizophrenia when someone really is planting voices inside your head. And I couldn't help wondering how long this had been going on. I had to think that this wasn't Dr. Bishop's last experiment, but her life's work. I had to think she'd been looking for someone like me since 1991, that she'd found me back then in her study, that she'd watched me spend fifteen years struggling to make a small difference and turning my back on everything that a guy like Frank Walters had the power to offer, and that she'd picked me as her heir for exactly these reasons.

Because that's the wonderful thing about paranoia: it makes you feel so special.

27

I'm going to have to be a little more honest about Mindland, now. Initially, I screamed out that I didn't want to be there. I doubt it was true, even at the time. I was scared in that first trip. I have a little bit of a phobia about heights. Flying in a chariot isn't the best thing for that. And, like all mortals, I fear death, so becoming metaphysical and ascending anywhere invites thoughts into the unknown, thoughts that are petrifying no matter who you are and how you brace yourself for them. So there was the fear.

But there was something else, some kind of internal lump, soft and squishy, warm and inviting, the kind of thing that makes us venture into the unknown, that gives memories meaning and wouldn't let me stay away. That lump seemed to be saying, "Buddy, you got to ride a chariot with Plato and hear a Trickster tale from an original ancient. It was every bit as cool as you thought it would be." I guess, because of this lump, I'd barely pedaled my bike to the bike path at the edge of the psych hospital grounds before I started making plans to come back.

The second time I went into Mindland, it was a mess. I didn't understand the rules. I didn't know how to guide my mind without my body there to slow it down. I didn't realize that, the first time, Dr. Bishop had been guiding me. This time, I was on my own.

I walked out the same door that led me to the back of the bowling alley and onto the same Mediterranean field with all the gatekeepers of Western thought. Almost instantly, I was yanked out of there, like I'd been jerked off the stage by an old vaudevillian hook. I couldn't find a way to settle into a time and place. The wind started swirling, kicking up dirt and dust in the field around me. The horizon was lost in the haze. Voices, sounds, images replaced the dirt and dust. They formed into a dozen or so dust devils. Or, more specifically, tiny, ethereal tornadoes composed not of physical detritus but of brands, logos, sound bites, and the like. They grew and crashed into one another and me. It all accelerated to dizzying speeds.

I closed my eyes and tried to think. How had Dr. Bishop guided me? First, she sent me to familiar places. The ancients. Exactly what I'd expect in Mindland. But it had made sense. A real sense. More concrete than a dream sense. And how do we make sense of the chaos outside of Mindland, outside of dreams?

Stories. The first thing I had to do was to put this chaos around me into a story. A narrative I could follow. Even if I didn't have my physical body to move me through things, a story had a structure I could understand. It would slow things down and keep things in order long enough for me to negotiate it all. And so I told myself the story of what was happening as it happened.

I'm in a maelstrom surrounded by clutter and pop culture dust devils. I'm metaphysical so I can't get hurt. I can open my eyes. As soon as I did, the dust devils spread out. They didn't go away, but they gave me room. I looked to the tortured ground, the torn posters and magazine advertisements and broken toasters and blenders and plastic toy packaging that had drifted down from the dust devils and now carpeted the once green grass. The clutter was no deeper than a fine falling snow, so I could walk across it. I started walking away from the cottage door. A dust devil steered a staggering path toward me. I stopped to see what it might be up to. It circled me once, tipped its open mouth toward me as if to try to suck me into the funnel. When I stayed rooted to the ground, it backed away four or five feet and rose straight up another three feet. A pair of woman's legs slid out of the bottom. Her feet were adorned with clunky black shoes. White tights stretched to her knees. The dust devil gradually rose, leaving not only the legs but a black, schoolgirl skirt to wrap around the legs, an exposed midriff, the bottom half of a uniform blouse tied into a knot just above the midriff, the rest of the blouse barely covering an apparently surgically-enhanced breast, and, finally, the head of a young woman. She looked vaguely familiar, but if pressed to come up with a name, I would not have been able to do it. She took one step toward me and lifted a finger with a blood red painted fingernail to a pair of lips made up in the same shade of blood red. "Well," she said.

I could not comprehend why, of all the detritus swirling around, she was the most prominent, the one to be deposited in front of me. I gave her a slight nod and tried to look beyond her, through the dust and trash toward something more meaningful.

She said, "Do you want to see me naked?"

"It's not that I don't," I said, suddenly concerned about whether or not I hurt this young woman's feelings. "I'm sure you're very attractive in your own right. It's just that, I didn't come here to see you naked. I came for other things."

She glanced down at her clunky shoe, twisted her foot as if she were extinguishing a cigarette, and looked back up at me, all with her finger still next to her mouth. She raised her eyebrows. "Do you want to hear me sing?"

"No!" I said, responding faster and more forcefully than I should have, if I really were trying to keep from hurting her feelings. At the moment, not hearing her music was more important.

The storm of dust devils spread further back. A bit of sunlight cracked through the cluttered air. Masses of people started to gather at the fringes. Music emerged from somewhere. A standard, repetitive, synthesized beat. She was going to sing. I could find no way to stop her or the music, but I desperately wanted to.

At that point, I had enough. Like Dorothy in the *Wizard of Oz* screaming for her dog Toto, I called out for Clint Dempsey.

This thrust me back into the hallway of the cottage. A little yellow light glowed above a doorway. I walked through. It led me down the steps again, back into the basement of the Williams Building. There, I entered a locker room. A handful of young men, mostly mid-to-late twenties, all lean and wiry, wearing the whites of the Fulham Football Club. They strapped on cleats and stretched their hamstrings one last time and took tiny sips of water and stared at the concrete and prepared for a game. Clint Dempsey—the soccer player, not the dog—sat among them. "Today," he told himself. "Today, I'm going to score. Today, I'm going to shoot every chance I get. Today, I'll score a hat trick." He stared at his cleats and repeatedly visualized what it would take, how John Terry and the Chelsea defense would be there, doing everything they could to keep Clint Dempsey off the ball, to keep the ball out of the net. And Clint Dempsey visualized the angles he would take to beat Terry to the ball, the moves he would use to elude the defense, the way his left leg would travel through the path of the ball with such force that it would bring his whole body with him and he'd fly through the shot and land again on his left foot.

I eavesdropped on Clint Dempsey's thoughts for a second or two before I indulged in my own visualizations. I realized that just by hollering out a name, I could slide into that person's mind, his situations and thoughts. That's how I'd found out about Dr. Bishop's cancer. That's how I witnessed Clint Dempsey's obsession. That's how I could figure out…

I started to call out Frank Walters' name. I got halfway through the Frank before I recognized how intelligent the guy was, what a formidable opponent. I'd need to sharpen my skills before encountering Walters in Mindland. So I picked a weaker mind. I called out, "Connor Jarred."

This thrust me into a scene I wasn't quite ready for because I hadn't accounted for time. I hadn't done the math. I could wander around Clint Dempsey's conscious mind because he was in England, which is nine hours ahead of California, so my middle-of-the-night cottage hours coincided with his late morning preparations for an early afternoon game. Ape Man was in the same time zone as me. His mind was unconscious, deep into a dream. Maybe nightmare would be a better word.

I found myself standing atop a ruffled sleeping bag inside a canvas, four-person tent. The faint glow of a dying campfire flickered against the front flap. A small kerosene lantern lit the rest of the scene. A large man lay on a coarse army surplus blanket. His navy blue shorts gathered in a bunch around his right ankle. He propped himself up on one elbow. His other hand cradled his belly fat, holding it away from his groin, making room for the head of the young boy that bobbed up and down there. Most of the boy's face was obscured by his mop of red hair. This kid couldn't have been more than ten or eleven. The Maori tattoo was lacking, but the face was unmistakable just the same.

Besides that, I was in this kid's thoughts. Just as I'd eavesdropped on Clint Dempsey's obsessions and was able to visualize Clint Dempsey's visualizations, I shared this kid's terror. I traced his thoughts as they searched for a way out of this tent and into the high desert that surrounded it and back to the dirt road that would lead to a main road that would take him eventually to a highway and home. I felt his sense of futility. I felt the intensity of the moment for him, down to the last detail: the erection that filled his mouth and the bush of pubic hair that tickled his nose and the hand that slapped the back of his head if it stopped bobbing.

The large man let go of his belly and reached around for the boy's thigh and yanked down the boy's plaid bermudas. The kid's flaccid member hung in front of his hairless scrotum. The large man licked his forefinger and used it to rub tiny circles around the boy's sphincter. This gave the boy an almost instant erection. He started to cry.

I had enough. I called out, "Get me out of this place!"

Luckily, it worked. I landed back in my little footlocker in the RW Winfield one-lane bowling alley.

28

The third time I went to Mindland, I just goofed off. I'd known before going in that I could sneak into other people's minds and snoop around. It even occurred to me that I could make suggestions in these people's minds and maybe they'd follow those suggestions, just like Dr. Bishop had apparently been doing in my mind when she convinced me to sell her fake secrets to Walters. During the day that separated my second trip and my third, I sat in my office at the psych hospital, winding up the spring on my toy bird, watching its beak inch a breath away from the desktop, then perform a back flip. I thought of all the possibilities. A sense of power ballooned in my chest. Every time I tried to pop it, the power balloon healed itself and re-inflated. The third trip, I figured, had to be just for fun.

When I emerged from the footlocker, I hollered, "Rip Van Winkle," and almost immediately found myself on a bench in front of a hotel. The sign above the hotel showed a painting of King George III, but on his head was the blue tricorn hat of an American Revolutionary, and in his hand was a sword. Faint shadows of a scepter bled through the paint under the sword. Under this portrait, the words "George Washington" had been painted. The hotel, I knew from reading Irving's story a thousand times, was Mr. Doolittle's inn. Any minute now, Rip would be along. At least that's what I hoped.

The Kaatskill mountains rose above the town in the distance. A veil of gray clouds settled atop their peaks. The waning sunlight cast shades of blue and purple along the ridges of the mountains. The rest of the sky glistened, bathed in gold. The shadows and magical hues struck me as somehow fake, touched up in an unsettling vibrancy designed to cast me into a world adjacent to my own.

Subtle details set me further off kilter. A tar sidewalk shone through the straw and pine needles at my feet; the bench beneath me was covered in a thick layer of varnish that I doubt existed in the 18th century. Small electric lights lined the walking path to my left. A brown trashcan sat alongside a green trashcan bearing the three arrows that indicated its role as a home for recyclables. Even Mr. Doolittle's inn cast an electric candle light on an ancient Budweiser sign.

Rip emerged amid this blend of authenticity and anachronism. He bore the same contradictory markings of the scene around him. While he looked like a flesh and blood person, something about him was off. He appeared more like an aging theme park employee than an 18th century farmer. His clothes were made of cotton and synthetic fibers. Makeup rather than burst blood vessels reddened his nose. He was getting up there in the years, though, and his beard was real. He yawned.

I looked into his thoughts, but nothing came out.

"That won't work here," he said.

"What's that?"

"Mind reading. You can do it with real people here, but I'm not real."

I looked at Rip. He looked as real as anything else. Dust settled into the coarse fibers of his coat. Rust flaked off his fowling gun. That sweet stench of body odor floated between us. I reached out for the one spot that seems to be fair game for contact: his shoulder. I patted it. The muscles and dirt and oil under my fingers felt like muscles and dirt and oil. I said, "What do you mean, you're not real?"

"I'm a myth," Rip said. "I don't generate thoughts. I just absorb the ones you give me."

"Can you still answer questions?"

"I can give it a shot."

Mr. Doolittle emerged from his inn, carrying a ceramic jug. He nodded to Rip and me. I nodded back. Rip held out his arms for the jug. Mr. Doolittle passed it along. He sat on the lacquered bench, next to Rip. He pulled out a stick and started whittling. A dusky orange light sprinkled his knife's blade. Rip took a pull off the jug.

"How did you become a myth?"

"Well, you know, the story is an old one. You can mine Chinese or Jewish legend and find stories about guys sleeping for decades and coming back to find everything changed. Irving got his story from a German folktale. I'm just one more rewriting of that legend."

"No. You're different than that," I said. Because I'd studied all of those Eastern legends at the university. I knew the difference between old myths and new ones. "I don't think you ever slept longer than ten or twelve hours in your life."

"How can you say that? I'm Rip Van Winkle."

"Look at the facts: you and your wife didn't get along, you were having affairs all over town…"

Rip stopped me with a mischievous smile. "Are you sure of that?"

"I'm pretty sure. That's what Washington Irving seems to be telling me."

Rip shrugged. A corner of his lip raised, pushing up his crackling skin, compacting the stage makeup on the ball of his cheek. He said, "Irving?"

I felt somehow part of a performance and like I'd just missed my cue. I thought back to the story and thought about Irving's sly remarks about Rip's infidelities. This reminded me that Irving didn't tell the tale at all. Diedrich Knickerbocker did. Or at least Irving claimed to find the story among Knickerbocker's papers. And, come to think of it, Irving didn't claim that so much as Geoffrey Crayon, the fictional author of *The Sketch Book*, did. So where did that leave me? With a fictional narrator calling up a fictional narrator to tell the story adapted from ancient legend and a German folktale into new American mythology and my mind in Mindland trying to make sense of it. I was thrown.

Rip shook me out of this. He said, "Go on."

"Okay." I shifted my focus back to the story. "So you and your wife didn't get along, you may or may not have been having affairs all around town, you weren't interested in working or raising your kids, and a war that seemed to have nothing to do with you was slowly brewing. So you wandered off. You skipped out on the war and the childrearing. You showed back up in town the week after your wife died and just in time to be a grandfather. Sounds to me like the classic case of a deadbeat dad."

Rip drank from his jug and shrugged. "You have your story and I have mine. And it doesn't matter. Everyone will believe Knickerbocker over you."

Mr. Doolittle stopped whittling long enough to pat Rip's knee, then turned his attention back to his knife and stick. Slivers of wood gathered at his feet.

"Don't get me wrong. I'm not judging you," I said. "I just want to know how you did it. Any careful reading of your story paints you as a drunk, a lousy father, maybe even an adulterer and a draft dodger. Yet, you're one of the most popular figures in American culture. We teach our kids to love you. How did that happen?"

Rip waved his hand at the scene in front of me. The sun sat perched upon the Kaatskills in the exact spot it was when we began this conversation, promising a perpetual sunset and a night that would never come. "Look at this world you created for me," Rip said. "You wanted to meet me in the 18th century, but you have no idea what it looks like. So where do you stick me? Frontierland?"

"I didn't stick you here."

"Whose mind are we in?"

I shrugged, genuinely lost in my search for an answer to that question. I said, "Go on."

"Okay, well, you go around looking for authenticity and you may or may not be looking for it in Frontierland. You look for the real Rip Van Winkle, but I'm a fictional character, a hodgepodge of everything that's come before me. And you just pick one moment in my evolution: Knickerbocker's story. You forget that I've been turned into a cartoon. I'm the hero of a kid's story. I'm a myth. Just like all myths, I'm always changing."

"But you're also Rip Van Winkle. Washington Irving created you. He gave you a name and stuck you in America. It was written. You can't change the words now."

Rip offered the jug to me. A sticky drip of brown streaked its side. I declined. "Your loss," he said. He drank a little more. Ale residue stained his gray and black beard. "Don't get too hung up on words on a page. They're just an illusion of permanence. What power do they have over a

Disney cartoon?"

I scratched my chin and looked up at the King George/George Washington painting above Rip. I raised my eyebrows and thought for a second. My plan had been to visit Rip first and Don Quixote second. Staring at the liver spots and dust-caked wrinkles of Rip's hands, thinking of the Frontierland I'd created and of Rip's last statement deflated me. I wanted to head back to my footlocker.

Rip jerked me out of my escape before I had a chance to make it. He added, "Anyway, we're just dancing around the real point here."

"Which is what?" I asked.

"Why are you trying to learn how to become what I've become?"

"What's that?"

"A loveable bastard."

Mr. Doolittle laughed from his end of the bench. It was a quick laugh, done almost before he started. The rich Kaatskill forests swallowed most of the sounds around us. All I could hear was Doolitttle's whittling. *Slip, slip, slip.*

Starting with the fourth time I journeyed into Mindland, I stopped goofing off. I got right down to business.

29

I sat at a table in the nicest downtown restaurant wearing, for the first time in my life, a suit that had not been purchased for me by a parent. Sure, Lola had picked it out and it had come off the rack at a department store, but it had been tailored to fit me right and I finally figured out a way to wear a suit without thinking the whole time, *goddamn it, I'm wearing a suit*. The director of one of the largest endowments in the nation sat across the table from me. Our business was done. His endowment would fund the Alzheimer's research at the hospital for another two or three years, at least. He'd even given me contacts to secure genuine embryonic stem cells for the research. Nothing was left but for him to finish his coffee and his story. I couldn't help feeling big time.

The endowment director told me about his mother, who'd recently died. She'd been in the awkward position of being a very healthy octogenarian when Alzheimer's took over. Her final five years had been marked by the torturous decline of her mind while her body worked just fine. "I used to wonder which would be worse: having your body give out on you while your mind is fine or having your mind go while your body is still relatively healthy," the endowment director told me. "Now I know."

I closed my eyes, gave a quick nod, and lifted my glance back up to meet his. Unlike my suit and tie, my sympathy was no façade. I meant it. I felt closer to the healthy body, diseased mind than this guy could possibly imagine. Every time I climbed back out of Mindland, I felt like I was snapping out of some kind of madness. My drive to fund the battle against mental illnesses and manias and delusions went beyond altruism. I was starting to feel like I had a personal stake in them.

The endowment director finished his coffee and checked his watch.

I looked outside the restaurant window at the image seated on the downtown bench. He'd been haunting me for the past ten minutes or so. At first, I'd hoped he was a ghost, a delusion, a construct of a guilty conscience. As time wore on, though, I was able to steal enough glances at that downtown bench to recognize that no phantom sat there. It was the flesh and blood Frank Walters.

The endowment director offered to drive me back to the psych hospital. This was out of character for a guy like the endowment director, but not out of character for this particular guy. Even though he oversaw a foundation that handled more money than many small countries have, even though he himself had the kind of wealth that few Americans can really conceive of, he was a lonely guy. He needed to hang out with someone. For some reason, he liked to hang out with me. I'd run into him a few weeks earlier while doing business with one of his assistants. The director and I happened to start chatting about soccer—the 2006 World Cup, in fact, and Clint Dempsey's goal—and we strangely hit it off. Next thing I knew we were doing lunch, the hospital was getting funded, and I'd finally found a friend who would talk to me about soccer. It was a good situation. "I appreciate the offer," I said, "but I have a little business to take care of while I'm in town."

The director nodded and shook my hand. I thanked him again for his generosity and told him I'd be in touch soon. We parted ways in front of the restaurant. As he turned the corner down California Street, I lingered on Main. I waited for him to take another turn into the parking lot halfway down California. Then, I sat down on the bench next to Frank Walters.

"Fancy meeting you here," Walters said.

Early on, this would have been unsettling. I would have wondered how this blind man knew it was me. Could he smell me? Did he know the sound of my walk well enough to recognize it out of a crowd of hundreds on this downtown street? Did he have some kind of sixth sense?

By now, though, I knew Walters well enough to see how his tricks worked. He knew it was me who sat down on the bench because no one else would sit next to an impeccably dressed blind man on a downtown bench at 1:30 on a Tuesday afternoon. He also knew to say perfectly vague things that a stranger would not think odd but I would think were directed specifically at me, like, "Fancy meeting you here."

"Just happened to be in the neighborhood," I said.

"I was banking on that."

Of course he was. Walters' time was money in the bank. It may not have been the big money that the endowment director had, but money is relative. It means different things to different people. Walters had a lot of money relative to what I had. And the amount of money Walters had was not enough relative to the amount of money he wanted. The fact that he'd spend an hour in the middle of his workday—time when he could have been making more of that money he wanted—to drive up here, wait outside a restaurant for me for another quarter of an hour, and know that he had another half-hour to drive home all meant that he was banking no small sum on meeting me. The fact that he'd left Ape Man in the car, the fact that he came armed with nothing more than his wits and his voice meant that he was serious about something. I ran all of this through my mind, but I said nothing. Let him listen for my breath just to make sure I'm still here.

"Well, I can see that you're a busy man. You want me to get right down to business."

"Nah," I said. "I'm not that busy. My work for today is done. I don't even have to go back to the office."

"Congratulations on the endowment."

Again, this was exactly the kind of thing that would've thrown me when I first met Walters. I would have wondered how much he knew about the endowment, what his connections were, what his abilities were to kill the deal, all of that. I would have slid into a quick, paranoid panic and given him a few seconds of upper hand. Not on this day, though. This day was all about trying to keep him unsettled. I said, "You know, I think I'm going to celebrate with an ice cream. Do you want an ice cream?"

"I'll pass."

I stood. "I am going to get an ice cream. Would you like to come with me?"

"I'll pass."

"Okay, well, I'm going to head over there. If you're still here when

I get back, we'll have a chat. But, please, don't feel like you have to wait for me."

Walters' lips got tense. He tightened his grip on his cane. He said nothing. He only nodded.

I walked over to the next block and went into the ice cream shop. A bored young woman who looked to be a year or two out of high school stood behind the counter. I paused for a second to question what I was doing in this shop, knowing that I had just eaten and didn't need more food, knowing that my stomach couldn't handle a scoop of ice cream anymore, anyway. But my imagination had conjured an image and it was worth eight bucks to make that image a reality. I ordered two cups of ice cream.

While the young woman wordlessly doled out the scoops, I took a moment to collect my thoughts. I wondered how Walters really knew where I'd be today. I decided to settle on the simplest solution first. That's what my time lingering in the minds of others was teaching me: usually the most direct solution to a problem is the right one. Take Walters' suits, for example. How did he dress like that? It had seemed like such a mystery to me that a blind man could be so impeccably dressed. So I looked into it. As it turns out, Walters had worked out a deal with a costume designer in Hollywood. Walters set the costume designer up with work in commercials, the costume designer kicked back suits to Walters. And who dressed him? Well, I'd actually witnessed it one morning in Mindland. I saw Ape Man select a suit, take it out of the plastic from the cleaners, and pass it over to Walters. While Walters put on his pants and shirt, Ape Man tied a tie around his own neck. He then loosened the tie, took it off, slid it over Walters' head, and tightened it. The whole scene was strangely touching: the intimacy of monsters.

So back to how Walters knew where I'd be. Well, the most direct solution would be that he probably called the administrative assistant who worked in my department and asked where I was. She would've told him. She would've had no reason not to.

I paid the ice cream girl and tipped her a buck and walked back down the block to where Frank Walters sat impatiently on a bench.

I sat next to him again. "I know you said you'd pass, but I got you a cup of ice cream anyway," I said. "It's strawberry cheesecake."

Walters took the cup of ice cream I handed him. He even spooned out a bite. And this was the image I had. I wanted Walters to have an ice cream in his hand while he tried to sound so tough laying down his threats. At least this was the best I could do to realize the image I'd had. Really, I wanted him to be licking an ice cream cone when he delivered his threats but giving an ice cream cone to an impeccably dressed blind man seemed cruel. I didn't want to be cruel. I wanted to be disarming.

So I spooned my ice cream and Walters spooned his. We sat side by side on a downtown bench. I wore my suit and tie. Walters wore his. A middle-aged blond man rode past on a beach cruiser. A group of scantily clad young women chatted outside a local boutique. A homeless guy across the street played accordion and sang. His open accordion case invited spare change. Passersby largely avoided the guy and his case. I tried not to act scared because, really, Walters terrified me. I'd known him long enough now to know that the little things about him that had intimidated me—the way he could maneuver so easily despite his sightlessness, the fact that he knew so much about my life—were insignificant compared to the big truth of who Walters really was.

I braced myself for his threat because I knew what he knew: that big things had gone down the night before in Mindland.

On my seventh trip, I set my sights on Walters. I climbed out of the footlocker and hollered, "Frank Walters," and a dull yellow bulb lit above a doorway. I walked down the stairs into the basement of the Williams Building. That's where I came face-to-face with complete darkness. No shadows, no hints of light in the corner, nothing for the pupils to expand wide enough to see, no difference between eyes open and eyes closed. Not only was there no light at all, there was a sense that there never had been light. This was my welcome into the world of Walters' mind.

It cast me out of any kind of comfort zone. It was so different from my mind and thought processes because, of course, I can see, and most people who can see think in images, not words. When I think of, say, a chair, I don't think of the word *chair*. I picture a chair in my mind. All of my thoughts start out this way. I add the words later. But for

Walters, who had been blind since birth, images weren't forthcoming. He thought in sounds, feelings, tastes, smells. Which we all do—we all think in sounds, feelings, tastes, and smells. But for Walters, he thought *only* in these ways. No visuals. So the absence of light wasn't an emptiness. Far from it. Sounds designated spaces. Thoughts abounded. A whole world existed. It's just that sight was absent from it.

For someone who has been able to see his whole life, this world was horrifying. After a second, I learned to calm down a bit and just go with it. As I became a little more comfortable with the darkness, something occurred to me. There was nothing wrong with my physical eyes. I was only blind through my metaphysical eyes, and only while I was in Walters' mind. And if that was true for me—if my experiences through others' minds in Mindland allowed me to sense exactly what they sensed—the same would be true for Walters. That is, if I could see, but I was blind in Walters' mind, than the opposite should be true for Walters: if he was blind, he could still see through other people's minds in Mindland. This must be why he wants an in to Mindland so bad. If he's here, he can see.

I pushed that thought as far back in my mind as possible. I didn't want to be the dick who kept a blind man from seeing. I wanted to be the guy who stopped a potential tyrant from imposing his will on the world. So I stayed focused to the task at hand.

I'd expected Walters to be asleep. It was after two in the morning. I didn't bank on Walters being an insomniac. Maybe that would have made sense to me if I'd thought ahead. And I had thought ahead. I just hadn't thought of everything. So Walters' dreams eluded me. Instead, I followed Walters into his kitchen. I recognized his sense of space and knowledge of obstacles. I felt his arm reach out above the stove and feel for a teakettle. I felt the cool wooden handle of the teakettle. I felt him reach for a faucet and fill the kettle and place it on a burner and turn a handle and listen to the hiss of gas and the tearing sound of the gas igniting under the burner. I listened for him to lean back against an obstacle that must have been a kitchen island and wait for the whistle of the kettle and then make his tea, which he knew would be herbal by the smell of the jasmine leaves. When he sat at the kitchen table and blew the top of his tea, I interrupted his thoughts. I whispered, "Dr. Bishop's research." His mind took the cue.

He ran through the reports in his head and came back with the same correct conclusion: that the research had been falsified, that these efforts to falsify the research would only have taken place if the research had been working, if Dr. Bishop had found a way into the collective unconscious. He thought briefly of the money that could be made by inserting advertisements into the collective unconscious. His mind then wandered back to his mug of tea.

I whispered again. "Daydream," I told Walters. "It will relax you. Imagine that the grant writer is here at your table. Tell him your plans like it's all a B-movie and you know that he'll be erased from the film before you ride off to your heroic end."

Walters broke into a smile. Of course, I couldn't see it. I could only feel what Walters felt when his cheeks got light and the corners of his lips rose.

"It would make no sense to waste this technology on advertising," Walters told the grant writer in his mind. "Why sell the path to power? Why sell it to anyone? If you can get in, money is easy enough to get."

"How so?"

"You're a grant writer. You know this. If you can make a good enough suggestion, people will give you money. You only focus on the wealthy, the ones who are looking to donate anyway. But think of how much money people like televangelists have pulled out of the pocketbooks of the poor. Imagine you're me—a blind man. You could start The Frank Walters Institute for the Blind. Make it a for-profit corporation. Convince everyone to donate five or ten or twenty dollars to the institute."

"You could do that," I said. Because this had occurred to me. I had thought about sneaking into the endowment director's head and making sure that the deal went through. I'd opted not to. I'd like to say that I'd opted not to out of some kind of moral high ground, but I can't say that for certain. I probably just felt like the deal would go through anyway and pushing harder would likely quell things. Nothing kills a deal like a smack of desperation.

"You could do that and a whole lot more," Walters told the imaginary and not-so imaginary me.

"Like what?"

"You could influence anyone you want. You could sneak into the minds of the media moguls and make, say, Rupert Murdoch do your bidding. You could influence the decisions of the president or various congressmen. You could place yourself on the boards of several large corporations and run them. You could donate a few hours a night to it and end up running the world."

"Would you really want to?" I asked.

"Of course. Everyone wants to rule the world."

"I don't," I said.

"You're lying to yourself. You think you could do all this good. You think you could end starvation and create a more egalitarian society. You have all kinds of visions. Everyone does. And anyone who gets the chance to run it all will take it."

"I disagree," I said. "I just don't see where the joy would be in running things."

Frank Walters reached across the table, placed his hand on the cold wood. He grabbed his cane and swung it around him. He hit no obstacle. "Where are you?" he asked, out loud. "How did you get into my house?"

I took this as my cue to get the hell out of Frank Walters' mind.

I had made a big mistake. I tried to put a thought into Walters' head that he wasn't capable of generating himself. He had to know I'd been inside, which meant that he was only one or two inductive leaps away from realizing that Dr. Bishop had not only found a way into Mindland, she'd shown me how to get there, too. And so, there Frank Walters sat, eating his strawberry cheesecake ice cream and enjoying the moment before he laid down his major threat.

I took one more stab at disarming him. I said, "Do you ever watch movies about time machines?"

"I don't watch movies."

Which surprised me. Of course, he couldn't *watch* movies, but even people who can see don't just watch movies. They listen to them, too. But I guess for a guy like Walters, if he's going to listen to something, he'll listen to something that doesn't rely so heavily on visuals, like an audio book or something. So I changed my tack a bit. I said, "It's not just movies. There are books about time machines, too. And all of the stories about them wrestle with the same problems: if you're going to go back in time, you're going to change the present and perhaps even change it so much that you yourself will no longer exist. Or they talk about the problems of time and space being linked together. And so on. But there's one thing that they never seem to come right out and acknowledge: that there can be only one time machine."

Walters played along. He asked, "How do you mean?"

"If there's one time machine, you can go back in time and change things and make them better for yourself in the future, maybe. Or you can go back and place bets on sporting events that you know the outcome of. Or whatever. But if I have a time machine, too, I can go back and undo anything that you did. And if there are five or ten or a hundred time machines, then everyone would be going back and changing things and undoing what's been undone and the world would become so unstable that it would be unrecognizable."

"Okay," Walters said. "That makes sense."

A shaggy dog that was not Clint Dempsey and that had no visible master came up to me and sniffed my knee. I ran my fingers around his neck, searching for a collar. I didn't feel one. I set my ice cream cup on the ground near the bench. The dog dug his nose into the ice cream. I fought the urge to ask Walters about my dog.

"So you see what I'm saying?" I asked.

"I have no idea what you're doing. You're acting very brazen for a man as vulnerable as you are. You're buying ice cream and talking about time machines and wasting my time."

"No, this is about you," I said. "It's about the elephant sitting on this bench between us."

"Lola?" Walters asked. "Is Lola the elephant?"

I knew what he was up to—playing with my biggest fear, poking my most sensitive area. I volleyed that shot right back at him and said, "No. The elephant is not your nephew Connor, either."

This took Walters aback for a split second. He flinched. Then he said, "I'll bite. Explain what you're thinking."

I rubbed the dog's neck. He kept licking the scoop of ice cream. I didn't add anything to my time machine discussion. Maybe my hint was too vague for Walters. Maybe he couldn't follow the same thought process I'd followed. After all, he'd never been in my mind. Not like I'd been in his. So perhaps he couldn't make the inductive leap that I'd made: that the path into Mindland is like a time machine. It can only work if no more than one person can go in. A second person could keep undoing what the first person had done. More than two people would lead to way too much instability.

And if the second person wanted to use that technology to become immensely powerful, he'd need to eliminate the first person.

The second person in this scenario would be Frank Walters and the first person, of course, would be me.

Surely, at some level, Walters knew this. He knew that he'd have to kill me if he wanted to pull off any of his plans. At some level, he had to know that I knew this. I didn't explain myself to Walters. I just watched the dog lick the empty cup at my feet.

Walters finished his ice cream, set the cup on the bench next to him, and patted my knee. "Anyway," he said. "I just wanted to let you know that I know. Dr. Bishop found a way in. She showed it to you. And you crept into my mind just like she tried to."

I nodded but didn't say anything.

Walters waited a beat and added, "And I want you to know that I'll stop at nothing to find out what you know."

"Hell," I said. "You didn't need to come all the way up here just to tell me that."

30

Before there was an Ape Man, there was a twelve-year-old boy named Connor Jarred struggling through an awkward adolescence made more awkward by his parents' misbehavior. His mother had begun having an affair with a landscaper who lived in Costa Mesa. She'd visit the landscaper in the early afternoons, shortly after picking up Connor at school. She'd stop at an ice cream shop, buy Connor a sundae or a banana split, and leave him in her Mercedes station wagon while she whiled away an hour in the landscaper's half of a duplex. Connor knew exactly what they were doing in there. He may have been twelve, but he'd been introduced to sex. He'd come across a stash of magazines in the closet of his father's den and spent several hours studying every page; he'd stumbled across a box of pornographic betamax videotapes at a Santa Ana swap meet, paid ten bucks for the bundle, and set up his parents' old betamax player in his bedroom; he'd further benefited from late-night cable. So, although Connor knew little about depths of emotion and complexities inherent in the act, he was aware of the basic mechanics— or at least how they're performed for a camera—and of the basic lies told to engage in those acts. He said nothing to anyone and ate his ice cream.

Despite Connor's silence, his father was not unaware of his wife's infidelities. He was prevented from taking the higher ground on extramarital affairs, however, as long as he continued to pay the rent on his girlfriend's apartment in Santa Ana. He could take the higher ground when it came to his son, who was becoming more and more of a disappointment to him every day. Not only was Connor a goofy kid with all his freckles and his mop of red hair cut short in the front and dangling down to his shoulders in back and his awkward limbs gotten more gangly from a recent growth spurt, but all the damn ice cream had taken him beyond the point of pudgy that could be stretched out when he shot up taller. Plus the whiteheads were bubbling up on the surface of Connor's skin like a pox. Connor's father did what he thought was best for his son. He started picking Connor up from school and leaving him in the car outside a Santa Ana apartment building.

Waiting out his father's infidelities was worse for Connor than waiting out his mother's. The lack of ice cream was far from the chief consideration. His parents' unraveling marriage wasn't even the problem. As Connor would learn in the subsequent years, the ball of hate that held his parents together was far too large to ever unravel completely. Extramarital affairs were like foreplay to them. What really bothered the twelve-year-old Connor on those Santa Ana afternoons was the neighborhood he'd been dropped in. Waiting in the car with the windows rolled up and the doors locked was not an option. The first time he'd tried that, a group of local kids had kicked at the passenger door, taunting Connor, shaking the car, and leaving the door panel looking like a relief map of the moon. Connor's father would not stand for it. He told Connor, "I don't care how many of them there are. Next time, you get off your ass and fight for yourself and my car." When Connor resisted this suggestion, his father added, "If you don't, I'll make your face look like my car door."

So Connor learned to fight, usually against older kids, usually two or three of them at a time. He burned off the ice cream weight of his mother's affairs in a barrage of side-armed punches and fistfuls of hair. Gradually, he learned how to straighten his punches, twist his wrist at impact to tear the skin of his opponent. He learned weak points and the power of kicking and holds that would cause others to submit. He also learned that the fights could be endless. Every day. If the neighborhood kids didn't come to him outside his father's girlfriend's apartment, he'd go to them, wandering up the hill to the park behind the middle school, finding groups of three or four kids in their school uniforms, finding any pretense to drag grass stains onto their blue polyester pants, to spread blood—his or theirs, it didn't matter—on to those button-up, short sleeve white shirts. It usually ended with Connor curled up on the grass, absorbing a flurry of kicks from black patent leather shoes.

This was where I came in. Or, at least a twelve-year-old version of me, looking strikingly like a thirty-seven-year-old version of me, only smaller.

I walked through the smog of a Santa Ana afternoon, across the speckled browns and greens of the park, among smatterings of bald white men with sleeve tattoos and forties of Mickeys malt liquor and adolescents in school uniforms and skateboarders grinding the edge of a low wall and empty concrete park benches and pick-up basketball games where the players lacked the definitive element of nets to determine whether or not the ball really had gone through the hoop. Three kids formed a half-circle around Connor. He held his fists just above his eye level and kept his forearms high, having learned that it's quicker and easier to drop your arms to protect your stomach than to raise them to protect your head. I stepped into the middle of the circle before the first punch was thrown. I looked first at the three kids gathered around Connor and said, "You'll fight another day, guys."

To Connor's amazement, they actually listened to me, gradually backing away until they felt it was safe to turn and walk off. Connor stayed in fighting position. I pointed at a white Jaguar with a fully repaired passenger door panel as it drove down the side street adjacent to the park. The right turn signal began to blink. Connor watched the car swing onto a main street that led to the freeway. It was not the first time his father had abandoned Connor in Santa Ana. Typically, he would then have to find a pay phone, call his mom, and fight all comers in the park until his mom arrived, usually an hour later.

Connor dropped his arms. "I gotta call my mom," he said.

"Come with me," I said.

Connor followed. We strolled past the gang of skins and their huge bottles of Mickeys, past the skateboarders, past the school kids. Though all three groups had approached Connor before, though he'd fought all of them and lost and lived to fight them and lose to them again, none of the groups cast him so much as a glance while he walked with me. Connor kept his hackles up.

I led him out of the park and down the hill toward the main drag.

The neighborhood was alive with people lifting weights in their front yard or buried under the hoods of their sputtering American cars or digging weeds out of a tiny tomato patch or scattering feed into the cages of fighting roosters in that unique blend of rural leftovers and urban main dish that Connor never tasted in the repeating cul-de-sacs of his Irvine housing development.

I pointed toward the tiny yard in front of a square yellow house thick with stucco, shaded by a red tile roof. Two black and tan Lakeland terriers ran up to the chainlink fence bordering the sidewalk. They faced us and their mouths yapped, but no sound came from them. I leaned against the bus stop bench, facing the terriers. Connor fell in line next to me. We both watched the silent yapping mouths.

"According to the story I heard," I said, "these dogs barked so much at bus riders that their owners had their voice boxes removed."

Connor stared at the dogs. They struggled to bark and failed to produce any sound that could be heard over the scraping of metal and concrete from the skateboarders, the sounds of basketballs rattling off backboards, the rumbling of nine million cars chugging through this mass of Southern California sprawl. "Why didn't any of those guys fight you?" Connor finally asked.

"If you genuinely want power, you don't fight," I told him. "No one in power fights. You either get someone else to fight for you, or you think your way out of a situation."

Connor looked around this neighborhood so foreign to him. "Who around here would fight for me?"

"No one."

"So what am I supposed to do?"

"Think," I said. I shook my thumb in the general direction of the bus stop sign behind me. It glistened like a white pebble on a full-moon night. "Think, why should I fight for territory if I could just leave it? Think about Hansel and Gretel, how they found their way out of the woods. If they had been able to stick to stones, they never would've had to fight the witch. And you don't even need the stones. You have bus signs on every block. They're set in concrete. No birds will peck them away. You can forever follow them back to Irvine."

Connor's glance pinballed from the silent dogs to me to the approaching OCTA bus. He said no more than the terriers. I handed him a dollar. "Give this to the bus driver and ask her how to get back home. She'll guide you."

Connor took the dollar. I wandered off.

When the bus finally dropped him off down the block from his house, his father's Jaguar and his mother's Mercedes were parked in the driveway. He unlocked the front door and walked into a chorus of groans and dirty talk. Apparently, his father's affairs reminded his mother that she'd always gone for the bad boys. Connor sat among the sounds of sex feeling like the bouncy red gym ball that his parents flung at each other in a game with rules he couldn't understand. He wished he were back at the Santa Ana park, throwing arms at whoever would fight him.

Of course, there were problems with this memory that I'd stuck in the Ape Man's mind. The biggest of these being that I didn't know Connor when he was twelve years old, and five hundred miles separated my Folsom adolescence from his Santa Ana afternoons. These problems didn't concern me, though. Human memory is fickle and malleable. Our imagination fills the gaps that reason can't reconcile. I knew that all I had to do was gather enough of the fragments hidden in the dusky closets of Ape Man's unconscious to create a story that he'd believe. And it was important to insert myself in the story. To show Ape Man not only that I'd done good deeds for him in the past, but that I could be trusted. I could help him, even.

For my purposes, the facts of the past were insignificant compared to the story I could make him believe about it. And, if I'm going to be honest about this, my motives weren't strictly calculated. I wanted to torment him. I wanted him to feel the pain that I felt every time my left hand ached to toss a ball for Clint Dempsey. So I fed him this memory. I made sure the kids he fought were white and that he lost to them every time and that I was the only person who could save him.

I planted this memory in his head so that he'd trust me because I'm as flawed and prone to petty schemes as the rest of my species. And because that asshole either killed my dog or took him and wouldn't give him back.

31

I stopped by Lola's apartment unexpected and caught her painting. I hadn't seen much of her process, but apparently she liked to work on several paintings at once. Some canvases were stretched on the floor, some half-finished but hanging on the wall, and five standing on easels with no stools in front. The apartment was tiny, three hundred square feet at most, and that included the kitchen, bathroom, and closet. It looked cluttered at first. A second glance showed that it wasn't cluttered at all. Everything was set up for maximum movement between paintings. Nothing that wasn't used for painting lived in the apartment. There wasn't even a chair to sit on.

Lola squatted over the canvas on the floor in the posture of a little kid inspecting an anthill. She smiled up to me but didn't stop painting. "What's up?" she asked.

I never came by Lola's apartment. I typically let it be her space. But on this day, I wanted to deal with something before it became a problem. There was an ethical gray area shadowing me. It had to do with Lola and Dr. Benengeli. I'd become friends with Dr. Benengeli at the same time that Lola and I had become lovers, but the relationships were mutually exclusive. The three of us hadn't spent time together since that long-ago afternoon of finger painting on psych hospital picnic tables. I wanted to change that.

I told her that I had tickets to go down to Los Angeles that weekend and see a production of *Waiting for Godot*. "A big hospital donor's son is the director," I said. "When she called to tell me about it, I bought tickets."

"How much did she donate to the hospital?"

"Enough for the hospital to buy out all the seats for the entire run of the play and not miss the money. But that's not how charities work."

Lola bit her lip and stared down. She was clearly thinking. I doubted her thoughts were about the play or the donor. She looked at her paintbrush. She stood, walked to a canvas on the wall, and worked that color into the scene. As she did this, she said, "You should take Dr. Benengeli."

"We can. I have four tickets."

Lola kept painting. "You know it's a two-hour play where nothing happens, don't you?"

"I read it," I said. "I've never seen it."

"Not only does nothing happen in the first act, but the same nothing happens in the second act."

"You don't have to go, if you don't want."

Lola's paintbrush dried out on the canvas on the wall. She went back to her palette and her canvas on the floor, squatting over it like she was building sandcastles. "I want to go," she said. "I love the play. I just wanted to make sure you knew."

Four of us rode down to LA in Dr. Benengeli's car. As soon as Lola and I got in the back seat, Dr. Benengeli went through the introduction. She said, "Lola, this is my partner, Marcela."

Marcela rode shotgun. Lola sat directly behind her. She smiled and scooted forward to shake Marcela's hand. She asked, "What kind of partnership? Do you have a private practice or something?"

I touched Lola's shoulder gently, feeling the soft cotton shirt stretched tightly over the curve. I shook my head.

Lola caught on. "Oh," she said. "You're a couple." She pointed a forefinger at her temple and made a goofy noise that sounded somewhere between a gunshot and a Bronx salute. "And here all this time I thought Dr. Benengeli was moving in on my man."

"She is," Marcela said.

Dr. Benengeli smiled. She glanced at me through the rearview mirror and winked. "The both of us are."

"Stop, you two," Lola said. "You're going to get the poor guy excited."

I leaned back in my seat. So it was going to be that kind of night.

Much of the ride down consisted of teasing me because I thought a play in Hollywood would be a fancy affair. I'd even started ironing a shirt. Lola loved this information. Dr. Benengeli and Marcela got a laugh out of it. Lola had told me that I was okay in what I was wearing, which was only a pair of Dickies and a long sleeve t-shirt with the name and logo of a punk rock record label on it. I wasn't quite the hipster the three women in the car were. I was the only one who didn't know that a playhouse in Hollywood would be more of a warehouse on a back street where I could pick up some crystal meth before the performance if I so chose, and where Dr. Benengeli would be sure to not only lock her car but put an anti-theft device on the steering wheel. Jokes at my expense stretched all the way down to Agoura Hills.

Very early in the play, I had to stop myself from crying. It had nothing to do with the razzing I'd gotten on the ride down. I'd actually enjoyed that. It helped me understand something about therapeutic relationships. I'd figured something weird would hang in the air between Dr. Benengeli and Lola because Dr. Benengeli had run a couple of group therapy sessions that Lola attended. But there was nothing there. They acted perfectly natural with each other, about as free as I would act if I went to a play with the physical therapist who massaged my neck back into shape after I got whiplash.

The tears trying to sneak their way out of my eyes had everything to do with the play. It was during a scene between the two main characters, Vladimir and Estragon. Vladimir asked Estragon if he'd read the Bible. Estragon admitted he'd only looked at the pictures, specifically the map. The pale blue of the Dead Sea was so beautiful. He thought they could've honeymooned there. Something about the wistfulness of the way the actor said it got me a little choked up.

By the second act, all four of us seemed to be having a different experience with the play. Dr. Benengeli was fuming. She'd whispered to us between acts that the director had it all wrong, that the play was supposed to be funnier. Vladimir and Estragon should be clowns, she said. Like Laurel and Hardy, she said. "Not all sad and dramatic like they're both goddamn Hamlet!" Her whisper to us sounded more like a stage whisper. A few other patrons shot a dagger or two in her direction.

Lola wasn't bothered by the way the actors took on the roles. She sat in her chair with her back rigid, leaning forward a little as if she wanted to scoot down right to the front edge of the stage and become a part of the show. Marcela wasn't bothered, either. In fact, the performance relaxed her so much that she nestled into a long nap. And as for me, well, I was crying.

It was a stifled, repressed cry. Slow, fat tears slipping out of ducts for the first time since I was a little kid. I couldn't stop them. There was just something about Vladimir and Estragon—Didi and Gogo, as they call each other—that had so much familiarity behind them. The way they talked was a whole other form of communication. The words came out like caresses. The meaning of individual words wasn't as important as the sense that the words hummed a kind reassurance, a kind of way of saying, "We share this life together. Whatever voids we face, whatever emptiness surrounds us, it's okay. Even if life seems meaningless, your life means something to me." Didi and Gogo showed love in the long term, which was something I never saw on stage or in books. Love stories are almost always about beginnings or endings. There's never one right in the middle. Except for this one.

I watched the two actors talk of nothing, talk of waiting, talk of leaving while staying still, talk of pain and desire. In a very sad way, it made me think of what I lost when my marriage ended: that comfort and caress that takes years—decades, lifetimes—to build. So there I was, the most absurd person in this Theater of the Absurd, crying in a production of *Waiting for Godot*.

Maybe the worst part about it all was Frank Walters sitting in the back row, off to my right. The Ape Man sat next to him, keeping him apprised of each fat, pitiful tear.

At least the drive home was more pleasant. Lola and Dr. Benengeli spent the time talking about the actor who played Godot, and how great it was when he finally hit the stage. To my surprise, Marcela acted as if she hadn't been asleep, and agreed with Lola and Dr. Benengeli.

Marcela said, "Yeah. Godot was my favorite character, too. That actor was so charming." This just inspired them more. They kept coming up with increasingly outlandish scenes starring Godot, and Marcela kept going along with it. Part of me wanted to tell Marcela that they were pulling her leg, that there is no Godot, that he never shows up. Lola and Dr. Benengeli were having so much fun that I couldn't stop them.

I just smiled and watched the freeway lights as we hurtled northward toward home.

32

The day after the play, Dr. Bishop checked into a medical hospital for what would be, in all likelihood, her last time. She left Eric in charge of putting her office affairs in order. Eric asked me to help him. I agreed.

I swung by Dr. Bishop's office at the end of my workday. Eric sat in Dr. Bishop's big leather chair, running papers through an industrial-sized shredder. Clear plastic bags full of shredded paper surrounded him. He looked at me and looked at the bags. "It's hard to believe," he said. "A whole life's work."

I nodded.

"You mind taking them out to the dumpster?"

I nodded again. I grabbed four bags full of shredded paper, two in each hand, and turned to leave the room.

"Wait," Eric said. He stood from the chair. "Let's leave this here and break down the lab."

I set down the bags and headed into the lab, which was adjacent to Dr. Bishop's office.

The squirrels had been released back into their clearing. The wires had been removed from their cages. The cages were gone, though I don't know where. On a plain, gray table in the northeast corner of the lab sat several flattened boxes, tape, bubble-wrap, and fifty or so surveillance cameras. Eric walked toward this table. I followed him. "I have to ask," I said. "Where on earth did you and your mom get fifty surveillance cameras?"

"Left over from the scandal," Eric said.

"Then I have to ask a second question. What was the scandal?"

"You don't know?" Eric picked up the first camera and started wrapping it in bubble-wrap.

"Nope. I have no idea."

"Where were you living? Under a rock?"

"Fresno," I said. I followed Eric's movements, wrapping up a camera of my own.

"And you didn't see anything about it?"

I shrugged. I thought about why I hadn't heard of the scandal at Winfield. It had occurred about eight years earlier, so I ran the mental rewind to that year and what I had been paying attention to. Because I'd been working at that community space, Fresno community issues mattered a lot to me then. I'd stayed apprised of those. Because the community space also had a small bookstore that helped keep us alive, I was aware of some international issues. I knew where everyone stood in the slicing up of Yugoslavia. I knew about ethnic Albanians and Serbs in Kosovo and atrocities in Bosnia and the US/NATO bombings of hospitals and schools and the Chinese embassy in Sarajevo. But I knew nothing about the closing of a private university a few hundred miles away. I thought about why the scandal had escaped me. "I guess I just didn't pay attention," I said. "I didn't know anyone who went to school here."

"What about Lola?"

"I was ten years out of touch with Lola by then."

Eric nodded. "It's a long story," he said. "I'll try to give you the short version.

"We had a chancellor at Winfield, a real piece of work. He cut tenure for all the professors, started firing the ones who were at the top of the salary range and replacing them with younger part-timers. He busted the union for all us service workers. Refused to negotiate with us. Fired everyone and said he'd only hire us back as independent contractors. And you know what that means. No benefits, no insurance, shit pay." Eric shook his head.

"Did you go back?"

"I'm no scab. It was the only year of my adult life when I didn't work on these grounds. So I wasn't here for the scandal, but I saw it coming. If you're gonna piss off everyone like this chancellor did, you better clear all them skeletons out of your closet first. And the chancellor left this big, ugly skeleton right there. Left the light on in his closet, too."

I took one of the flattened boxes, folded and taped it into shape, and packed into the box the four cameras Eric and I had prepared. I picked up another camera. Eric kept wrapping and talking.

"A few years before he busted all the unions, he'd hired two maintenance guys to install surveillance cameras in the dorms. But only in the women's dorms, and only in the places where it was clear what he wanted to use those cameras for. He taped a bunch of the girls taking showers and sleeping with their boyfriends and… Well, not *sleeping* with their boyfriends. But you know what I mean. He built his own little library of naked undergrads. Only when he fired everyone in our union, he fired the two guys he'd hired to install those cameras. They were part of the union, too. Then he hired those two back as scabs, but for lower wages. Those guys got pissed and showed the campus police where all the cameras were. The chancellor had busted the campus police's union, too, which pissed off not only the campus officers, but it pissed off the county police force because those guys are all union and they didn't want a non-union shop in their county. So, *bam*." Eric snapped his fingers. "Those two guys sang, all the cameras came out of their hiding places, investigators found the chancellor's video vault. Shit hit the fan. It was nuts."

Eric lifted his baseball cap, ran his leathery fingers through his gray-blond hair. "You should've seen that vault," he said. "It was a big room, the size of a bedroom. Fifteen feet by fifteen feet, maybe. No windows. Floor-to-ceiling shelves full of videotapes. Eight years of videos. Eight years of girls taking showers and college kids fucking. Supposedly, he liked to watch girls use the bathroom, too. But who knows? The only things in the room besides the videotapes were a TV, a VCR, and a leather chair."

"Wow," I said.

"No kidding." Eric packed one camera into the box and started wrapping the next. "Anyway, the police called the local paper. They sent a photographer out to take pictures of the room. Rumor has it he stuck a box of tissues by the leather chair before he took the photo. I don't know if it's true. I know there was a box of tissues in the picture. I just don't know who put it there. Regardless, it was a huge scandal. Kids were upset. Parents were upset. A bunch of parents sued the school and won. The university declared bankruptcy. It was a mess."

"What happened to the chancellor?"

"Nothing, really," Eric said. "You know the story. Rich people don't go to jail. He got probation or a suspended sentence or something like that. He's down in LA now, vice president of something at some big corporation."

I shook my head. "I can't believe he didn't give those two guys enough money to keep their mouths shut."

"He was a cheap bastard. His bribe didn't even add up to the amount of money he'd cut their pay. So they took the bribe and ratted him out, anyway."

"Good for them."

Eric shook his head. "They were fuckers. They should've been arrested, too. They never should've installed those cameras to begin with. What's the saying? 'Better the blind man who pisses out the window than the knowing servant who raises it for him.'"

"Is that a saying?" I asked.

Eric laughed. "Sure. Why not?"

I sealed the first box, which was now full of cameras, and built the second box. Eric and I kept wrapping, packing, boxing.

That night, I had to take a deeper look into the chancellor. Well, I didn't *have* to. I wanted to. The more time I spent in Mindland, the better I became at rationalizing. I'd want to, say, snoop around the chancellor's unconscious thoughts, so I'd tell myself that the chancellor would help me understand the mind of the wealthy. Which, to be honest, I couldn't understand at all. I couldn't think in terms of yachts or Swiss watches or whatever wealthy people think in terms of, which probably isn't even yachts and Swiss watches. So the chancellor would help me understand what was so great about all this wealth, why people wanted it so badly, why Walters was willing to kill me to get at it. At least that's what I told myself. I also told myself that these rationalizations were fine as long as I didn't start believing them in earnest.

After I'd completed my business in Mindland, I stuck around to have some fun. I called out the chancellor's name. I was whipped back into the basement of the Williams Building. A dull yellow bulb shone above the room of the chancellor's thoughts. He's a good enough place to start. He's probably sleeping. I can probably watch his dreams a little. I liked doing that: watching dreams. It had that same kind of mindlessness that watching television has, only dreams aren't trying to sell me anything. I figured it was a nice enough way to round out this trip into Mindland.

I followed the steps to the basement, entered a room under a dull yellow bulb, and slid inside the chancellor's dreams. Which, as it turned out, were nightmares.

Nightmares are scariest when they're our own. They're catered to our particular fears and obsessions. Watching someone else's nightmares isn't unlike watching a Luis Buñuel film, only faster. Men morph into little girls, monsters appear and devour, the dreamer fails to run or throw a punch, fails to escape situations that get exponentially worse, and it all happens at such a breakneck speed that a scene is replaced as soon as it appears.

And so went the chancellor's nightmares. Worse and worse until he woke up alone and sweating. I watched him get out of bed, walk to his bathroom, and wash his face. Despite the nightmares, the guy had clearly landed on his feet. His bedroom was nearly the size of my apartment. All his furniture was handmade from hardwoods. Even his pajamas were silk. Before I could catch myself, I mumbled, "Man, if you want to get rid of these nightmares, you should start giving back to the people you harmed."

He dried his face and said aloud to his reflection in the mirror. "I should give back to the people I harmed."

At this point, I could have left matters alone. I did not. I kept whispering into his mind. "Use your corporation," I said. "Start a foundation for artists. Make Lola Diaz, the girl who painted the murals in McCabe Hall, the first recipient of the fellowship."

The chancellor walked back to his king-size bed and crawled into it alone. "Hmm," he said. "Lola Diaz." And he drifted off to sleep.

I stuck around to watch another nightmare.

Not to get too far ahead of my tale, but sure enough, two weeks after this night, Lola got a letter in the mail from the chancellor. His corporation had created a fund for artists, and she would receive the first fellowship. According to the letter, the idea had come to the chancellor in a dream. And how much was this fellowship for? Just about the amount you would expect a wealthy man to pay to assuage his nightmares.

When Lola showed me the letter, I smiled and hugged her. But, really, it took another ten minutes before I stopped shaking.

33

It was hard not to snoop. It really was. When Dr. Bishop showed me the way into this world, she filled my life with temptations that I would've rather not battled. Suddenly, I had power. Suddenly, I could sneak into people's minds and control their actions. On the one hand, like Walters said, I could convince myself that I could use this technology for good, but I didn't really believe that. Everyone who gets power falls for that same rationalization: that they know what's best for everyone, that they may be manipulating people a little bit, sure, but it's for the greater good.

I couldn't forget that we have a word to describe the act of taking away people's power to make their own decisions, of manipulating people to act against their own free will. It's called tyranny. It's never for the greater good.

So, of course, the easiest thing for me to do would've been to stay out of Mindland altogether. Walters had forced my hand, though. I couldn't stay out. I had to learn how to wield this technology at least well enough to ward off Walters. I had to keep going in.

And while I was there, it was hard not to snoop. I really wanted to know some things that were none of my business. Like, for example, was Lola part of the Winfield scandal? Had the chancellor been soiling his tissues to the image of Lola and some college beau having sex in front of a security camera? Had that tape gotten out? Was this one of the ghosts haunting Lola? And what exactly had her father done to her? How did he do it? How much? All of these things poked at my curiosity and insecurities, and I wanted to know. And Lola's mind was just a holler and a dull yellow light bulb and a trip to the Williams basement away.

Still, I couldn't do it. I had to respect Lola. Above everyone else, I had to respect her.

I did snoop a little, of course. I couldn't help myself. On my seventh or eighth trip into Mindland, I emerged from the footlocker and hollered the name of my old buddy in the ad industry, Brandon Burch. I figured he'd be an easy enough target. He wouldn't recognize me in his brain; I wouldn't find anything too compromising. It would all be innocent enough.

Down in the Williams basement, I found Brandon sitting on a leather couch in the kind of bachelor pad that middle-aged men have when they have plenty of money and no particular sense of style. His couch covered one whole wall of the condo, turned the corner, and filled another half of a wall. It was puffy and too dark to harbor any real stains. Brandon's feet were propped up on a black, glass-topped coffee table. He flipped through the channels until he got to a commercial advertising videos of drunk young women who raised their tops for the camera. He stopped there and watched for a minute.

I'd expected to find him sleeping. I guess insomnia was a virus running through the advertising industry. I sat cautiously on a puffy armchair that matched the puffy couch. I didn't say anything. With Walters, I'd learned one lesson about talking to a conscious person in Mindland. With the chancellor, I'd learned another lesson. I listened for Brandon's thoughts. I was surprised to find him ruminating on death.

Someone he'd worked with—a mentor, I gathered—had recently died. The funeral was in two days. Brandon thought about the funeral and thoughts horrifying to Brandon lingered just below these surface meditations. I delved beneath his surface, listened to his fears that he would end up like his mentor, that he *was* ending up like his mentor: alone in a two-bedroom condo with one empty bedroom and wood floors that always felt cold under his bare feet and a bunch of doors that separated rooms for no reason because it wasn't like anyone else ever came to this apartment ever. A sadness lingered in Brandon, flashing into his vision like the head in a Whac-A-Mole game destined to reemerge from a new hole every time Brandon took the hammer and smacked it down. And Brandon had stopped hammering the mole a long time ago.

He just flipped the channels and meditated on the flashing lights of his huge flat-screen TV and tried to forget the days when he first started working in advertising—a failing musician with a new day job and the rationalization that he'd only do the day job until the new band and the move to Los Angeles all panned out for him; a guy who, after all, really could play his guitar well and actually did know how to sing and could pen little jingles that crept into people's brains and repeated themselves regardless of attempts to dislodge the tune; a guy who wrote a jingle for a big box store's ad campaign, a jingle so incessant, so tormenting that even Brandon couldn't get out of his head. Below all of this in Brandon's insomniac mind was the fear that he feared the most: that he had become the person he'd always hated. That he'd hated this person for good reasons: because what little imagination and creativity he had was for sale, because what he bought with the money he made selling his talent was more or less worthless to him, because he had one chance to ride this rock around the sun for seventy or so circles and he was squandering that chance chasing ends that were ultimately unsatisfying. Now, Brandon couldn't help mourning the death of the man who'd led him into this world. And the funeral was in two days.

So much for snooping.

The next day, I called Brandon from my office in the psych hospital. He picked up the phone and said, "Oak View State Psychiatric Hospital."

"Yes, sir, this is Oak View," I said. "We'll be sending a couple of our associates to speak to you today. You'll recognize them by their white coats. It's in your best interest to just do what they say."

"You'll never take me alive."

"The hell with it," I said, breaking character. "You're too crazy for this place, anyway."

Brandon laughed a quick, insincere laugh. "What are you really calling about?"

"I'm heading to Los Angeles tomorrow. Burbank, actually. I thought maybe we could meet up, grab lunch, something."

"I have to go to a funeral tomorrow afternoon."

"Who died?"

"Some fucker," Brandon said. "No one."

"Is the funeral anywhere near Burbank?"

"It's in Burbank. Forest Lawn Cemetery. Why? Wanna come?"

"Sure," I said. That was the whole idea behind my call in the first place. I had no other business in Burbank beyond being with a friend at a funeral. "Can you pick me up at the Burbank train station?"

"Figures you'd be the only one in the world to come into Los Angeles without a car. What time does the train come in?"

I checked the schedule and gave Brandon the time. He told me he'd be there.

The train was delayed for forty-five minutes outside of Simi Valley. The police there had chased two kids into the train tunnel. The juveniles and the police were engaged in an armed standoff. At least that's what the conductor had announced. I waited in my seat, surrounded by boxy apartment buildings and the faux old train station, by the dry brush and jagged hills of the valley beyond. I had a Japanese paperback with me. It was all about a lonely guy searching for a lost pinball machine. I got so wrapped up in the novel that I forgot about the police pursuit, the fear I had of Simi Valley policemen—Simi Valley being where the jury acquitted the policemen who beat Rodney King, after all—and the kids in the tunnel, the train delay, the upcoming funeral, everything. I followed this lost Japanese guy and his quixotic pursuit and felt like I was right there with him. Or more accurately, I felt like I *was* him. Together, we stumbled and weaved around the labyrinth in our minds. We groped blindly for meaning. He told me that good questions have no answers. I found a little comfort in that.

I got so lost in that book that I didn't notice the train moving again. I barely looked up as the valley gave way to warehouses, sound stages, box stores, freeways, dry riverbanks, burrito stands, and gas stations. If I hadn't finished the book before reaching the Burbank station, I may have kept riding right past it. As things stood, I looked up in time to exit the train and catch sight of Brandon, arms crossed, framed by the Burbank airport, poised to attack me for still not having a car. I slid my paperback into my backpack and walked across the platform. Brandon didn't move.

He was decked out in a black suit. With the suit, his sunglasses, and his bald head, he looked like a federal agent. Still, old habits are hard to break, so I said to him, "Fester!"

A smile shattered his countenance. He stuck out his hand to shake mine. I grabbed his hand and pulled him close for a hug.

"Good to see the train's running on time as usual," Brandon said. He pointed toward his car. We started walking.

I told him about the police showdown in Simi Valley.

"Fuck it," Brandon said. "At least we got to skip the church service." He pushed a remote control and unlocked the doors of his Lexus sedan. I climbed into the passenger side. He climbed into the driver's side and started the car.

"Sorry about making you miss that."

"Are you kidding? Apologizing because you made me miss church? Shit. I should thank you."

We pulled out of the parking lot and Brandon drove us to Forest Lawn cemetery. Our conversation was stilted and groping, the way conversations tend to be with old friends who haven't seen each other for a while, old friends who have become strangers.

We got to the cemetery behind the hearse, but apparently within a minute or two of the procession. Groups of single men, all in black suits, drifted over to a tent and some chairs positioned around an open grave. Brandon and I left the car and drifted into these flows. I watched the faces of the men. No one seemed particularly bereaved. I caught snatches of dirty jokes, talk of the company's open bar after the funeral, comments expressing the desire for a short service. Someone behind me said, "I hope they plant this bastard quick. My kid's got a little league game tonight."

Brandon winced at these words. It was a tiny wince that came and went in the span of time it takes for a hummingbird to flap his wings. I was polite enough to act like I didn't notice. We circled around the open grave. The priest said a few generic words and read a psalm. No one cried. The casket was lowered into the ground. I watched it gradually descend and felt bad for Brandon and realized that my coming here, my masquerading as a friend even though he and I hadn't really been friends for years, was as quixotic as every other effort that I'd made to make the world a better place. The fact that no one seemed to care put a finer point on it all.

After the crowd left for their little league games and open bars, Brandon and I wandered around the cemetery. Brandon had been there several times before, apparently. He offered to show me the graves of Lucille Ball, Freddie Prinze, Liberace, Marvin Gaye. I declined to see them all. One tombstone was just like another. We walked across the plush grass, sweating in our black suits, talking about little bits of nothing. Brandon asked me if I was still married, a question that always bugged me when I was still married because it seemed to have such a sense of doom. It seemed to imply that marriage wasn't at all what it pretended to be. The question bugged me even more when he asked it, and I wasn't still married. It had an I-told-you-so quality to it. I swallowed my pride, though, and said, "Nope. We got divorced a few months back."

"Seeing anyone new?"

"Yeah."

"Did you meet her in the nuthouse?"

"Yeah."

"Was she an inmate?"

"A patient. But, yes."

Brandon looked to see if I was kidding. When he saw I wasn't, he said, "You always did go for the train wreck girls, didn't you?"

I nodded. Even when I'd been married, I'd get little crushes on an occasional woman in my life. The crushes were nothing I had any intention of acting on. They'd just blossom and wilt in my chest. And once the flower of the crush had withered down to dried potpourri, I'd realize that I always did fall for the girls with the biggest piles of baggage. I think that realization kept me married longer than I otherwise would've been. I felt like, if not my wife, I'd just be with some other tormented woman and her purse full of painful memories.

I didn't like Brandon pointing this out, but it was fair game. After I'd wandered into his mind and eavesdropped, it was only right that he point things out that I tried to keep below the surface of my own conscious thoughts.

We kept wandering among the tombstones. I idly read the names. They meant little to me. A parade of lives that didn't really touch mine. Just as my tombstone will probably mean nothing to most people who see it whenever that day comes. It'll just be an empty name and a couple of dates. And that's if I even get a tombstone at all, now that they've gone the way of the telegraph. I almost tripped over Bobby Fuller's grave marker and stopped there. "Wait a minute," I said. "Is this *the* Bobby Fuller? The 'I Fought the Law' guy?"

"Really?" Brandon said. "Scatman Crothers means nothing to you, but Bobby Fuller is impressive?"

"It's a great song."

Brandon decided to sit down in the grass there. I sat there, too. Brandon told me the story of Bobby Fuller's death, about how it may have been a murder. I knew nothing about it. I just knew his songs. I listened to Brandon's story. For a second, I flashed back to the days of Pop Culture and the References, the days spent on the road, the fights and the stories, all the songs we played and floors we slept on and beers we drank. It seemed like a whole other life, a world away from where we were now: a middle-aged grant writer and a middle-aged copywriter in our funeral suits.

Brandon finished his story. Daylight hung around us, obscured through the yellow smog, enriched by the plush lawn, twinkling off the metal grave markers. I said, "What do you think of when you think of Cincinnati?"

"One asshole of a city," Brandon said. "Why?"

"Do you remember a show we played there?"

Brandon gazed off down the hill, the gears of his mind trying to churn out a memory. I waited. He said, "Vaguely. A crappy warehouse. No one came. Was that Cincinnati?"

I shrugged.

Brandon gave a little laugh. "I guess that could've been about ten cities, huh?"

I nodded.

"What do you think of when you think of Cincinnati?" Brandon asked.

"You and Pop were fighting. I wandered off on my own and bought a Stiff Little Fingers record. The girl from the record store was really pretty. She came out to the show and danced to every song. It felt to me like the best show we ever played."

"Cincinnati, huh? Was the girl a cute, chubby little chick? Big round face?"

"Yeah," I said, getting a little excited. "Do you remember?"

"Nah," Brandon said. "I just figure that, if you dug her, she had to be a little chubby chick with a big round face."

"So you don't remember that show?"

"No."

"Not at all?"

"Not at all. That memory exists for you and you alone."

I plucked a few strands of grass and let them flutter away in the wind. "So what if I forget about it? What happens to that part of the past?"

Brandon stood and brushed off the seat of his pants. "Come on," he said. "I don't have time for these stupid fucking questions. The agency is springing for free drinks."

The agency, as it turned out, was Dickinson and Associates. It was Frank Walters' company. And the guy who died was Walters' second in command on the fifteenth floor. I saw Walters briefly at the reception. If Walters knew I was there, he didn't give any indication.

Ape Man knew I was there. He spent half the afternoon staring at Brandon and me.

34

Lola was in my apartment when I got home from work. She had just gotten out of the shower. Her hair was still wet. She wore white clamdiggers and a camisole. Camisole was a word that Lola had taught me. A few weeks earlier—actually, it was the day after my first trip into Mindland—I had asked Lola, "What do you call these shirts that you're always wearing?"

"They're not shirts," she'd said. "They're camisoles."

And from that point on, I could think about Lola more accurately instead of thinking, 'Wow, Lola looks great in that shirt,' which was all wrong because the word "shirt" made me picture a t-shirt. Lola looked great in a t-shirt, too. But it was the wrong image for my head. I wanted to picture the loose, silky tops she wore. The ones that had the thin straps dividing the line between her nape and her shoulders. The ones that showed off the pale skin below her neck and between her breasts. The ones that really made me think, 'Wow, she looks great in that.' The camisole.

This camisole Lola wore was a soft purple, the color of a grape juice stain that has faded on your white t-shirt after the fifteenth or twentieth time in the laundry. She still carried her towel and dried the ends of her hair. I brought a couple of bags into the kitchen and set a pot half-full of water on the stove to boil. Lola sat in a kitchen chair. "You're cooking tonight?"

"Spinach lasagna," I said. I took the groceries out of the bag, lined them up on the counter, took out a cutting board, and started on the garlic. Lola watched me. I could see bits of paint in the grooves of her knuckles. "What were you working on today?"

"Mostly on that same painting. The one on the floor. I'm calling it *Untitled #2*."

"What's the first *Untitled*?"

"There is no first *Untitled*. But that's just such a beginner's-sounding title. I don't like it. It makes me feel like I'm on my first painting ever."

"But *Untitled #2* doesn't make you feel like you're on your second painting ever?"

"It does. That's why I always use that title until I'm finished with the painting. It always gives me that great feeling that I'm on a second time around." Lola folded her towel and hung it on the back of the chair next to her. She tucked her hair behind her ears. "It's like, I don't know. It's like, the first time you do something, it's always a jumbled mess. You don't know what you're doing. You're groping your way through the darkness. You don't know the rules or the shortcuts. It's no good. And, by the third time you do something, it starts to get that stain of a habit on it. But the second time… Baby, that's where the magic is."

I browned the garlic and some eggplant on top of it. I asked Lola to explain what she'd painted on *Untitled #2*. She told me all about the colors she'd used, the details she'd agonized over, the little figures that leapt from her subconscious onto the canvas. I cooked and listened to her. Times like this, I would think about my divorce and what really shook me up about it. I would realize that I didn't miss my ex-wife so much as I missed being married: missed having someone at home when I got there; missed having someone to cook for and who would cook for me; missed having someone else's stories to fill up the apartment; missed having someone else's clothes on my floor and funny lotions and bottles I couldn't quite understand in my shower; missed another human's warmth in my bed in the middle of the night; missed having to attend awkward events and having to watch horrible movies just because someone wanted me there beside her. I missed the meaning your life takes on when you're not just living it for yourself anymore. When I'd been with my ex-wife, we each had our individual lives, but together, we'd formed a third identity. A *we* grew from her and me. When we split up, it felt like she and I had killed that little *we*. That's what I missed. And now, with Lola more or less moved in—using her studio apartment as a genuine studio and spending her evenings here with me—I could feel a new little *we* growing from Lola and me. In a way, I guess it was like bringing in Clint Dempsey once my ex-wife and I had put Nietzsche to sleep.

When the lasagna was layered and in the oven and Lola was done explaining everything about *Untitled #2*, I sat at the table across from her. She turned in her seat to face me. "I met your neighbor today," she said.

"Oh, yeah? Who?"

"The blind guy. What's his name?"

"Frank?"

Lola looked up at the ceiling fan above us and thought this over. "No," she said. "Frank doesn't sound right."

It had to be Walters, though. I said, "Was he dressed up?"

"Oh my god, was he. I wanted to ask him if I could touch his shirt. It seemed so soft. And the rest of that suit? Christ. He must've spent a few grand on that."

"And did he have a skinhead guy with him? A guy with a big tattoo on his face?"

"Yeah. You know him, right?"

"I know him."

Lola picked up a fat candle from the middle of the kitchen table. She spun it around on its glass-dish base like a slow moving record. I pushed the matches across the table. She lit a match and used it to light the candle. Her lips pursed. She blew out the match. "Anyway," she said. "The poor guy. He came into the wrong house. He just opened our front door and walked in here. I had to tell him that he had the wrong place. The poor guy looked so sad when I told him that."

"I bet he recovered pretty quickly, huh?"

"He did. He even knew my name. He said, 'I'm sorry, Lola.' And he just backed out the door. The funny thing is, you'd think the guy with him—the skinhead, the one who could *see*—would've told him that he was opening the wrong door."

I picked up the spent match and twirled it between the pads of my fingers. "You'd think."

Lola smiled. She brushed her hair off her shoulders, exposing the soft purple strap of her camisole. "But you told him about me, huh? How sweet."

I set the match on the table in front of me. "How sweet," I said. I couldn't even look Lola in the eye when I said it.

News of Frank Walters didn't sit well with me. I could hardly eat my lasagna. I couldn't pay any attention to the DVD that Lola watched, couldn't even muster up a groan when the protagonist realized that he loved the underfed girl and raced to tell her before her plane left and she was gone forever. Later that night, Lola and I were in bed. She was naked, with her legs spread wide. My head was between her legs. My nose nuzzled her sweet spot and my tongue explored everything just below. She ran her fingers through my hair, occasionally trying to grab on to it and pull, but I'd cut it too short for her to get a real handful. I was naked, too, but in no real hurry to move on to the next step. And that's when it occurred to me that Frank Walters and his Ape Man could bust in at any moment and ruin everything. And this should've been the perfect time for me. Lola and I were in that Untitled #2 phase, when we'd worked past the initial awkwardness and made our mistakes and learned the rules and shortcuts, but before the stain of habit seeped in. I did everything I could to focus on the good around me. I kept my eyes and mind on Lola for the next half-hour.

When she fell asleep, I crept out of bed, dressed, and left the apartment. As I locked the door behind me, I was determined. Tonight, this thing with Frank Walters was going to end.

I rode my bike toward the beach, racing across the pedestrian bridge over the freeway and down the promenade. No pedestrians were out this late at night. A few groups of homeless people milled around in different alcoves, trying to stay hidden from the wind, waiting for the police to come along and scatter them, send them down to the riverbed where they'd sleep through the night. I whipped past them, a ghost dressed in jeans, a black hoodie, and black sneakers. I had lights for my bike, but I kept them off. There were three ways to get from the promenade to the bike trail that I wanted. Each night, I varied which path I took. I didn't think that Walters was following me. I didn't want to take any chances, either way. I wound down the promenade, along the riverbed, back behind a few warehouses, and onto the trail that led up the mountains north of town. The trail was separated from the street. No one could follow me on it without a bicycle, and a second bicycle would've been conspicuous at this time of night. I figured no one knew I was there. I pedaled up the gradual slope, keeping a solid pace. The hospital was ten miles up this trail. A lot of it would be uphill. I'd been taking this ride every night for a few weeks, though. Once the initial soreness worked its way out of my muscles, the ride was easy. Just me and the moon and the oil rigs pumping on the hills to my left. I pedaled and I thought about Walters and Dr. Bishop and me.

We were the last three left who believed in Dr. Bishop's discovery. I'd done a little more research on Dr. Toru—her former colleague at Stanford, the one who'd started selling the information to Walters. I found out that she'd spent a couple of years after Dr. Bishop's retirement writing essays that completely discredited Dr. Bishop's research. She'd abandoned the concept of consciously entering the collective unconscious and painted the experiments as a batty old scientist's flights of fantasy. As far as Dr. Toru was concerned, the brain factory—fMRIs, EEGs, neuromarketing—was where it was at nowadays. The psychological community seemed to be in agreement. I wondered if Dr. Bishop had had a hand in all of that, if maybe she'd been lingering around in Mindland for much longer than she let on, if maybe she'd found a way to enter it years ago, and was only now admitting to it because Walters was hot on her trail and she needed me to shake him. Or because the cancer was winning the battle and she needed one more person to go inside and verify that she hadn't been dreaming it all, that she really had entered and someone else could follow her into a shared unconscious.

There were ways for me to solve these mysteries, but I wasn't at all prepared to face the answers. My desire for ignorance was justified. Especially considering the most troubling bit of information that popped up in front of my face periodically: Dr. Bishop's former colleague, Dr. Amanda Toru, was spending her late fifties checking in and out of psychiatric institutions.

I thought of Dr. Toru and our encounter on psych hospital grounds and the conspicuous absence of keys or a visitor's badge on her person. I feared the day would come when I'd be at Oak View without my own keys dangling from my hip, telling tales of the giants in Dr. Bishop's research and everyone else turning those giants into windmills in their minds. So I let it go. I stayed focused on Walters.

He was such a dangerous guy. He wanted to rule the world. He'd found the technology that would allow him to rule it. Now, with Dr. Bishop in the hospital, only one person stood between him and a power that most people can only dream of. Me. From his perspective, I had to be a pretty surmountable obstacle. Who was I? An anonymous guy with a forgettable office job and an apartment that had housed so many tenants it may as well have a revolving door on it. I had to be one of the easiest people to erase from this world. Who would even call for the investigation? The only person who seemed to see me on a regular basis and care whether I lived or died had just gotten out of a psych hospital. Even if Lola had known everything I'd been up to, who would have believed her when she told my story? So, for Walters—a guy so fixated on getting exactly what he wanted; so desperate to escape his fifteenth-floor purgatory—Mindland and all the power he could gain from it was right at his fingertips. All he would have to do is torment Lola until I showed him the way to RW Winfield's cottage. And I knew myself. I wouldn't let him torment Lola long. I wouldn't let her be a martyr. I'd sing right away. Even though I knew the consequences. This was my reasoning, anyway. This was why I felt like the world was too small for both Walters and me to live in it.

Scariest of all was the thing I'd been thinking of every night for the past week, since I'd gone to that funeral with Brandon and looked eye-to-eye at the Ape Man and knew Walters was right on the edge of getting what he wanted, the thing I'd been thinking as I pedaled up this six-foot-wide, paved bike path flanked to the left by oil rigs and to the right by the industrial yards of the companies operating those rigs. If Walters wanted to run the world, I was the only obstacle he had to overcome. But I'd also been thinking, and this is the scary thing, that the flipside of that statement was true. I could rule the world, if I wanted to. I could have that power that others can only dream of. Walters was my only obstacle.

I entered the Oak View State Psychiatric Hospital from the northeast corner, rode through the arboretum, and locked my bike against a tree outside the RW Winfield cottage. I unlocked the door. It swung open with only a slight squeak from the ancient hinges. I scanned the arboretum behind me. Natural grasses, indigenous trees, flowers with dreamlike colors in the moonlight, but there were no people around. I stepped into the cottage and shut the door behind me. The ancient brass key fit into the lock. I locked the door.

I didn't need the penlight any more. I'd been in this cottage for more than a dozen times over the past few weeks. My routine felt like second nature by now. I skipped the first seventeen steps of Dr. Bishop's nineteen-step plan. They'd been red herrings, anyway. I probably didn't even need the footlocker or to be in the one-lane bowling alley. I climbed in, anyway, just in case. Two minutes later, I stood in Mindland. Welcome back.

There was no point in stalling or wandering around. Tonight, I'd end things. I yelled out, "Connor Jarred." A dull yellow light flickered over a doorway. I raced down and entered. A parade of images flashed in front of me, impossible to separate or make sense of individually. Collectively, they amounted to REM. Ape Man was dreaming. Dreams didn't help me. They were too random, too hard to control. Most of us forget our dreams almost instantly. Even if we remember them, we tell ourselves, "It was just a dream," and move on with our waking life. So I made the sound of an alarm clock in Ape Man's head and he woke up.

I had figured out a few little tricks in Mindland. The first was figuring out how to plant memories. All I had to do was eavesdrop on a thought, then weave my thoughts into it. The key was to keep things visual, to project the words and images over memories as if they were a movie. I would begin by showing the scene that triggered the thought. When Ape Man was visualizing it, I would cast my images over his images. Memory is fragile enough as it is. It's malleable. And dealing with a weak mind like Ape Man's, memory was a lump of clay on a spinning wheel. I could make it into what I wanted. There was one memory in particular I was working on.

The poor guy had been molested on a camping trip when he was a little kid. He'd never dealt with this. He, in fact, spent a lot of time trying to repress it. The memory continued to haunt him, even before I started making sure it haunted him. He couldn't seem to keep it repressed. And, just as I'd done for the last several nights, I projected the memory into Ape Man's mind.

We found ourselves sitting in the high desert, surrounded by a circle of two-man and four-man tents, chaparral, the wobbly, cartoon arms of saguaros. A campfire burned in front of us. Ape Man and I sat on lawn chairs. I looked nothing like I do outside of Mindland. I looked, I guess, like one of Ape Man's childhood friends. In this memory, I was ten or eleven years old. Ape Man was the same age, but he looked like a thirty-year-old Ape Man shrunk down to ten-year-old size. He was bald. He wore his obligatory white shirt and red suspenders. The light from the campfire licked the tribal tattoo on his face. The adult who was supervising the camping trip was in the big tent behind us. Ape Man kept looking nervously over his shoulder, waiting to be called into that tent.

The humane thing to do would've been to spend this time convincing Ape Man that it wasn't his fault, that he could get help for this, that he could get past it, that the memory would keep haunting him until he faced it. Part of me wanted to do that. I thought of myself as the kind of person who helped people solve problems, not someone who exacerbated them for my own purposes. But I guess there was more to me than I thought, a dark little voice inside that got to have a say once in a while.

So I reminded myself that I wasn't here to do the humane thing. I was here to protect Lola and myself by any means at my disposal. I projected a new image onto the molester. I turned him into Frank Walters.

For the first few nights, I had difficulty passing Walters off as the molester. Repetition has a way of turning lies into truth. By this night, I didn't have to project at all. Frank Walters rustled around in the tent behind us. Ape Man waited to be called. I said to him, "Tonight's the night, Connor. You have to stop him."

"I can't stop him," Ape Man said.

"You can. I'll tell you how. It's simple. You just have to destroy all the information he gets from the mental hospitals. That's what gives him the power to get into your mind like this. Destroy all that information, and he'll lose the power."

Ape Man stared at me. Every night, he had trouble with this. He said, "Huh?"

"Destroy the information, and he can't hurt you."

"How's that?"

"Listen to me. Just destroy the information."

"Then he can't hurt me?"

"Then he can't hurt you."

Walters clambered out of the tent. He shouted, "Connor!"

Ape Man stood.

"Be tough," I said.

He nodded.

"Destroy the information," I said.

He nodded. "Destroy it all." He had a look of determination on his face. It was a look I'd never seen on him before: courage behind those sky blue eyes. I could feel the fear leaving him. It seemed like, on this night, he would act. Ape Man turned away from me and went into the tent. Frank Walters followed him inside.

The first couple of times Ape Man and I went through this scenario, I would leave his mind once the memory was planted. It seemed like my work was done. My fear was that, if I stuck around too long, he'd know I was there. He had to know a little of what Walters was up to. Someone had to be reading all of those psychological essays to Walters. Someone had to read the reports I'd sent to Walters. Ape Man had been right next to Walters through it all. Sure, it was possible that he didn't understand what he was reading and what Walters was up to. But I doubted that. Ape Man wasn't stupid. He was unreasonably angry and suffered from an unhealthy dose of cognitive dissonance, but he wasn't stupid. He knew some of what Walters was up to. He had to. So I feared that, if I stayed in his mind snooping around too much, I'd be discovered.

That wasn't the case. Not really.

I'd figured this one out, too. In order to manipulate me, Dr. Bishop would have been in my conscious mind. She would have directed a few daydreams. In retrospect, I could think back to some of my daydreams and guess which ones Dr. Bishop had a hand in. But I never suspected her while it was happening. Even after I knew what her research was, I didn't suspect her. Walters had only picked up on me in his mind because I'd been so awkward about it. I'd tried to talk to him and Mindland manipulation works best with projected images, not conversations. It was beyond my capacity to plant images in the mind of a blind man, so all Walters had to do was recognize when the voices in his head were coming from me. Also, Walters probably knew I was there because we all create our realities to a certain extent and the reality that Walters created included me sneaking around in his mind. Ape Man wouldn't have gone this far, though, so I could stick with him.

One thing Ape Man wrestled with was his participation in Walters' white-collar world. I knew this by snooping on his conscious thoughts. He often daydreamed about conversations with one of his skinhead buddies, a guy who always talked about blue-collar ethics, about the workers sticking together and class war and all that. Of course, I knew that Ape Man came from money, but I also knew it didn't matter. The guy was a study in contradiction. I guess we all are, to some extent. So I played with that. As long as I stayed close to skinhead rhetoric, I could masquerade as this guy in Ape Man's daydreams.

Ape Man snapped out of his memories of childhood trauma. He climbed out of bed and walked out of his bedroom. I whispered, "Is Uncle Frank awake?" in his head. Ape Man walked down the hallway, paused outside Walters' bedroom door, and listened to the rhythmic hum of Walters' snoring. Ape Man kept walking down the hallway and into the kitchen. The kitchen was easier to recognize through Ape Man's eyes: the granite countertop of the kitchen island that Walters had leaned against while his water boiled, the gas stove with a red tea kettle on it, the oak cabinets that housed his mugs and everything else. Like Walters' wardrobe, the kitchen was impeccable, tasteful, a beautiful sight that Walters would never see. Ape Man didn't pay attention. He went to the refrigerator, grabbed a bottle of Newcastle Brown, and sat at the kitchen table.

I joined him in his thoughts, saying, "Another sleepless night, CJ?"

Ape Man shook his head. He took a long, deep drink from his bottle of beer.

"It's all this rich boy shit. You forgot your roots. Now you got nothing left but a life of sucking some rich fuck's cock. That's what those nightmares are about."

Ape Man tried to shake these thoughts from his head, but as long as I stayed there, he'd keep having them. No amount of beer he drank could wash me away. I could feel him heating up, the adrenaline burning through his veins. He fought the flashing images of the memory he'd just sweated himself out of. The quick images of a little Ape Man screaming, "Destroy it all!"

Ape Man fiddled with a day-old copy of the *Los Angeles Times* that had been lying on the kitchen table since he had read it to Walters that morning. Ape Man ran his fingers along the edges of the pages and let the ink stain his fingertips.

"You could throw that paper on the stove," I told him. "Put an end to all this fancy bullshit built on the backs of the working class."

I expected some hesitation on Ape Man's part. I'd even created further, deeper arguments that I could wield against Ape Man's initial resistance. Truth be told, I feared that I wouldn't be able to pull it off. These actions went against so many of my inclinations, so much of who I thought I was, that I wasn't at all sure I could overcome any resistance that Ape Man produced. But he didn't argue, and he didn't question my ideas. He didn't resist at all. I guess that a person who becomes a skinhead and a bodyguard doesn't typically get there by ruminating over the subtleties of issues and coming to a rational decision about them. A person gets there by acting first and denying his regrets later.

Ape Man lifted his beer and chugged the rest of it. He thought, "Destroy it all." He tossed a section of the newspaper on the stove and lit all four burners. The paper burst into flames that reached beyond the range hood and licked the oak cabinets. Within a few seconds, the thin bottom of the cabinets caught fire and new flames spread across the cabinet doors.

I thought to myself, maybe this is enough. Maybe if Walters sees me burn his house down, it will scare him off my trail. Maybe I can torment Ape Man enough to keep Walters away.

Ape Man had a different idea, though.

He grabbed another section of the *Times*, rolled it into a thick tube, and lit one end. He headed back down the hallway to Walters' room. I knew what Ape Man was thinking. Of course I did. I probably could have stopped him. I probably should have. My initial plan was just to have Ape Man burn the house down and hope that a smoke alarm or something would wake Walters. Walters was an agile guy. He knew his house well. He could escape whether the house was on fire or not. I tried to tell myself that I didn't want Walters dead. I just wanted him scared to death.

Regardless, I knew where Ape Man was going with that burning tube and who he planned to set on fire. I could've stopped him. But I didn't. I didn't want to face what all this Mindland business was turning me into. I just got the hell out of this guy's brain.

35

Eric waited for me outside the cottage. This surprised me. It was nearly one in the morning. I expected the whole campus to be empty, asleep. Eric sat on the same bench I'd sat on with Dr. Bishop two weeks earlier. A paper bag lay by his foot. He reached inside and grabbed a bottle of pale ale. "Join me?"

I took a seat next to him. He handed me the bottle. I used the bottle opener on my key chain to open one for me and one for Eric. "Thanks."

"Don't mention it."

We didn't say a word for a minute or two. The fog of having been in Mindland hadn't yet lifted in my brain. I still felt a bit horrified.

Later, when the story hit the news, when Ape Man was in custody and blaming me, when detectives investigated the incidentals, when my name came up and a detective decided to follow that lead, when he visited my office and interviewed me, I was glad that Eric had happened to be outside the cottage at this moment. He'd given me a solid alibi for the night of the fire.

I couldn't have known any of this ahead of time. I just sipped my beer and tried to relax there in the arboretum. "How's your mom doing?" I asked.

Eric shook his head. "She'll never leave her hospital bed again."

I knew this. I just wasn't expecting Eric to speak so bluntly. I said, "It's a shame."

Eric nodded.

"She's a great woman."

Eric nodded again.

"I'd like to visit her."

"You should. She asks about you every day."

"I can't," I said. "I went there yesterday. They said only family is allowed."

Eric folded the paper bag down over the beer at his feet. He brushed a leaf off his shoe. "I'll take care of that," he said. "I'll say you're a cousin from out of town. Make sure they let you in."

"Thanks."

Moonlight and pine needles and patches of silence fell around us. I thought of Lola, sleeping alone. I hoped she wouldn't wake. I don't know if she'd noticed me sneaking out at night. She hadn't said anything. I thought if I could just get back unnoticed tonight, then it'd be the last time. All of this will be over.

Eric picked up an acorn from the bench. He tossed it at the cottage door. "Do you believe any of this?" he asked.

"Any of what?"

"Any of this Mindland crap."

I shrugged.

"You must, right?" he said. "You must believe it if you keep going down into the bowling alley."

I shrugged again. Eric looked at me. He didn't have to say it for me to know what he was getting at. His mother was dying and he was serious, here. I knew something and he deserved to know. I lied. I said, "I want to believe it. I want to believe it for her sake, you know." I shook my head, stared at my feet. "But it's just not working. I can't get in."

"I know," Eric said. "I tried, too. Followed all nineteen of her steps. It didn't work. All I felt was that footlocker around me. It felt like a coffin."

I knew that about Eric. Dr. Bishop had told me that I was her second choice for this mission. She'd first tried to help Eric into Mindland, but he couldn't take that nineteenth step. She said that one of the reasons she chose me had to do with my study of Eastern spirituality. I'd long since learned to meditate. I practiced it often. I guess this was key. "Has anyone else tried to get into Mindland?" I asked, trying to sound casual, probably not pulling it off.

Eric shook his head. "Not that I know of." He picked up another acorn, rolled it around in his hands, and tossed it at the door. "This is impossible. There is no Mindland. I'm gonna tear this sucker down tomorrow."

"The cottage?"

"Yep."

"The bowling alley underneath?"

"The whole fucking thing."

"How? Why?"

"Mom's orders. The last thing she signed. I got a crew coming tomorrow to take it all down, piece by piece. We'll haul in earth to fill up that old, warped-lane alley."

"What are you going to do with Winfield's remains?"

"Box them up and mail them to a great-granddaughter who's still living on his wealth."

"And your mom wanted this?"

Eric nodded. He drank some beer. We both took a few minutes for our thoughts. Then Eric broke the silence. He said, "I've destroyed all of her research. It's all gone."

"I figured you'd be done by now," I said. I'd seen the bed of his truck piled high with plastic bags full of shredded paper. A scientific legacy on its way to the recycling plant.

"I've even ground up the hard drives of the computers she'd been working on. When this sucker comes down tomorrow, there won't be anything left."

"Your mom will still be left."

"For a few days, anyway."

Eric and I sat in the arboretum and polished off the whole six-pack. It was the first time in years that I'd drank three beers in one sitting. I was a little wobbly as I raced my bike down the mountain toward my apartment.

And, at that exact moment, down in Malibu, the fire department arrived on the property of Frank Walters. Only the charred skeleton of his house remained. Walters and everything he owned had burned up in the fire. All that was left was Walters' nephew, standing on the curb in front of Walters' house, watching the smoldering ash. Crying.

36

Eric walked me to Dr. Bishop's hospital room the next morning. We were both a little tired from our midnight excursion in the arboretum. Eric said, "I'm gonna get breakfast at that little diner on Telegraph. Take all the time you need." He slid out of the room, leaving me alone with what was left of Dr. Bishop.

She lay in her hospital bed surrounded by a monitor for her heart, a respirator for her lungs, tubes pumping nutrients in and ushering waste out, flower arrangements wilting, get-well cards wishing the impossible. Her gray hair was greasy and matted from where the nurses must have cradled her head to change the pillowcase underneath. Her hospital gown swallowed what was left of her skin and bones. This was the first time I'd seen her without makeup. I'd grown accustomed to a Dr. Bishop who looked professional, sharp. This person in the hospital bed seemed almost like a stranger. Sunlight glistened off a long white hair that had grown underneath her chin. Her mouth was agape: coffee-stained teeth and old fillings on display. This was all too intimate for me.

I asked myself why I'd come. Dr. Bishop wouldn't be able to talk or hear what I had to say. She was more or less a cyborg at this point. The path of her life from here on out had been reduced to sliding down the slope of a slow morphine drip. Part of me had wanted to tell her that everything would be okay now. But sitting in a hospital chair, watching the respirator pump air slowly into her lungs, it was clear that everything would *not* be okay for her. She was on her deathbed. All the peace anyone could give her now came in the form of an opiate.

I couldn't bring myself to speak to her. I was too conflicted. Should I thank her for opening the world of Mindland up to me, for showing me that we're not all alone in this world, that our minds can exist beyond our bodies so there's real, scientific hope for an afterlife? Should I curse her for getting into my mind and convincing me to abandon my marriage and my life's work just so I could kill some guy she needed dead? Should I mourn the destruction of her research into the collective unconscious or castigate her for meddling in affairs best left alone? Should I even bother speaking when I didn't know what to say and she couldn't hear anyway?

I sat in the chair and watched the machines keep Dr. Bishop alive in only the most literal sense of the word. I breathed in rhythm with the respirator. I gradually nodded off and napped until my neck was sore.

When I awoke, I was still alone in the room with Dr. Bishop. Just the two of us. I thought about apologizing for falling asleep alongside her deathbed, of explaining that I hadn't been sleeping well lately because I'd been spending my nights in Mindland. But, of course, she'd been sleeping this whole time, too. There was no need to apologize.

A slow trickle of yellow fluid filled a bag near the wall. Enough was enough. I used the wooden arms of the hospital chair to push myself up, stood alongside Dr. Bishop's bed, and tapped the metal frame twice. "Lady," I whispered, "you set me up." Then I bent over and kissed her forehead.

I spent the afternoon sitting in my office, winding up a toy bird, watching his beak creep close to the desk, watching his back flip. When the spring wound down, I wound it back up. I couldn't seem to bring myself to do anything else. The phone rang. I saw before answering it that the call was coming from Dickinson and Associates. I thought it might be Frank Walters. By this point, a heavy dose of denial had kicked in and Walters was still alive in my mind. I answered the phone the way I always answered it: "Oak View State Psychiatric Hospital, Grant Writing Department."

"What did you do to Walters?"

"Huh?"

"We know it was you. What did you do to him?"

The voice seemed familiar. More than familiar. It was a voice that I'd heard tell a hundred stories, sing a thousand songs. The voice had spent a lot of time rattling around in my ears, but I couldn't place it. The caller ID was throwing me off. I asked, "Who is this?"

"I'm asking the questions here. Come clean. Tell me everything you know about Frank Walters."

I could hear a giggle behind those last words. As soon as I realized that someone was trying to play a trick on me, I placed the voice. "What's up, Brandon? Working for Dickinson and Associates now?"

"Good old Dicks and Ass. It's true. I made my pact with the devil. But did you hear?" Brandon paused.

"Hear what?"

"I'm not just working here. I'm running the fifteenth floor."

"What are you talking about?"

"The day after that funeral we went to, your buddy Walters called me into his office. He offered me my old mentor's position. It's a big step up for me. If I play my cards right, I may even move up to the top level. Rub elbows with Mr. Dickinson and all his associates. Why the hell not? I'm still young."

"Congratulations," I said. For a second, I worried about my old buddy. He'd been so harried with fear that he'd turn into his mentor, and now he was doing exactly that. On purpose. It didn't make sense. And there was something else that didn't make sense in my fog of denial. I asked, "But how are you running things? What about Walters? Isn't he still the honcho of the mid-level?"

"Not anymore. He was killed last night."

"Killed? What? Like an accident?" I asked, forcing myself to accept what I already knew.

"Something like that. That crazy skinhead nephew of his burned down the house. Walters didn't have time to get out."

"Wow. So ten days, you go from the art department to middle management. Crazy."

"Upper-middle management. But that's not the half of it," Brandon said. He told me about Ape Man calling him in the middle of the night. Brandon rushed straight out to Agoura Hills, found the fire department spraying the brush all around Walters' property, the house still engulfed in flames but a lost cause. Ape Man sat on the curb surrounded by the police. Brandon couldn't wedge his way into the conversation, so he made a middle-of-the-night call to a defense attorney whom Brandon had penned a jingle for. The guy was both a shyster and one of the top defense attorneys in Los Angeles. The perfect mix, according to Brandon. By 2:30 AM, Brandon, the defense attorney, and Ape Man sat together in an interrogation room at the Lost Hills Sheriff Station. Brandon insisted on being part of the meeting. "Information," Brandon told me. "It's the most valuable commodity in business today."

"And what information did you get?" I asked.

"You think I'm just going to tell you what I had to pay a lawyer $360 an hour to find out? Never."

"It's okay by me," I said. I'd already been in all three of their minds: Brandon, Ape Man, and Walters. With or without the footlocker in the bowling alley, I could go back. Into Ape Man's and Brandon's mind, anyway.

"Your name kept coming up," Brandon said.

"Really?" I wound up the little bird, just as a way of keeping distracted enough to sound nonchalant. He crept down toward the desk. "Are you sure it was me? I have a pretty common name."

The wind-up bird did a back flip.

"Oh, I know who Connor was talking about," Brandon said. "What were you involved in?"

"Nothing," I said. "We had a psychologist here who was batty. She had all these dreams about mental telepathy, that kind of thing. Walters bought into it. It was insane. I think he killed my dog."

Brandon ignored my last comment. He asked, "Who was the shrink?"

"A woman named Dr. Bishop."

"Can I schedule an appointment with her?"

"I doubt it." I told Brandon that I'd been to the hospital that morning to visit her, and that there wasn't even enough of her left to say goodbye to.

"Maybe I'll come up your way for a funeral. Repay the favor."

"No need," I said. "I won't even go to the funeral myself." I was lying, of course. I'd go to the funeral, but the last thing I wanted was Brandon standing next to me, trying to sniff out information about Mindland while I tried to decide whether or not to cry.

"What do you think of it all?" Brandon asked.

"About the telepathy stuff? Walters?"

"Yeah."

"I already told you. It's insane."

"Hmmm." Brandon seemed to chew on this for a few seconds. I didn't say anything. I could hear weird white noises on the other end of the line: shuffling papers or scratching stubble or something. "Well," Brandon said to buy more time, to fill the line with a few more white noises, then, finally, "Maybe we could meet up for lunch."

Brandon offered to take me to the same chain restaurant where Walters had taken me on our first meeting. Oh, no. Here we go again.

37

The best thing about Brandon's call was that it served as a warning. Sooner or later, the police would pay me a visit. They did it sooner.

Two days after Ape Man burned down the house, a visitor stopped by my office. I was in the middle of a follow-up call to a state agency about a land grant. If everything went through, the hospital would take over several acres of farmland on the western edge of the facility. It was all part of my dream of making Oak View as self-sufficient as possible. The first step: having the patients farm their own food. I was so swept up in this possibility that when the unknown man walked in, I just put up a finger and finished my call. The next few minutes were spent discussing annual precipitation figures and environmental impact studies, which were done back in the Winfield days but seemed recent enough for the initial planning stage. I told the director of the state agency, "Think of the old Victory Gardens from the World War II era. I'm proposing Victory Gardens for the patients here."

The director seemed to love this last line. He sounded more excited by the metaphor than all the facts, figures, and economic projections I'd been sending him. I expected as much. That's why I spent so much time coming up with the metaphor and linking it to the time that most Americans think of as the apex of our culture. The director was so taken that he emailed me all the proper forms while we were still on the phone. He even gave me his direct extension and scheduled a time for a future telephone discussion. I noted the time in my increasingly full calendar.

During this phone call, I kept one eye on the unknown man waiting in my office. Truth be told, I didn't even entertain the possibility that he might be a detective. He didn't match my image of what a detective is supposed to look like. He didn't have a noticeably cheap suit, tobacco-stained fingers, cigarette ashes rubbed into polyester slacks, barber hairstyle #2, or mismatched socks. He didn't even have a perpetual scowl on an indeterminately middle-aged face. This guy couldn't have looked more different. He wore hippie sandals, cargo shorts, and an aloha shirt. He scratched his chin as he flipped through the paperbacks on my shelves, lingering over the words long enough to demonstrate a genuine interest in them. He also appeared to be a few years younger than me: early thirties at the oldest.

I assumed he was a new employee. The aloha shirt on Hawaiian Shirt Friday cemented the assumption in my mind. I finished my call and offered the visitor a seat in the state-issued, metal-and-vinyl chair in front of my desk. He sat down. I said, "Sorry about that. I'd been on hold for almost forty-five minutes before I got through. I couldn't just hang up."

"It's no problem," the guy said. He handed me a business card that announced him as a member of the Los Angeles County Police Department. A homicide detective.

I took a second to readjust my story about this man in front of me, deleting the new employee notion, casting him as the detective I'd been awaiting, and dismissing the notion of detectives I'd developed during multiple viewings of Elliott Gould in *The Long Goodbye*. I said, "I hate it when people do that to me. When I come to their office and they just stick a finger in the air and keep talking on the phone. I hated doing it myself."

The detective shrugged. "I could've called ahead and told you I was coming."

"Still. I apologize."

The detective waved off the apology, asked me if I knew Frank Walters and his nephew, Connor Jarred, if I knew about the fire, if I knew why he was there. I did. I'd been half-expecting at least a call from the police since I'd first heard from Brandon. I ran through all the possible conversations in my head so many times I started to worry that any answers I gave the police might sound rehearsed. I also reached a point in my thoughts about all of this where I realized that it was highly doubtful any police officers in the country would accept Ape Man's alibi: that it wasn't really him who did it, that it was me inside his head, taking control. My understanding of the police—which may have been real or may have been entirely based on crime novels I'd read and bad cop dramas on television—was that police generally arrest the easiest likely suspect and gather only the evidence to convict him. They had Ape Man in custody. High-priced lawyer or not, no metaphysical defense was likely to get him off this hook. At least this is the way it was likely to play out in a novel or on television. Who knew about the world outside of fiction? Anyway, for my purposes, it hardly mattered what I said to this detective.

I was concerned about the interview with him, but I wasn't exactly worried. RW Winfield's cottage had been torn down for less than four hours before I went looking for another way into Mindland. I'd discovered that any dark place where it would be safe to leave my body while my mind wandered would work just as well as the footlocker. So if I messed it all up with the detective, I could simply creep into his mind at night and convince him that I was innocent. I tried not to think about that last point. I said, "Brandon Burch told me that you guys might be coming around."

"You know Mr. Burch?"

"We used to play in a band together. Pop Culture and the References." I wished I had a copy of one of the records we released or one of the fanzines that ran an interview with us to hand to him. It seemed like the kind of thing that would happen if this were a television show. The camera would focus on a picture of Brandon and me both looking as if we were in our mid-thirties but dressed to denote an earlier time and the folly of following the fashions of another decade. I wanted to stay within the formula. I just couldn't.

The detective said, "Never heard of you guys."

"That's why I'm here at Oak View and Brandon's working in advertising."

The detective smiled. "So do you know what Mr. Jarred says about you?"

I shook my head.

"He says that you crept into his head and convinced him to kill Mr.

Walters."

"Oh, really?" I laughed a little while I said it. It was a nervous laugh but I also thought it was funny in that it was ridiculous enough to fit into what Lola called "my odd little world."

The detective looked embarrassed. "I'm just repeating what he said."

"I understand." I swept up the papers dealing with the land grant, stacked them neatly into a file folder, and slid the file folder to the left side of my desk. "You know, we have some empty beds here. Mr. Jarred's welcome to come stay for a while."

"Don't be surprised if the state takes you up on that," the detective said, though we both knew that convicts with mental illnesses didn't end up at sunny, restful Oak View. They usually ended up in prison, like any other convict. "But I do have to ask you some questions."

I nodded.

The detective pulled out a notebook and read the first question. "What do you know about the collective unconscious?"

"It all comes from Karl Jung, right? Archetypes and that kind of thing. It's how he explained why fairy tales are so similar from one culture to another, isn't it?"

The detective shrugged.

I said, "You'd really be better off asking one of the psychologists about it."

"What about Dr. Bishop and the collective unconscious?"

"Well, now, that's different. What Dr. Bishop studied wasn't really the collective unconscious. It was more like telepathy or ESP. Like, she did this experiment where she set up a camera in my foyer to see if my dog could sense me coming home."

"And could he?"

"That's the funny thing. He usually could. But I usually came home at the same time every day. Plus, I commute by bus, so he could've just gotten excited every time the #6 rolled down Main Street." I paused for a second. The detective sat in the chair like the guy who'd pulled the shortest straw. I added, "Connor Jarred killed my dog. I think. Maybe he just kidnapped him. I can't figure out what happened to the pup, anyway."

"Really?"

I nodded. "He and Walters had this crazy idea that they could use telepathy in advertising. Put the thoughts right into your head that you wanted to buy this or that product. It seemed silly to me. I kinda just laughed them off until they took my dog. After that, I did my best to avoid them." I wondered if I'd said too much, given myself a motive, at least, or raised a little suspicion in the detective. I wanted to ask him about Clint Dempsey, if a dog's body had turned up in the wreckage of the house, if the detective knew anything. But I told myself to be calm. If Clint Dempsey were alive, I could find him.

The detective didn't look the least bit suspicious. I think the word "telepathy" was helping me, too. Even though what Dr. Bishop was working on wasn't really telepathy, using that word seemed to be a good way to discredit everything she'd done, at least in the minds of laymen. The word seemed to be working.

"I see," the detective said. He looked at his notebook, flipped a page, scanned the words there, and let out a heavy sigh. His thoughts were painted on his face.

"I'm not the only one who thinks all this is silly, am I?" I asked.

"You and me both, I think."

I stood from the chair. "As long as you're here, let me give you a tour of the facility. It's a pretty neat place."

The detective checked his watch and said, "Sure."

I led the detective through the maze of the Williams Building and out into the warm spring day. A soft breeze blew in from the west and carried with it the faint aroma of the Pacific. I walked the detective all around the hospital grounds, showing him the research facilities and the cafeteria and the gym and the different units and the outdoor stage and the buildings that hadn't been renovated yet. We chatted the whole time. He asked me about the Winfield scandal. When he saw that I didn't really know much about it, he told me a few anecdotes that one of his colleagues had told him. This led to me showing him Lola's paintings in the abandoned McCabe Hall. Eventually, we stumbled over Dr. Bishop's old research room and went inside. Of course, most of the stuff had been cleared out: no more computers, desks, cages rigged up to shock the squirrels. No more squirrels. All that remained was Dr. Bishop's old motorcycle helmet. I picked it up and told the detective the story of her experiment.

"And she got paid to do this?" the detective asked.

"No," I said. "She did it in her spare time." I spun the helmet around in my hands. One of Dr. Bishop's gray hairs clung to the inside pads of the helmet. I thought to pull the hair out, then decided to leave it. Her final artifact.

"The craziest thing about Walters and all of this," I said, "is that advertising already works really, really well. Think of all the stuff that you believe just because you haven't questioned the ads you've seen. Think about something like a diamond, right? It's a rock. That's it. A pretty rock, but still, a rock. And look how much people will pay for one. And a tiny little one, at that. The diamonds you buy aren't even big enough to be good for what rocks are generally good for. But look at all the harm the diamond industry does to the world. It's madness. And if you have an industry that can convince you to blow thousands of dollars on a shiny rock that has no practical utility, even if you know apartheid dug that rock out of the ground for you, how much more effective does that industry need to be?"

The detective nodded. "I hadn't really thought about that."

"And you're a detective. Your whole job is to detect suspicious activity. If you're not questioning this stuff, then you know it's all flying over the head of the average Joe."

The detective's head kept bobbing on his shoulders as if he were agreeing with one thought after another in his head. He didn't say anything, though.

After we'd spent about an hour touring the grounds, the detective finally asked me where I'd been the night when Ape Man burned the house down. I told him I'd show him and headed for the arboretum. The springtime sun cast hazy shadows among the gathering of indigenous trees. A bluebird landed on a nearby black elder and picked at the petals of a small white flower that may have had dreams of becoming a berry someday. I pointed out the bench where Dr. Bishop had first promised to lead me into Mindland and told the detective that I'd been sitting there with Eric, talking about Eric's mom dying, drinking beer. I told the detective that Eric could corroborate my story, but the detective had to be patient. Eric worked on his own schedule. Sometimes, it took days or weeks for him to respond. "But if I committed the murder telepathically, I guess it doesn't matter where I did it from, huh?" I added.

The detective laughed and said, "It's so ridiculous. I almost feel crazy coming up here."

I stopped walking and said, "That's the scary thing about working in a psych hospital. Everyone starts to seem crazy after a while."

38

After Dr. Bishop's funeral, Lola seemed okay with coming by the psych hospital. We often had lunch together at a picnic bench among the squirrels or revisited her paintings in McCabe Hall or hung out with Eric. Within a few months, everything settled down. The detective stayed in Agoura Hills. Ape Man copped an insanity plea and got himself a cell in at the California Men's Colony. I stayed in the clear.

Brandon kept calling, trying to take me out to lunch at chain restaurants or tempt me with the cast-off fringe benefits of his business— everything from the expensive wardrobe pieces left over from a commercial shoot to the winning raffle ticket that could claim a brand new Toyota Prius. Rejecting Brandon was different from rejecting Walters. I was no more inclined to give Brandon information than I had been for Walters, but I still wanted to keep an earlier version of Brandon alive in my mind, a Brandon who toured the continent with me, screaming silly punk rock songs and answering to the name Fester. As long as that little Brandon lived in my memory, I couldn't hate the mid-level advertising executive he'd become. So I let him keep trying to get the information, all the while knowing that I could probably convince him that this Mindland stuff was all absurd. Or if he couldn't be convinced, I could just torment him nightly in Mindland until my voice in his head earned him a room at Oak View. One way or another, I'd deal with him.

My work required me to be on duty forty hours a week, but the actual work I did took far less than forty hours. I found a bit of autonomy during the in-between times. I wandered around the hospital grounds, chatting with people, looking for interesting nooks and crannies. I read and researched different things I was curious about. I spent a lot of time in the archives, wading through Dr. Bishop's papers—the ones that Eric hadn't burned—that dealt with her life and her research prior to the Mindland studies. I spent a lot more time thinking about going back into Mindland, thinking about all the things I could do there. Little things: helping Lola forget about her childhood pain, helping Eric deal with the death of his mother, helping the Ape Man through his incarceration. Big things: convincing a president to stop a stupid war, getting Congress to spend more money on education and health care, maybe even convincing insurance companies that mental illnesses were real illnesses and needed to be covered. I daydreamed about sliding back into that big, open field with all of the teachers of antiquity and taking my own stump, teaching my own rules, laying down my own philosophy. I spent hours at my desk on the third and a half floor of the Williams Building, winding up my little toy bird, watching it do back flips, and dreaming about saving the world. When temptation grew too strong, when Mindland seemed too close, too inviting, when my dreams took me to the point where I wanted to act on them, I usually left the office and found other people to talk to. Often, I'd wander over to Dr. Benengeli's rehearsals. Her newest play was *Waiting for Godot*.

A few days before opening night, Lola came to the psych hospital to join me for lunch. She brought two bottles of iced tea and homemade fish and chips wrapped in brown butcher paper. We sat on the old bench where we'd watched the rehearsals of *Rosencrantz and Guildenstern Are Dead*. Summer breezes fluttered through the branches of the gray pine. In front of us, a shadow cut the stage in half. Most of the actors lingered in the shade around the perimeter. The sunlight pinged off the wiry white hair of one of the actors. It tickled his bow tie and muted the maroon fibers of his sweater vest. Lola pointed at the actor and said, "Is that The Professor?"

I'd seen a few rehearsals up close. I knew the answer. "Yes, it is."

"Really? As detached from reality as that guy is, Dr. Benengeli gave him a part?"

"A big part. He's Estragon."

"Isn't that one of the leads?"

"Yes."

"Pretty risky casting move."

"You know Dr. Benengeli," I said. "She likes to play fast and loose." As if on cue, Dr. Benengeli scooted a wooden orange crate to center stage. She pulled The Professor close. She stepped on the box, placed her left hand on her breast, and spread her exceptionally small right arm in front of her in a mimicry of declamation. She climbed off the crate. The Professor climbed onto the crate and mimicked her mimicry. Even from a distance, he looked unstable. Dr. Benengeli kept a steadying hand on The Professor's elbow. I took a sip of my tea and added, "Plus, there's an Estragon understudy."

Lola sprinkled malt vinegar onto her fish, took a bite, watched a bit more of the rehearsal, and chewed. When she was done, she said, "So who's the other main character? What's his name?"

"Vladimir."

"Who's playing him?"

"Walk over there. You're not going to believe it."

"A movie star?"

I nodded, as if I'd heard of the movie star or even remembered his name. When one of the secretaries told me about him, she listed a half-dozen movies that I'd not only missed seeing but hadn't even heard of. Matters were made worse when I'd met the movie star at a previous rehearsal. The Professor introduced us, then wandered off. The movie star and I were left alone in front of the stage. After a few awkward seconds, I said the only thing that came to my mind, which was, "So, you're an actor?" He laughed as if I were being coy. I smiled, left it at that, and drifted away. I hadn't told Lola about that encounter because I feared she would rent a handful of movies that I didn't particularly want to see just so I'd know who this actor was.

Lola set her fish and chips and butcher paper and bottle of malt vinegar on the bench and started toward the stage. I watched the brazen sway of her hips as she walked away. She took maybe fifteen steps, then stopped suddenly. Her hand covered her mouth. She twisted around and rushed back to me.

"Is that who I think it is?"

I nodded.

"Wow! We have to go to opening night."

"Well, you know I'm in the play, too?"

"Really?" Lola raised an eyebrow and latched her gaze onto mine. "And who are you playing? Pozzo?"

"Nope," I said. "I got the title role."

"Godot?"

I smiled.

Lola slapped me on the thigh gently but still with enough force to make the keys on my belt loop jingle. She grinned like I was kidding.

Acknowledgements

Thanks to Patricia Geary, Jack Lopez, Justin Bryant, Mickey Hess, and Todd Taylor for reading the manuscript and giving me helpful feedback. Thanks to all the former employees of the Camarillo State Mental Hospital and the current employees of another psychiatric hospital who let me interview them for this book. Thanks also to my publisher, Jennifer Joseph, for making my manuscript a book. Special thanks to the City of Ventura for awarding me an artist's grant that facilitated the writing of this novel. Biggest thanks of all to my wife, Felizon Vidad, for working in a couple of psych hospitals so that I'd have an idea for a new novel, for her careful reading and fact-checking, and for everything else.